By the author

Fiction

The Andromeda Strain

The Terminal Man

The Great Train Robbery

Eaters of the Dead

Non-fiction

Five Patients

Jasper Johns

CONGO

CONGO

MICHAEL CRICHTON

ALFRED A. KNOPF   New York   1980

THIS IS A BORZOI BOOK
PUBLISHED BY ALFRED A. KNOPF, INC.

Library of Congress Cataloging in Publication Data

Crichton, Michael, [date]   Congo.

Bibliography: p.   I. Title.
PS3553.R48C6   1980   813'.54   80-7972
ISBN 0-394-51392-4

Manufactured in the United States of America

FIRST TRADE EDITION

For Bob Gottlieb

The more experience and insight I obtain into human nature, the more convinced do I become that the greater portion of a man is purely animal.

—Henry Morton Stanley, 1887

The large male [gorilla] held my attention. . . . He gave an impression of dignity and restrained power, of absolute certainty in his majestic appearance. I felt a desire to communicate with him. . . . Never before had I had this feeling on meeting an animal. As we watched each other across the valley, I wondered if he recognized the kinship that bound us.

—George B. Schaller, 1964

Contents

Introduction   xi

Prologue: The Place of Bones   3

DAY 1: HOUSTON   9
DAY 2: SAN FRANCISCO   33
DAY 3: TANGIER   75
DAY 4: NAIROBI   105
DAY 5: MORUTI   141
DAY 6: LIKO   171
DAY 7: MUKENKO   197
DAY 8: KANYAMAGUFA   209
DAY 9: ZINJ   229
DAY 10: ZINJ   243
DAY 11: ZINJ   267
DAY 12: ZINJ   281
DAY 13: MUKENKO   311

Epilogue: The Place of Fire   341
References   345

Introduction

Only prejudice, and a trick of the Mercator projection, prevents us from recognizing the enormity of the African continent. Covering nearly twelve million square miles, Africa is almost as large as North America and Europe combined. It is nearly twice the size of South America. As we mistake its dimensions, we also mistake its essential nature: the Dark Continent is mostly hot desert and open grassy plains.

In fact, Africa is called the Dark Continent for one reason only: the vast equatorial rain forests of its central region. This is the drainage basin of the Congo River, and one-tenth of the continent is given over to it—a million and a half square miles of silent, damp, dark forest, a single uniform geographical feature nearly half the size of the continental United States. This primeval forest has stood, unchanged and unchallenged, for more than sixty million years.

Even today, only half a million people inhabit the Congo Basin, and they are mostly clustered in villages along the banks of the slow muddy rivers that flow through the jungle. The great expanse of the forest remains inviolate, and to this day thousands of square miles are still unexplored.

This is true particularly of the northeastern corner of the Congo basin, where the rain forest meets the Virunga volcanoes, at the edge of the Great Rift Valley. Lacking estab-

lished trade routes or compelling features of interest, Virunga
was never seen by Western eyes until less than a hundred years
ago.

The race to make "the most important discovery of the
1980s" in the Congo took place during six weeks of 1979.
This book recounts the thirteen days of the last American
expedition to the Congo, in June, 1979—barely a hundred
years after Henry Morton Stanley first explored the Congo in
1874–77. A comparison of the two expeditions reveals much
about the changing—and unchanging—nature of African
exploration in the intervening century.

Stanley is usually remembered as the newsman who found
Livingstone in 1871, but his real importance lay in later ex-
ploits. Moorehead calls him "a new kind of man in Africa . . .
a businessman-explorer. . . . Stanley was not in Africa to
reform the people nor to build an empire, and he was not
impelled by any real interest in such matters as anthropology,
botany or geology. To put it bluntly, he was out to make a
name for himself."

When Stanley set out again from Zanzibar in 1874, he
was again handsomely financed by newspapers. And when he
emerged from the jungle at the Atlantic Ocean 999 days later,
having suffered incredible hardships and the loss of more than
two-thirds of his original party, both he and his newspapers
had one of the great stories of the century: Stanley had traveled the entire length of the Congo River.

But two years later, Stanley was back in Africa under very
different circumstances. He traveled under an assumed name;
he made diversionary excursions to throw spies off his trail;
the few people who knew he was in Africa could only guess
that he had in mind "some grand commercial scheme."

In fact, Stanley was financed by Leopold II of Belgium,
who intended to acquire *personally* a large piece of Africa.
"It is not a question of Belgian colonies," Leopold wrote
Stanley. "It is a question of creating a new State, as big as

possible. . . . The King, as a private person, wishes to possess properties in Africa. Belgium wants neither a colony nor territories. Mr. Stanley must therefore buy lands or get them conceded to him. . . ."

This incredible plan was carried out. By 1885, one American said that Leopold "possesses the Congo just as Rockefeller possesses Standard Oil." The comparison was apt in more ways than one, for African exploration had become dominated by business.

It has remained so to this day. Stanley would have approved the 1979 American expedition, which was conducted in secrecy, with an emphasis on speed. But the differences would have astonished him. When Stanley passed near Virunga in 1875, it had taken him almost a year to get there; the Americans got their expedition on site in just over a week. And Stanley, who traveled with a small army of four hundred, would have been amazed at an expedition of only twelve— and one of them an ape. The territories through which the Americans moved a century later were autonomous political states; the Congo was now Zaire, and the Congo River the Zaire River. In fact, by 1979 the word "Congo" technically referred only to the drainage basin of the Zaire River, although Congo was still used in geological circles as a matter of familiarity, and for its romantic connotations.

Despite these differences, the expeditions had remarkably similar outcomes. Like Stanley, the Americans lost two-thirds of their party, and emerged from the jungle as desperately as Stanley's men a century before. And like Stanley, they returned with incredible tales of cannibals and pygmies, ruined jungle civilizations, and fabulous lost treasures.

I would like to thank R. B. Travis, of Earth Resources Technology Services in Houston, for permission to use videotaped debriefings; Dr. Karen Ross, of ERTS, for further background on the expedition; Dr. Peter Elliot, of the Department of Zoology, University of California at Berkeley, and the Project Amy staff, including Amy herself; Dr. William Wens, of Kasai Mining & Manufacturing, Zaire; Dr. Smith Jefferson, of the Department of Medical Pathology, University of Nairobi, Kenya; and Captain Charles Munro, of Tangier, Morocco.

I am further indebted to Mark Warwick, of Nairobi, for his initial interest in this project; Alan Binks, of Nairobi, for graciously offering to take me into the Virunga region of Zaire; Joyce Small for arranging my transport, usually at short notice, to obscure parts of the world; and finally my special thanks to my assistant, Judith Lovejoy, whose untiring efforts through very difficult times were crucial to the completion of this book.

M.C.

CONGO

Prologue:
The Place of Bones

Dawn came to the Congo rain forest.

The pale sun burned away the morning chill and the clinging damp mist, revealing a gigantic silent world. Enormous trees with trunks forty feet in diameter rose two hundred feet overhead, where they spread their dense leafy canopy, blotting out the sky and perpetually dripping water to the ground below. Curtains of gray moss, and creepers and lianas, hung down in a tangle from the trees; parasitic orchids sprouted from the trunks. At ground level, huge ferns, gleaming with moisture, grew higher than a man's chest and held the low ground fog. Here and there was a spot of color: the red acanthema blossoms, which were deadly poison, and the blue dicindra vine, which only opened in early morning. But the basic impression was of a vast, oversized, gray-green world—an alien place, inhospitable to man.

Jan Kruger put aside his rifle and stretched his stiff muscles. Dawn came quickly at the equator; soon it was quite light, although the mist remained. He glanced at the expedition campsite he had been guarding: eight bright orange nylon tents, a blue mess tent, a supply tarp lashed over boxed equipment in a vain attempt to keep them dry. He saw the other guard, Misulu, sitting on a rock; Misulu waved sleepily. Nearby was the transmitting equipment: a silver dish antenna, the black transmitter box, the snaking coaxial cables running to the portable video camera mounted on the collapsible tripod. The Americans used this equipment to transmit daily reports by satellite to their home office in Houston.

Kruger was the *bwana mukubwa*, hired to take the expedition into the Congo. He had led expeditions before: oil companies, map-survey parties, timber-mining teams, and geological parties like this one. Companies sending teams into the field wanted someone who knew local customs and local dialects well enough to handle the porters and arrange the travel. Kruger was well suited for this job; he spoke Kiswahili as well as Bantu and a little Bagindi, and he had been to the Congo many times, although never to Virunga.

Kruger could not imagine why American geologists would want to go to the Virunga region of Zaire, in the northeast corner of the Congo rain forest. Zaire was the richest country in black Africa, in minerals—the world's largest producer of cobalt and industrial diamonds, the seventh largest producer of copper. In addition there were major deposits of gold, tin, zinc, tungsten and uranium. But most of the minerals were found in Shaba and Kasai, not in Virunga.

Kruger knew better than to ask why the Americans wanted to go to Virunga, and in any case he had his answer soon enough. Once the expedition passed Lake Kivu and entered the rain forest, the geologists began scouring river and streambeds. Searching placer deposits meant that they were looking for gold, or diamonds. It turned out to be diamonds.

But not just any diamonds. The geologists were after what they called Type IIb diamonds. Each new sample was immediately submitted to an electrical test. The resulting conversations were beyond Kruger—talk of dielectric gaps, lattice ions, resistivity. But he gathered that it was the electrical properties of the diamonds that mattered. Certainly the samples were useless as gemstones. Kruger had examined several, and they were all blue from impurities.

For ten days, the expedition had been tracing back placer deposits. This was standard procedure: if you found gold or diamonds in streambeds, you moved upstream toward the presumed erosive source of the minerals. The expedition had moved to higher ground along the western slopes of the Virunga volcanic chain. It was all going routinely until one day around noon when the porters flatly refused to proceed further.

This part of Virunga, they said, was called *kanyamagufa*, which meant "the place of bones." The porters insisted that any men foolish enough to go further would have their bones broken, particularly their skulls. They kept touching their cheekbones, and repeating that their skulls would be crushed.

The porters were Bantu-speaking Arawanis from the nearest large town, Kisangani. Like most town-dwelling natives, they had all sorts of superstitions about the Congo jungle. Kruger called for the headman.

"What tribes are here?" Kruger asked, pointing to the jungle ahead.

"No tribes," the headman said.

"No tribes at all? Not even Bambuti?" he asked, referring to the nearest group of pygmies.

"No men come here," the headman said. "This is *kanyamagufa*."

"Then what crushes the skulls?"

"*Dawa*," the headman said ominously, using the Bantu term for magical forces. "Strong *dawa* here. Men stay away."

Kruger sighed. Like many white men, he was thoroughly sick of hearing about *dawa*. *Dawa* was everywhere, in plants and rocks and storms and enemies of all kinds. But the belief in *dawa* was prevalent throughout much of Africa and strongly held in the Congo.

Kruger had been obliged to waste the rest of the day in tedious negotiation. In the end, he doubled their wages and promised them firearms when they returned to Kisangani, and they agreed to continue on. Kruger considered the incident an irritating native ploy. Porters could generally be counted on to invoke some local superstition to increase their wages, once an expedition was deep enough into the field to be dependent on them. He had budgeted for this eventuality and, having agreed to their demands, he thought no more about it.

Even when they came upon several areas littered with shattered fragments of bone—which the porters found frightening—Kruger was not concerned. Upon examination, he found the bones were not human but rather the small delicate bones of colobus monkeys, the beautiful shaggy black-and-white creatures that lived in the trees overhead. It was true that there were a lot of bones, and Kruger had no idea why they should be shattered, but he had been in Africa a long time, and he had seen many inexplicable things.

Nor was he any more impressed with the overgrown fragments of stone that suggested a city had once stood in this area. Kruger had come upon unexplored ruins before, too. In Zimbabwe, in Broken Hill, in Maniliwi, there were the remains of cities and temples that no twentieth-century scientist had ever seen and studied.

He camped the first night near the ruins.

The porters were panic-stricken, insisting that the evil forces would attack them during the night. Their fear was caught by the American geologists; to pacify them, Kruger had posted two guards that night, himself and the most trustworthy porter, Misulu. Kruger thought it was all a lot of rot, but it had seemed the politic thing to do.

And just as he expected, the night had passed quietly. Around midnight there had been some movement in the bush, and some low wheezing sounds, which he took to be a leopard. Big cats often had respiratory trouble, particularly in the jungle. Otherwise it was quiet, and now it was dawn: the night was over.

A soft beeping sound drew his attention. Misulu heard it

too, and glanced questioningly at Kruger. On the transmitting equipment, a red light blinked. Kruger got up and crossed the campsite to the equipment. He knew how to operate it; the Americans had insisted that he learn, as an "emergency procedure." He crouched over the black transmitter box with its rectangular green LED.

He pressed buttons, and the screen printed TX HX, meaning a transmission from Houston. He pressed the response code, and the screen printed CAMLOK. That meant that Houston was asking for video camera transmission. He glanced over at the camera on its tripod and saw that the red light on the case had blinked on. He pressed the carrier button and the screen printed SATLOK, which meant that a satellite transmission was being locked in. There would now be a six-minute delay, the time required to lock the satellite-bounced signal.

He'd better go wake Driscoll, the head geologist, he thought. Driscoll would need a few minutes before the transmission came through. Kruger found it amusing the way the Americans always put on a fresh shirt and combed their hair before stepping in front of the camera. Just like television reporters.

Overhead, the colobus monkeys shrieked and screamed in the trees, shaking the branches. Kruger glanced upward, wondering what had set them going. But it was normal for colobus monkeys to fight in the morning.

Something struck him lightly in the chest. At first he thought it was an insect but, glancing down at his khaki shirt, he saw a spot of red, and a fleshy bit of red fruit rolled down his shirt to the muddy ground. The damned monkeys were throwing berries. He bent over to pick it up. And then he realized that it was not a piece of fruit at all. It was a human eyeball, crushed and slippery in his fingers, pinkish white with a shred of white optic nerve still attached at the back.

He swung his gun around and looked over to where Misulu was sitting on the rock. Misulu was not there.

Kruger moved across the campsite. Overhead, the colobus monkeys fell silent. He heard his boots squish in the mud as he moved past the tents of sleeping men. And then he heard the wheezing sound again. It was an odd, soft sound, carried on the swirling morning mist. Kruger wondered if he had been mistaken, if it was really a leopard.

And he saw Misulu. Misulu lay on his back, in a kind of halo of blood. His skull had been crushed from the sides, the facial bones shattered, the face narrowed and elongated, the mouth open in an obscene yawn, the one remaining eye wide and bulging. The other eye had exploded outward with the force of the impact.

Kruger felt his heart pounding as he bent to examine the body. He wondered what could have caused such an injury. And then he heard the soft wheezing sound again, and this time he felt quite sure it was not a leopard. Then the colobus monkeys began their shrieking, and Kruger leapt to his feet and screamed.

DAY 1: HOUSTON

June 13, 1979

1. ERTS Houston

Ten thousand miles away, in the cold, windowless main data room of Earth Resources Technology Services, Inc., of Houston, Karen Ross sat hunched over a mug of coffee in front of a computer terminal, reviewing the latest Landsat images from Africa. Ross was the ERTS Congo Project Supervisor, and as she manipulated the satellite images in artificial contrast colors, blue and purple and green, she glanced at her watch impatiently. She was waiting for the next field transmission from Africa.

It was now 10:15 p.m. Houston time, but there was no indication of time or place in the room. Day or night, the main data facility of ERTS remained the same. Beneath banks of special kalon fluorescent lights, programming crews in sweaters worked at long rows of quietly clicking computer terminals, providing real-time inputs to the field parties that ERTS maintained around the world. This timeless quality was understood to be necessary for the computers, which required a constant temperature of 60 degrees, dedicated electrical lines, special color-corrected lights that did not interfere with circuitry. It was an environment made for machines; the needs of people were secondary.

But there was another rationale for the main facility design. ERTS wanted programmers in Houston to identify with the field parties, and if possible to live on their schedules. Inputting baseball games and other local events was discouraged; there was no clock which showed Houston time, although on the far wall eight large digital clocks recorded local time for the various field parties.

The clock marked CONGO FIELD PARTY read 06:15 a.m. when the overhead intercom said, "Dr. Ross, CCR bounce."

She left the console after punching in the digital password blocking codes. Every ERTS terminal had a password control, like a combination lock. It was part of an elaborate system to prevent outside sources tapping into their enormous data bank. ERTS dealt in information, and as R. B. Travis, the head of ERTS, was fond of saying, the easiest way to obtain information was to steal it.

She crossed the room with long strides. Karen Ross was nearly six feet tall, an attractive though ungainly girl. Only twenty-four years old, she was younger than most of the programmers, but despite her youth, she had a self-possession that most people found striking—even a little unsettling. Karen Ross was a genuine mathematical prodigy.

At the age of two, while accompanying her mother to the supermarket, she had worked out in her head whether a ten-ounce can at 19¢ was cheaper than a one-pound-twelve-ounce can at 79¢. At three, she startled her father by observing that, unlike other numbers, zero meant different things in different positions. By eight, she had mastered algebra and geometry; by ten, she had taught herself calculus; she entered M.I.T. at thirteen and proceeded to make a series of brilliant discoveries in abstract mathematics, culminating in a treatise, "Topological Prediction in n-Space," which was useful for decision matrices, critical path analyses, and multidimensional mapping. This interest had brought her to the attention of ERTS, where she was made the youngest field supervisor in the company.

Not everyone liked her. The years of isolation, of being the youngest person in the room, had left her aloof and rather distant. One co-worker described her as "logical to a fault." Her chilly demeanor had earned her the title "Ross Glacier," after the Antarctic formation.

And her youth still held her back—at least, age was Travis's excuse when he refused to let her lead the Congo expedition into the field, even though she had derived all the Congo database, and by rights should have been the onsite team leader. "I'm sorry," Travis had said, "but this contract's too big, and I just can't let you have it." She had pressed, reminding him of her successes leading teams the year before to Pahang and Zambia. Finally he had said, "Look, Karen, that site's ten thousand miles away, in four-plus terrain. We need more than a console hotdogger out there."

She bridled under the implication that that was all she was—a console hotdogger, fast with the buttons, good at playing with Travis's toys. She wanted to prove herself in a four-plus field situation. And the next time she was determined to make Travis let her go.

Ross pressed the button for the third-floor elevator, marked "CX Access Only." She caught an envious glance from one of the programmers while she waited for the elevator to arrive. Within ERTS, status was not measured by salary, title, the size of one's office, or the other usual corporate indicators of power. Status at ERTS was purely a matter of access to information—and Karen Ross was one of eight people in the company who had access to the third floor at any time.

She stepped onto the third-floor elevator, glancing up at the scanner lens mounted over the door. At ERTS the elevators traveled only one floor, and all were equipped with passive scanners; it was one way that ERTS kept track of the movements of personnel while they were in the building. She said "Karen Ross" for the voice monitors, and turned in a full circle for the scanners. There was a soft electronic bleep, and the door slid open at the third floor.

She emerged into a small square room with a ceiling video monitor, and faced the unmarked outer door of the Communications Control Room. She repeated "Karen Ross," and inserted her electronic identicard in the slot, resting her fingers on the metallic edge of the card so the computer could record galvanic skin potentials. (This was a refinement instituted three months earlier, after Travis learned that Army experiments with vocal cord surgery had altered voice characteristics precisely enough to false-positive Voiceident programs.) After a cycling pause, the door buzzed open. She went inside.

With its red night lights, Communications Control was like a soft, warm womb—an impression heightened by the cramped, almost claustrophobic quality of the room, packed with electronic equipment. From floor to ceiling, dozens of video monitors and LEDs flickered and glowed as the technicians spoke in hushed tones, setting dials and twisting knobs. The CCR was the electronic nerve center of ERTS: all communications from field parties around the world were routed through here. Everything in the CCR was recorded, not only incoming data but room voice responses, so the exact conversation on the night of June 13, 1979, is known.

One of the technicians said to her, "We'll have the transponders hooked in in a minute. You want coffee?"

"No," Ross said.

"You want to be out there, right?"

"I earned it," she said. She stared at the video screens, at the bewildering display of rotating and shifting forms as the technicians began the litany of locking in the bird bounce, a transmission from satellite in orbit, 320 miles over their heads.

"Signal key."

"Signal key. Password mark."

"Password mark."

"Carrier fix."

"Carrier fix. We're rolling."

She paid hardly any attention to the familiar phrases. She watched as the screens displayed gray fields of crackling static. "Did we open or did they open?" she asked.

"We initiated," a technician said. "We had it down on the call sheet to check them at dawn local time. So when they didn't initiate, we did."

"I wonder why they didn't initiate," Ross said. "Is something wrong?"

"I don't think so. We put out the initiation trigger and they picked it up and locked in within fifteen seconds, all the appropriate codes. Ah, here we go."

At 6:22 a.m. Congo time, the transmission came through: there was a final blur of gray static and then the screens cleared. They were looking at a part of the camp in the Congo, apparently a view from a tripod-mounted video camera. They saw two tents, a low smoldering fire, the lingering wisps of a foggy dawn. There was no sign of activity, no people.

One of the technicians laughed. "We caught them still sleeping. Guess they do need you there." Ross was known for her insistence on formalities.

"Lock your remote," she said.

The technician punched in the remote override. The field camera, ten thousand miles away, came under their control in Houston.

"Pan scan," she said.

At the console, the technician used a joystick. They watched as the video images shifted to the left, and they saw more of the camp. The camp was destroyed: tents crushed and torn, supply tarp pulled away, equipment scattered in the mud. One tent burned brightly, sending up clouds of black smoke. They saw several dead bodies.

"Jesus," one technician said.

"Back scan," Ross said. "Spot resolve to six-six."

On the screens, the camera panned back across the camp. They looked at the jungle. They still saw no sign of life.

"Down pan. Reverse sweep."

Onscreen, the camera panned down to show the silver dish of the portable antenna, and the black box of the transmitter. Nearby was another body, one of the geologists, lying on his back.

"Jesus, that's Roger. . . ."

"Zoom and T-lock," Ross said. On the tape, her voice sounds cool, almost detached.

The camera zoomed in on the face. What they saw was grotesque, the head crushed and leaking blood from eyes and nose, mouth gaping toward the sky.

"What did *that?*"

At that moment, a shadow fell across the dead face onscreen. Ross jumped forward, grabbing the joystick and hitting the zoom control. The image widened swiftly; they could see the outline of the shadow now. It was a man. And he was moving.

"Somebody's there! Somebody's still alive!"

"He's limping. Looks wounded."

Ross stared at the shadow. It did not look to her like a limping man; something was wrong, she couldn't put her finger on what it was. . . .

"He's going to walk in front of the lens," she said. It was almost too much to hope for. "What's that audio static?"

They were hearing an odd sound, like a hissing or a sighing.

"It's not static, it's in the transmission."

"Resolve it," Ross said. The technicians punched buttons, altering the audio frequencies, but the sound remained peculiar and indistinct. And then the shadow moved, and the man stepped in front of the lens.

"Diopter," Ross said, but it was too late. The face had

already appeared, very near the lens. It was too close to focus without a diopter. They saw a blurred, dark shape, nothing more. Before they could click in the diopter, it was gone.

"A native?"

"This region of the Congo is uninhabited," Ross said.

"*Something* inhabits it."

"Pan scan," Ross said. "See if you can get him onscreen again."

The camera continued to pan. She could imagine it sitting on its tripod in the jungle, motor whirring as the lens head swung around. Then suddenly the image tilted and fell sideways.

"He knocked it over."

"Damn!"

The video image crackled, shifting lines of static. It became very difficult to see.

"Resolve it! Resolve it!"

They had a final glimpse of a large face and a dark hand as the silver dish antenna was smashed. The image from the Congo shrank to a spot, and was gone.

2. Interference Signature

During June of 1979, Earth Resources Technology had field teams studying uranium deposits in Bolivia, copper deposits in Pakistan, agricultural field utilization in Kashmir, glacier advance in Iceland, timber resources in Malaysia, and diamond deposits in the Congo. This was not unusual for ERTS; they generally had between six and eight groups in the field at any time.

Since their teams were often in hazardous or politically unstable regions, they were vigilant in watching for the first signs of "interference signatures." (In remote-sensing terminology, a "signature" is the characteristic appearance of an object or geological feature in a photograph or video image.) Most interference signatures were political. In 1977, ERTS had airlifted a team out of Borneo during a local Communist uprising, and again from Nigeria in 1978 during a military coup. Occasionally the signatures were geological; they had pulled a team from Guatemala in 1976 after the earthquake there.

In the opinion of R. B. Travis, called out of bed in the late hours of June 13, 1979, the videotapes from the Congo were "the worst interference signature ever," but the signature origin remained mysterious. All they knew was that the camp had been destroyed in a mere six minutes—the time between the signal initiation from Houston and the reception in the Congo. The rapidity was frightening; Travis's first instruction was to figure out "what the hell happened out there."

A heavyset man of forty-eight, Travis was accustomed to crises. By training he was an engineer with a background in satellite construction for RCA and later Rockwell; in his thirties he had shifted to management, becoming what aerospace engineers called a "Rain Dancer." Companies manufacturing satellites contracted eighteen to twenty-four months in advance for a launch rocket to put the satellite in orbit—and then hoped that the satellite, with its half-million working parts, would be ready on the assigned day. If it was not, the only alternative was to pray for bad weather delaying the launch, to dance for rain.

Travis had managed to keep a sense of humor after a decade of high-tech problems; his management philosophy was summarized by a large sign mounted behind his desk, which read "S.D.T.A.G.W." It stood for "Some Damn Thing Always Goes Wrong."

But Travis was not amused on the night of June 13. His entire expedition had been lost, all the ERTS party killed— eight of his people, and however many local porters were with them. *Eight people!* The worst disaster in ERTS history, worse even than Nigeria in '78. Travis felt fatigued, mentally drained, as he thought of all the phone calls ahead of him. Not the calls he would make, but those he would receive. Would so-and-so be back in time for a daughter's graduation, a son's Little League playoff? Those calls would be routed to Travis, and he would have to listen to the bright expectation in the voices, the hopefulness, and his own careful answers—he wasn't sure, he understood the problem, he would do his best, of course, of course. . . . The coming deception exhausted him in advance.

Because Travis couldn't tell anyone what had happened for at least two weeks, perhaps a month. And then he would be making phone calls himself, and visits to the homes, and attending the memorial services where there would be no casket, a deadly blank space, a gap, and the inevitable questions from families and relatives that he couldn't answer while they scrutinized his face, looking for the least muscle twitch, or hesitation, or sign.

What could he tell them?

That was his only consolation—perhaps in a few weeks, Travis could tell them more. One thing was certain: if he were to make the dreadful calls tonight, he could tell the families nothing at all, for ERTS had no idea what had gone wrong. That fact added to Travis's sense of exhaustion. And there were details: Morris, the insurance auditor, came in and said "What do you want to do about the terms?" ERTS took out term life insurance policies for every expedition member, and also for local porters. African porters received U.S. $15,000 each in insurance, which seemed trivial until one recognized that African per capita income averaged U.S. $180 per year. But Travis had always argued that local expedition people should share risk benefits—even if it meant paying widowed families a small fortune, in their terms. Even if it cost ERTS a small fortune for the insurance.

"Hold them," Travis said.

"Those policies are costing us *per day*—"

"Hold them," Travis said.

"For how long?"

"Thirty days," Travis said.

"Thirty *more* days?"

"That's right."

"But we know the holders are dead." Morris could not reconcile himself to the waste of money. His actuarial mind rebelled.

"That's right," Travis said. "But you'd better slip the porters' families some cash to keep them quiet."

"Jesus. How much are we talking about?"

"Five hundred dollars each."

"How do we account that?"

"Legal fees," Travis said. "Bury it in legal, local disposition."

"And the American team people that we've lost?"

"They have Master Charge," Travis said. "Stop worrying."

Roberts, the British-born ERTS press liaison, came into his office. "You want to open this can up?"

"No," Travis said. "I want to kill it."

"For how long?"

"Thirty days."

"Bloody hell. Your own staff will leak inside thirty days," Roberts said. "I promise you."

"If they do, you'll squash it," Travis said. "I need another thirty days to make this contract."

"Do we know what happened out there?"

"No," Travis said. "But we will."

"How?"

"From the tapes."

"Those tapes are a mess."

"So far," Travis said. And he called in the specialty teams of console hotdoggers. Travis had long since concluded that although ERTS could wake up political advisers around the world, they were most likely to get information in-house. "Everything we know from the Congo field expedition," he said, "is registered on that final videotape. I want a seven-band visual and audio salvage, starting right now. Because that tape is all we have."

The specialty teams went to work.

3. Recovery

ERTS referred to the process as "data recovery," or sometimes as "data salvage." The terms evoked images of deep-sea operations, and they were oddly appropriate.

To recover or salvage data meant that coherent meaning was pulled to the surface from the depths of massive electronic information storage. And, like salvage from the sea, it was a slow and delicate process, where a single false step meant the irretrievable loss of the very elements one was trying to bring up. ERTS had whole salvage crews skilled in the art of data recovery. One crew immediately went to work on the audio recovery, another on the visual recovery.

But Karen Ross was already engaged in a visual recovery. The procedures she followed were highly sophisticated, and only possible at ERTS.

Earth Resources Technology was a relatively new company, formed in 1975 in response to the explosive growth of information on the Earth and its resources. The amount of material handled by ERTS was staggering: just the Landsat imagery alone amounted to more than five hundred thousand pictures, and sixteen new images were acquired every hour, around the clock. With the addition of conventional and draped aerial photography, infrared photography, and artificial aperture side-looking radar, the total information available to ERTS exceeded two million images, with new input on the order of thirty images an hour. All this information had to be catalogued, stored, and made available for instantaneous retrieval. ERTS was like a library which acquired seven hundred new books a day. It was not surprising that the librarians worked at fever pitch around the clock.

Visitors to ERTS never seemed to realize that even with computers, such data-handling capacity would have been impossible ten years earlier. Nor did visitors understand the basic nature of the ERTS information—they assumed that the pictures on the screens were photographic, although they were not.

Photography was a nineteenth-century chemical system for recording information using light-sensitive silver salts. ERTS utilized a twentieth-century electrical system for recording information, analogous to chemical photographs, but very different. Instead of cameras, ERTS used multispectral scanners; instead of film, they used CCTs—computer compatible tapes. In fact, ERTS did not bother with "pictures" as they were ordinarily understood from old-fashioned photographic technology. ERTS bought "data scans" which they converted to "data displays," as the need arose.

Since the ERTS images were just electrical signals recorded on magnetic tape, a great variety of electrical image manipulation was possible. ERTS had 837 computer programs to alter imagery: to enhance it, to eliminate unwanted elements, to bring out details. Ross used fourteen programs on the Congo videotape—particularly on the static-filled section in which the hand and face appeared, just before the antenna was smashed.

First she carried out what was called a "wash cycle," getting rid of the static. She identified the static lines as occurring at specific scan positions, and having a specific gray-scale value. She instructed the computer to cancel those lines.

The resulting image showed blank spaces where the static was removed. So she did "fill-in-the-blanks"—instructing the computer to introject imagery, according to what was around the blank spaces. In this operation the computer made a logical guess about what was missing.

She now had a static-free image, but it was muddy and indistinct, lacking definition. So she did a "high-priced spread"—intensifying the image by spreading the gray-scale values. But for some reason she also got a phase distortion that she had to cancel, and that released spiking glitches previously suppressed, and to get rid of the glitches she had to run three other programs. . . .

Technical details preoccupied her for an hour, until suddenly the image "popped," coming up bright and clean. She caught her breath as she saw it. The screen showed a dark, brooding face with heavy brows, watchful eyes, a flattened nose, prognathous lips.

Frozen on the video screen was the face of a male gorilla.

Travis came over, shaking his head. "We finished the audio recovery on that hissing noise. The computer confirms it as human breathing, with at least four separate origins. But it's damned strange. According to the analysis, the sound is coming from inhalation, not exhalation, the way people usually make sounds."

"The computer is wrong," Ross said. "It's not human." She pointed to the screen, and the face of the gorilla.

Travis showed no surprise. "Artifact," he said.

"It's no artifact."

"You did fill-in-the-blanks, and you got an artifact. The tag team's been screwing around with the software at lunch again." The tag team—the young software programmers—had a tendency to convert data to play highly sophisticated versions of pinball games. Their games sometimes got subrouted into other programs.

Ross herself had complained about it. "But this image is real," she insisted, pointing to the screen.

"Look," Travis said, "last week Harry did fill-in-the-blanks on the Karakorum Mountains and he got back a lunar landing game. You're supposed to land next to the McDonald's stand, all very amusing." He walked off. "You'd better meet the others in my office. We're setting advance times to get back in."

"I'm leading the next team."

Travis shook his head. "Out of the question."

"But what about this?" she said, pointing to the screen.

"I'm not buying that image," Travis said. "Gorillas don't behave that way. It's got to be an artifact." He glanced at his watch. "Right now, the only question I have is how fast we can put a team back in the Congo."

4. Return Expedition

Travis had never had any doubts in his mind about going back in; from the first time he saw the videotapes from the Congo, the only question was how best to do it. He called in all the section heads: Accounts, Diplo, Remote, Geo, Logistics, Legal. They were all yawning and rubbing their eyes. Travis began by saying, "I want us back in the Congo in ninety-six hours."

Then he leaned back in his chair and let them tell him why it couldn't be done. There were plenty of reasons.

"We can't assemble the air cargo units for shipment in less than a hundred and sixty hours," Cameron, the logistics man said.

"We can postpone the Himalaya team, and use their units," Travis said.

"But that's a mountain expedition."

"You can modify the units in nine hours," Travis said.

"But we can't get equipment to fly it out," Lewis, the transport master, said.

"Korean Airlines has a 747 cargo jet available at SFX. They tell me it can be down here in nine hours."

"They have a plane just sitting there?" Lewis said, incredulous.

"I believe," Travis said, "that they had a last-minute cancellation from another customer."

Irwin, the accountant, groaned. "What'd that cost?"

"We can't get visas from the Zaire Embassy in Washington in time," Martin, the diplomatic man, said. "And there is serious doubt they'd issue them to us at all. As you know, the first set of Congo visas were based on our mineral exploration rights with the Zaire government, and our MER are non-exclusive. We were granted permission to go in, and so were the Japanese, the Germans, and the Dutch, who've formed a mining consortium. But it's strictly first come, first served. First ore-body strike takes the contract. If Zaire finds out that our expedition is in trouble, they'll just cancel us out and let the Euro-Japanese consortium try their luck. There are three hundred Japanese trade officials in Kinshasa right now, spending yen like water."

"I think that's right," Travis said. "If it became known that our expedition is in trouble."

"It'll become known the minute we apply for visas."

"We won't apply for them. As far as anybody knows," Travis said, "we still have an expedition in Virunga. If we put a second small team into the field fast enough, nobody will ever know that it wasn't the original team."

"But what about the specific personnel visas to cross the borders, the manifests—"

"Details," Travis said. "That's what liquor is for," referring to bribes, which were often liquor. In many parts of the world, expedition teams went in with crates of liquor and boxes of those perennial favorites, transistor radios and Polaroid cameras.

"Details? How're you going to cross the border?"

"We'll need a good man for that. Maybe Munro."

"Munro? That's playing rough. The Zaire government hates Munro."

"He's resourceful, and he knows the area."

Martin, the diplomatic expert, cleared his throat and said, "I'm not sure I should be here for this discussion. It looks to me as if you are proposing to enter a sovereign state with an illegal party led by a former Congo mercenary soldier. . . ."

"Not at all," Travis said. "I'm obliged to put a support party into the field to assist my people already there. Happens all the time. I have no reason to think anybody is in trouble; just a routine support party. I haven't got time to go through official channels. I may not be showing the best judgment in whom I hire, but it's nothing more serious than that."

By 11:45 p.m. on the night of June 13, the main sequencing of the next ERTS expedition had been worked out and confirmed by the computer. A fully loaded 747 could leave Houston at 8 p.m. the following evening, June 14; the plane could be in Africa on June 15 to pick up Munro "or someone like him"; and the full team could be in place in the Congo on June 17.

In ninety-six hours.

From the main data room, Karen Ross could look through the glass walls into Travis's office and see the arguments taking place. In her logical way, she concluded that Travis had "Q'd" himself, meaning that he had drawn false conclusions from insufficient data, and had said Q.E.D. too soon. Ross felt there

was no point in going back into the Congo until they knew
what they were up against. She remained at her console,
checking the image she had recovered.

Ross bought this image—but how could she make Travis
buy it?

In the highly sophisticated data-processing world of
ERTS, there was a constant danger that extracted information would begin to "float"—that the images would cut loose
from reality, like a ship cut loose from its moorings. This
was true particularly when the database was put through
multiple manipulations—when you were rotating 106 pixels in
computer-generated hyper space.

So ERTS evolved other ways to check the validity of
images they got back from the computer. Ross ran two check
programs against the gorilla image. The first was called
APNF, for Animation Predicted Next Frame.

It was possible to treat videotape as if it were movie film, a
succession of stills. She showed the computer several "stills" in
succession, and then asked it to create the Predicted Next
Frame. This PNF was then checked against the actual next
frame.

She ran eight PNFs in a row, and they worked. If there
was an error in the data handling, it was at least a consistent
error.

Encouraged, she next ran a "fast and dirty three-space."
Here the flat video image was assumed to have certain three-
dimensional characteristics, based on gray-scale patterns. In
essence, the computer decided that the shadow of a nose, or a
mountain range, meant that the nose or mountain range protruded above the surrounding surface. Succeeding images
could be checked against these assumptions. As the gorilla
moved, the computer verified that the flat image was, indeed,
three-dimensional and coherent.

This proved beyond a doubt that the image was real.

She went to see Travis.

. . .

"Let's say I buy this image," Travis said, frowning. "I still don't see why you should take the next expedition in."

Ross said, "What did the other team find?"

"The other team?" Travis asked innocently.

"You gave that tape to another salvage team to confirm my recovery," Ross said.

Travis glanced at his watch. "They haven't pulled anything out yet." And he added, "We all know you're fast with the database."

Ross smiled. "That's why you need me to take the expedition in," she said. "I know the database, because I generated the database. And if you intend to send another team in right away, before this gorilla thing is solved, the only hope you have is for the team leader to be fast onsite with the data. This time, you *need* a console hotdogger in the field. Or the next expedition will end up like the last one. Because you still don't know what happened to the last expedition."

Travis sat behind his desk, and stared at her for a long time. She recognized his hesitation as a sign that he was weakening.

"And I want to go outside," Ross said.

"To an outside expert?"

"Yes. Somebody on our grant list."

"Risky," Travis said. "I hate to involve outside people at this point. You know the consortium is breathing down our necks. You up the leak ratios."

"It's important," Ross insisted.

Travis sighed. "Okay, if you think it's important." He sighed again. "Just don't delay your team."

Ross was already packing up her hard copy.

. . .

Alone, Travis frowned, turning over his decision in his mind. Even if they ran the next Congo expedition slam-bam, in and out in less than fifteen days, their fixed costs would still exceed three hundred thousand dollars. The Board was going to scream—sending an untried, twenty-four-year-old kid, a *girl*, into the field with this kind of responsibility. Especially on a project as important as this one, where the stakes were enormous, and where they had already fallen behind on every timeline and cost projection. And Ross was so cold, she was likely to prove a poor field leader, alienating the others in the team.

Yet Travis had a hunch about the Ross Glacier. His management philosophy, tempered in his rain-dancing days, was always to give the project to whoever had the most to gain from success—or the most to lose from failure.

He turned to face his console, mounted beside his desk. "Travis," he said, and the screen glowed.

"Psychograph file," he said.

The screen showed call prompts.

"Ross, Karen," Travis said.

The screen flashed THINKING A MOMENT . That was the programmed response which meant that information was being extracted. He waited.

Then the psychograph summary printed out across the screen. Every ERTS employee underwent three days of intensive psychological testing to determine not only skills but potential biases. The assessment of Ross would, he felt, be reassuring to the Board.

HIGHLY INTELLIGENT / LOGICAL / FLEXIBLE / RESOURCEFUL / DATA INTUITIVE / THOUGHT PROCESSES SUITED TO RAPIDLY CHANGING REALTIME CONTEXTS / DRIVEN TO SUCCEED AT DEFINED GOALS / CAPABLE SUSTAINED MENTAL EFFORT /

It looked like the perfect description of the next Congo team leader. He scanned down the screen, looking for the negatives. These were less reassuring.

YOUTHFUL-RUTHLESS / TENUOUS HUMAN RAPPORT / DOMINEERING / INTELLECTUALLY ARROGANT / INSENSITIVE / DRIVEN TO SUCCEED AT ANY COST /

And there was a final "flopover" notation. The very concept of personality flopover had been evolved through ERTS testing. It suggested that any dominant personality trait could be suddenly reversed under stress conditions: parental personalities could flop over and turn childishly petulant, hysterical personalities could become icy calm—or logical personalities could become illogical.

FLOPOVER MATRIX: DOMINANT {POSSIBLY UNDESIRABLE} OBJECTIV-ITY MAY BE LOST ONCE DESIRED GOAL IS PERCEIVED CLOSE AT HAND / DESIRE FOR SUCCESS MAY PROVOKE DANGEROUSLY ILLOGICAL RESPONSES / PARENTAL FIGURES WILL BE ESPECIALLY DENIGRATED / SUBJECT MUST BE MONITORED IN LATE STAGE GOAL-ORIENTED PROCEDURES /

Travis looked at the screen, and decided that such a circumstance was highly unlikely in the coming Congo expedition.

Karen Ross was exhilarated by her new authority. Shortly before midnight, she called up the grant lists on her office terminal. ERTS had animal experts in various areas whom they supported with nominal grants from a non-profit foundation called the Earth Resources Wildlife Fund. The grant lists were arranged taxonomically. Under "Primates" she found fourteen names, including several in Borneo, Malaysia, and

Africa as well as the United States. In the United States there
was only one gorilla researcher available, a primatologist
named Dr. Peter Elliot, at the University of California at
Berkeley.

The file onscreen indicated that Elliot was twenty-nine
years old, unmarried, an associate professor without tenure in
the Department of Zoology. Principal Research Interest was
listed as "Primate Communications (Gorilla)." Funding was
made to something called Project Amy.

She checked her watch. It was just midnight in Houston,
10 p.m. in California. She dialed the home number on the
screen.

"Hello," a wary male voice said.

"Dr. Peter Elliot?"

"Yes . . ." The voice was still cautious, hesitant. "Are you
a reporter?"

"No," she said. "This is Dr. Karen Ross in Houston; I'm
associated with the Earth Resources Wildlife Fund, which
supports your research."

"Oh, yes . . ." The voice remained cautious. "You're sure
you're not a reporter? It's only fair to tell you I'm recording
this telephone call as a potential legal document."

Karen Ross hesitated. The last thing she needed was some
paranoid academic recording ERTS developments. She said
nothing.

"You're American?" he said.

"Of course."

Karen Ross stared at the computer screens, which flashed
VOICE IDENTIFICATION CONFIRMED: ELLIOT, PETER, 29 YEARS.

"State your business," Elliot said.

"Well, we're about to send an expedition into the Virunga
region of the Congo, and—"

"Really? When are you going?" The voice suddenly
sounded excited, boyish.

"Well, as a matter of fact we're leaving in two days, and—"

"I want to go," Elliot said.

Ross was so surprised she hardly knew what to say. "Well, Dr. Elliot, that's not why I'm calling you, as a matter of fact—"

"I'm planning to go there anyway," Elliot said. "With Amy."

"Who's Amy?"

"Amy is a gorilla," Peter Elliot said.

DAY 2: SAN FRANCISCO
June 14, 1979

1. Project Amy

It is unfair to suggest, as some primatologists later did, that Peter Elliot had to "get out of town" in June, 1979. His motives, and the planning behind the decision to go to the Congo, are a matter of record. Professor Elliot and his staff had decided on an African trip at least two days before Ross called him.

But it is certainly true that Peter Elliot was under attack: from outside groups, the press, academic colleagues, and even members of his own department at Berkeley. Toward the end, Elliot was accused of being a "Nazi criminal" engaged in the "torture of dumb [sic] animals." It is no exaggeration to say that Elliot had found himself, in the spring of 1979, fighting for his professional life.

Yet his research had begun quietly, almost accidentally. Peter Elliot was a twenty-three-year-old graduate student in the Department of Anthropology at Berkeley when he first read about a year-old gorilla with amoebic dysentery who had been flown from the Minneapolis zoo to the San Francisco School of Veterinary Medicine for treatment. That was in 1973, in the exciting early days of primate language research.

The idea that primates might be taught language was very old. In 1661, Samuel Pepys saw a chimpanzee in London and wrote in his diary that it was "so much like a man in most things that . . . I do believe that it already understands much English, and I am of the mind it might be taught to speak or make signs." Another seventeenth-century writer went further, saying, "Apes and Baboons . . . can speak but will not for fear they should be imployed, and set to work."

Yet for the next three hundred years attempts to teach apes to talk were notably unsuccessful. They culminated in an ambitious effort by a Florida couple, Keith and Kathy Hayes, who for six years in the early 1950s raised a chimpanzee named Vicki as if she were a human infant. During that time, Vicki learned four words—"mama," "papa," "cup," and "up." But her pronunciation was labored and her progress slow. Her difficulties seemed to support the growing conviction among scientists that man was the only animal capable of language. Typical was the pronouncement of George Gaylord Simpson: "Language is . . . the most diagnostic single trait of man: all normal men have language; no other now living organisms do."

This seemed so self-evident that for the next fifteen years nobody bothered to try teaching language to an ape. Then in 1966, a Reno, Nevada, couple named Beatrice and Allen Gardner reviewed movies of Vicki speaking. It seemed to them that Vicki was not so much incapable of language as incapable of speech. They noticed that while her lip movements were awkward, her hand gestures were fluid and expressive. The obvious conclusion was to try sign language.

In June, 1966, the Gardners began teaching American Sign Language (Ameslan), the standardized language of the deaf, to an infant chimpanzee named Washoe. Washoe's progress with ASL was rapid; by 1971, she had a vocabulary of 160 signs, which she used in conversation. She also made up new word combinations for things she had never seen before: when shown watermelon for the first time, she signed it "water fruit."

The Gardners' work was highly controversial; it turned out that many scientists had an investment in the idea that apes were incapable of language. (As one researcher said, "My God, think of all those eminent names attached to all those scholarly papers for all those decades—and everyone agreeing that only man had language. What a mess.")

Washoe's skills provoked a variety of other experiments in teaching language. A chimpanzee named Lucy was taught to communicate through a computer; another, Sarah, was taught to use plastic markers on a board. Other apes were studied as well. An orangutan named Alfred began instruction in 1971; a lowland gorilla named Koko in 1972; and in 1973 Peter Elliot began with a mountain gorilla, Amy.

At his first visit to the hospital to meet Amy, he found a pathetic little creature, heavily sedated, with restraining straps on her frail black arms and legs. He stroked her head and said gently, "Hello, Amy, I'm Peter."

Amy promptly bit his hand, drawing blood.

From this inauspicious beginning emerged a singularly successful research program. In 1973, the basic teaching technique, called molding, was well understood. The animal was shown an object and the researcher simultaneously molded the animal's hand into the correct sign, until the association was firmly made. Subsequent testing confirmed that the animal understood the meaning of the sign.

But if the basic methodology was accepted, the application was highly competitive. Researchers competed over the rate of sign acquisition, or vocabulary. (Among human beings, vocabulary was considered the best measure of intelligence.) The rate of sign acquisition could be taken as a measure of either the scientist's skill or the animal's intelligence.

It was by now clearly recognized that different apes had different personalities. As one researcher commented, "Pongid studies are perhaps the only field in which academic gossip centers on the students and not the teachers." In the increasingly competitive and disputatious world of primate research, it was said that Lucy was a drunk, that Koko was an ill-mannered brat, that Lana's head was turned by her celebrity ("she only works when there is an interviewer present"), and that Nim was so stupid he should have been named Dim.

At first glance, it may seem odd that Peter Elliot should have come under attack, for this handsome, rather shy man—the son of a Marin County dry cleaner—had avoided controversy during his years of work with Amy. Elliot's publications were modest and temperate; his progress with Amy was well documented; he showed no interest in publicity, and was not among those researchers who took their apes on the Carson or the Griffin show.

But Elliot's diffident manner concealed not only a quick intelligence, but a fierce ambition as well. If he avoided controversy, it was only because he didn't have time for it—he had been working nights and weekends for years, and driving his staff and Amy just as hard. He was very good at the business of science, getting grants; at all the animal behaviorist conferences, where others showed up in jeans and plaid lumberjack shirts, Elliot arrived in a three-piece suit. Elliot intended to be the foremost ape researcher, and he intended Amy to be the foremost ape.

Elliot's success in obtaining grants was such that by 1975 he employed four people working full time with Amy. By 1978, Project Amy had an annual budget of $160,000 and a staff of eight, including a child psychologist and a computer programmer. A staff member of the Bergren Institute later said that Elliot's appeal lay in the fact that he was "a good investment; for example, Project Amy got fifty percent more computer time for our money because he went on line with his time-sharing terminal at night and on weekends, when the time was cheaper. He was very cost-effective. And dedicated, of course: Elliot obviously cared about nothing in life except his work with Amy. That made him a boring conversationalist but a very good bet, from our standpoint. It's hard to decide who's truly brilliant; it's easier to see who's driven, which in the long run may be more important. We anticipated great things from Elliot."

Peter Elliot's difficulties began on the morning of February 2, 1979. Amy lived in a mobile home on the Berkeley campus; she spent nights there alone, and usually provided an effusive greeting the next day. However, on that morning the Project Amy staff found her in an uncharacteristic sullen mood; she was irritable and bleary-eyed, behaving as if she had been wronged in some fashion.

Elliot felt that something had upset her during the night. When asked, she kept making signs for "sleep box," a new word pairing he did not understand. That in itself was not unusual; Amy made up new word pairings all the time, and they were often hard to decipher. Just a few days before, she had bewildered them by talking about "crocodile milk." Eventually they realized that Amy's milk had gone sour, and that since she disliked crocodiles (which she had only seen in picture books), she somehow decided that sour milk was "crocodile milk."

Now she was talking about "sleep box." At first they thought she might be referring to her nestlike bed. It turned out she was using "box" in her usual sense, to refer to the television set.

Everything in her trailer, including the television, was controlled on a twenty-four-hour cycle by the computer. They ran a check to see if the television had been turned on during the night, disturbing her sleep. Since Amy liked to watch television, it was conceivable that she had managed to turn it on herself. But Amy looked scornful as they examined the actual television in the trailer. She clearly meant something else.

Finally they determined that by "sleep box" she meant

"sleep pictures." When asked about these sleep pictures, Amy signed that they were "bad pictures" and "old pictures," and that they "make Amy cry."

She was dreaming.

The fact that Amy was the first primate to report dreams caused tremendous excitement among Elliot's staff. But the excitement was short-lived. Although Amy continued to dream on succeeding nights, she refused to discuss her dreams; in fact, she seemed to blame the researchers for this new and confusing intrusion into her mental life. Worse, her waking behavior deteriorated alarmingly.

Her word acquisition rate fell from 2.7 words a week to 0.8 words a week, her spontaneous word formation rate from 1.9 to 0.3. Monitored attention span was halved. Mood swings increased; erratic and unmotivated behavior became commonplace; temper tantrums occurred daily. Amy was four and a half feet tall, and weighed 130 pounds. She was an immensely strong animal. The staff began to wonder if they could control her.

Her refusal to talk about her dreams frustrated them. They tried a variety of investigative approaches: they showed her pictures from books and magazines; they ran the ceiling-mounted video monitors around the clock, in case she signed something significant while alone (like young children, Amy often "talked to herself"); they even administered a battery of neurological tests, including an EEG.

Finally they hit on finger painting.

This was immediately successful. Amy was enthusiastic about finger painting, and after they mixed cayenne pepper with the pigments, she stopped licking her fingers. She drew images swiftly and repetitively, and she seemed to become somewhat more relaxed, more her old self.

David Bergman, the child psychologist, noted that "what Amy actually draws is a cluster of apparently related images:

inverted crescent shapes, or semicircles, which are always associated with an area of vertical green streaks. Amy says the green streaks represent 'forest,' and she calls the semicircles 'bad houses' or 'old houses.' In addition she often draws black circles, which she calls 'holes.' "

Bergman cautioned against the obvious conclusion that she was drawing old buildings in the jungle. "Watching her make drawings one after another, again and again, convinces me of the obsessive and private nature of the imagery. Amy is troubled by these pictures, and she is trying to get them out, to banish them to paper."

In fact, the nature of the imagery remained mysterious to the Project Amy staff. By late April, 1979, they had concluded that her dreams could be explained in four ways. In order of seriousness, they were:

1. *The dreams are an attempt to rationalize events in her daily life.* This was the usual explanation of (human) dreams, but the staff doubted that it applied in Amy's case.

2. *The dreams are a transitional adolescent manifestation.* At seven years of age, Amy was a gorilla teenager, and for nearly a year she had shown many typical teenage traits, including rages and sulks, fussiness about her appearance, a new interest in the opposite sex.

3. *The dreams are a species-specific phenomeon.* It was possible that all gorillas had disturbing dreams, and that in the wild the resultant stresses were handled in some fashion by the behavior of the group. Although gorillas had been studied in the wild for the past twenty years, there was no evidence for this.

4. *The dreams are the first sign of incipient dementia.* This was the most feared possibility. To train an ape effectively, one had to begin with an infant; as the years progressed, researchers waited to see if their animal would grow up to be bright or stupid, recalcitrant or pliable, healthy or sickly. The

health of apes was a constant worry; many programs collapsed
after years of effort and expense when the apes died of physical
or mental illness. Timothy, an Atlanta chimp, became psy-
chotic in 1976 and committed suicide by coprophagia, chok-
ing to death on his own feces. Maurice, a Chicago orang,
became intensely neurotic, developing phobias that halted
work in 1977. For better or worse, the very intelligence that
made apes worthwhile subjects for study also made them as
unstable as human beings.

But the Project Amy staff was unable to make further
progress. In May, 1979, they made what turned out to be a
momentous decision: they decided to publish Amy's drawings,
and submitted her images to the *Journal of Behavioral Sci-
ences*.

2. Breakthrough

"Dream Behavior in a Mountain Gorilla" was never published. The paper was routinely forwarded to three scientists on the editorial board for review, and one copy somehow (it is still unclear just how) fell into the hands of the
Primate Preservation Agency, a New York group formed
in 1975 to prevent the "unwarranted and illegitimate exploi-
tation of intelligent primates in unnecessary laboratory
research."*

On June 3, the PPA began picketing the Zoology Department at Berkeley, and calling for the "release" of Amy. Most
of the demonstrators were women, and several young children
were present; videotapes of an eight-year-old boy holding a

---

* The following account of Elliot's persecution draws heavily on J. A.
Peebles, "Infringement of Academic Freedom by Press Innuendo and Hearsay:
The Experience of Dr. Peter Elliot," in the *Journal of Academic Law and
Psychiatry* 52, no. 12 (1979): 19–38.

placard with Amy's photograph and shouting "Free Amy! Free Amy!" appeared on local television news.

In a tactical error, the Project Amy staff elected to ignore the protests except for a brief press release stating that the PPA was "misinformed." The release went out under the Berkeley Information Office letterhead.

On June 5, the PPA released comments on Professor Elliot's work from other primatologists around the country. (Many later denied the comments or claimed they were misquoted.) Dr. Wayne Turman, of the University of Oklahoma at Norman, was quoted as saying that Elliot's work was "fanciful and unethical." Dr. Felicity Hammond, of the Yerkes Primate Research Center in Atlanta, said that "neither Elliot nor his research is of the first rank." Dr. Richard Aronson at the University of Chicago called the research "clearly fascist in nature."

None of these scientists had read Elliot's paper before commenting; but the damage, particularly from Aronson, was incalculable. On June 8, Eleanor Vries, the spokesperson for the PPA, referred to the "criminal research of Dr. Elliot and his Nazi staff"; she claimed Elliot's research caused Amy to have nightmares, and that Amy was being subjected to torture, drugs, and electroshock treatments.

Belatedly, on June 10, the Project Amy staff prepared a lengthy press release, explaining their position in detail and referring to the unpublished paper. But the University Information Office was now "too busy" to issue the release.

On June 11, the Berkeley faculty scheduled a meeting to consider "issues of ethical conduct" within the University. Eleanor Vries announced that the PPA had hired the noted San Francisco attorney Melvin Belli "to free Amy from subjugation." Belli's office was not available for comment.

On the same day, the Project Amy staff had a sudden, unexpected breakthrough in their understanding of Amy's dreams.

. . .

Through all the publicity and commotion, the group had continued to work daily with Amy, and her continued distress— and flaring temper tantrums—was a constant reminder that they had not solved the initial problem. They persisted in their search for clues, although when the break finally came, it happened almost by accident.

Sarah Johnson, a research assistant, was checking prehistoric archaeological sites in the Congo, on the unlikely chance that Amy might have seen such a site ("old buildings in the jungle") in her infancy, before she was brought to the Minneapolis zoo. Johnson quickly discovered the pertinent facts about the Congo: the region had not been explored by Western observers until a hundred years ago; in recent times, hostile tribes and civil war had made scientific inquiry hazardous; and finally, the moist jungle environment did not lend itself to artifact preservation.

This meant remarkably little was known about Congolese prehistory, and Johnson completed her research in a few hours. But she was reluctant to return so quickly from her assignment, so she stayed on, looking at other books in the anthropology library—ethnographies, histories, early accounts. The earliest visitors to the interior of the Congo were Arab slave traders and Portuguese merchants, and several had written accounts of their travels. Because Johnson could read neither Arabic nor Portuguese, she just looked at the plates.

And then she saw a picture that, she said, "sent a chill up my spine."

It was a Portuguese engraving originally dated 1642 and reprinted in an 1842 volume. The ink was yellowing on frayed brittle paper, but clearly visible was a ruined city in the jungle, overgrown with creeper vines and giant ferns. The doors and windows were constructed with semicircular arches, exactly as Amy had drawn them.

. . .

"It was," Elliot said later, "the kind of opportunity that comes to a researcher once in his lifetime—if he's lucky. Of course we knew nothing about the picture; the caption was written in flowing script and included a word that looked like 'Zinj,' and the date 1642. We immediately hired translators skilled in archaic Arabic and seventeenth-century Portuguese, but that wasn't the point. The point was we had a chance to verify a major theoretical question. Amy's pictures seemed to be a clear case of specific genetic memory."

Genetic memory was first proposed by Marais in 1911, and it had been vigorously debated ever since. In its simplest form, the theory proposed that the mechanism of genetic inheritance, which governed the transmission of all physical traits, was not limited to physical traits alone. Behavior was clearly genetically determined in lower animals, which were born with complex behavior that did not have to be learned. But higher animals had more flexible behavior, dependent on learning and memory. The question was whether higher animals, particularly apes and men, had any part of their psychic apparatus fixed from birth by their genes.

Now, Elliot felt, with Amy they had evidence for such a memory. Amy had been taken from Africa when she was only seven months old. Unless she had seen this ruined city in her infancy, her dreams represented a specific genetic memory which could be verified by a trip to Africa. By the evening of June 11, the Project Amy staff was agreed. If they could arrange it—and pay for it—they would take Amy back to Africa.

On June 12, the team waited for the translators to complete work on the source material. Checked translations were expected to be ready within two days. But a trip to Africa for Amy and two staff members would cost at least thirty thousand dollars, a substantial fraction of their total annual operating budget. And transporting a gorilla halfway around the world involved a bewildering tangle of customs regulations and bureaucratic red tape.

Clearly, they needed expert help, but they were not sure where to turn. And then, on June 13, a Dr. Karen Ross from one of their granting institutions, the Earth Resources Wildlife Fund, called from Houston to say that she was leading an expedition into the Congo in two days' time. And although she showed no interest in taking Peter Elliot or Amy with her, she conveyed—at least over the telephone—a confident familiarity with the way expeditions were assembled and managed in far-off places around the world.

When she asked if she could come to San Francisco to meet with Dr. Elliot, Dr. Elliot replied that he would be delighted to meet with her, at her convenience.

3. Legal Issues

Peter Elliot remembered June 14, 1979, as a day of sudden reverses. He began at 8 a.m. in the San Francisco law firm of Sutherland, Morton & O'Connell, because of the threatened custody suit from the PPA—a suit which became all the more important now that he was planning to take Amy out of the country.

He met with John Morton in the firm's wood-paneled library overlooking Grant Street. Morton took notes on a yellow legal pad. "I think you're all right," Morton began, "but let me get a few facts. Amy is a gorilla?"

"Yes, a female mountain gorilla."

"Age?"

"She's seven now."

"So she's still a child?"

Elliot explained that gorillas matured in six to eight years, so that Amy was late adolescent, the equivalent of a sixteen-year-old human female.

Morton scratched notes on a pad. "Could we say she's still a minor?"

"Do we want to say that?"

"I think so."

"Yes, she's still a minor," Elliot said.

"Where did she come from? I mean originally."

"A woman tourist named Swenson found her in Africa, in a village called Bagimindi. Amy's mother had been killed by the natives for food. Mrs. Swenson bought her as an infant."

"So she was not bred in captivity," Morton said, writing on his pad.

"No. Mrs. Swenson brought her back to the States and donated her to the Minneapolis zoo."

"She relinquished her interest in Amy?"

"I assume so," Elliot said. "We've been trying to reach Mrs. Swenson to ask about Amy's early life, but she's out of the country. Apparently she travels constantly; she's in Borneo. Anyway, when Amy was sent to San Francisco, I called the Minneapolis zoo to ask if I could keep her for study. The zoo said yes, for three years."

"Did you pay any money?"

"No."

"Was there a written contract?"

"No, I just called the zoo director."

Morton nodded. "Oral agreement . . ." he said, writing. "And when the three years were up?"

"That was the spring of 1976. I asked the zoo for an extension of six years, and they gave it to me."

"Again orally?"

"Yes. I called on the phone."

"No correspondence?"

"No. They didn't seem very interested when I called. To

tell you the truth, I think they had forgotten about Amy. The
zoo has four gorillas, anyway."

Morton frowned. "Isn't a gorilla a pretty expensive animal? I mean, if you wanted to buy one for a pet or for the
circus."

"Gorillas are on the endangered list; you can't buy them
as pets. But yes, they'd be pretty expensive."

"How expensive?"

"Well, there's no established market value, but it would be
twenty or thirty thousand dollars."

"And all during these years, you have been teaching her
language?"

"Yes," Peter said. "American Sign Language. She has a
vocabulary of six hundred and twenty words now."

"Is that a lot?"

"More than any known primate."

Morton nodded, making notes. "You work with her every
day in ongoing research?"

"Yes."

"Good," Morton said. "That's been very important in the
animal custody cases so far."

For more than a hundred years, there had been organized
movements in Western countries to stop animal experimentation. They were led by the anti-vivisectionists, the RSPCA, the
ASPCA. Originally these organizations were a kind of lunatic
fringe of animal lovers, intent on stopping all animal research.

Over the years, scientists had evolved a standard defense
acceptable to the courts. Researchers claimed that their
experiments had the goal of bettering the health and welfare
of mankind, a higher priority than animal welfare. They
pointed out that no one objected to animals being used as
beasts of burden or for agricultural work—a life of drudgery
to which animals had been subjected for thousands of years.
Using animals in scientific experiments simply extended the
idea that animals were the servants of human enterprises.

In addition, animals were literally brutes. They had no self-awareness, no recognition of their existence in nature. This meant, in the words of philosopher George H. Mead, that "animals have no rights. We are at liberty to cut off their lives; there is no wrong committed when an animal's life is taken away. He has not lost anything. . . ."

Many people were troubled by these views, but attempts to establish guidelines quickly ran into logical problems. The most obvious concerned the perceptions of animals further down the phylogenetic scale. Few researchers operated on dogs, cats, and other mammals without anesthesia, but what about annelid worms, crayfish, leeches, and squid? Ignoring these creatures was a form of "taxonomic discrimination." Yet if these animals deserved consideration, shouldn't it also be illegal to throw a live lobster into a pot of boiling water?

The question of what constituted cruelty to animals was confused by the animal societies themselves. In some countries, they fought the extermination of rats; and in 1968 there was the bizarre Australian pharmaceutical case.* In the face of these ironies, the courts hesitated to interfere with animal experimentation. As a practical matter, researchers were free to do as they wished. The volume of animal research was extraordinary: during the 1970s, sixty-four million animals were killed in experiments in the United States each year.

But attitudes had slowly changed. Language studies with dolphins and apes made it clear that these animals were not only intelligent but self-aware; they recognized themselves in

---

* A new pharmaceutical factory was built in Western Australia. In this factory all the pills came out on a conveyor belt; a person had to watch the belt, and press buttons to sort the pills into separate bins by size and color. A Skinnerian animal behaviorist pointed out that it would be simple to teach pigeons to watch the pills and peck colored keys to do the sorting process. Incredulous factory managers agreed to a test; the pigeons indeed performed reliably, and were duly placed on the assembly line. Then the RSPCA stepped in and put a stop to it on the grounds that it represented cruelty to animals; the job was turned over to a human operator, for whom it did not, apparently, represent cruelty.

mirrors and photographs. In 1974, scientists themselves formed
the International Primate Protection League to monitor research involving monkeys and apes. In March, 1978, the Indian
government banned the export of rhesus monkeys to research
laboratories around the world. And there were court cases
which concluded that in some instances animals did, indeed,
have rights.

The old view was analogous to slavery: the animal was
the property of its owner, who could do whatever he wished.
But now ownership became secondary. In February, 1977,
there was a case involving a dolphin named Mary, released by
a lab technician into the open ocean. The University of Hawaii
prosecuted the technician, charging loss of a valuable research
animal. Two trials resulted in hung juries; the case was
dropped.

In November, 1978, there was a custody case involving a
chimpanzee named Arthur, who was fluent in sign language.
His owner, Johns Hopkins University, decided to sell him and
close the program. His trainer, William Levine, went to court
and obtained custody on the grounds that Arthur knew language and thus was no longer a chimpanzee.

"One of the pertinent facts," Morton said, "was that when
Arthur was confronted by other chimpanzees, he referred to
them as 'black things.' And when Arthur was twice asked to
sort photographs of people and photographs of chimps, he
sorted them correctly except that both times he put his own
picture in the stack with the people. He obviously did not
consider himself a chimpanzee, and the court ruled that he
should remain with his trainer, since any separation would
cause him severe psychic distress."

"Amy cries when I leave her," Elliot said.

"When you conduct experiments, do you obtain her permission?"

"Always." Elliot smiled. Morton obviously had no sense
of day-to-day life with Amy. It was essential to obtain her

permission for any course of action, even a ride in a car. She was a powerful animal, and she could be willful and stubborn.

"Do you keep a record of her acquiescence?"

"Videotapes."

"Does she understand the experiments you propose?"

He shrugged. "She says she does."

"You follow a system of rewards and punishments?"

"All animal behaviorists do."

Morton frowned. "What forms do her punishments take?"

"Well, when she's a bad girl I make her stand in the corner facing the wall. Or else I send her to bed early without her peanut-butter-and-jelly snack."

"What about torture and shock treatments?"

"Ridiculous."

"You never physically punish the animal?"

"She's a pretty damn big animal. Usually I worry that she'll get mad and punish *me*."

Morton smiled and stood. "You're going to be all right," he said. "Any court will rule that Amy is your ward and that you must decide any ultimate disposition in her case." He hesitated. "I know this sounds strange, but could you put Amy on the stand?"

"I guess so," Elliot said. "Do you think it will come to that?"

"Not in this case," Morton said, "but sooner or later it will. You watch: within ten years, there will be a custody case involving a language-using primate, and the ape will be in the witness-box."

Elliot shook his hand, and said as he was leaving, "By the way, would I have any problem taking her out of the country?"

"If there *is* a custody case, you could have trouble taking her across state lines," Morton said. "Are you planning to take her out of the country?"

"Yes."

"Then my advice is to do it fast, and don't tell anyone," Morton said.

Elliot entered his office on the third floor of the Zoology Department building shortly after nine. His secretary, Carolyn, said: "A Dr. Ross called from that Wildlife Fund in Houston; she's on her way to San Francisco. A Mr. Hakamichi called three times, says it's important. The Project Amy staff meeting is set for ten o'clock. And Windy is in your office."

"Really?"

James Weldon was a senior professor in the Department, a weak, blustery man. "Windy" Weldon was usually portrayed in departmental cartoons as holding a wet finger in the air: he was a master at knowing which way the wind was blowing. For the past several days, he had avoided Peter Elliot and his staff.

Elliot went into his office.

"Well, Peter my boy," Weldon said, reaching out to give his version of a hearty handshake. "You're in early."

Elliot was instantly wary. "I thought I'd beat the crowds," he said. The picketers did not show up until ten o'clock, sometimes later, depending on when they had arranged to meet the TV news crews. That was how it worked these days: protest by appointment.

"They're not coming any more," Weldon smiled.

He handed Elliot the late city edition of the *Chronicle*, a front-page story circled in black pen. Eleanor Vries had resigned her position as regional director of the PPA, pleading overwork and personal pressures; a statement from the PPA in New York indicated that they had seriously misconstrued the nature and content of Elliot's research.

"Meaning what?" Elliot asked.

"Belli's office reviewed your paper and Vries's public statements about torture, and decided that the PPA was exposed to a major libel suit," Weldon said. "The New York office is terrified. They'll be making overtures to you later today. Personally, I hope you'll be understanding."

Elliot dropped into his chair. "What about the faculty meeting next week?"

"Oh, that's essential," Weldon said. "There's no question that the faculty will want to discuss unethical conduct—on the part of the media, and issue a strong statement in your support. I'm drawing up a statement now, to come from my office."

The irony of this was not lost on Elliot. "You sure you want to go out on a limb?" he asked.

"I'm behind you one thousand percent, I hope you know that," Weldon said. Weldon was restless, pacing around the office, staring at the walls, which were covered with Amy's finger paintings. Windy had something further on his mind. "She's still making these same pictures?" he asked, finally.

"Yes," Elliot said.

"And you still have no idea what they mean?"

Elliot paused; at best it was premature to tell Weldon what they thought the pictures meant. "No idea," he said.

"Are you sure?" Weldon asked, frowning. "I think somebody knows what they mean."

"Why is that?"

"Something very strange has happened," Weldon said. "Someone has offered to buy Amy."

"To *buy* her? What are you talking about, to buy her?"

"A lawyer in Los Angeles called my office yesterday and offered to buy her for a hundred and fifty thousand dollars."

"It must be some rich do-gooder," Elliot said, "trying to save Amy from torture."

"I don't think so," Weldon said. "For one thing, the offer came from Japan. Someone named Hakamichi—he's in electronics in Tokyo. I found that out when the lawyer called back this morning, to increase his offer to two hundred and fifty thousand dollars."

"Two hundred and fifty thousand dollars?" Elliot said. "For Amy?" Of course it was out of the question. He would never sell her. But why would anyone offer so much money?

Weldon had an answer. "This kind of money, a quarter of a million dollars, can only be coming from private enterprise. Industry. Clearly, Hakamichi has read about your work and found a use for speaking primates in an industrial context." Windy stared at the ceiling, a sure sign he was about to wax eloquent. "I think a new field might be opening up here, the training of primates for industrial applications in the real world."

Peter Elliot swore. He was not teaching Amy language in order to put a hard hat on her head and a lunch pail in her hand, and he said so.

"You're not thinking it through," Weldon said. "What if we are on the verge of a new field of applied behavior for the great apes? Think what it means. Not only funding to the Department, and an opportunity for applied research. Most important, there would be a reason to keep these animals alive. You know that the great apes are becoming extinct. The chimps in Africa are greatly reduced in number. The orangs of Borneo are losing their natural habitat to the timber cutters and will be extinct in ten years. The gorilla is down to three thousand in the central African forests. These animals will all disappear in our lifetime—*unless there is a reason to keep them alive,* as species. You may provide that reason, Peter my boy. Think about it."

Elliot did think about it, and he discussed it at the Project Amy staff meeting at ten o'clock. They considered possible industrial applications for apes, and possible advantages to employers, such as the lack of unions and fringe benefits. In the late twentieth century, these were major considerations. (In 1978, for each new automobile that rolled off the Detroit assembly lines, the cost of worker health benefits exceeded the cost of all the steel used to build the car.)

But they concluded that a vision of "industrialized apes" was wildly fanciful. An ape like Amy was not a cheap and stupid version of a human worker. Quite the opposite: Amy was a highly intelligent and complex creature out of her element in the modern industrial world. She demanded a great deal of supervision; she was whimsical and unreliable; and her health was always at risk. It simply didn't make sense to use her in industry. If Hakamichi had visions of apes wielding soldering irons on a microelectronic assembly line, building TVs and hi-fi sets, he was sorely misinformed.

The only note of caution came from Bergman, the child psychologist. "A quarter of a million is a lot of money," he said, "and Mr. Hakamichi is probably no fool. He must have learned about Amy through her drawings, which imply she is neurotic and difficult. If he's interested in her, I'd bet it's *because of her drawings*. But I can't imagine why those drawings should be worth a quarter of a million dollars."

Neither could anyone else, and the discussion turned to the drawings themselves, and the newly translated texts. Sarah Johnson, in charge of research, started out with the flat comment "I have bad news about the Congo."*

For most of recorded history, she explained, nothing was known about the Congo. The ancient Egyptians on the upper Nile knew only that their river originated far to the south, in a region they called the Land of Trees. This was a mysterious place with forests so dense they were as dark as night in the middle of the day. Strange creatures inhabited this perpetual gloom, including little men with tails, and animals half black and half white.

For nearly four thousand years afterward, nothing more substantial was learned about the interior of Africa. The Arabs

---

* Johnson's principal reference was the definitive work by A. J. Parkinson, *The Congo Delta in Myth and History* (London: Peters, 1904).

came to East Africa in the seventh century A.D., in search of gold, ivory, spices, and slaves. But the Arabs were merchant seamen and did not venture inland. They called the interior Zinj—the Land of the Blacks—a region of fable and fantasy. There were stories of vast forests and tiny men with tails; stories of mountains that spewed fire and turned the sky black; stories of native villages overwhelmed by monkeys, which would have congress with the women; stories of great giants with hairy bodies and flat noses; stories of creatures half leopard, half man; stories of native markets where the fattened carcasses of men were butchered and sold as a delicacy.

Such stories were sufficiently forbidding to keep the Arabs on the coast, despite other stories equally alluring: mountains of shimmering gold, riverbeds gleaming with diamonds, animals that spoke the language of men, great jungle civilizations of unimaginable splendor. In particular, one story was repeated again and again in early accounts: the story of the Lost City of Zinj.

According to legend, a city known to the Hebrews of Solomonic times had been a source of inconceivable wealth in diamonds. The caravan route to the city had been jealously guarded, passed from father to son, as a sacred trust for generation after generation. But the diamond mines were exhausted and the city itself now lay in crumbling ruins, somewhere in the dark heart of Africa. The arduous caravan routes were long since swallowed up by jungle, and the last trader who remembered the way had carried his secret with him to the grave many hundreds of years before.

This mysterious and alluring place the Arabs called the Lost City of Zinj.* Yet despite its enduring fame, Johnson could find few detailed descriptions of the city. In 1187 Ibn

---

* The fabled city of Zinj formed the basis for H. Rider Haggard's popular novel *King Solomon's Mines*, first published in 1885. Haggard, a gifted linguist, had served on the staff of the Governor of Natal in 1875, and he presumably heard of Zinj from the neighboring Zulus at that time.

Baratu, an Arab in Mombasa, recorded that "the natives of the region tell . . . of a lost city far inland, called Zinj. There the inhabitants, who are black, once lived in wealth and luxury, and even the slaves decorated themselves with jewels and especially blue diamonds, for a great store of diamonds is there."

In 1292, a Persian named Mohammed Zaid stated that "a large diamond [the size] of a man's clenched fist . . . was exhibited on the streets of Zanzibar, and all said it had come from the interior, where the ruins of a city called Zinj may be found, and it is here that such diamonds may be found in profusion, scattered upon the ground and also in rivers. . . ."

In 1334, another Arab, Ibn Mohammed, stated that "our number made arrangements to seek out the city of Zinj, but quitted our quest upon learning that the city was long since abandoned, and much ruined. It is said that the aspect of the city is wondrous strange, for doors and windows are built in the curve of a half-moon, and the residences are now overtaken by a violent race of hairy men who speak in whispers no known language. . . ."

Then the Portuguese, those indefatigable explorers, arrived. By 1544, they were venturing inland from the west coast up the mighty Congo River, but they soon encountered all the obstacles that would prevent exploration of central Africa for hundreds of years to come. The Congo was not navigable beyond the first set of rapids, two hundred miles inland (at what was once Léopoldville, and is now Kinshasa). The natives were hostile and cannibalistic. And the hot steaming jungle was the source of disease—malaria, sleeping sickness, bilharzia, blackwater fever—which decimated foreign intruders.

The Portuguese never managed to penetrate the central Congo. Neither did the English, under Captain Brenner, in 1644; his entire party was lost. The Congo would remain for two hundred years as a blank spot on the civilized maps of the world.

But the early explorers repeated the legends of the interior, including the story of Zinj. A Portuguese artist, Juan Diego de Valdez, drew a widely acclaimed picture of the Lost City of Zinj in 1642. "But," Sarah Johnson said, "he also drew pictures of men with tails, and monkeys having carnal knowledge of native women."

Somebody groaned.

"Apparently Valdez was crippled," she continued. "He lived all his life in the town of Setúbal, drinking with sailors and drawing pictures based on his conversations."

Africa was not thoroughly explored until the mid-nineteenth century, by Burton and Speke, Baker and Livingstone, and especially Stanley. No trace of the Lost City of Zinj was found by any of them. Nor had any trace of the apocryphal city been found in the hundred years since.

The gloom that descended over the Project Amy staff meeting was profound. "I told you it was bad news," Sarah Johnson said.

"You mean," Peter Elliot said, "that this picture is based on a description, and we don't know whether the city actually exists or not."

"I'm afraid so," Sarah Johnson said. "There is no proof that the city in the picture exists at all. It's just a story."

4. Resolution

Peter Elliot's unquestioned reliance on twentieth-century hard data—facts, figures, graphs—left him unprepared for the possibility that the 1642 engraving, in all its detail, was merely the fanciful speculation of an uninhibited artist. The news came as a shock.

Their plans to take Amy to the Congo suddenly appeared childishly naïve; the resemblance of her sketchy, schematic drawings to the 1642 Valdez engraving was obviously coincidental. How could they ever have imagined that a Lost City of Zinj was anything but the stuff of ancient fable? In the seventeenth-century world of widening horizons and new wonders, the idea of such a city would have seemed perfectly reasonable, even compelling. But in the computerized twentieth century, the Lost City of Zinj was as unlikely as Camelot or Xanadu. They had been fools ever to take it seriously. "The lost city doesn't exist," he said.

"Oh, it exists, all right," she said. "There's no doubt about *that.*"

Elliot glanced up quickly, and then he saw that Sarah Johnson had not answered him. A tall gangly girl in her early twenties stood at the back of the room. She might have been considered beautiful except for her cold, aloof demeanor. This girl was dressed in a severe, businesslike suit, and she carried a briefcase, which she now set on the table, popping the latches.

"I'm Dr. Ross," she announced, "from the Wildlife Fund, and I'd like your opinion of these pictures."

She passed around a series of photographs, which were viewed by the staff with an assortment of whistles and sighs. At the head of the table, Elliot waited impatiently until the photographs came down to him.

They were grainy black-and-white images with horizontal scanning line streaks, photographed off a video screen. But the image was unmistakable: a ruined city in the jungle, with curious inverted crescent-shaped doors and windows.

5. Amy

"By satellite?" Elliot repeated, hearing the tension in his voice.

"That's right, the pictures were transmitted by satellite from Africa two days ago."

"Then you know the location of this ruin?"

"Of course."

"And your expedition leaves in a matter of hours?"

"Six hours and twenty-three minutes, to be exact," Ross said, glancing at her digital watch.

Elliot adjourned the meeting, and talked privately with Ross for more than an hour. Elliot later claimed that Ross had "deceived" him about the purpose of the expedition and the hazards they would face. But Elliot was eager to go, and probably not inclined to be too fussy about the reasons behind Ross's coming expedition, or the dangers involved. As a skilled grantsman, he had long ago grown comfortable with situations where other peoples' money and his own motivations did not exactly coincide. This was the cynical side of academic life: how much pure research had been funded because it might cure cancer? A researcher promised anything to get his money.

Apparently it never occurred to Elliot that Ross might be using him as coldly as he was using her. From the start Ross was never entirely truthful; she had been instructed by Travis to explain the ERTS Congo mission "with a little data drop-out." Data dropout was second nature to her; everyone at ERTS had learned to say no more than was necessary. Elliot treated her as if she were an ordinary funding agency, and that was a serious mistake.

In the final analysis, Ross and Elliot misjudged each other, for each presented a deceptive appearance, and in the same way. Elliot appeared so shy and retiring that one Berkeley faculty member had commented, "It's no wonder he's devoted his life to apes; he can't work up the nerve to talk to people." But Elliot had been a tough middle linebacker in college, and his diffident academic demeanor concealed a head-crunching ambitious drive.

Similarly, Karen Ross, despite her youthful cheerleader beauty and soft, seductive Texas accent, possessed great intelligence and a deep inner toughness. (She had matured early, and a high-school teacher had once appraised her as "the very flower of virile Texas womanhood.") Ross felt responsible for the previous ERTS expedition, and she was determined to rectify past errors. It was at least possible that Elliot and Amy could help her when she got onsite; that was reason enough to take them with her. Beyond that, Ross was concerned about the consortium, which was obviously seeking Elliot, since Hakamichi was calling. If she took Elliot and Amy with her, she removed a possible advantage to the consortium—again, reason enough to take them with her. Finally, she needed a cover in case her expedition was stopped at one of the borders—and a primatologist and an ape provided a perfect cover.

But in the end Karen Ross wanted only the Congo diamonds—and she was prepared to say anything, do anything, sacrifice anything to get them.

In photographs taken at San Francisco airport, Elliot and Ross appear as two smiling, youthful academics, embarking on a lark of an expedition to Africa. But in fact, their motivations were different, and grimly held. Elliot was reluctant to tell her how theoretical and academic his goals were—and Ross was reluctant to admit how pragmatic were hers.

In any case, by midday on June 14, Karen Ross found herself riding with Peter Elliot in his battered Fiat sedan along Hallowell Road, going past the University athletic field. She had some misgivings: they were going to meet Amy.

Elliot unlocked the door with its red sign DO NOT DISTURB ANIMAL EXPERIMENTATION IN PROGRESS. Behind the door, Amy was grunting and scratching impatiently. Elliot paused.

"When you meet her," he said, "remember that she is a gorilla and not a human being. Gorillas have their own etiquette. Don't speak loudly or make any sudden movements until she gets used to you. If you smile, don't show your teeth, because bared teeth are a threat. And keep your eyes downcast, because direct stares from strangers are considered hostile. Don't stand too close to me or touch me, because she's very jealous. If you talk to her, don't lie. Even though she uses sign language, she understands most human speech, and we usually just talk to her. She can tell when you're lying and she doesn't like it."

"She doesn't like it?"

"She dismisses you, won't talk to you, and gets bitchy."

"Anything else?"

"No, it should be okay." He smiled reassuringly. "We have this traditional greeting, even though she's getting a little big for it." He opened the door, braced himself, and said, "Good morning, Amy."

A huge black shape came leaping out through the open door into his arms. Elliot staggered back under the impact. Ross was astonished by the size of the animal. She had been imagining something smaller and cuter. Amy was as large as an adult human female.

Amy kissed Elliot on the cheek with her large lips, her black head seeming enormous alongside his. Her breath steamed his glasses. Ross smelled a sweetish odor, and watched as he gently unwrapped her long arms from around his shoulders. "Amy happy this morning?" he asked.

Amy's fingers moved quickly near her cheek, as if she were brushing away flies.

"Yes, I was late today," Elliot said.

She moved her fingers again, and Ross realized that Amy was signing. The speed was surprising; she had expected something much slower and more deliberate. She noticed that Amy's eyes never left Elliot's face. She was extraordinarily attentive, focusing on him with total animal watchfulness. She seemed to absorb everything, his posture, his expression, his tone of voice, as well as his words.

"I had to work," Elliot said. She sighed again quickly, like human gestures of dismissal. "Yes, that's right, people work." He led Amy back into the trailer, and motioned for Karen Ross to follow. Inside the trailer, he said, "Amy, this is Dr. Ross. Say hello to Dr. Ross."

Amy looked at Karen Ross suspiciously.

"Hello, Amy," Karen Ross said, smiling at the floor. She felt a little foolish behaving this way, but Amy was large enough to frighten her.

Amy stared at Karen Ross for a moment, then walked away, across the trailer to her easel. She had been finger-painting, and now resumed this activity, ignoring them.

"What's that mean?" Ross said. She distinctly felt she was being snubbed.

"We'll see," Elliot said.

After a few moments, Amy ambled back, walking on her knuckles. She went directly to Karen Ross, sniffed her crotch, and examined her minutely. She seemed particularly interested in Ross's leather purse, which had a shiny brass clasp. Ross said later that "it was just like any cocktail party in Houston. I was being checked out by another woman. I had the feeling that any minute she was going to ask me where I bought my clothes."

That was not the outcome, however. Amy reached up and deliberately streaked globs of green finger paint on Ross's skirt.

"I don't think this is going too well," Karen Ross said.

Elliot had watched the progress of this first meeting with more apprehension than he was willing to admit. Introducing new humans to Amy was often difficult, particularly if they were women.

Over the years, Elliot had come to recognize many distinctly "feminine" traits in Amy. She could be coy, she responded to flattery, she was preoccupied with her appearance, loved makeup, and was very fussy about the color of the sweaters she wore in the winter. She preferred men to women, and she was openly jealous of Elliot's girl friends. He rarely brought them around to meet her, but sometimes in the morning she would sniff him for perfume, and she always commented if he had not changed his clothing overnight.

This situation might have been amusing if not for the fact that Amy made occasional unprovoked attacks on strange women. And an attack by Amy was never amusing.

Amy returned to the easel and signed, *No like woman no like Amy no like go away away.*

"Come on, Amy, be a good gorilla," Peter said.

"What did she say?" Ross asked, going to the sink to wash the finger paint from her dress. Peter noticed that she did not squeal and shriek as many visitors did when they received an unfriendly greeting from Amy.

"She said she likes your dress," he said.

Amy shot him a look, as she always did whenever Elliot mistranslated her. *Amy not lie. Peter not lie.*

"Be nice, Amy," he said. "Karen is a nice human person."

Amy grunted, and returned to her work, painting rapidly.

"What happens now?" Karen Ross said.

"Give her time." He smiled reassuringly. "She needs time to adjust."

He did not bother to explain that it was much worse with chimpanzees. Chimps threw feces at strangers, and even at workers they knew well; they sometimes attacked to establish dominance. Chimpanzees had a strong need to determine who was in charge. Fortunately, gorillas were much less formal in their dominance hierarchies, and less violent.

At that moment, Amy ripped the paper from the easel and shredded it noisily, flinging the pieces around the room.

"Is this part of the adjustment?" Karen Ross asked. She seemed more amused than frightened.

"Amy, cut it out," Peter said, allowing his tone to convey irritation. "Amy . . ."

Amy sat in the middle of the floor, surrounded by the paper. She tore it angrily and signed, *This woman. This woman.* It was classic displacement behavior. Whenever gorillas did not feel comfortable with direct aggression, they did something symbolic. In symbolic terms, she was now tearing Karen Ross apart.

And she was getting worked up, beginning what the Project Amy staff called "sequencing." Just as human beings first became red-faced, and then tensed their bodies, and then shouted and threw things before they finally resorted to direct physical aggression, so gorillas passed through a stereotyped behavioral sequence on the way to physical aggression. Tearing up paper, or grass, would be followed by lateral crablike movements and grunts. Then she would slap the ground, making as much noise as possible.

And then Amy would charge, if he didn't interrupt the sequence.

"Amy," he said sternly. "Karen button woman."

Amy stopped shredding. In her world, "button" was the acknowledged term for a person of high status.

Amy was extremely sensitive to individual moods and behavior, and she had no difficulty observing the staff and deciding who was superior to whom. But among strangers, Amy as a gorilla was utterly impervious to formal human status cues; the principal indicators—clothing, bearing, and speech—had no meaning to her.

As a young animal, she had inexplicably attacked policemen. After several biting episodes and threatened lawsuits, they finally learned that Amy found police uniforms with their shiny buttons clownlike and ridiculous; she assumed that anyone so foolishly dressed must be of inferior status and safe to attack. After they had taught her the concept of "button," she treated anyone in uniform with deference.

Amy now stared at "button" Ross with new respect. Surrounded by the torn paper, she seemed suddenly embarrassed, as if she had made a social error. Without being told, she went and stood in the corner, facing the wall.

"What's that about?" Ross said.

"She knows she's been bad."

"You make her stand in the corner, like a child? She didn't mean any harm." Before Elliot could warn against it, she went over to Amy. Amy stared steadfastly at the corner.

Ross unshouldered her purse and set it on the floor within Amy's reach. Nothing happened for a moment. Then Amy took the purse, looked at Karen, then looked at Peter.

Peter said, "She'll wreck whatever's inside."

"That's all right."

Amy immediately opened the brass clasp, and dumped the contents on the floor. She began sifting through, signing, *Lipstick lipstick, Amy like Amy want lipstick want.*

"She wants lipstick."

Ross bent over and found it for her. Amy removed the cap and smeared a red circle on Karen's face. She then smiled and grunted happily, and crossed the room to her mirror, which was mounted on the floor. She applied lipstick.

"I think we're doing better," Karen Ross said.

Across the room, Amy squatted by the mirror, happily making a mess of her face. She grinned at her smart image, then applied lipstick to her teeth. It seemed a good time to ask her the question. "Amy want take trip?" Peter said.

Amy loved trips, and regarded them as special treats. After an especially good day, Elliot often took her for a ride to a nearby drive-in, where she would have an orange drink, sucking it through the straw and enjoying the commotion she caused among the other people there. Lipstick and an offer of a trip was almost too much pleasure for one morning. She signed, *Car trip?*

"No, not in the car. A long trip. Many days."

Leave house?

"Yes, leave house. Many days."

This made her suspicious. The only times she had left the house for many days had been during hospitalizations for pneumonia and urinary-tract infections; they had not been pleasant trips. She signed, *Where go trip?*

"To the jungle, Amy."

There was a long pause. At first he thought she had not understood, but she knew the word for jungle, and she should be able to put it all together. Amy signed thoughtfully to herself, repetitively as she always did when she was mulling things over: *Jungle trip trip jungle go trip jungle go.* She set aside her lipstick. She stared at the bits of paper on the floor, and then she began to pick them up and put them in the wastebasket.

"What does that mean?" Karen Ross asked.

"That means Amy wants to take a trip," Peter Elliot said.

6. Departure

The hinged nose of the Boeing 747 cargo jet lay open like a jaw, exposing the cavernous, brightly lit interior. The plane had been flown up from Houston to San Francisco that afternoon; it was now nine o'clock at night, and puzzled workers were loading on the large aluminum travel cage, boxes of vitamin pills, a portable potty, and cartons of toys. One workman pulled out a Mickey Mouse drinking cup and stared at it, shaking his head.

Outside on the concrete, Elliot stood with Amy, who covered her ears against the whine of the jet engines. She signed to Peter, *Birds noisy.*

"We fly bird, Amy," he said.

Amy had never flown before, and had never seen an airplane at close hand. *We go car,* she decided, looking at the plane.

"We can't go by car. We fly."

Fly where fly? Amy signed.

"Fly jungle."

This seemed to perplex her, but he did not want to explain further. Like all gorillas, Amy had an aversion to water, refusing to cross even small streams. He knew she would be distressed to hear that they would be flying over large bodies of water. Changing the subject, he suggested they board the plane and look around. As they climbed the sloping ramp up the nose, Amy signed, *Where button woman?*

He had not seen Ross for the last five hours, and was surprised to discover that she was already on board, talking on a telephone mounted on a wall of the cargo hold, one hand cupped over her free ear to block the noise. Elliot overheard her say, "Well, Irving seems to think it's enough. . . . Yes, we have four nine-oh-seven units and we are prepared to match and absorb. Two micro HUDs, that's all. . . . Yes, why not?" She finished the call, turned to Elliot and Amy.

"Everything okay?" he asked.

"Fine. I'll show you around." She led him deeper into the cargo hold, with Amy at his side. Elliot glanced back and saw the chauffeur coming up the ramp with a series of numbered metal boxes marked INTEC, INC. followed by serial numbers.

"This," Karen Ross said, "is the main cargo hold." It was filled with four-wheel-drive trucks, Land Cruisers, amphibious vehicles, inflatable boats, and racks of clothing, equipment, food—all tagged with computer codes, all loaded in modules. Ross explained that ERTS could outfit expeditions to any geographical and climatic condition in a matter of hours. She kept emphasizing the speed possible with computer assembly.

"Why the rush?" Elliot asked.

"It's business," Karen Ross said. "Four years ago, there were no companies like ERTS. Now there are nine around the world, and what they all sell is competitive advantage, meaning speed. Back in the sixties, a company—say, an oil company—might spend months or years investigating a possible site. But that's no longer competitive; business decisions are made in weeks or days. The pace of everything has speeded up. We're already looking to the nineteen-eighties, where we'll provide answers in *hours*. Right now the average ERTS contract runs a little under three weeks, or five hundred hours. But by 1990 there will be 'close of business' data—an executive can call us in the morning for information anywhere in the world, and have a complete report transmitted by computer to his desk before close of business that evening, say ten to twelve hours."

As they continued the tour, Elliot noticed that although the trucks and vehicles caught the eye first, much of the aircraft storage space was given over to aluminum modules marked "C3I."

"That's right," Ross said. "Command-Control Communications and Intelligence. They're micronic components, the most expensive budget item we carry. When we started outfitting expeditions, twelve percent of the cost went to electronics. Now it's up to thirty-one percent, and climbing every year. It's field communications, remote sensing, defense, and so on."

She led them to the rear of the plane, where there was a modular living area, nicely furnished, with a large computer console, and bunks for sleeping.

Amy signed, *Nice house.*

"Yes, it is nice."

They were introduced to Jensen, a young bearded geologist, and to Irving Levine, who announced that he was the "triple E." The two men were running some kind of probability study on the computer but they paused to shake hands with Amy, who regarded them gravely, and then turned her attention to the screen. Amy was captivated by the colorful screen images and bright LEDs, and kept trying to punch the buttons herself. She signed, *Amy play box.*

"Not now, Amy," Elliot said, and swatted her hands away.

Jensen asked, "Is she always this way?"

"I'm afraid so," Elliot said. "She likes computers. She's worked around them ever since she was very young, and she thinks of them as her private property." And then he added, "What's a triple E?"

"Expedition electronics expert," Irving said cheerfully. He was a short man with an impish quick smile. "Doing the best I can. We picked up some stuff from Intec, that's about all. God knows what the Japs and the Germans will throw at us."

"Oh, damn, there she goes," Jensen said, laughing as Amy pushed the buttons.

Elliot said, "Amy no!"

"It's just a game. Probably not interesting to apes," Jensen said. And he added, "She can't hurt anything."

Amy signed, *Amy good gorilla*, and pushed the buttons on the computer again. She appeared relaxed, and Elliot was grateful for the distraction the computer provided. He was always amused by the sight of Amy's heavy dark form before a computer console. She would touch her lower lip thoughtfully before pushing the buttons, in what seemed a parody of human behavior.

Ross, practical as always, brought them back to mundane matters. "Will Amy sleep on one of the bunks?"

Elliot shook his head. "No. Gorillas expect to make a fresh bed each night. Give her some blankets, and she'll twist them into a nest on the floor and sleep there."

Ross nodded. "What about her vitamins and medications? Will she swallow pills?"

"Ordinarily you have to bribe her, or hide the pills in a piece of banana. She tends to gulp banana, without chewing it."

"Without chewing." Ross nodded as if that were important. "We have a standard issue," she said. "I'll see that she gets them."

"She takes the same vitamins that people do, except that she'll need lots of ascorbic acid."

"We issue three thousand units a day. That's enough? Good. And she'll tolerate anti-malarials? We have to start them right away."

"Generally speaking," Elliot said, "she has the same reaction to medication as people."

Ross nodded. "Will the cabin pressurization bother her? It's set at five thousand feet."

Elliot shook his head. "She's a mountain gorilla, and they live at five thousand to nine thousand feet, so she's actually altitude-adapted. But she's acclimated to a moist climate and she dehydrates quickly; we'll have to keep forcing fluids on her."

"Can she use the head?"

"The seat's probably too high for her," Elliot said, "but I brought her potty."

"She'll use her potty?"

"Sure."

"I have a new collar for her; will she wear it?"

"If you give it to her as a gift."

As they reviewed other details of Amy's requirements, Elliot realized that something had happened during the last few hours, almost without his knowing it: Amy's unpredictable, dream-driven neurotic behavior had fallen away. It was as if the earlier behavior was irrelevant; now that she was going on a trip, she was no longer moody and introspective, her interests were outgoing; she was once again a youthful female gorilla. He found himself wondering whether her dreams, her depression—finger paintings, everything—were a result of her confined laboratory environment for so many years. At first the laboratory had been agreeable, like a crib for young children. But perhaps in later years it pinched. Perhaps, he thought, Amy just needed a little excitement.

Excitement was in the air: as he talked with Ross, Elliot felt something remarkable was about to happen. This expedition with Amy was the first example of an event primate researchers had predicted for years—the Pearl thesis.

Frederick Pearl was a theoretical animal behaviorist. At a meeting of the American Ethnological Society in New York in 1972, he had said, "Now that primates have learned sign language, it is only a matter of time until someone takes an animal into the field to assist the study of wild animals of the same species. We can imagine language-skilled primates acting as interpreters or perhaps even as ambassadors for mankind, in contact with wild creatures."

Pearl's thesis attracted considerable attention, and funding from the U.S. Air Force, which had supported linguistic research since the 1960s. According to one story, the Air Force had a secret project called CONTOUR, involving possible contact with alien life forms. The official military position was that UFOs were of natural origin—but the military was covering its bets. Should alien contact occur, linguistic fundamentals were obviously critically important. And taking primates into the field was seen as an example of contact with "alien intelligence"; hence the Air Force funding.

Pearl predicted that fieldwork would be undertaken before 1976, but in fact no one had yet done it. The reason was that on closer examination, no one could figure out quite what the advantages were—most language-using primates were as baffled by wild primates as human beings were. Some, like the chimpanzee Arthur, denied any association with their own kind, referring to them as "black things." (Amy, who had been taken to the zoo to view other gorillas, recognized them but was haughty, calling them "stupid gorillas" once she found that when she signed to them, they did not reply.)

Such observations led another researcher, John Bates, to

say in 1977 that "we are producing an educated animal élite which demonstrates the same snobbish aloofness that a Ph.D. shows toward a truck driver. . . . It is highly unlikely that the generation of language-using primates will be skillful ambassadors in the field. They are simply too disdainful."

But the truth was that no one really knew what would happen when a primate was taken into the field. Because no one had done it: Amy would be the first.

At eleven o'clock, the ERTS cargo plane taxied down the runway at San Francisco International, lifted ponderously into the air, and headed east through the darkness toward Africa.

DAY 3: TANGIER
June 15, 1979

1. Ground Truth

Peter Elliot had known Amy since infancy. He prided himself on his ability to predict her responses, although he had only known her in a laboratory setting. Now, as she was faced with new situations, her behavior surprised him.

Elliot had anticipated Amy would be terrified of the takeoff, and had prepared a syringe with Thoralen tranquilizer. But sedation proved unnecessary: Amy watched Jensen and Levine buckle their seat belts, and she immediately buckled herself in, too; she seemed to regard the procedure as an amusing, if simpleminded, game. And although her eyes widened when she heard the full roar of the engines, the human beings around her did not seem disturbed, and Amy imitated their bored indifference, raising her eyebrows and sighing at the tedium of it all.

Once airborne, however, Amy looked out the window and immediately panicked. She released her seat belt and scurried back and forth across the passenger compartment, moving from window to window, knocking people aside in whimpering terror while she signed, *Where ground ground where ground?* Outside, the ground was black and indistinct. *Where ground?* Elliot shot her with Thoralen and then began grooming her, sitting her down and plucking at her hair.

In the wild, primates devoted several hours each day to

grooming one another, removing ticks and lice. Grooming behavior was important in ordering the group's social dominance structure—there was a pattern by which animals groomed each other, and with what frequency. And, like back rubs for people, grooming seemed to have a soothing, calming effect. Within minutes, Amy had relaxed enough to notice that the others were drinking, and she promptly demanded a "green drop drink"—her term for a martini with an olive—and a cigarette. She was allowed this on special occasions such as departmental parties, and Elliot now gave her a drink and a cigarette.

But the excitement proved too much for her: an hour later, she was quietly looking out the window and signing *Nice picture* to herself when she vomited. She apologized abjectly, *Amy sorry Amy mess Amy Amy sorry.*

"It's all right, Amy," Elliot assured her, stroking the back of her head. Soon afterward, signing *Amy sleep now,* she twisted the blankets into a nest on the floor and went to sleep, snoring loudly through her broad nostrils. Lying next to her, Elliot thought, how do other gorillas get to sleep with this racket?

Elliot had his own reaction to the journey. When he had first met Karen Ross, he assumed she was an academic like himself. But this enormous airplane filled with computerized equipment, the acronymic complexity of the entire operation suggested that Earth Resources Technology had powerful resources behind it, perhaps even a military association.

Karen Ross laughed. "We're much too organized to be military." She then told him the background of the ERTS interest in Virunga. Like the Project Amy staff, Karen Ross had also stumbled upon the legend of the Lost City of Zinj. But she had drawn very different conclusions from the story.

During the last three hundred years, there had been several attempts to reach the lost city. In 1692, John Marley, an English adventurer, led an expedition of two hundred into the Congo; it was never heard from again. In 1744, a Dutch expedition went in; in 1804, another British party led by a Scottish aristocrat, Sir James Taggert, approached Virunga from the north, getting as far as the Rawana bend of the Ubangi River. He sent an advance party farther south, but it never returned.

In 1872, Stanley passed near the Virunga region but did not enter it; in 1899, a German expedition went in, losing more than half its party. A privately financed Italian expedition disappeared entirely in 1911. There had been no more recent searches for the Lost City of Zinj.

"So no one has ever found it," Elliot said.

Ross shook her head. "I think several expeditions found the city," she said. "But nobody ever got back out again."

Such an outcome was not necessarily mysterious. The early days of African exploration were incredibly hazardous. Even carefully managed expeditions lost half of their party or more. Those who did not succumb to malaria, sleeping sickness, and blackwater fever faced rivers teeming with crocodiles and hippos, jungles with leopards and suspicious, cannibalistic natives. And, for all its luxuriant growth, the rain forest provided little edible food; a number of expeditions had starved to death.

"I began," Ross said to Elliot, "with the idea that the city existed, after all. Assuming it existed, where would I find it?"

The Lost City of Zinj was associated with diamond mines, and diamonds were found with volcanoes. This led Ross to look along the Great Rift Valley—an enormous geological fault thirty miles wide, which sliced vertically up the eastern third of the continent for a distance of fifteen hundred miles. The Rift Valley was so huge that its existence was not recog-

nized until the 1890s, when a geologist named Gregory noticed that the cliff walls thirty miles apart were composed of
the same rocks. In modern terms the Great Rift was actually
an abortive attempt to form an ocean, for the eastern third of
the continent had begun splitting off from the rest of the
African land mass two hundred million years ago; for some
reason, it had stopped before the break was complete.

On a map the Great Rift depression was marked by two
features: a series of thin vertical lakes—Malawi, Tanganyika,
Kivu, Mobutu—and a series of volcanoes, including the only
active volcanoes in Africa at Virunga. Three volcanoes in the
Virunga chain were active: Mukenko, Mubuti, and Kana-
garawi. They rose 11,000–15,000 feet above the Rift Valley to
the east, and the Congo Basin to the west. Thus Virunga
seemed a good place to look for diamonds. Her next step was
to investigate the ground truth.

"What's ground truth?" Peter asked.

"At ERTS, we deal mostly in remote sensing," she explained. "Satellite photographs, aerial run-bys, radar side scans.
We carry millions of remote images, but there's no substitute
for ground truth, the experience of a team actually on the site,
finding out what's there. I started with the preliminary expedition we sent in looking for gold. They found diamonds as
well." She punched buttons on the console, and the screen
images changed, glowing with dozens of flashing pinpoints of
light.

"This shows the placer deposit locations in streambeds
near Virunga. You see the deposits form concentric semicircles leading back to the volcanoes. The obvious conclusion is
that diamonds were eroded from the slopes of the Virunga
volcanoes, and washed down the streams to their present
locations."

"So you sent in a party to look for the source?"

"Yes." She pointed to the screen. "But don't be deceived
by what you see here. This satellite image covers fifty thou-

sand square kilometers of jungle. Most of it has never been seen by white men. It's hard terrain, with visibility limited to a few meters in any direction. An expedition could search that area for years, passing within two hundred meters of the city and failing to see it. So I needed to narrow the search sector. I decided to see if I could find the city."

"Find the city? From satellite pictures?"

"Yes," she said. "And I found it."

The rain forests of the world had traditionally frustrated remote-sensing technology. The great jungle trees spread an impenetrable canopy of vegetation, concealing whatever lay beneath. In aerial or satellite pictures, the Congo rain forest appeared as a vast, undulating carpet of featureless and monotonous green. Even large features, rivers fifty or a hundred feet wide, were hidden beneath this leafy canopy, invisible from the air.

So it seemed unlikely she would find any evidence for a lost city in aerial photographs. But Ross had a different idea: she would utilize the very vegetation that obscured her vision of the ground.

The study of vegetation was common in temperate regions, where the foliage underwent seasonal changes. But the equatorial rain forest was unchanging: winter or summer, the foliage remained the same. Ross turned her attention to another aspect, the differences in vegetation albedo.

Albedo was technically defined as the ratio of electromagnetic energy reflected by a surface to the amount of energy incident upon it. In terms of the visible spectrum, it was a measure of how "shiny" a surface was. A river had a high albedo, since water reflected most of the sunlight striking it. Vegetation absorbed light, and therefore had a low albedo. Starting in 1977, ERTS developed computer programs which measured albedo precisely, making very fine distinctions.

Ross asked herself the question: If there was a lost city, what signature might appear in the vegetation? There was an obvious answer: late secondary jungle.

The untouched or virgin rain forest was called primary jungle. Primary jungle was what most people thought of when they thought of rain forests: huge hardwood trees, mahogany and teak and ebony, and underneath a lower layer of ferns and palms, clinging to the ground. Primary jungle was dark and forbidding, but actually easy to move through. However, if the primary jungle was cleared by man and later abandoned, an entirely different secondary growth took over. The dominant plants were softwoods and fast-growing trees, bamboo and thorny tearing vines, which formed a dense and impenetrable barrier.

But Ross was not concerned about any aspect of the jungle except its albedo. Because the secondary plants were different, secondary jungle had a different albedo from primary jungle. And it could be graded by age: unlike the hardwood trees of primary jungle, which lived hundreds of years, the softwoods of secondary jungle lived only twenty years or so. Thus as time went on, the secondary jungle was replaced by another form of secondary jungle, and later by still another form.

By checking regions where late secondary jungle was generally found—such as the banks of large rivers, where innumerable human settlements had been cleared and abandoned—Ross confirmed that the ERTS computers could, indeed, measure the necessary small differences in reflectivity.

She then instructed the ERTS scanners to search for albedo differences of .03 or less, with a unit signature size of a hundred meters or less, across the fifty thousand square kilometers of rain forest on the western slopes of the Virunga volcanoes. This job would occupy a team of fifty human aerial photographic analysts for thirty-one years. The computer scanned 129,000 satellite and aerial photographs in under nine hours.

And found her city.

In May, 1979, Ross had a computer image showing a very old secondary jungle pattern laid out in a geometric, gridlike form. The pattern was located 2 degrees north of the equator, longitude 30 degrees, on the western slopes of the active volcano Mukenko. The computer estimated the age of the secondary jungle at five hundred to eight hundred years.

"So you sent an expedition in?" Elliot said.

Ross nodded. "Three weeks ago, led by a South African named Kruger. The expedition confirmed the placer diamond deposits, went on to search for the origin, and found the ruins of the city."

"And then what happened?" Elliot asked.

He ran the videotape a second time.

Onscreen he saw black-and-white images of the camp, destroyed, smoldering. Several dead bodies with crushed skulls were visible. As they watched, a shadow moved over the dead bodies, and the camera zoomed back to show the outline of the lumbering shadow. Elliot agreed that it looked like the shadow of a gorilla, but he insisted, "Gorillas couldn't do this. Gorillas are peaceful, vegetarian animals."

They watched as the tape ran to the end. And then they reviewed her final computer-reconstituted image, which clearly showed the head of a male gorilla.

"That's ground truth," Ross said.

Elliot was not so sure. He reran the last three seconds of videotape a final time, staring at the gorilla head. The image was fleeting, leaving a ghostly trail, but something was wrong with it. He couldn't quite identify what. Certainly this was atypical gorilla behavior, but there was something else. . . . He pushed the freeze-frame button and stared at the frozen image. The face and the fur were both gray: unquestionably gray.

"Can we increase contrast?" he asked Ross. "This image is washed out."

"I don't know," Ross said, touching the controls. "I think this is a pretty good image." She was unable to darken it.

"It's very gray," he said. "Gorillas are much darker."

"Well, this contrast range is correct for video."

Elliot was sure this creature was too light to be a mountain gorilla. Either they were seeing a new race of animal, *or a new species.* A new species of great ape, gray in color, aggressive in behavior, discovered in the eastern Congo. . . . He had come on this expedition to verify Amy's dreams—a fascinating psychological insight—but now the stakes were suddenly much higher.

Ross said, "You don't think this is a gorilla?"

"There are ways to test it," he said. He stared at the screen, frowning, as the plane flew onward in the night.

2. B-8 Problems

"You want me to *what*?" Tom Seamans said, cradling the phone in his shoulder and rolling over to look at his bedside clock. It was 3 a.m.

"Go to the zoo," Elliot repeated. His voice sounded garbled, as if coming from under water.

"Peter, where are you calling from?"

"We're somewhere over the Atlantic now," Elliot said. "On our way to Africa."

"Is everything all right?"

"Everything is fine," Elliot said. "But I want you to go to the zoo first thing in the morning."

"And do what?"

"Videotape the gorillas. Try to get them in movement. That's very important for the discriminant function, that they be moving."

"I'd better write this down," Seamans said. Seamans handled the computer programming for the Project Amy staff, and he was accustomed to unusual requests, but not in the middle of the night. "What discriminant function?"

"While you're at it, run any films we have in the library of gorillas—any gorillas, wild or in zoos or whatever. The more specimens the better, so long as they're moving. And for a baseline, you'd better use chimps. Anything we have on chimps. Transfer it to tape and put it through the function."

"What function?" Seamans yawned.

"The function you're going to write," Elliot said. "I want a multiple variable discriminant function based on total imagery—"

"You mean a pattern-recognition function?" Seamans had written pattern-recognition functions for Amy's language use, enabling them to monitor her signing around the clock. Seamans was proud of that program; in its own way, it was highly inventive.

"However you structure it," Elliot said. "I just want a function that'll discriminate gorillas from other primates like chimps. A species-differentiating function."

"Are you kidding?" Seamans said. "That's a B-8 problem." In the developing field of pattern-recognition computer programs, so-called B-8 problems were the most difficult; whole teams of researchers had devoted years to trying to teach computers the difference between "B" and "8"—precisely because the difference was so obvious. But what was obvious to the human eye was not obvious to the computer scanner. The scanner had to be told, and the specific instructions turned out to be far more difficult than anyone anticipated, particularly for handwritten characters.

Now Elliot wanted a program that would distinguish between similar visual images of gorillas and chimps. Seamans could not help asking, "Why? It's pretty obvious. A gorilla is a gorilla, and a chimp is a chimp."

"Just do it," Elliot said.

"Can I use size?" On the basis of size alone, gorillas and chimps could be accurately distinguished. But visual functions could not determine size unless the distance from the recording instrument to the subject image was known, as well as the focal length of the recording lens.

"No, you can't use size," Elliot said. "Element morphology only."

Seamans sighed. "Thanks a lot. What resolution?"

"I need ninety-five-percent confidence limits on species assignment, to be based on less than three seconds of black-and-white scan imagery."

Seamans frowned. Obviously, Elliot had three seconds of videotape imagery of some animal and he was not sure whether it was a gorilla or not. Elliot had seen enough gorillas over the years to know the difference: gorillas and chimps were utterly different animals in size, appearance, movement, and behavior. They were as different as intelligent oceanic mammals—say, porpoises and whales. In making such discriminations, the human eye was far superior to any computer program that could be devised. Yet Elliot apparently did not trust his eye. What was he thinking of?

"I'll try," Seamans said, "but it's going to take a while. You don't write that kind of program overnight."

"I need it overnight, Tom," Elliot said. "I'll call you back in twenty-four hours."

3. Inside the Coffin

In one corner of the 747 living module was a sound-baffled fiberglass booth, with a hinged hood and a small CRT screen; it was called "the coffin" because of the claustrophobic feeling that came from working inside it. As the airplane crossed the mid-Atlantic, Ross stepped inside the coffin. She had a last

look at Elliot and Amy—both asleep, both snoring loudly—
and Jensen and Levine playing "submarine chase" on the
computer console, as she lowered the hood.

Ross was tired, but she did not expect to get much sleep
for the next two weeks, which was as long as she thought the
expedition would last. Within fourteen days—336 hours—
Ross's team would either have beaten the Euro-Japanese consortium or she would have failed and the Zaire Virunga
mineral exploration rights would be lost forever.

The race was already under way, and Karen Ross did not
intend to lose it.

She punched Houston coordinates, including her own
sender designation, and waited while the scrambler inter-
locked. From now on, there would be a signal delay of five
seconds at both ends, because both she and Houston would be
sending in coded burst transmissions to elude passive listeners.

The screen glowed: TRAVIS.

She typed back: ROSS. She picked up the telephone re-
ceiver.

"It's a bitch," Travis said, although it was not Travis's
voice, but a computer-generated flat audio signal, without expression.

"Tell me," Ross said.

"The slants are rolling," Travis's surrogate voice said.

She knew his slang: Travis called all competition "slants";
in most instances during the past four years, the competition
had been Japanese. (Travis was fond of saying, "In the eigh-
ties, it's the Japs. In the nineties, it'll be the Chinks. Either
way it's slants, and they all work Sundays and to hell with the
football game. We gotta keep up.")

"Details," Ross said, and waited for the five-second delay.
She could imagine Travis in the CCR in Houston, hearing her
own computer-generated voice. That flat voice required a
change in speech patterns; what was ordinarily conveyed by
phrasing and emphasis had to be made explicit.

"They know you're on your way," Travis's voice whined. "They are pushing their own schedule. The Germans are behind it—your friend Richter. I'm arranging a feeding in a matter of minutes. That's the good news."

"And the bad news?"

"The Congo has gone to hell in the last ten hours," Travis said. "We have a nasty GPU."

"Print," she said.

On the screen, she saw printed GEOPOLITICAL UPDATE, followed by a dense paragraph. It read:

```
ZAIRE EMBASSY WASHINGTON STATES EASTERN BORDERS VIA RWANDA
CLOSED / NO EXPLANATION / PRESUMPTION IDI AMIN TROOPS FLEEING
TANZANIAN INVASION UGANDA INTO EASTERN ZAIRE / CONSEQUENT
DISRUPTION / BUT FACTS DIFFER / LOCAL TRIBES {KIGANI} ON RAM-
PAGE / REPORTED ATROCITIES AND CANNIBALISM ETC / FOREST-
DWELLING PYGMIES UNRELIABLE / KILLING ALL VISITORS CONGO
RAIN FOREST / ZAIRE GOVERNMENT DISPATCHED GENERAL MUGURU
{AKA BUTCHER OF STANLEYVILLE} / PUT DOWN KIGANI REBELLION 'AT
ALL COSTS' / SITUATION HIGHLY UNSTABLE / ONLY LEGAL ENTRY
INTO ZAIRE NOW WEST THROUGH KINSHASA / YOU ARE ON YOUR OWN /
ACQUISITION WHITE HUNTER MUNRO NOW PARAMOUNT IMPORTANCE
WHATEVER COST / KEEP HIM FROM CONSORTIUM WILL PAY ANYTHING /
YOUR SITUATION EXTREME DANGER / MUST HAVE MUNRO TO SURVIVE /
```

She stared at the screen. It was the worst possible news. She said, "Have you got a time course?"

```
EURO-JAPANESE CONSORTIUM NOW COMPRISES HAKAMICHI {JAPAN} /
GERLICH {GERMANY} / VOORSTER {AMSTERDAM} / UNFORTUNATELY
HAVE RESOLVED DIFFERENCES NOW IN COMPLETE ACCORD / MONITOR-
ING US CANNOT ANTICIPATE SECURE TRANSMISSIONS ANYTIME HENCE-
FORTH / ANTICIPATE ELECTRONIC COUNTERMEASURES AND WARFARE
TACTICS IN PURSUIT OF TWO-B GOAL / THEY WILL ENTER CONGO
{RELIABLE SOURCE} WITHIN 48 HOURS NOW SEEKING MUNRO /
```

"When will they reach Tangier?" she asked.

"In six hours. You?"

"Seven hours. And Munro?"

"We don't know about Munro," Travis said. "Can you booby him?"

"Absolutely," Ross said. "I'll arrange the booby now. If Munro doesn't see things our way, I promise you it'll be seventy-two hours before he's allowed out of the country."

"What've you got?" Travis asked.

"Czech submachine guns. Found on the premises, with his prints on them, carefully applied. That should do it."

"That should do it," Travis agreed. "What about your passengers?" He was referring to Elliot and Amy.

"They're fine," Ross said. "They know nothing."

"Keep it that way," Travis said, and hung up.

4. Feeding Time

"It's feeding time," Travis called cheerfully. "Who's at the trough?"

"We've got five tap dancers on Beta dataline," Rogers said. Rogers was the electronic surveillance expert, the bug catcher.

"Anybody we know?"

"Know them all," Rogers said, slightly annoyed. "Beta line is our main cross-trunk line in-house, so whoever wants to tap in to our system will naturally plug in there. You get more bits and pieces that way. Of course we aren't using Beta any more except for routine uncoded garbage—taxes and payroll, that stuff."

"We have to arrange a feed," Travis said. A feed meant putting false data out over a tapped line, to be picked up. It was a delicate operation. "You have the slants on the line?"

"Sure. What do you want to feed them?"

"Coordinates for the lost city," Travis said.

Rogers nodded, mopping his brow. He was a portly man who sweated profusely. "How good do you want it?"

"Damn good," Travis said. "You won't fool the slants with static."

"You don't want to give them the actual co-ords?"

"God, no. But I want them reasonably close. Say, within two hundred kilometers."

"Can do," Rogers said.

"Coded?" Travis said.

"Of course."

"You have a code they can break in twelve to fifteen hours?"

Rogers nodded. "We've got a dilly. Looks like hell, but then when you work it, it pops out. Got an internal weakness in concealed lettering frequency. At the other end, looks like we made a mistake, but it's very breakable."

"It can't be too easy," Travis warned.

"Oh, no, they'll earn their yen. They'll never suspect a feed. We ran it past the army and they came back all smiles, teaching us a lesson. Never knew it was a setup."

"Okay," Travis said, "put the data out, and let's feed them. I want something that'll give them a sense of confidence for the next forty-eight hours or more—until they figure out that we've screwed them."

"Delighted," Rogers said, and he moved off to Beta terminal.

Travis sighed. The feeding would soon begin, and he hoped it would protect his team in the field—long enough for them to get to the diamonds first.

5. Dangerous Signatures

The soft murmur of voices woke him.

"How unequivocal is that signature?"

"Pretty damn unequivocal. Here's the pissup, nine days ago, and it's not even epicentered."

"That's cloud cover?"

"No, that's not cloud cover, it's too black. That's ejecta from the signature."

"Hell."

Elliot opened his eyes to see dawn breaking as a thin red line against blue-black through the windows of the passenger compartment. His watch read 5:11—five in the morning, San Francisco time. He had slept only two hours since calling Seamans. He yawned and glanced down at Amy, curled up in her nest of blankets on the floor. Amy snored loudly. The other bunks were unoccupied.

He heard soft voices again, and looked toward the computer console. Jensen and Levine were staring at a screen and talking quietly. "Dangerous signature. We got a computer projection on that?"

"Coming. It'll take a while. I asked for a five-year runback, as well as the other pissups."

Elliot climbed out of his cot and looked at the screen. "What're pissups?" he said.

"PSOPs are prior significant orbital passes by the satellite," Jensen explained. "They're called pissups because we usually ask for them when we're already pissing upwind. We've been looking at this volcanic signature here," Jensen said, pointing to the screen. "It's not too promising."

"What volcanic signature?" Elliot asked.

They showed him the billowing plumes of smoke—dark green in artificial computer-generated colors—which belched from the mouth of Mukenko, one of the active volcanoes of the Virunga range. "Mukenko erupts on the average of once every three years," Levine said. "The last eruption was March, 1977, but it looks like it's gearing up for another full eruption in the next week or so. We're waiting now for the probability assessment."

"Does Ross know about this?"

They shrugged. "She knows, but she doesn't seem worried. She got an urgent GPU—geopolitical update—from Houston about two hours ago, and she went directly into the cargo bay. Haven't seen her since."

Elliot went into the dimly lit cargo bay of the jet. The cargo bay was not insulated and it was chilly: the trucks had a thin frost on metal and glass, and his breath hissed from his mouth. He found Karen Ross working at a table under low pools of light. Her back was turned to him, but when he approached, she dropped what she was doing and turned to face him.

"I thought you were asleep," she said.

"I got restless. What's going on?"

"Just checking supplies. This is our advanced technology unit," she said, lifting up a small backpack. "We've developed a miniaturized package for field parties; twenty pounds of equipment contains everything a man needs for two weeks: food, water, clothing, everything."

"Even water?" Elliot asked.

Water was heavy: seven-tenths of human body weight was water, and most of the weight of food was water; that was why dehydrated food was so light. But water was far more critical to human life than food. Men could survive for weeks without food, but they would die in a matter of hours without water. And water was heavy.

Ross smiled. "The average man consumes four to six liters a day, which is eight to thirteen pounds of weight. On a two-week expedition to a desert region, we'd have to provide two hundred pounds of water for each man. But we have a NASA water-recycling unit which purifies all excretions, including urine. It weighs six ounces. That's how we do it."

Seeing his expression, she said, "It's not bad at all. Our purified water is cleaner than what you get from the tap."

"I'll take your word for it." Elliot picked up a pair of strange looking sunglasses. They were very dark and thick, and there was a peculiar lens mounted over the forehead bridge.

"Holographic night goggles," Ross said. "Employing thin-film diffraction optics." She then pointed out vibration-free camera lenses with optical systems that compensated for movement, strobe infrared lights, and miniature survey lasers no larger than a pencil eraser. There was also a series of small tripods with rapid-geared motors mounted on the top, and brackets to hold something, but she did not explain these devices beyond saying they were "defensive units."

Elliot drifted toward the far table, where he found six submachine guns set out under the lights. He picked one up; it was heavy, and gleaming with grease. Clips of ammunition lay stacked nearby. Elliot did not notice the lettering on the stock; the machine guns were Russian AK-47s manufactured under license in Czechoslovakia.

He glanced at Ross.

"Just precautions," Ross said. "We carry them on every expedition. It doesn't mean anything."

Elliot shook his head. "Tell me about your GPU from Houston," he said.

"I'm not worried about it," she said.

"I am," Elliot said.

As Ross explained it, the GPU was just a technical report. The Zaire government had closed its eastern borders during the previous twenty-four hours; no tourist or commercial traffic could enter the country from Rwanda or Uganda; everyone now had to enter the country from the west, through Kinshasa.

No official reason was given for closing the eastern border, although sources in Washington speculated that Idi Amin's troops, fleeing across the Zaire border from the Tanzanian invasion of Uganda, might be causing "local difficulties." In central Africa, local difficulties usually meant cannibalism and other atrocities.

"Do you believe that?" Elliot asked. "Cannibalism and atrocities?"

"No," Ross said. "It's all a lie. It's the Dutch and the Germans and the Japanese—probably your friend Hakamichi. The Euro-Japanese electronics consortium knows that ERTS is close to discovering important diamond reserves in Virunga. They want to slow us down as much as they can. They've got the fix in somewhere, probably in Kinshasa, and closed the eastern border. It's nothing more than that."

"If there's no danger, why the machine guns?"

"Just precautions," she said again. "We'll never use machine guns on this trip, believe me. Now why don't you get some sleep? We'll be landing in Tangier soon."

"Tangier?"

"Captain Munro is there."

6. Munro

The name of "Captain" Charles Munro was not to be found on the list of the expedition leaders employed by any of the usual field parties. There were several reasons for this, foremost among them his distinctly unsavory reputation.

Munro had been raised in the wild Northern Frontier Province of Kenya, the illegitimate son of a Scottish farmer

and his handsome Indian housekeeper. Munro's father had
the bad luck to be killed by Mau Mau guerillas in 1956.* Soon
afterward, Munro's mother died of tuberculosis, and Munro
made his way to Nairobi where in the late 1950s he worked as
a white hunter, leading parties of tourists into the bush. It was
during this time that Munro awarded himself the title of "Captain," although he had never served in the military.

Apparently, Captain Munro found humoring tourists un-
congenial; by 1960, he was reported running guns from
Uganda into the newly independent Congo. After Moise
Tshombe went into exile in 1963, Munro's activities became
politically embarrassing, and ultimately forced him to disappear from East Africa in late 1963.

He appeared again in 1964, as one of General Mobutu's
white mercenaries in the Congo, under the leadership of
Colonel "Mad Mike" Hoare. Hoare assessed Munro as a
"hard, lethal customer who knew the jungle and was highly
effective, when we could get him away from the ladies." Following the capture of Stanleyville in Operation Dragon
Rouge, Munro's name was associated with the mercenary
atrocities at a village called Avakabi. Munro again disappeared for several years.

In 1968, he re-emerged in Tangier, where he lived splen-
didly and was something of a local character. The source of
Munro's obviously substantial income was unclear, but he was
said to have supplied Communist Sudanese rebels with East
German light arms in 1971, to have assisted the royalist
Ethiopians in their rebellion in 1974–1975, and to have as-
sisted the French paratroopers who dropped into Zaire's
Shaba province in 1978.

His mixed activities made Munro a special case in Africa

---

* Although more than nineteen thousand people were killed in the Mau
Mau uprisings, only thirty-seven whites were killed during seven years of terror-
ism. Each dead white was properly regarded more as a victim of circumstance than of emerging black politics.

in the 1970s; although he was *persona non grata* in a half-dozen African states, he traveled freely throughout the continent, using various passports. It was a transparent ruse: every border official recognized him on sight, but these officials were equally afraid to let him enter the country or to deny him entry.

Foreign mining and exploration companies, sensitive to local feeling, were reluctant to hire Munro as an expedition leader for their parties. It was also true that Munro was by far the most expensive of the bush guides. Nevertheless, he had a reputation for getting tough, difficult jobs done. Under an assumed name, he had taken two German tin-mining parties into the Cameroons in 1974; and he had led one previous ERTS expedition into Angola during the height of the armed conflict in 1977. He quit another ERTS field group headed for Zambia the following year after Houston refused to meet his price: Houston had canceled the expedition.

In short, Munro was acknowledged as the best man for dangerous travel. That was why the ERTS jet stopped in Tangier.

At the Tangier airport, the ERTS cargo jet and its contents were bonded, but all ongoing personnel except Amy passed through customs, carrying their personal belongings. Jensen and Levine were pulled aside for searches; trace quantities of heroin were discovered in their hand baggage.

This bizarre event occurred through a series of remarkable coincidences. In 1977, United States customs agents began to employ neutron backscatter devices, as well as chemical vapor detectors, or sniffers. Both were hand-held electronic devices manufactured under contract by Hakamichi Electronics in Tokyo. In 1978, questions arose about the accuracy of these devices; Hakamichi suggested that they be tested at other ports of entry around the world, including Singapore, Bangkok, Delhi, Munich, and Tangier.

Thus Hakamichi Electronics knew the capabilities of the detectors at Tangier airport, and they also knew that a variety of substances, including ground poppy seeds and shredded turnip, would produce a false-positive registration on airport sensors. And the "false-positive net" required forty-eight hours to untangle. (It was later shown that both men had somehow acquired traces of turnip on their briefcases.)

Both Irving and Jensen vigorously denied any knowledge of illicit material, and appealed to the local U.S. consular office. But the case could not be resolved for several days; Ross telephoned Travis in Houston, who determined that it was "a slant plant" and a "Dutch herring." There was nothing to be done except to carry on, and continue with the expedition as best they could.

"They think this will stop us," Travis said, "but it won't."

"Who's going to do the geology?" Ross asked.

"You are," Travis said.

"And the electronics?"

"You're the certified genius," Travis said. "Just make sure you have Munro. He's the key to everything."

The song of the muezzin floated over the pastel jumble of houses in the Tangier Casbah at twilight, calling the faithful to evening prayer. In the old days, the muezzin himself appeared in the minarets of the mosque, but now a recording played over loudspeakers: a mechanized call to the Muslim ritual of obeisance.

Karen Ross sat on the terrace of Captain Munro's house overlooking the Casbah and waited for her audience with the man himself. Beside her, Peter Elliot sat in a chair and snored noisily, exhausted from the long flight.

They had been waiting nearly three hours, and she was worried. Munro's house was of Moorish design, and open to the outdoors. From the interior she could hear voices, faintly carried by the breeze, speaking some Oriental language.

One of the graceful Moroccan servant girls that Munro seemed to have in infinite supply came onto the terrace carrying a telephone. She bowed formally. Ross saw that the girl had violet eyes; she was exquisitely beautiful, and could not have been more than sixteen. In careful English the girl said, "This is your telephone to Houston. The bidding will now begin."

Karen nudged Peter, who awoke groggily. "The bidding will now begin," she said.

Peter Elliot was surprised from the moment of his first entrance into Munro's house. He had anticipated a tough military setting and was amazed to see delicate carved Moroccan arches and soft gurgling fountains with sunlight sparkling on them.

Then he saw the Japanese and Germans in the next room, staring at him and at Ross. The glances were distinctly unfriendly, but Ross stood and said, "Excuse me a moment," and she went forward and embraced a young blond German man warmly. They kissed, chattered happily, and in general appeared to be intimate friends.

Elliot did not like this development, but he was reassured to see that the Japanese—identically dressed in black suits —were equally displeased. Noticing this, Elliot smiled benignly, to convey a sense of approval for the reunion.

But when Ross returned, he demanded, "Who was that?"

"That's Richter," she said. "The most brilliant topologist in Western Europe; his field is n-space extrapolation. His work's extremely elegant." She smiled. "Almost as elegant as mine."

"But he works for the consortium?"

"Naturally. He's German."

"And you're talking with him?"

"I was delighted for the opportunity," she said. "Karl has a fatal limitation. He can only deal with pre-existing data. He takes what he is given, and does cartwheels with it in n-space. But he cannot imagine anything new at all. I had a professor at M.I.T. who was the same way. Tied to facts, a hostage to reality." She shook her head.

"Did he ask about Amy?"

"Of course."

"And what did you tell him?"

"I told him she was sick and probably dying."

"And he believed that?"

"We'll see. There's Munro."

Captain Munro appeared in the next room, wearing khakis, smoking a cigar. He was a tall, rugged-looking man with a mustache, and soft dark watchful eyes that missed nothing. He talked with the Japanese and Germans, who were evidently unhappy with what he was saying. Moments later, Munro entered their room, smiling broadly.

"So you're going to the Congo, Dr. Ross."

"We are, Captain Munro," she said.

Munro smiled. "It seems as though everyone is going."

There followed a rapid exchange which Elliot found incomprehensible. Karen Ross said, "Fifty thousand U.S. in Swiss francs against point oh two of first-year adjusted extraction returns."

Munro shook his head. "A hundred in Swiss francs and point oh six of first-year return on the primary deposits, crude-grade accounting, no discounting."

"A hundred in U.S. dollars against point oh one of the first-year return on all deposits, with full discounting from point of origin."

"Point of origin? In the middle of the bloody Congo? I

would want three years from point of origin: what if you're shut down?"

"You want a piece, you gamble. Mobutu's clever."

"Mobutu's barely in control, and I am still alive because I am no gambler," Munro said. "A hundred against point oh four of first year on primary with front-load discount only. Or I'll take point oh two of yours."

"If you're no gambler, I'll give you a straight buy-out for two hundred."

Munro shook his head. "You've paid more than that for your MER in Kinshasa."

"Prices for everything are inflated in Kinshasa, including mineral exploration rights. And the current exploration limit, the computer CEL, is running well under a thousand."

"If you say so." He smiled, and headed back into the other room, where the Japanese and Germans were waiting for his return.

Ross said quickly, "That's not for them to know."

"Oh, I'm sure they know it anyway," Munro said, and walked into the other room.

"Bastard," she whispered to his back. She talked in low tones on the telephone. "He'll never accept that. . . . No, no, he won't go for it . . . they want him bad. . . ."

Elliot said, "You're bidding very high for his services."

"He's the best," Ross said, and continued whispering into the telephone. In the next room, Munro was shaking his head sadly, turning down an offer. Elliot noticed that Richter was very red in the face.

Munro came back to Karen Ross. "What was your projected CEL?"

"Under a thousand."

"So you say. Yet you know there's an ore intercept."

"I don't know there's an ore intercept."

"Then you're foolish to spend all this money to go to the Congo," Munro said. "Aren't you?"

Karen Ross made no reply. She stared at the ornate ceiling of the room.

"Virunga's not exactly a garden spot these days," Munro continued. "The Kigani are on the rampage, and they're cannibals. Pygmies aren't friendly any more either. Likely to find an arrow in your back for your troubles. Volcanoes always threatening to blow. Tsetse flies. Bad water. Corrupt officials. Not a place to go without a very good reason, hmm? Perhaps you should put off your trip until things settle down."

Those were precisely Peter Elliot's sentiments, and he said so.

"Wise man," Munro said, with a broad smile that annoyed Karen Ross.

"Evidently," Karen Ross said, "we will never come to terms."

"That seems clear." Munro nodded.

Elliot understood that negotiations were broken off. He got up to shake Munro's hand and leave—but before he could do that, Munro walked into the next room and conferred with the Japanese and Germans.

"Things are looking up," Ross said.

"Why?" Elliot said. "Because he thinks he's beaten you down?"

"No. Because he thinks we know more than they do about the site location and are more likely to hit an ore body and pay off."

In the next room, the Japanese and Germans abruptly stood, and walked to the front door. At the door, Munro shook hands with the Germans, and bowed elaborately to the Japanese.

"I guess you're right," Elliot said to Ross. "He's sending them away."

But Ross was frowning, her face grim. "They can't do this," she said. "They can't just quit this way."

Elliot was confused again. "I thought you wanted them to quit."

"Damn," Ross said. "We've been screwed." She whispered into the telephone, talking to Houston.

Elliot didn't understand it at all. And his confusion was not resolved when Munro locked the door behind the last of the departing men, then came back to Elliot and Ross to say that supper was served.

They ate Moroccan-style, sitting on the floor and eating with their fingers. The first course was a pigeon pie, and it was followed by some sort of stew.

"So you sent the Japanese off?" Ross said. "Told them no?"

"Oh, no," Munro said. "That would be impolite. I told them I would think about it. And I will."

"Then why did they leave?"

Munro shrugged. "Not my doing, I assure you. I think they heard something on the telephone which changed their whole plan."

Karen Ross glanced at her watch, making a note of the time. "Very good stew," she said. She was doing her best to be agreeable.

"Glad you like it. It's *tajin*. Camel meat."

Karen Ross coughed. Peter Elliot noticed that his own appetite had diminished. Munro turned to him. "So you have the gorilla, Professor Elliot?"

"How did you know that?"

"The Japanese told me. The Japanese are fascinated by your gorilla. Can't figure the point of it, drives them mad. A young man with a gorilla, and a young woman who is search-ing for—"

"Industrial-grade diamonds," Karen Ross said.

"Ah, industrial-grade diamonds." He turned to Elliot. "I

enjoy a frank conversation. Diamonds, fascinating." His manner suggested that he had been told nothing of importance.

Ross said, "You've got to take us in, Munro."

"World's full of industrial-grade diamonds," Munro said. "You can find them in Africa, India, Russia, Brazil, Canada, even in America—Arkansas, New York, Kentucky—everywhere you look. But you're going to the Congo."

The obvious question hung in the air.

"We are looking for Type IIb boron-coated blue diamonds," Karen Ross said, "which have semiconducting properties important to microelectronics applications."

Munro stroked his mustache. "Blue diamonds," he said, nodding. "It makes sense."

Ross said that of course it made sense.

"You can't dope them?" Munro asked.

"No. It's been tried. There was a commercial boron-doping process, but it was too unreliable. The Americans had one and so did the Japanese. Everyone gave it up as hopeless."

"So you've got to find a natural source."

"That's right. I want to get there as soon as possible," Ross said, staring at him, her voice flat.

"I'm sure you do," Munro said. "Nothing but business for our Dr. Ross, eh?" He crossed the room and, leaning against one of the arches, looked out on the dark Tangier night. "I'm not surprised at all," he said. "As a matter of—"

At the first blast of machine-gun fire, Munro dived for cover, the glassware on the table splattered, one of the girls screamed, and Elliot and Ross threw themselves to the marble floor as the bullets whined around them, chipping the plaster overhead, raining plaster dust down upon them. The blast lasted thirty seconds or so, and it was followed by complete silence.

When it was over, they got up hesitantly, staring at one another.

"The consortium plays for keeps." Munro grinned. "Just
my sort of people."

Ross brushed plaster dust off her clothes. She turned to
Munro. "Five point two against the first two hundred, no de-
ductions, in Swiss francs, adjusted."

"Five point seven, and you have me."

"Five point seven. Done."

Munro shook hands with them, then announced that he
would need a few minutes to pack his things before leaving for
Nairobi.

"Just like that?" Ross asked. She seemed suddenly concerned, glancing again at her watch.

"What's your problem?" Munro asked.

"Czech AK-47s," she said. "In your warehouse."

Munro showed no surprise. "Better get them out," he said.
"The consortium undoubtedly has something similar in the
works, and we've got a lot to do in the next few hours." As he
spoke, they heard the police klaxons approaching from a distance. Munro said, "We'll take the back stair."

An hour later, they were airborne, heading toward Nairobi.

DAY 4: NAIROBI
June 16, 1979

1. Timeline

It was farther across Africa from Tangier to Nairobi than it was across the Atlantic Ocean from New York to London—3,600 miles, an eight-hour flight. Ross spent the time at the computer console, working out what she called "hyperspace probability lines."

The screen showed a computer-generated map of Africa, with streaking multicolored lines across it. "These are all timelines," Ross said. "We can weight them for duration and delay factors." Beneath the screen was a total-elapsed-time clock, which kept shifting numbers.

"What's that mean?" Elliot asked.

"The computer's picking the fastest route. You see it's just identified a timeline that will get us on site in six days eighteen hours and fifty-one minutes. Now it's trying to beat that time."

Elliot had to smile. The idea of a computer predicting *to the minute* when they would reach their Congo location seemed ludicrous to him. But Ross was totally serious.

As they watched, the computer clock shifted to 5 days 22 hours 24 minutes.

"Better," Ross said, nodding. "But still not very good." She pressed another button and the lines shifted, stretching like rubber bands over the African continent. "This is the consortium route," she said, "based on our assumptions about the expedition. They're going in big—thirty or more people, a full-scale undertaking. And they don't know the exact location of the city; at least, we don't think they know. But they have a substantial start on us, at least twelve hours, since their aircraft is already forming up in Nairobi."

The clock registered total elapsed time: 5 days 09 hours 19 minutes. Then she pressed a button marked DATE and it shifted to 06 21 79 0814. "According to this, the consortium will reach the Congo site a little after eight o'clock in the morning on June 21."

The computer clicked quietly; the lines continued to stretch and pull, and the clock read a new date: 06 21 79 1224.

"Well," she said, "that's where we are now. Given maximum favorable movements for us and them, the consortium will beat us to the site by slightly more than four hours, five days from now."

Munro walked past, eating a sandwich. "Better lock another path," he said. "Or go radical."

"I hesitate to go radical with the ape."

Munro shrugged. "Have to do something, with a timeline like that."

Elliot listened to them with a vague sense of unreality: they were discussing a difference of hours, five days in the future. "But surely," Elliot said, "over the next few days, with all the arrangements at Nairobi, and then getting into the jungle—you can't put too much faith in those figures."

"This isn't like the old days of African exploration," Ross said, "where parties disappeared into the wilds for months. At most, the computer is off by minutes—say, roughly half an hour in the total five-day projection." She shook her head. "No. We have a problem here, and we've got to do something about it. The stakes are too great."

"You mean the diamonds."

She nodded, and pointed to the bottom of the screen,

where the words BLUE CONTRACT appeared. He asked her what
the Blue Contract was.

"One hell of a lot of money," Ross said. And she added, "I
think." For in truth she did not really know.

Each new contract at ERTS was given a code name. Only
Travis and the computer knew the name of the company buying the contract; everyone else at ERTS, from computer programmers to field personnel, knew the projects only by their
color-code names: Red Contract, Yellow Contract, White
Contract. This was a business protection for the firms involved. But the ERTS mathematicians could not resist a lively
guessing game about contract sources, which was the staple of
daily conversation in the company canteen.

The Blue Contract had come to ERTS in December,
1978. It called for ERTS to locate a natural source of industrial-grade diamonds in a friendly or neutralist country. The
diamonds were to be Type IIb, "nitrogen-poor" crystals.
No dimensions were specified, so crystal size did not matter;
nor were recoverable quantities specified: the contractor
would take what he could get. And, most unusual, there was
no UECL.

Nearly all contracts arrived with a unit extraction cost
limit. It was not enough to find a mineral source; the minerals
had to be extractable at a specified unit cost. This unit cost
in turn reflected the richness of the ore body, its remoteness,
the availability of local labor, political conditions, the possible
need to build airfields, roads, hospitals, schools, mines, or
refineries.

For a contract to come in without a UECL meant only one
thing: somebody wanted blue diamonds so badly he didn't
care what they cost.

Within forty-eight hours, the ERTS canteen had explained
the Blue Contract. It turned out that Type IIb diamonds were
blue from trace quantities of the element boron, which ren-
dered them worthless as gemstones but altered their electronic

properties, making them semiconductors with a resistivity on the order of 100 ohms centimeters. They also had light-transmissive properties.

Someone then found a brief article in *Electronic News* for November 17, 1978: "McPhee Doping Dropped." It explained that the Waltham, Massachusetts, firm of Silec, Inc., had abandoned the experimental McPhee technique to dope diamonds artificially with a monolayer boron coating. The McPhee process had been abandoned as too expensive and too unreliable to produce "desirable semiconducting properties." The article concluded that "other firms have underestimated problems in boron monolayer doping; Hakamichi (Tokyo) abandoned the Nagaura process in September of this year." Working backward, the ERTS canteen fitted additional pieces of the puzzle into place.

Back in 1971, Intec, the Santa Clara microelectronics firm, had first predicted that diamond semiconductors would be important to a future generation of "superconducting" computers in the 1980s.

The first generation of electronic computers, ENIAC and UNIVAC, built in the wartime secrecy of the 1940s, employed vacuum tubes. Vacuum tubes had an average life span of twenty hours, but with thousands of glowing hot tubes in a single machine, some computers shut down every seven to twelve minutes. Vacuum-tube technology imposed a limit on the size and power of planned second-generation computers.

But the second generation never used vacuum tubes. In 1947, the invention of the transistor—a thumbnail-sized sandwich of solid material which performed all the functions of a vacuum tube—ushered in an era of "solid state" electronic devices which drew little power, generated little heat, and were smaller and more reliable than the tubes they replaced. Silicon technology provided the basis for three generations of increasingly compact, reliable, and cheap computers over the next twenty years.

But by the 1970s, computer designers began to confront the inherent limitations of silicon technology. Although circuits had been shrunk to microscopic dimensions, computation speed was still dependent on circuit length. To miniaturize circuits still more, where distances were already on the order of millionths of an inch, brought back an old problem: heat. Smaller circuits would literally melt from the heat produced. What was needed was some method to eliminate heat and reduce resistance at the same time.

It had been known since the 1950s that many metals when cooled to extremely low temperatures became "superconducting," permitting the unimpeded flow of electrons through them. In 1977, IBM announced it was designing an ultra-high-speed computer the size of a grapefruit, chilled with liquid nitrogen. The superconducting computer required a radically new technology, and a new range of low-temperature construction materials.

Doped diamonds would be used extensively throughout.

Several days later, the ERTS canteen came up with an alternative explanation. According to the new theory, the 1970s had been a decade of unprecedented growth in computers. Although the first computer manufacturers in the 1940s had predicted that four computers would do the computing work of the entire world for the foreseeable future, experts anticipated that by 1990 there would actually be *one billion* computers—most of them linked by communications networks to other computers. Such networks didn't exist, and might even be theoretically impossible. (A 1975 study by the Hanover Institute concluded there was insufficient metal in the earth's crust to construct the necessary computer transmission lines.)

According to Harvey Rumbaugh, the 1980s would be characterized by a critical shortage of computer data transmission systems: "Just as the fossil fuel shortage took the industrialized world by surprise in the 1970s, so will the data transmission shortage take the world by surprise in the next ten years. People were denied *movement* in the 1970s; but they will be denied *information* in the 1980s, and it remains to be seen which shortage will prove more frustrating."

Laser light represented the only hope for handling these massive data requirements, since laser channels carried twenty thousand times the information of an ordinary metal coaxial trunk line. Laser transmission demanded whole new technologies—including thin-spun fiber optics, and doped semiconducting diamonds, which Rumbaugh predicted would be "more valuable than oil" in the coming years.

Even further, Rumbaugh anticipated that within ten years *electricity itself would become obsolete.* Future computers would utilize only light circuits, and interface with light-transmission data systems. The reason was speed. "Light," Rumbaugh said, "moves at the speed of light. Electricity doesn't. We are living in the final years of microelectronic technology."

Certainly microelectronics did not look like a moribund technology. In 1979, microelectronics was a major industry throughout the industrialized world, accounting for eighty billion dollars annually in the United States alone; six of the top twenty corporations in the Fortune 500 were deeply involved in microelectronics. These companies had a history of extraordinary competition and advance, over a period of less than thirty years.

In 1958, a manufacturer could fit 10 electronic components onto a single silicon chip. By 1970, it was possible to fit 100 units onto a chip of the same size—a tenfold increase in slightly more than a decade.

But by 1972, it was possible to fit 1,000 units on a chip, and by 1974, 10,000 units. It was expected that by 1980, there would be one million units on a single chip the size of a thumbnail, but, using electronic photoprojection, this goal was actually realized in 1978. By the spring of 1979, the new

goal was ten million units—or, even better, one billion units—
on a single silicon chip by 1980. But nobody expected to wait
past June or July of 1979 for this development.
Such advances within an industry are unprecedented.
Comparison to older manufacturing technologies makes this
clear. Detroit was content to make trivial product design
changes at three-year intervals, but the electronics industry
routinely expected *order of magnitude* advances in the same
time. (To keep pace, Detroit would have had to increase
automobile gas mileage from 8 miles per gallon in 1970 to
80,000,000 miles per gallon in 1979. Instead, Detroit went
from 8 to 16 miles per gallon during that time, further evidence of the coming demise of the automotive industry as the
center of the American economy.)

In such a competitive market, everyone worried about foreign
powers, chiefly Japan, which since 1973 had maintained a
Japanese Cultural Exchange in Santa Clara—actually a cover
organization for blatant and well-financed industrial espionage.
The Blue Contract could only be understood in the light
of an industry making major advances every few months.
Travis had said that the Blue Contract was "the biggest thing
we'll see in the next ten years. Whoever finds those diamonds
has a jump on the technology for at least five years. *Five
years.* Do you know what that means?"
Ross knew what it meant. In an industry where competitive edges were measured in months, companies had made
fortunes by beating competitors by a matter of weeks with
some new technique or device; Syntel in California had been
the first to make a 256K memory chip while everyone else was
still making 16K chips and dreaming of 64K chips. Syntel
kept their advantage for only sixteen weeks, but realized a
profit of more than a hundred and thirty million dollars.

"And we're talking about *five years*," Travis said. "That's an advantage measured in billions of dollars, maybe tens of billions of dollars. If we can get to those diamonds."

These were the reasons for the extraordinary pressure Ross felt as she continued to work with the computer. At the age of twenty-four, she was team leader in a high-technology race involving a half-dozen nations around the globe, all secretly pitting their business and industrial resources against one another.

The stakes made any conventional race seem ludicrous. Travis told her before she left, "Don't be afraid when the pressure makes you crazy. You have *billions of dollars* riding on your shoulders. Just do the best you can."

Doing the best she could, she managed to reduce the expedition timeline by another three hours and thirty-seven minutes—but they were still slightly behind the consortium projection. Not too far to make up the time, especially with Munro's cold-blooded shortcuts, but nevertheless behind—which could mean total disaster in a winner-take-all race.

And then she received bad news.

The screen printed PIGGYBACK SLURP / ALL BETS OFF .

"Hell," Ross said. She felt suddenly tired. Because if there really had been a piggyback slurp, their chances of winning the race were vanishing—before any of them had even set foot in the rain forests of central Africa.

2. Piggyback Slurp

Travis felt like a fool.

He stared at the hard copy from Goddard Space Flight Center, Greenbelt, Maryland:

ERTS WHY ARE YOU SENDING US ALL THIS MUKENKO DATA WE DON'T REALLY CARE THANKS ANYWAY DESIST AT LEISURE.

That had arrived an hour ago from GSFC/Maryland, but it was already too late by more than five hours.

"Damn!" Travis said, staring at the telex.

The first indication to Travis that anything was wrong was when the Japanese and Germans broke off negotiations with Munro in Tangier. One minute they had been willing to pay anything; the next minute they could hardly wait to leave. The break-off had come abruptly, discontinuously; it implied the sudden introduction of new data into the consortium computer files.

New data from where?

There could be only one explanation—and now it was confirmed in the GSFC telex from Greenbelt.

ERTS WHY ARE YOU SENDING ALL THIS MUKENKO DATA

There was a simple answer to that: ERTS *wasn't* sending any data. At least, not willingly. ERTS and GSFC had an arrangement to exchange data updates—Travis had made that deal in 1978 to obtain cheaper satellite imagery from orbiting Landsats. Satellite imagery was his company's single greatest expense. In return for a look at derived ERTS data, GSFC agreed to supply satellite CCTs at 30 percent reduced gross cost.

It seemed like a good deal at the time, and the coded locks were specified in the agreement.

But now the potential drawbacks loomed large before Travis; his worst fears were confirmed. Once you put a line over two thousand miles from Houston to Greenbelt, you begged for a piggyback data slurp. Somewhere between Texas and Maryland someone had inserted a terminal linkup—probably in the carrier telephone lines—and had begun to slurp out data on a piggyback terminal. This was the form of industrial espionage they most feared.

A piggyback-slurp terminal tapped in between two legitimate terminals, monitoring the back and forth transmissions. After a time, the piggyback operator knew enough to begin making transmissions on line, slurping out data from both ends, pretending to be GSFC to Houston, and Houston to GSFC. The piggyback terminal could continue to function until one or both legitimate terminals realized that they were being slurped.

Now the question was how much data had been slurped out in the last seventy-two hours?

He had called for twenty-four-hour scanner checks, but they were disheartening. It looked as though the ERTS computer had yielded up not only original database elements, but also data-transformation histories—the sequence of operations performed on the data by ERTS over the last four weeks.

If that was true, it meant that the Euro-Japanese consortium piggyback knew what transformations ERTS had carried out on the Mukenko data—and therefore they knew where the lost city was located, with pinpoint accuracy. They now knew the location of the city as precisely as Ross did.

Timelines had to be adjusted, unfavorably to the ERTS team. And the updated computer projections were unequivocal—Ross or no Ross, the likelihood of the ERTS team reaching the site ahead of the Japanese and Germans was now almost nil.

From Travis's viewpoint, the entire ERTS expedition was now a futile exercise, and a waste of time. There was no hope of success. The only unfactorable element was the gorilla Amy, and Travis's instincts told him that a gorilla named Amy would not prove decisive in the discovery of mineral deposits in the northeastern Congo.

It was hopeless.

Should he recall the ERTS team? He stared at the console by his desk. "Call cost-time," he said.

The computer blinked COST-TIME AVAILABLE.

"Congo Field Survey," he said.

The screen printed out numbers for the Congo Field Survey: expenditures by the hour, accumulated costs, committed future costs, cutoff points, future branch-point deletions. . . . The project was now just outside Nairobi, and was running an accumulated cost of slightly over $189,000.

Cancellation would cost $227,455.

"Factor BF," he said.

The screen changed. BF. He now saw a series of probabilities. "Factor BF" was *bona fortuna*, good luck—the imponderable in all expeditions, especially remote, dangerous expeditions.

THINKING A MOMENT, the computer flashed.

Travis waited. He knew that the computer would require several seconds to perform the computations to assign weights to random factors that might influence the expedition, still five or more days from the target site.

His beeper buzzed. Rogers, the tap dancer, said, "We've traced the piggyback slurp. It's in Norman, Oklahoma, nominally at the North Central Insurance Corporation of America. NCIC is fifty-one percent owned by a Hawaiian holding company, Halekuli, Inc., which is in turn wholly owned by mainland Japanese interests. What do you want?"

"I want a very bad fire," Travis said.

"Got you," Rogers said. He hung up the phone.

The screen flashed ASSESSED FACTOR BF and a probability: .449. He was surprised: that figure meant that ERTS had an almost even chance of attaining the target site before the consortium. Travis didn't question the mathematics; .449 was good enough.

The ERTS expedition would continue to the Congo, at

least for the time being. And in the meantime he would do whatever he could to slow down the consortium. Off the top of his head, Travis could think of one or two ideas to accomplish that.

3. Additional Data

The jet was moving south over Lake Rudolf in northern Kenya when Tom Seamans called Elliot.

Seamans had finished his computer analysis to discriminate gorillas from other apes, principally chimpanzees. He had then obtained from Houston a videotape of three seconds of a garbled video transmission which seemed to show a gorilla smashing a dish antenna and staring into a camera.

"Well?" Elliot said, looking at the computer screen. The data flashed up:

```
DISCRIMINANT FUNCTION GORILLA / CHIMP
FUNCTIONAL GROUPINGS DISTRIBUTED AS:
GORILLA: .9934
CHIMP: .1132
TEST VIDEOTAPE {HOUSTON}: .3349
```

"Hell," Elliot said. At those figures, the study was equivocal, useless.

"Sorry about that," Seamans said over the phone. "But part of the trouble comes from the test material itself. We had to factor in the computer derivation of that image. The image has been cleaned up, and that means it's been regularized; the critical stuff has been lost. I'd like to work with the original digitized matrix. Can you get me that?"

Karen Ross was nodding yes. "Sure," Elliot said.

"I'll go another round with it," Seamans said. "But if you

want my gut opinion, it is never going to turn out. The fact is that gorillas show a considerable individual variation in facial structure, just as people do. If we increase our sample base, we're going to get more variation, and a larger population interval. I think you're stuck. You can never prove it's not a gorilla—but for my money, it's not."

"Meaning what?" Elliot asked.

"It's something new," Seamans said. "I'm telling you, if this was really a gorilla, it would have showed up .89 or .94, somewhere in there, on this function. But the image comes out at .39. That's just not good enough. It's not a gorilla, Peter."

"Then what is it?"

"It's a transitional form. I ran a function to measure where the variation was. You know what was the major differential? Skin color. Even in black-and-white, it's not dark enough to be a gorilla, Peter. This is a whole new animal, I promise you."

Elliot looked at Ross. "What does this do to your time-line?"

"For the moment, nothing," she said. "Other elements are more critical, and this is unfactorable."

The pilot clicked on the intercom. "We are beginning our descent into Nairobi," he said.

4. Nairobi

Five miles outside Nairobi, one can find the wild game of the East African savannah. And within the memory of many Nairobi residents the game could be found closer still—gazelles, buffalo, and giraffe wandering around backyards, and the occasional leopard slipping into one's bedroom. In those days, the city still retained the character of a wild colonial station; in its heyday, Nairobi was a fast-living place indeed: "Are you married or do you live in Kenya?" went the standard question. The men were hard-drinking and rough, the women beautiful and loose, and the pattern of life no more predictable than the fox hunts that ranged over the rugged countryside each weekend.

But modern Nairobi is almost unrecognizable from the time of those freewheeling colonial days. The few remaining Victorian buildings lie stranded in a modern city of half a million, with traffic jams, stoplights, skyscrapers, supermarkets, same-day dry cleaners, French restaurants, and air pollution.

The ERTS cargo plane landed at Nairobi International Airport at dawn on the morning of June 16, and Munro contacted porters and assistants for the expedition. They intended to leave Nairobi within two hours—until Travis called from Houston to inform them that Peterson, one of the geologists on the first Congo expedition, had somehow made it back to Nairobi.

Ross was excited by the news. "Where is he now?" she asked.

"At the morgue," Travis said.

Elliot winced as he came close: the body on the stainless-steel table was a blond man his own age. The man's arms had been crushed; the skin was swollen, a ghastly purple color. He glanced at Ross. She seemed perfectly cool, not blinking or turning away. The pathologist stepped on a foot pedal, activating a microphone overhead. "Would you state your name, please."

"Karen Ellen Ross."

"Your nationality and passport number?"

"American, F 1413649."

"Can you identify the man before you, Miss Ross?"

"Yes," she said. "He is James Robert Peterson."

"What is your relation to the deceased James Robert Peterson?"

"I worked with him," she said dully. She seemed to be examining a geological specimen, scrutinizing it unemotionally. Her face showed no reaction.

The pathologist faced the microphone. "Identity confirmed as James Robert Peterson, male Caucasian, twenty-nine years old, nationality American." He turned back to Ross. "When was the last time you saw Mr. Peterson?"

"In May of this year. He was leaving for the Congo."

"You have not seen him in the last month?"

"No," she said. "What happened?"

The pathologist touched the puffy purple injuries on his arms. His fingertips sank in, leaving indentations like teeth in the flesh. "Damned strange story," the pathologist said.

The previous day, June 15, Peterson had been flown to Nairobi airport aboard a small charter cargo plane, in end-stage terminal shock. He died several hours later without regaining consciousness. "Extraordinary he made it at all. Apparently the aircraft made an unscheduled stop for a mechanical problem at Garona field, a dirt track in Zaire. And then this fellow comes stumbling out of the woods, collapsing at their feet." The pathologist pointed out that the bones had been shattered in both arms. The injuries, he explained, were not new; they had occurred at least four days earlier, perhaps more. "He must have been in incredible pain."

Elliot said, "What could cause that injury?"

The pathologist had never seen anything like it. "Superficially, it resembles mechanical trauma, a crush injury from an automobile or truck. We see a good deal of those here; but mechanical crush injuries are never bilateral, as they are in this case."

"So it wasn't a mechanical injury?" Karen Ross asked.

"Don't know what it was. It's unique in my experience," the pathologist said briskly. "We also found traces of blood under his nails, and a few strands of gray hair. We're running a test now."

Across the room, another pathologist looked up from his microscope. "The hair is definitely not human. Cross section doesn't match. Some kind of animal hair, close to human."

"The cross section?" Ross said.

"Best index we have of hair origin," the pathologist said. "For instance, human pubic hair is more elliptical in cross section than other body hair, or facial hair. It's quite characteristic—admissible in court. But especially in this laboratory, we come across a great deal of animal hair, and we're expert in that as well."

A large stainless-steel analyzer began pinging. "Blood's coming through," the pathologist said.

On a video screen they saw twin patterns of pastel-colored streaks. "This is the electrophoresis pattern," the pathologist explained. "To check serum proteins. That's ordinary human blood on the left. On the right we have the blood sample from under the nails. You can see it's definitely not human blood."

"Not human blood?" Ross said, glancing at Elliot.

"It's *close* to human blood," the pathologist said, staring at the pattern. "But it's not human. Could be a domestic or farm animal—a pig, perhaps. Or else a primate. Monkeys and apes are very close serologically to human beings. We'll have a computer analysis in a minute."

On the screen, the computer printed ALPHA AND BETA SERUM GLOBULINS MATCH: GORILLA BLOOD.

The pathologist said, "There's your answer to what he had under his nails. Gorilla blood."

5. Examination

"She won't hurt you," Elliot told the frightened orderly. They were in the passenger compartment of the 747 cargo jet. "See, she's smiling at you."

Amy was indeed giving her most winning smile, being careful not to expose her teeth. But the orderly from the private clinic in Nairobi was not familiar with these fine points of gorilla etiquette. His hands shook as he held the syringe.

Nairobi was the last opportunity for Amy to receive a thorough checkup. Her large, powerful body belied a constitutional fragility, as her heavy-browed, glowering face belied a meek, rather tender nature. In San Francisco, the Project Amy staff subjected her to a thorough medical regimen—urine samples every other day, stool samples checked weekly for occult blood, complete blood studies monthly, and a trip to the dentist every three months for removal of the black tartar that accumulated from her vegetarian diet.

Amy took it all in stride, but the terrified orderly did not know that. He approached her holding the syringe in front of him like a weapon. "You sure he won't bite?"

Amy, trying to be helpful, signed *Amy promise no bite.* She was signing slowly, deliberately, as she always did when confronted by someone who did not know her language.

"She promises not to bite you," Elliot said.

"So you say," the orderly said. Elliot did not bother to explain that he hadn't said it; she had.

After the blood samples were drawn, the orderly relaxed a little. Packing up, he said, "Certainly is an ugly brute."

"You've hurt her feelings," Elliot said.

And, indeed, Amy was signing vigorously, *What ugly?* "Nothing, Amy," Elliot said. "He's just never seen a gorilla before."

The orderly said, "I beg your pardon?"

"You've hurt her feelings. You'd better apologize."

The orderly snapped his medical case shut. He stared at Elliot and then at Amy. "Apologize to *him?*"

"Her," Elliot said. "Yes. How would you like to be told you're ugly?"

Elliot felt strongly about this. Over the years, he had come to feel acutely the prejudices that human beings showed toward apes, considering chimpanzees to be cute children, orangs to be wise old men, and gorillas to be hulking, dangerous brutes. They were wrong in every case.

Each of these animals was unique, and did not fit the human stereotypes at all. Chimps, for example, were much more callous than gorillas ever were. Because chimps were extroverts, an angry chimp was far more dangerous than an angry gorilla; at the zoo, Elliot would watch in amazement as human mothers pushed their children closer to look at the chimps, but recoiled protectively at the sight of the gorillas. These mothers obviously did not know that wild chimpanzees caught and ate human infants—something gorillas never did.

Elliot had witnessed repeatedly the human prejudice against gorillas, and had come to recognize its effect on Amy. Amy could not help the fact that she was huge and black and heavy-browed and squash-faced. Behind the face people considered so repulsive was an intelligent and sensitive consciousness, sympathetic to the people around her. It pained her when people ran away, or screamed in fear, or made cruel remarks.

The orderly frowned. "You mean that he understands English?"

"Yes, *she* does." The gender change was something else Elliot didn't like. People who were afraid of Amy always assumed she was male.

The orderly shook his head. "I don't believe it."

"Amy, show the man to the door."

Amy lumbered over to the door and opened it for the orderly, whose eyes widened as he left. Amy closed the door behind him.

Silly human man, Amy signed.

"Never mind," Elliot said. "Come, Peter tickle Amy." And for the next fifteen minutes, he tickled her as she rolled on the floor and grunted in deep satisfaction. Elliot never noticed the door open behind him, never noticed the shadow falling across the floor, until it was too late and he turned his head to look up and saw the dark cylinder swing down, and his head erupted with blinding white pain and everything went black.

6. Kidnapped

He awoke to a piercing electronic shriek.

"Don't move, sir," a voice said.

Elliot opened his eyes and stared into a bright light shining down on him. He was still lying on his back in the aircraft; someone was bent over him.

"Look to the right . . . now to the left. . . . Can you flex your fingers?"

He followed the instructions. The light was taken away and he saw a black man in a white suit crouched beside him. The man touched Elliot's head; his fingers came away red with blood. "Nothing to be alarmed about," the man said; "it's quite superficial." He looked off. "How long would you estimate he was unconscious?"

"Couple of minutes, no more," Munro said.

The high-pitched squeal came again. He saw Ross moving around the passenger section, wearing a shoulder pack, and holding a wand in front of her. There was another squeal. "Damn," she said, and plucked something from the molding around the window. "That's five. They really did a job."

Munro looked down at Elliot. "How do you feel?" he asked.

"He should be put under observation for twenty-four hours," the black man said. "Just as a precaution."

"Twenty-four hours!" Ross said, moving around the compartment.

Elliot said, "Where is she?"

"They took her," Munro said. "They opened the rear door, inflated the pneumatic slide, and were gone before any-one realized what happened. We found this next to you."

Munro gave him a small glass vial with Japanese mark-ings. The sides of the vial were scratched and scored; at one end was a rubber plunger, at the other end a broken needle.

Elliot sat up.

"Easy there," the doctor said.

"I feel fine," Elliot said, although his head was throbbing. He turned the vial over in his hand. "There was frost on it when you found it?"

Munro nodded. "Very cold."

"CO_2," Elliot said. It was a dart from a gas gun. He shook his head. "They broke the needle off in her." He could imag-ine Amy's screams of outrage. She was unaccustomed to any-thing but the tenderest treatment. Perhaps that was one of the shortcomings of his work with her; he had not prepared her well enough for the real world. He sniffed the vial, smelled a pungent odor. "Lobaxin. Fast-acting soporific, onset within fifteen seconds. It's what they'd use." Elliot was angry. Lobaxin was not often used on animals because it caused liver damage. And they had broken the needle—

He got to his feet and leaned on Munro, who put his arm around him. The doctor protested.

"I'm fine," Elliot said.

Across the room, there was another squeal, this one loud and prolonged. Ross was moving her wand over the medicine cabinet, past the bottles of pills and supplies. The sound seemed to embarrass her; quickly she moved away, shutting the cabinet.

She crossed the passenger compartment, and a squeal was heard again. Ross removed a small black device from the underside of one seat. "Look at this. They must have brought an extra person just to plant the bugs. It'll take hours to sterilize the plane. We can't wait."

She went immediately to the computer console and began typing.

Elliot said, "Where are they now? The consortium?"

"The main party left from Kubala airport outside Nairobi six hours ago," Munro said.

"Then they didn't take Amy with them."

"Of course they didn't take her," Ross said, sounding annoyed. "They've got no use for her."

"Have they killed her?" Elliot asked.

"Maybe," Munro said quietly.

"Oh, *Jesus* . . ."

"But I doubt it," Munro continued. "They don't want any publicity, and Amy's famous—as famous in some circles as an ambassador or a head of state. She's a talking gorilla, and there aren't many of those. She's been on television news, she's had her picture in the newspapers. . . . They'd kill you before they killed her."

"Just so they don't kill her," Elliot said.

"They won't," Ross said, with finality. "The consortium isn't interested in Amy. They don't even know why we brought her. They're just trying to blow our timeline—but they won't succeed."

Something in her tone suggested that she planned to leave Amy behind. The idea appalled Elliot. "We've got to get her back," he said. "Amy is my responsibility, I can't possibly abandon her here—"

"Seventy-two minutes," Ross said, pointing to the screen. "We have exactly one hour and twelve minutes, before we blow the timeline." She turned to Munro. "And we have to switch over to the second contingency."

"Fine," Munro said. "I'll get the men working on it."

"In a new plane," Ross said. "We can't take this one, it's

contaminated." She was punching in call letters to the computer console, her fingers clicking on the buttons. "We'll take it straight to point M," Ross said. "Okay?"

"Absolutely," Munro said.

Elliot said, "I won't leave Amy. If you're going to leave her behind, you'll have to leave me as well—" Elliot stopped.

Printed on the screen was the message FORGET GORILLA PROCEED TO NEXT CHECKPOINT URGENT APE NOT SIGNIFICANT TIME-LINE OUTCOME COMPUTER VERIFICATION REPEAT PROCEED WITHOUT AMY.

"You can't leave her behind," Elliot said. "I'll stay behind, too."

"Let me tell you something," Ross said. "I never believed that Amy was important to this expedition—or you either. From the very beginning she was just a diversion. When I came to San Francisco, I was followed. You and Amy provided a diversion. You threw the consortium into a spin. It was worth it. Now it's not worth it. We'll leave you both behind if we have to. I couldn't care less."

7. Bugs

"Well, goddam it," Elliot began, "do you mean to tell me that . . ."

"That's right," Ross said coldly. "You're expendable." But even as she spoke, she grabbed his arm firmly and led him out of the airplane while she held her finger to her lips.

Elliot realized that she intended to pacify him in private, but he was determined not to back down from his position. Amy *was* his responsibility, and to hell with all the diamonds and international intrigue. Outside on the concrete runway he repeated stubbornly, "I'm not leaving without Amy."

"Neither am I." Ross walked quickly across the runway toward a police helicopter.

Elliot hurried to catch up. "What?"

"Don't you understand *anything?*" Ross said. "That airplane's *not clean.* It's full of bugs, and the consortium's listening in. I made that speech for their benefit."

"But who was following you in San Francisco?"

"Nobody. They're going to spend hours trying to figure out who was."

"Amy and I weren't just a diversion?"

"Not at all," she said. "Look: we don't know what happened to the last ERTS Congo team, but no matter what you or Travis or anyone else says, *I* think gorillas were involved. And I think that Amy will help us when we get there."

"As an ambassador?"

"We need information," Ross said. "And she knows more about gorillas than we do."

"But can you find her in an hour and ten minutes?"

"Hell, no," Ross said, checking her watch. "This won't take more than twenty minutes."

"Lower! Lower!"

Ross was shouting into her radio headset as she sat alongside the police helicopter pilot. The helicopter was circling the tower of Government House, turning and moving north, toward the Hilton.

"This is not acceptable, madam," the pilot said politely. "We fly below airspace limitations."

"You're too damn high!" Ross said. She was looking at a box on her knees, with four compass-point digital readouts. She flicked switches quickly, while the radio crackled with angry complaints from Nairobi tower.

"East now, due east," she instructed, and the helicopter

tilted and moved east, toward the poor outskirts of the city.

In the back, Elliot felt his stomach twist with each banking turn of the helicopter. His head pounded and he felt awful, but he had insisted on coming. He was the only person knowledgeable enough to minister to Amy if she was in medical trouble.

Now, sitting alongside the pilot, Ross said, "Got a reading," and she pointed to the northeast. The helicopter thumped over crude shacks, junked automobile lots, dirt roads. "Slower now, slower . . ."

The readouts glowed, the numbers shifting. Elliot saw them all go to zero, simultaneously.

"Down!" Ross shouted, and the helicopter descended in the center of a vast garbage dump.

The pilot remained with the helicopter; his final words were disquieting. "Where there's garbage, there's rats," he said.

"Rats don't bother me," Ross said, climbing out with her box in her hand.

"Where there's rats, there's cobras," the pilot said.

"Oh," Ross said.

She crossed the dump with Elliot. There was a stiff breeze; papers and debris ruffled at their feet. Elliot's head ached, and the odors arising from the dump nauseated him.

"Not far now," Ross said, watching the box. She was excited, glancing at her watch.

"Here!"

She bent over and picked through the trash, her hand making circles, digging deeper in frustration, elbow-deep in the trash.

Finally she came up with a necklace—a necklace she had given Amy when they first boarded the airplane in San Francisco. She turned it over, examining the plastic name tag on it, which Elliot noticed was unusually thick. There were fresh scratches on the back.

"Hell," Ross said. "Sixteen minutes shot." And she hurried back to the waiting helicopter.

Elliot fell into step beside her. "But how can you find her if they got rid of her necklace bug?"

"Nobody," Ross said, "plants only one bug. This was just a decoy, they were supposed to find it." She pointed to the scratches on the back. "But they're clever, they reset the frequencies."

"Maybe they got rid of the second bug too," Elliot said.

"They didn't," Ross said. The helicopter lifted off, a thuddering whirr of blades, and the paper and trash of the dump swirled in circles beneath them. She pressed her mouthpiece to her lips and said to the pilot, "Take me to the largest scrap-metal source in Nairobi."

Within nine minutes, they had picked up another very weak signal, located within an automobile junkyard. The helicopter landed in the street outside, drawing dozens of shouting children. Ross went with Elliot into the junkyard, moving past the rusting hulks of cars and trucks.

"You're sure she's here?" Elliot said.

"No question. They have to surround her with metal, it's the only thing they can do."

"Why?"

"Shielding." She picked her way around the broken cars, pausing frequently to refer to her electronic box.

Then Elliot heard a grunt.

It came from inside an ancient rust-red Mercedes bus. Elliot climbed through the shattered doors, the rubber gaskets crumbling in his hands, into the interior. He found Amy on her back, tied with adhesive tape. She was groggy, but complained loudly when he tore the tape off her hair.

He located the broken needle in her right chest and plucked

it out with forceps. Amy shrieked, then hugged him. He heard the far-off whine of a police siren.

"It's all right, Amy, it's all right," he said. He set her down and examined her more carefully. She seemed to be okay.

And then he said, "Where's the second bug?"

Ross grinned. "She swallowed it."

Now that Amy was safe, Elliot felt a wave of anger. "You made her swallow it? An electronic bug? Don't you realize that she is a very delicate animal and her health is extremely precarious—"

"Don't get worked up," Ross said. "Remember the vitamins I gave you? You swallowed one, too." She glanced at her watch. "Thirty-two minutes," she said. "Not bad at all. We have forty minutes before we have to leave Nairobi."

8. Present Point

Munro sat in the 747, punching buttons on the computer. He watched as the lines crisscrossed over the maps, ticking out datalines, timelines, information lock coordinates.

The computer ran through possible expedition routings quickly, testing a new one every ten seconds. After each data fit, outcomes were printed—cost, logistical difficulties, supply problems, total elapsed times from Houston, from Present Point (Nairobi), where they were now.

Looking for a solution.

It wasn't like the old days, Munro thought. Even five years ago, expeditions were still run on guesswork and luck. But now every expedition employed real-time computer planning; Munro had long since been forced to learn BASIC and TW/ GESHUND and other major interactive languages. Nobody did it by the seat of the pants any more. The business had changed.

Munro had decided to join the ERTS expedition precisely

because of those changes. Certainly he hadn't joined because of Karen Ross, who was stubborn and inexperienced. But ERTS had the most elaborate working database, and the most sophisticated planning programs. In the long run, he expected those programs to make the crucial difference. And he liked a smaller team; once the consortium was in the field, their working party of thirty was going to prove unwieldy.

But he had to find a faster timeline to get them in. Munro pressed the buttons, watching the data flash up. He set trajectories, intersections, junctions. Then, with a practiced eye, he began to eliminate alternatives. He closed out pathways, shut down airfields, eliminated truck routes, avoided river crossings.

The computer kept coming back with reduced times, but from Present Point (Nairobi) the total elapsed times were always too long. The best projection beat the consortium by thirty-seven minutes—which was nothing to rely on. He frowned, and smoked a cigar. Perhaps if he crossed the Liko River at Mugana . . .

He punched the buttons.

It didn't help. Crossing the Liko was *slower*. He tried trekking through the Goroba Valley, even though it was probably too hazardous to execute.

PROPOSED ROUTING EXCESSIVELY HAZARDOUS.

"Great minds think alike," Munro said, smoking his cigar. But it started him wondering: were there other, unorthodox approaches they had overlooked? And then he had an idea.

The others wouldn't like it, but it might work. . . .

Munro called the logistics equipment list. Yes, they were equipped for it. He punched in the routing, smiling as he saw the line streak straight across Africa, within a few miles of their destination. He called for outcomes.

PROPOSED ROUTING UNACCEPTABLE.

He pressed the override button, got the data outcomes anyway. It was just as he thought—they could beat the consortium by a full forty hours. Nearly two full days!

The computer went back to the previous statement:

PROPOSED ROUTING UNACCEPTABLE / ALTITUDE FACTORS / HAZARDS TO PERSONNEL EXCESSIVE / PROBABILITY SUCCESS UNDER LIMITS /

Munro didn't think that was true. He thought they could pull it off, especially if the weather was good. The altitude wouldn't be a problem, and the ground although rough would be reasonably yielding.

In fact, the more Munro thought about it, the more certain he was that it would work.

9. Departure

The little Fokker S-144 prop plane was pulled up alongside the giant 747 cargo jet, like an infant nursing at its mother's breast. Two cargo ramps were in constant motion as men transferred equipment from the larger plane to the smaller one. Returning to the airfield, Ross explained to Elliot that they would be taking the smaller plane, since the 747 had to be debugged, and since it was "too large" for their needs now.

"But the jet must be faster," Elliot said.

"Not necessarily," Ross said, but she did not explain further.

In any case, things were now happening very fast, and Elliot had other concerns. He helped Amy aboard the Fokker, and checked her thoroughly. She seemed to be bruised all over her body—at least she complained that everything hurt when he touched her—but she had no broken bones, and she was in good spirits.

Several black men were loading equipment into the airplane, laughing and slapping each other on the back, having a fine time. Amy was intrigued with the men, demanding to know *What joke?* But they ignored her, concentrating on the work at hand. And she was still groggy from her medication. Soon she fell asleep.

Ross supervised the loading, and Elliot moved toward the rear of the plane, where she was talking with a jolly black man, whom she introduced as Kahega.

"Ah," Kahega said, shaking Elliot's hand. "Dr. Elliot. Dr. Ross and Dr. Elliot, two doctors, very excellent."

Elliot was not sure why it was excellent.

Kahega laughed infectiously. "Very good *cover*," he announced. "Not like the old days with Captain Munro. Now two doctors—a medical mission, yes? Very excellent. Where are the 'medical supplies'?" He cocked an eyebrow.

"We have no medical supplies." Ross sighed.

"Oh, very excellent, doctor, I like your manner," Kahega said. "You are American, yes? We take what, M-16s? Very good rifle, M-16. I prefer it myself."

"Kahega thinks we are running guns," Ross said. "He just can't believe we aren't."

Kahega was laughing. "You are with Captain Munro!" he said, as if this explained everything. And then he went off to see about the other workmen.

"You sure we aren't running guns?" Elliot asked when they were alone.

"We're after something more valuable than guns," Ross said. She was repacking the equipment, working quickly. Elliot asked if he could help, but she shook her head. "I've got to do this myself. We have to get it down to forty pounds per person."

"Forty pounds? For everything?"

"That's what the computer projection allows. Munro's brought in Kahega and seven other Kikuyu assistants. With the three of us, that makes eleven people all together, plus Amy—she gets her full forty pounds. But it means a total of four hundred eighty pounds." Ross continued to weigh packs and parcels of food.

The news gave Elliot serious misgivings. The expedition was taking yet another turn, into still greater danger. His immediate desire to back out was checked by his memory of the video screen, and the gray gorillalike creature that he suspected was a new, unknown animal. That was a discovery worth risk. He stared out the window at the porters. "They're Kikuyu?"

"Yes," she said. "They're good porters, even if they never shut up. Kikuyu tribesmen love to talk. They're all brothers, by the way, so be careful what you say. I just hope Munro didn't have to tell them too much."

"The Kikuyu?"

"No, the NCNA."

"The NCNA," Elliot repeated.

"The Chinese. The Chinese are very interested in computers and electronic technology," Ross said. "Munro must be telling them something in exchange for the advice they're giving him." She gestured to the window, and Elliot looked out. Sure enough, Munro stood under the shadow of the 747 wing, talking with four Chinese men.

"Here," Ross said, "stow these in that corner." She pointed to three large Styrofoam cartons marked AMERICAN SPORT DIVERS, LAKE ELSINORE, CALIF.

"We doing underwater work?" Elliot asked, puzzled.

But Ross wasn't paying attention. "I just wish I knew what he was telling them," she said. But as it turned out, Ross needn't have worried, for Munro paid the Chinese in something more valuable to them than electronics information.

The Fokker lifted off from the Nairobi runway at 14:24 hours, three minutes ahead of their new timeline schedule.

· · ·

During the sixteen hours following Amy's recovery, the ERTS expedition traveled 560 miles across the borders of four countries—Kenya, Tanzania, Rwanda, and Zaire—as they went from Nairobi to the Barawanda Forest, at the edge of the Congo rain forest. The logistics of this complex move would have been impossible without the assistance of an outside ally. Munro said that he "had friends in low places," and in this case he had turned to the Chinese Secret Service, in Tanzania.

The Chinese had been active in Africa since the early 1960s, when their spy networks attempted to influence the course of the Congolese civil war because China wanted access to the Congo's rich supplies of uranium. Field operatives were run out of the Bank of China or, more commonly, the New China News Agency. Munro had dealt with a number of NCNA "war correspondents" when he was running arms from 1963 to 1968, and he had never lost his contacts.

The Chinese financial commitment to Africa was considerable. In the late 1960s, more than half of China's two billion dollars in foreign aid went to African nations. An equal sum was spent secretly; in 1973, Mao Tse-tung complained publicly about the money he had wasted trying to overthrow the Zaire government of President Mobutu.

The Chinese mission in Africa was meant to counter the Russian influence, but since World War II the Chinese bore no great love for the Japanese, and Munro's desire to beat the Euro-Japanese consortium fell on sympathetic ears. To celebrate the alliance, Munro had brought three grease-stained cardboard cartons from Hong Kong.

The two chief Chinese operatives in Africa, Li T'ao and Liu Shu-wen, were both from Hunan province. They found their African posting tedious because of the bland African food, and gratefully accepted Munro's gift of a case of tree ears fungus, a case of hot bean sauce, and a case of chili paste with garlic. The fact that these spices came from neutral Hong Kong, and were not the inferior condiments produced in Taiwan, was a subtle point; in any case, the gift struck exactly the proper note for an informal exchange.

NCNA operatives assisted Munro with paperwork, some difficult-to-obtain equipment, and information. The Chinese possessed excellent maps, and remarkably detailed information about conditions along the northeast Zaire border—since they were assisting the Tanzanian troops invading Uganda. The Chinese had told him that the jungle rivers were flooding, and had advised him to procure a balloon for crossings. But Munro did not bother to take their advice; indeed, he seemed to have some plan to reach his destination without crossing any rivers at all. Although how, the Chinese could not imagine.

At 10 p.m. on June 16, the Fokker stopped to refuel at Rawamagena airport, outside Kigali in Rwanda. The local traffic control officer boarded the plane with a clipboard and forms, asking their next destination. Munro said that it was Rawamagena airport, meaning that the aircraft would make a loop, then return.

Elliot frowned. "But we're going to land somewhere in the—"

"Sh-h-h," Ross said, shaking her head. "Leave it alone."

Certainly the traffic officer seemed content with this flight plan; once the pilot signed the clipboard, he departed. Ross explained that flight controllers in Rwanda were accustomed to aircraft that did not file full plans. "He just wants to know when the plane will be back at his field. The rest is none of his business."

Rawamagena airport was sleepy; they had to wait two hours for petrol to be brought, yet the normally impatient

Ross waited quietly. And Munro dozed, equally indifferent to the delay.

"What about the timeline?" Elliot asked.

"No problem," she said. "We can't leave for three hours anyway. We need the light over Mukenko."

"That's where the airfield is?" Elliot asked.

"If you call it an airfield," Munro said, and he pulled his safari hat down over his eyes and went back to sleep.

This worried Elliot until Ross explained to him that most outlying African airfields were just dirt strips cut into the bush. The pilots couldn't land at night, or in the foggy mornings, because there were often animals on the field, or encamped nomads, or another plane that had put down and was unable to take off again. "We need the light," she explained. "That's why we're waiting. Don't worry: it's all factored in."

Elliot accepted her explanation, and went back to check on Amy. Ross sighed. "Don't you think we'd better tell him?" she asked.

"Why?" Munro said, not lifting his hat.

"Maybe there's a problem with Amy."

"I'll take care of Amy," Munro said.

"It's going to upset Elliot when he finds out," Ross said.

"Of course it's going to upset him," Munro said. "But there's no point upsetting him until we have to. After all, what's this jump worth to us?"

"Forty hours, at least. It's dangerous, but it'll give us a whole new timeline. We could still beat them."

"Well, there's your answer," Munro said. "Now keep your mouth shut, and get some rest."

DAY 5: MORUTI
June 17, 1979

1. Zaire

Five hours out of Rawamagena, the landscape changed. Once past Goma, near the Zaire border, they found themselves flying over the easternmost fingers of the Congo rain forest. Elliot stared out the window, fascinated.

Here and there in the pale morning light, a few fragile wisps of fog clung like cotton to the canopy of trees. And occasionally they passed the dark snaking curve of a muddy river, or the straight deep red gash of a road. But for the most part they looked down upon an unbroken expanse of dense forest, extending away into the distance as far as the eye could see.

The view was boring, and simultaneously frightening—it was frightening to be confronted by what Stanley had called "the indifferent immensity of the natural world." As one sat in the air-conditioned comfort of an airplane seat, it was impossible not to recognize that this vast, monotonous forest was a giant creation of nature, utterly dwarfing in scale the greatest cities or other creations of mankind. Each individual green puff of a tree had a trunk forty feet in diameter, soaring two hundred feet into the air; a space the size of a Gothic cathedral was concealed beneath its billowing foliage. And Elliot knew that the forest extended to the west for nearly *two thousand miles*, until it finally stopped at the Atlantic Ocean, on the west coast of Zaire.

Elliot had been anticipating Amy's reaction to this first view of the jungle, her natural environment. She looked out the window with a fixed stare. She signed *Here jungle* with the same emotional neutrality that she named color cards, or objects spread out on her trailer floor in San Francisco. She was identifying the jungle, giving a name to what she saw, but he sensed no deeper recognition.

Elliot said to her, "Amy like jungle?"

Jungle here, she signed. *Jungle is.*

He persisted, probing for the emotional context that he was sure must be there. Amy like jungle?

Jungle here. Jungle is. Jungle place here Amy see jungle here.

He tried another approach. "Amy live jungle here?"

No. Expressionless.

"Where Amy live?"

Amy live Amy house. Referring to her trailer in San Francisco.

Elliot watched her loosen her seat belt, cup her chin on her hand as she stared lazily out the window. She signed, *Amy want cigarette.*

She had noticed Munro smoking.

"Later, Amy," Elliot said.

At seven in the morning, they flew over the shimmering metal roofs of the tin and tantalum mining complex at Masisi. Munro, Kahega, and the other porters went to the back of the plane, where they worked on the equipment, chattering excitedly in Swahili.

Amy, seeing them go, signed, *They worried.*

"Worried about what, Amy?"

They worried men worry they worried problems. After a while, Elliot moved to the rear of the plane to find Munro's men half buried under great heaps of straw, stuffing equipment into oblong torpedo-shaped muslin containers, then packing straw around the supplies. Elliot pointed to the muslin torpedoes. "What are these?"

"They're called Crosslin containers," Munro said. "Very reliable."

"I've never seen equipment packed this way," Elliot said, watching the men work. "They seem to be protecting our supplies very carefully."

"That's the idea," Munro said. And he moved up the aircraft to the cockpit, to confer with the pilot.

Amy signed, *Nosehair man lie Peter*. "Nosehair man" was her term for Munro, but Elliot ignored her. He turned to Kahega. "How far to the airfield?"

Kahega glanced up. "Airfield?"

"At Mukenko."

Kahega paused, thinking it over. "Two hours," he said. And then he giggled. He said something in Swahili and all his brothers laughed, too.

"What's funny?" Elliot said.

"Oh, Doctor," Kahega said, slapping him on the back. "You are humorous by your nature."

The airplane banked, making a slow wide circle in the air. Kahega and his brothers peered out the windows, and Elliot joined them. He saw only unbroken jungle—and then a column of green jeeps, moving down a muddy track far below. It looked like a military formation. He heard the word "Muguru" repeated several times.

"What's the matter?" Elliot said. "Is this Muguru?"

Kahega shook his head vigorously. "No hell. This damn pilot, I warn Captain Munro, this damn pilot lost."

"Lost?" Elliot repeated. Even the word was chilling.

Kahega laughed. "Captain Munro set him right, give him dickens."

The airplane now flew east, away from the jungle toward a wooded highland area, rolling hills and stands of deciduous trees. Kahega's brothers chattered excitedly, and laughed and slapped one another; they seemed to be having a fine time.

Then Ross came back, moving quickly down the aisle, her face tense. She unpacked cardboard boxes, withdrawing several basketball-sized spheres of tightly wrapped metal foil.

The foil reminded him of Christmas-tree tinsel. "What's that for?" Elliot asked.

And then he heard the first explosion, and the Fokker shuddered in the air.

Running to the window, he saw a straight thin white vapor trail terminating in a black smoke cloud off to their right. The Fokker was banking, tilting toward the jungle. As he watched, a second trail streaked up toward them from the green forest below.

It was a missile, he realized. A guided missile.

"Ross!" Munro shouted.

"Ready!" Ross shouted back.

There was a bursting red explosion, and his view through the windows was obscured by dense smoke. The airplane shook with the blast, but continued the turn. Elliot couldn't believe it: *someone was shooting missiles at them.*

"Radar!" Munro shouted. "Not optical! Radar!"

Ross gathered up the silver basketballs in her arms and moved back down the aisle. Kahega was opening the rear door, the wind whipping through the compartment.

"What the hell's happening?" Elliot said.

"Don't worry," Ross said over her shoulder. "We'll make up the time." There was a loud whoosh, followed by a third explosion. With the airplane still banked steeply, Ross tore the wrappings from the basketballs and threw them out into the open sky.

Engines roaring, the Fokker swung eight miles to the

south and climbed to twelve thousand feet, then circled the forest in a holding pattern. With each revolution, Elliot could see the foil strips hanging in the air like a glinting metallic cloud. Two more rockets exploded within the cloud. Even from a distance, the noise and the shock waves disturbed Amy; she was rocking back and forth in her seat, grunting softly.

"That's chaff," Ross explained, sitting in front of her portable computer console, punching buttons. "It confuses radar weapons systems. Those radar-guided SAMs read us as somewhere in the cloud."

Elliot heard her words slowly, as if in a dream. It made no sense to him. "But who's shooting at us?"

"Probably the FZA," Munro said. "Forces Zairoises Armoises—the Zaire army."

"The Zaire army? Why?"

"It's a mistake," Ross said, still punching buttons, not looking up.

"A mistake? They're shooting surface-to-air missiles at us and *it's a mistake*? Don't you think you'd better call them and tell them it's a mistake?"

"Can't," Ross said.

"Why not?"

"Because," Munro said, "we didn't want to file a flight plan in Rawamagena. That means we are technically in violation of Zaire airspace."

"Jesus Christ," Elliot said.

Ross said nothing. She continued to work at the computer console, trying to get the static to resolve on the screen, pressing one button after another.

"When I agreed to join this expedition," Elliot said, beginning to shout, "I didn't expect to get into a shooting war."

"Neither did I," Ross said. "It looks as if we both got more than we bargained for."

Before Elliot could reply, Munro put an arm around his shoulder and took him aside. "It's going to be all right," he told Elliot. "They're outdated sixties SAMs and most of them are blowing up because the solid propellant's cracked with age. We're in no danger. Just look after Amy, she needs your help now. Let me work with Ross."

Ross was under intense pressure. With the airplane circling eight miles from the chaff cloud, she had to make a decision quickly. But she had just been dealt a devastating—and wholly unexpected—setback.

The Euro-Japanese consortium had been ahead of them from the very start, by approximately eighteen hours and twenty minutes. On the ground in Nairobi, Munro had worked out a plan with Ross which would erase that difference and put the ERTS expedition on site *forty hours* ahead of the consortium team. This plan—which for obvious reasons she had not told Elliot—called for them to parachute onto the barren southern slopes of Mount Mukenko.

From Mukenko, Munro estimated it was thirty-six hours to the ruined city; Ross expected to jump at two o'clock that afternoon. Depending on cloud cover over Mukenko and the specific drop zone, they might reach the city as early as noon on June 19.

The plan was extremely hazardous. They would be jumping untrained personnel into a wilderness area, more than three days' walk from the nearest large town. If anyone suffered a serious injury, the chances of survival were slight. There was also a question about the equipment: at altitudes of 8,000–10,000 feet on the volcanic slopes, air resistance was reduced, and the Crosslin packets might not provide enough protection.

Initially Ross had rejected Munro's plan as too risky, but

he convinced her it was feasible. He pointed out that the parafoils were equipped with automated altimeter-release devices;
that the upper volcanic scree was as yielding as a sandy beach;
that the Crosslin containers could be overpacked; and that he
could carry Amy down himself.

Ross had double-checked outcome probabilities from the
Houston computer, and the results were unequivocal. The
probability of a successful jump was .7980, meaning there
was one chance in five that someone would be badly hurt.
However, *given a successful jump*, the probability of expedition success was .9943, making it virtually certain they would
beat the consortium to the site.

No alternate plan scored so high. She had looked at the
data and said, "I guess we jump."

"I think we do," Munro had said.

The jump solved many problems, for the geopolitical updates were increasingly unfavorable. The Kigani were now in
full rebellion; the pygmies were unstable; the Zaire army had
sent armored units into the eastern border area to put down the
Kigani—and African field armies were notoriously trigger-
happy. By jumping onto Mukenko, they expected to bypass
all these hazards.

But that was before the Zaire army SAMs began explod-
ing all around them. They were still eighty miles south of the
intended drop zone, circling over Kigani territory, wasting
time and fuel. It looked as if their daring plan, so carefully
worked out and confirmed by computer, was suddenly irrelevant.

And to add to her difficulties, she could not confer with
Houston; the computer refused to link up by satellite. She
spent fifteen minutes working with the portable unit, boosting
power and switching scrambler codes, until she finally realized
that her transmission was being electronically jammed.

For the first time in her memory, Karen Ross wanted to cry.

"Easy now," Munro said quietly, lifting her hands away from the buttons. "One thing at a time, no point in getting upset." Ross had been punching the buttons over and over again, unaware of what she was doing.

Munro was conscious of the deteriorating situation with both Elliot and Ross. He had seen it happen on expeditions before, particularly when scientists and technical people were involved. Scientists worked all day in laboratories where conditions could be rigorously regulated and monitored. Sooner or later, scientists came to believe that the outside world was just as controllable as their laboratories. Even though they knew better, the shock of discovering that the natural world followed its own rules and was indifferent to them represented a harsh psychic blow. Munro could read the signs.

"But this," Ross said, "is obviously a non-military aircraft, how can they do it?"

Munro stared at her. In the Congolese civil war, civilian aircraft had been routinely shot down by all sides. "These things happen," he said.

"And the jamming? Those bastards haven't got the capability to jam us. We're being jammed between our transmitter and our satellite transponder. To do that requires another satellite somewhere, and—" She broke off, frowning.

"You didn't expect the consortium to sit by idly," Munro said. "The question is, can you fix it? Have you got counter-measures?"

"Sure, I've got countermeasures," Ross said. "I can encode a burst bounce, I can transmit optically on an IR carrier, I can link a ground-base cable—but there's nothing I can put together in the next few minutes, and we need information now. Our plan is shot."

"One thing at a time," Munro repeated quietly. He saw the tension in her features, and he knew she was not thinking clearly. He also knew he could not do her thinking for her; he had to get her calm again.

In Munro's judgment, the ERTS expedition was already finished—they could not possibly beat the consortium to the Congo site. But he had no intention of quitting; he had led expeditions long enough to know that anything could happen, so he said, "We can still make up the lost time."

"Make it up? How?"

Munro said the first thing that came to mind: "We'll take the Ragora north. Very fast river, no problem."

"The Ragora's too dangerous."

"We'll have to see," Munro said, although he knew that she was right. The Ragora was much too dangerous, particularly in June. Yet he kept his voice calm, soothing, reassuring. "Shall I tell the others?" he asked finally.

"Yes," Ross said. In the distance, they heard another rocket explosion. "Let's get out of here."

Munro moved swiftly to the rear of the Fokker and said to Kahega, "Prepare the men."

"Yes, boss," Kahega said. A bottle of whiskey was passed around, and each of the men took a long swallow.

Elliot said, "What the hell is this?"

"The men are getting prepared," Munro said.

"Prepared for what?" Elliot asked.

At that moment, Ross came back, looking grim. "From here on, we'll continue on foot," she said.

Elliot looked out the window. "Where's the airfield?"

"There is no airfield," Ross said.

"What do you mean?"

"I mean there is no airfield."

"Is the plane going to put down in the fields?" Elliot asked.

"No," Ross said. "The plane is not going to put down at all."

"Then how do we get down?" Elliot asked, but even as he asked the question, his stomach sank, because he knew the answer.

"Amy will be fine," Munro said cheerfully, cinching Elliot's straps tightly around his chest. "I gave her a shot of your Thoralen tranquilizer, and she'll be quite calm. No problem at all, I'll keep a good grip on her."

"Keep a good grip on her?" Elliot asked.

"She's too small to fit a harness," Munro said. "I'll have to carry her down." Amy snored loudly, and drooled on Munro's shoulder. He set Amy on the floor; she lay limply on her back, still snoring.

"Now, then," Munro said. "Your parafoil opens automatically. You'll find you have lines in both hands, left and right. Pull left to go left, right to go right, and—"

"What happens to her?" Elliot asked, pointing to Amy.

"I'll take her. Pay attention now. If anything goes wrong, your reserve chute is here, on your chest." He tapped a cloth bundle with a small black digital box, which read 4757. "That's your rate-of-fall altimeter. Automatically pops your reserve chute if you hit thirty-six hundred feet and are still falling faster than two feet per second. Nothing to worry about: whole thing's automatic."

Elliot was chilled, drenched in sweat. "What about landing?"

"Nothing to it." Munro grinned. "You'll land automatically too. Stay loose and relax, take the shock in the legs. Equivalent of jumping off a ten-foot ledge. You've done it a thousand times."

Behind him Elliot saw the open door, bright sunlight glaring into the plane. The wind whipped and howled. Kahega's men jumped in quick succession, one after another. He glanced at Ross, who was ashen, her lower lip trembling as she gripped the doorway.

"Karen, you're not going to go along with—"

She jumped, disappearing into the sunlight. Munro said "You're next."

"I've never jumped before," Elliot said.

"That's the best way. You won't be frightened."

"But I *am* frightened."

"I can help you with that," Munro said, and he pushed Elliot out the plane.

Munro watched him fall away, his grin instantly gone. Munro had adopted his hearty demeanor only for Elliot's benefit. "If a man has to do something dangerous," he said later, "it helps to be angry. It's for his own protection, really. Better he should hate someone than fall apart. I wanted Elliot to hate me all the way down."

Munro understood the risks. The minute they left the aircraft, they also left civilization, and all the unquestioned assumptions of civilization. They were jumping not only through the air, but through time, backward into a more primitive and dangerous way of life—the eternal realities of the Congo, which had existed for centuries before them. "Those were the facts of life," Munro said, "but I didn't see any reason to worry the others before they jumped. My job was to get those people into the Congo, not scare them to death. There was plenty of time for that."

Elliot fell, scared to death.

His stomach jumped into his throat, and he tasted bile; the wind screamed around his ears and tugged at his hair; and the air was cold—he was instantly chilled and shivering. Below him the Barawana Forest lay spread across rolling hills. He felt no appreciation for the beauty before him, and in fact he closed his eyes, for he was plummeting at hideous speed toward the ground. But with his eyes shut he was more aware of the screaming wind.

Too much time had passed. Obviously the parafoil (whatever the hell that was) was not going to open. His life now depended on the parachute attached to his chest. He clutched it, a small tight bundle near his churning stomach. Then he pulled his hands away: he didn't want to interfere with its opening. He dimly remembered that people had died that way, when they interfered with the opening of their parachute.

The screaming wind continued; his body rushed sickeningly downward. *Nothing was happening.* He felt the fierce wind tugging at his feet, whipping his trousers, flapping his shirt against his arms. *Nothing was happening.* It had been at least three minutes since he'd jumped from the plane. He dared not open his eyes, for fear of seeing the trees rushing up close as his body crashed downward toward them in his final seconds of conscious life. . . .

He was going to throw up.

Bile dribbled from his mouth, but since he was falling head downward, the liquid ran up his chin to his neck and then inside his shirt. It was freezing cold. His shivering was becoming uncontrollable.

He snapped upright with a bone-twisting jolt.

For an instant he thought he had hit the ground, and then he realized that he was still descending through the air, but more slowly. He opened his eyes and stared at pale blue sky.

He looked down, and was shocked to see that he was still thousands of feet from the earth. Obviously he had only been falling a few seconds from the airplane above him—

Looking up, he could not see the plane. Directly overhead was a giant rectangular shape, with brilliant red, white, and blue stripes: the parafoil. Finding it easier to look up than down, he studied the parafoil intently. The leading edge was curved and puffy; the rear edge thin, fluttering in the breeze. The parafoil looked very much like an airplane wing, with cords running down to his body.

He took a deep breath and looked down. He was still very high over the landscape. There was some comfort in the slowness with which he was descending. It was really rather peaceful.

And then he noticed he wasn't moving down; he was moving sideways. He could see the other parafoils below, Kahega and his men and Ross; he tried to count them, and thought there were six, but he had difficulty concentrating. He appeared to be moving laterally away from them.

He tugged on the lines in his left hand, and he felt his body twist as the parafoil moved, taking him to the left.

Not bad, he thought.

He pulled harder on the left cords, ignoring the fact that this seemed to make him move faster. He tried to stay near the rectangles descending beneath him. He heard the scream of the wind in his ears. He looked up, hoping to see Munro, but all he could see was the stripes of his own parafoil.

He looked back down, and was astonished to find that the ground was a great deal closer. In fact, it seemed to be rushing up to him at brutal speed. He wondered where he had got the idea that he was drifting gently downward. There was nothing gentle about his descent at all. He saw the first of the parafoils crumple gently as Kahega touched ground, then the second, and the third.

It wouldn't be long before he landed. He was approaching the level of the trees, but his lateral movement was very fast. He realized that his left hand was rigidly pulling on the cords. He released his grip, and his lateral movement ceased. He drifted forward.

Two more parafoils crumpled on impact. He looked back to see Kahega and his men, already down, gathering up the cloth. They were all right; that was encouraging.

He was sliding right into a dense clump of trees. He pulled his cords and twisted to the right, his whole body tilting. He was moving very fast now. The trees could not be avoided. He was going to smash into them. The branches seemed to reach up like fingers, grasping for him.

He closed his eyes, and felt the branches scratching at his face and body as he crashed down, knowing that any second he was going to hit, that he was going to hit the ground and roll—

He never hit.

Everything became silent. He felt himself bobbing up and down. He opened his eyes and saw that he was swinging four feet above the ground. His parafoil had caught in the trees.

He fumbled with his harness buckles, and fell out onto the earth. As he picked himself up, Kahega and Ross came running over to ask if he was all right.

"I'm fine," Elliot said, and indeed he felt extraordinarily fine, more alive than he could ever remember feeling. The next instant he fell over on rubber legs and promptly threw up.

Kahega laughed. "Welcome to the Congo," he said.

Elliot wiped his chin and said, "Where is Amy?"

A moment later Munro landed, with a bleeding ear where Amy had bitten him in terror. But Amy was none the worse for the experience, and came running on her knuckles over to Elliot, making sure that he was all right, and then signing, *Amy fly no like.*

"Look out!"

The first of the torpedo-shaped Crosslin packets smashed down, exploding like a bomb when it hit the ground, spraying equipment and straw in all directions.

"There's the second one!"

Elliot dived for safety. The second bomb hit just a few yards away; he was pelted with foil containers of food and

rice. Overhead, he heard the drone of the circling Fokker airplane. He got to his feet in time to see the final two Crosslin
containers crash down, and Kahega's men running for safety,
with Ross shouting, "Careful, those have the lasers!"

It was like being in the middle of a blitz, but as swiftly as it
had begun it was over. The Fokker above them flew off, and
the sky was silent; the men began repacking the equipment
and burying the parafoils, while Munro barked instructions in
Swahili.

Twenty minutes later, they were moving single-file
through the forest, starting a two-hundred-mile trek that
would lead them into the unexplored eastern reaches of the
Congo, to a fabulous reward.

If they could reach it in time.

2. Kigani

Once past the initial shock of his jump, Elliot enjoyed the
walk through the Barawana Forest. Monkeys chattered in the
trees, and birds called in the cool air; the Kikuyu porters were
strung out behind them, smoking cigarettes and joking with
one another in an exotic tongue. Elliot found all his emotions
agreeable—the sense of freedom from a crass civilization; the
sense of adventure, of unexpected events that might occur at
any future moment; and finally the sense of romance, of a
quest for the poignant past while omnipresent danger kept
sensation at a peak of intense feeling. It was in this heightened
mood that he listened to the forest animals around him,
viewed the play of sunlight and shadow, felt the springy
ground beneath his boots, and looked over at Karen Ross,
whom he found beautiful and graceful in an utterly unexpected way.

Karen Ross did not look back at him.

As she walked, she twisted knobs on one of her black electronic boxes, trying to establish a signal. A second electronic box hung from a shoulder strap, and since she did not turn to look at him, he had time to notice that there was already a dark stain of sweat at her shoulder, and another running down the back of her shirt. Her dark blonde hair was damp, clinging unattractively to the back of her head. And he noticed that her trousers were wrinkled, streaked with dirt from the fall. She still did not look back.

"Enjoy the forest," Munro advised him. "This is the last time you'll feel cool and dry for quite a while."

Elliot agreed that the forest was pleasant.

"Yes, very pleasant." Munro nodded, with an odd expression on his face.

The Barawana Forest was not virginal. From time to time, they passed cleared fields and other signs of human habitation, although they never saw farmers. When Elliot mentioned that fact, Munro just shook his head. As they moved deeper into the forest Munro turned self-absorbed, unwilling to talk. Yet he showed an interest in the fauna, frequently pausing to listen intently to bird cries before signaling the expedition to continue on.

During these pauses, Elliot would look back down the line of porters with loads balanced on their heads, and feel acutely his kinship with Livingstone and Stanley and the other explorers who had ventured through Africa a century before. And in this, his romantic associations were accurate. Central African life was little changed since Stanley explored the Congo in the 1870s, and neither was the basic nature of expeditions to that region. Serious exploration was still carried out on foot; porters were still necessary; expenses were still daunting—and so were the dangers.

.   .   .

By midday, Elliot's boots had begun to hurt his feet, and he found that he was exceedingly tired. Apparently the porters were tired too, because they had fallen silent, no longer smoking cigarettes and shouting jokes to one another up and down the line. The expedition proceeded in silence until Elliot asked Munro if they were going to stop for lunch.

"No," Munro said.

"Good," Karen Ross said, glancing at her watch.

Shortly after one o'clock, they heard the thumping of helicopters. The reaction of Munro and the porters was immediate—they dived under a stand of large trees and waited, looking upwards. Moments later, two large green helicopters passed overhead; Elliot clearly read white stenciling: "FZA."

Munro squinted at the departing craft. They were American-made Hueys; he had not been able to see the armament. "It's the army," he said. "They're looking for Kigani."

An hour later, they arrived at a clearing where manioc was being grown. A crude wooden farmhouse stood in the center, with pale smoke issuing from a chimney and laundry on a wash line flapping in the gentle breeze. But they saw no inhabitants.

The expedition had circled around previous farm clearings, but this time Munro raised his hand to call for a halt. The porters dropped their loads and sat in the grass, not speaking.

The atmosphere was tense, although Elliot could not understand why. Munro squatted with Kahega at the edge of the clearing, watching the farmhouse and the surrounding fields. After twenty minutes, when there was still no sign of movement, Ross, who was crouched near Munro, became impatient. "I don't see why we are—"

Munro clapped his hand over her mouth. He pointed to the clearing, and mouthed one word: Kigani.

Ross's eyes went wide. Munro took his hand away.

They all stared at the farmhouse. Still there was no sign of life. Ross made a circular movement with her arm, suggesting that they circle around the clearing and move on. Munro shook his head, and pointed to the ground, indicating that she should sit. Munro looked questioningly at Elliot, and pointed to Amy, who foraged in the tall grass off to one side. He seemed to be concerned that Amy would make noise. Elliot signed to Amy to be quiet, but it was not necessary. Amy had sensed the general tension, and glanced warily from time to time toward the farmhouse.

Nothing happened for several more minutes; they listened to the buzz of the cicadas in the hot midday sun, and they waited. They watched the laundry flutter in the breeze.

Then the thin wisp of blue smoke from the chimney stopped.

Munro and Kahega exchanged glances. Kahega slipped back to where the porters sat, opened one load, and brought out a machine gun. He covered the safety with his hand, muffling the click as he released it. It was incredibly quiet in the clearing. Kahega resumed his place next to Munro and handed him the gun. Munro checked the safety, then set the gun on the ground. They waited several minutes more. Elliot looked at Ross but she was not looking at him.

There was a soft creak as the farmhouse door opened. Munro picked up the machine gun.

No one came out. They all stared at the open door, waiting. And then finally the Kigani stepped into the sunlight.

Elliot counted twelve tall muscular men armed with bows and arrows, and carrying long *pangas* in their hands. Their legs and chests were streaked with white, and their faces were solid white, which gave their heads a menacing, skull-like appearance. As the Kigani moved off through the tall manioc, only their white heads were visible, looking around tensely.

Even after they were gone, Munro remained watching the silent clearing for another ten minutes. Finally he stood and sighed. When he spoke, his voice seemed incredibly loud. "Those were Kigani," Munro said.

"What were they doing?" Ross said.

"Eating," Munro said. "They killed the family in that house, and then ate them. Most farmers have left, because the Kigani are on the rampage."

He signaled Kahega to get the men moving again, and they set off, skirting around the clearing. Elliot kept looking at the farmhouse, wondering what he would see if he went inside. Munro's statement had been so casual: *They killed the family . . . and then ate them.*

"I suppose," Ross said, looking over her shoulder, "that we should consider ourselves lucky. We're probably among the last people in the world to see these things."

Munro shook his head. "I doubt it," he said. "Old habits die hard."

During the Congolese civil war in the 1960s, reports of widespread cannibalism and other atrocities shocked the Western world. But in fact cannibalism had always been openly practiced in central Africa.

In 1897, Sidney Hinde wrote that "nearly all the tribes in the Congo Basin either are, or have been, cannibals; and among some of them the practice is on the increase." Hinde was impressed by the undisguised nature of Congolese cannibalism: "The captains of steamers have often assured me that whenever they try to buy goats from the natives, slaves are demanded in exchange; the natives often come aboard with tusks of ivory with the intention of buying a slave, complaining that *meat is now scarce in their neighborhood.*"

In the Congo, cannibalism was not associated with ritual or religion or war; it was a simple dietary preference. The Reverend Holman Bentley, who spent twenty years in the region, quoted a native as saying, "You white men consider pork to be the tastiest of meat, but pork is not to be compared with human flesh." Bentley felt that the natives "could not understand the objections raised to the practice. 'You eat fowls and goats, and we eat men; why not? What is the difference?' "

This frank attitude astonished observers, and led to bizarre customs. In 1910, Herbert Ward wrote of markets where slaves were sold "piecemeal whilst still alive. Incredible as it may appear, captives are led from place to place in order that individuals may have the opportunity of indicating, by external marks on the body, the portion they desire to acquire. The distinguishing marks are generally made by means of coloured clay or strips of grass tied in a peculiar fashion. The astounding stoicism of the victims, who thus witness the bargaining for their limbs piecemeal, is only equalled by the callousness with which they walk forward to meet their fate."

Such reports cannot be dismissed as late-Victorian hysteria, for all observers found the cannibals likable and sympathetic. Ward wrote that "the cannibals are not schemers and they are not mean. In direct opposition to all natural conjectures, they are among the best types of men." Bentley described them as "merry, manly fellows, very friendly in conversation and quite demonstrative in their affection."

Under Belgian colonial administration, cannibalism became much rarer—by the 1950s, there were even a few graveyards to be found—but no one seriously thought it had been eradicated. In 1956, H. C. Engert wrote, "Cannibalism is far from being dead in Africa. . . . I myself once lived in a cannibal village for a time, and found some [human] bones. The natives . . . were pleasant enough people. It was just an old custom which dies hard."

Munro considered the 1979 Kigani uprising a political insurrection. The tribesmen were rebelling against the demand by

the Zaire government that the Kigani change from hunting to
farming, as if that were a simple matter. The Kigani were a
poor and backward people; their knowledge of hygiene was
rudimentary; their diet lacked proteins and vitamins, and they
were prey to malaria, hookworm, bilharzia, and African sleeping sickness. One child in four died at birth, and few Kigani
adults lived past the age of twenty-five. The hardships of their
life required explanation, supplied by Angawa, or sorcerers.
The Kigani believed that most deaths were supernatural: either
the victim was under a sorcerer's spell, had broken some taboo,
or was killed by vengeful spirits from the dead. Hunting also
had a supernatural aspect: game was strongly influenced by the
spirit world. In fact, the Kigani considered the supernatural
world far more real than the day-to-day world, which they felt
to be a "waking dream," and they attempted to control the
supernatural through magical spells and potions, provided by
the Angawa. They also carried out ritual body alterations,
such as painting the face and hands white, to render an individual more powerful in battle. The Kigani believed that magic
also resided in the bodies of their adversaries, and so to overcome spells cast by other Angawa they ate the bodies of their
enemies. The magical power invested in the enemy thus became their own, frustrating enemy sorcerers.

These beliefs were very old, and the Kigani had long since
settled on a pattern of response to threat, which was to eat
other human beings. In 1890, they went on the rampage in
the north, following the first visits by foreigners bearing firearms, which had frightened off the game. During the civil war
in 1961, starving, they attacked and ate other tribes.

"And why are they eating people now?" Elliot asked
Munro.

"They want their right to hunt," Munro said. "Despite the
Kinshasa bureaucrats."

.   .   .

In the early afternoon, the expedition mounted a hill from which they could overlook the valleys behind them to the south. In the distance they saw great billowing clouds of smoke and licking flames; there were the muffled explosions of air-to-ground rockets, and the helicopters wheeling like mechanical vultures over a kill.

"Those are Kigani villages," Munro said, looking back, shaking his head. "They haven't a prayer, especially since the men in those helicopters and the troops on the ground are all from the Abawe tribe, the traditional enemy of the Kigani."

The twentieth-century world did not accommodate maneating beliefs; indeed, the government in Kinshasa, two thousand miles away, had already decided to "expunge the embarrassment" of cannibals within its borders. In June, the Zaire government dispatched five thousand armed troops, six rocket-armed American UH-2 helicopters, and ten armored personnel carriers to put down the Kigani rebellion. The military leader in charge, General Ngo Muguru, had no illusions about his directive. Muguru knew that Kinshasa wanted him to eliminate the Kigani as a tribe. And he intended to do exactly that.

During the rest of the day, they heard distant explosions of mortar and rockets. It was impossible not to contrast the modernity of this equipment with the bows and arrows of the Kigani they had seen. Ross said it was sad, but Munro replied that it was inevitable.

"The purpose of life," Munro said, "is to stay alive. Watch any animal in nature—all it tries to do is stay alive. It doesn't care about beliefs or philosophy. Whenever any animal's behavior puts it out of touch with the realities of its existence, it becomes extinct. The Kigani haven't seen that times have changed and their beliefs don't work. And they're going to be extinct."

"Maybe there is a higher truth than merely staying alive," Ross said.

"There isn't," Munro said.

They saw several other parties of Kigani, usually from a distance of many miles. At the end of the day, after they had crossed the swaying wooden bridge over the Moruti Gorge, Munro announced that they were now beyond the Kigani territory and, at least for the time being, safe.

3. Moruti Camp

In a high clearing above Moruti, the "place of soft winds," Munro shouted Swahili instructions and Kahega's porters began to unpack their loads. Karen Ross looked at her watch. "Are we stopping?"

"Yes," Munro said.

"But it's only five o'clock. There's still two hours of light left."

"We stop here," Munro said. Moruti was located at 1,500 feet; another two hours' walking would put them down in the rain forest below. "It's much cooler and more pleasant here."

Ross said that she did not care about pleasantness.

"You will," Munro said.

To make the best time, Munro intended to keep out of the rain forest wherever possible. Progress in the jungle was slow and uncomfortable; they would have more than enough experience with mud and leeches and fevers.

Kahega called to him in Swahili; Munro turned to Ross and said, "Kahega wants to know how to pitch the tents."

Kahega was holding a crumpled silver ball of fabric in his outstretched hand; the other porters were just as confused, rummaging through their loads, looking for familiar tent poles or stakes, finding none.

The ERTS camp had been designed under contract by a NASA team in 1977, based on the recognition that wilderness expedition equipment was fundamentally unchanged since the eighteenth century. "Designs for modern exploration are long overdue," ERTS said, and asked for state-of-the-art improvements in lightness, comfort, and efficiency of expedition gear. NASA had redesigned everything, from clothing and boots to tents and cooking gear, food and menus, first-aid kits, and communications systems for ERTS wilderness parties.

The redesigned tents were typical of the NASA approach. NASA had determined that tent weight consisted chiefly of the structural supports. In addition, single-ply tents were poorly insulated. If tents could be properly insulated, clothing and sleeping-bag weight could be reduced, as could the daily caloric requirements of expedition members. Since air was an excellent insulator, the obvious solution was an unsupported, pneumatic tent: NASA designed one that weighed six ounces.

Using a little hissing foot pump, Ross inflated the first tent. It was made from double-layer 20-mil silvered Mylar, and looked like a gleaming ribbed Quonset hut. The porters clapped their hands with delight; Munro shook his head, amused; Kahega produced a small silver unit, the size of a shoebox. "And this, Doctor? What is this?"

"We won't need that tonight. That's an air conditioner," Ross said.

"Never go anywhere without one," Munro said, still amused.

Ross glared at him. "Studies show," she said, "that the single greatest factor limiting work efficiency is ambient temperature, with sleep deprivation as the second factor."

"Really."

Munro laughed and looked to Elliot, but Elliot was studiously examining the view of the rain forest in the evening sun. Amy came up and tugged at his sleeve.

Woman and nosehair man fight, she signed.

Amy had liked Munro from the beginning, and the feeling was mutual. Instead of patting her on the head and treating her like a child, as most people did, Munro instinctively treated her like a female. Then, too, he had been around enough gorillas to have a feeling for their behavior. Although he didn't know ASL, when Amy raised her arms, he understood that she wanted to be tickled, and would oblige her for a few moments, while she rolled grunting with pleasure on the ground.

But Amy was always distressed by conflict, and she was frowning now. "They're just talking," Elliot assured her.

She signed, *Amy want eat.*

"In a minute." Turning back, he saw Ross setting up the transmitting equipment; this would be a daily ritual during the rest of the expedition, and one which never failed to fascinate Amy. Altogether, the equipment to send a transmission ten thousand miles by satellite weighed six pounds, and the electronic countermeasures, or ECM devices, weighed an additional three pounds.

First, Ross popped open the collapsed umbrella of the silver dish antenna, five feet in diameter. (Amy particularly liked this; as each day progressed, she would ask Ross when she would "open metal flower.") Then Ross attached the transmitter box, plugging in the krylon-cadmium fuel cells. Next she linked the anti-jamming modules, and finally she hooked up the miniaturized computer terminal with its tiny keyboard and three-inch video screen.

This miniature equipment was highly sophisticated. Ross's computer had a 189K memory and all circuitry was redundant; housings were hermetically sealed and shockproof; even the keyboard was impedance-operated, so there were no moving parts to get gummed up, or admit water or dust.

And it was incredibly rugged. Ross remembered their "field tests." In the ERTS parking lot, technicians would throw new equipment against the wall, kick it across the concrete, and leave it in a bucket of muddy water overnight. Anything found working the next day was certified as field-worthy.

Now, in the sunset at Moruti, she punched in code co-ordinates to lock the transmission to Houston, checked signal strength, and waited the six minutes until the transponders matched up. But the little screen continued to show only gray static, with intermittent pulses of color. That meant someone was jamming them with a "symphony."

In ERTS slang, the simplest level of electronic jamming was called "tuba." Like a kid next door practicing his tuba, this jamming was merely annoying; it occurred within limited frequencies, and was often random or accidental, but transmissions could generally pass through it. At the next level was "string quartet," where multiple frequencies were jammed in an orderly fashion; next was "big band," where the electronic music covered a wider frequency range; and finally "symphony," where virtually the full transmission range was blocked.

Ross was now getting hit by a "symphony." To break through demanded coordination with Houston—which she was unable to arrange—but ERTS had several prearranged routines. She tried them one after another and finally broke the jamming with a technique called interstitial coding. (Interstitial coding utilized the fact that even dense music had periods of silence, or interstices, lasting microseconds. It was possible to monitor the jamming signals, identify regularities in the interstices, and then transmit in bursts during the silences.)

Ross was gratified to see the little screen glow in a multi-colored image—a map of their position in the Congo. She punched in the field position lock, and a light blinked on the screen. Words appeared in "shortline," the compressed language devised for small-screen imagery. FILD TME-POSITN CHEK: PLS CONFRM LOCL TME 18:04 H 6/17/79. She confirmed that it was indeed just after 6 p.m. at their location. Immediately, overlaid lines produced a scrambled pattern as their Field Time-Position was measured against the computer simulation run in Houston before their departure.

Ross was prepared for bad news. According to her mental calculations, they had fallen some seventy-odd hours behind their projected timeline, and some twenty-odd hours behind the consortium.

Their original plan had called for them to jump onto the slopes of Mukenko at 2 p.m. on June 17, arriving at Zinj approximately thirty-six hours later, around midday of June 19. This would have put them onsite nearly two days before the consortium.

However, the SAM attack forced them to jump eighty miles south of their intended drop zone. The jungle terrain before them was varied, and they could expect to pick up time rafting on rivers, but it would still take a minimum of three days to go eighty miles.

That meant that they could no longer expect to beat the consortium to the site. Instead of arriving forty-eight hours ahead, they would be lucky if they arrived only twenty-four hours too late.

To her surprise, the screen blinked: FILD TME-POSITN CHEK: -09:04 H WEL DUN. They were only nine hours off their simulation timeline.

"What does that mean?" Munro asked, looking at the screen.

There was only one possible conclusion. "Something has slowed the consortium," Ross said.

On the screen they read EURO / NIPON CONSRTIM LEGL TRUBL GOMA AIRPRT ZAIR THEIR AIRCRFT FOUND RADIOACTIVE TUF LUK FOR THEM.

"Travis has been working back in Houston," Ross said. She could imagine what it must have cost ERTS to put in the fix at the rural airport in Goma. "But it means we can still do it, if we can make up the nine hours."

"We can do it," Munro said.

In the light of the setting equatorial sun, Moruti camp gleamed like a cluster of dazzling jewels—a silver dish antenna, and five silver-domed tents, all reflecting the fiery sun. Peter Elliot sat on the hilltop with Amy and stared at the rain forest spread out below them. As night fell, the first hazy strands of mist appeared; and as the darkness deepened and water vapor condensed in the cooling air, the forest became shrouded in dense, darkening fog.

DAY 6: LIKO
June 18, 1979

1. Rain Forest

The next morning they entered the humid perpetual gloom of the Congo rain forest.

Munro noted the return of old feelings of oppression and claustrophobia, tinged with a strange, overpowering lassitude. As a Congo mercenary in the 1960s, he had avoided the jungle wherever possible. Most military engagements had occurred in open spaces—in the Belgian colonial towns, along riverbanks, beside the red dirt roads. Nobody wanted to fight in the jungle; the mercenaries hated it, and the superstitious Simbas feared it. When the mercenaries advanced, the rebels often fled into the bush, but they never went very far, and Munro's troops never pursued them. They just waited for them to come out again.

Even in the 1960s the jungle remained *terra incognita*, an unknown land with the power to hold the technology of mechanized warfare beyond its periphery. And with good reason, Munro thought. Men just did not belong there. He was not pleased to be back.

Elliot, never having been in a rain forest, was fascinated. The jungle was different from the way he had imagined it to be. He was totally unprepared for the scale—the gigantic trees soaring over his head, the trunks as broad as a house, the thick snaking moss-covered roots. To move in the vast space beneath these trees was like being in a very dark cathedral: the sun was completely blocked, and he could not get an exposure reading on his camera.

He had also expected the jungle to be much denser than it was. Their party moved through it freely; in a surprising way it seemed barren and silent—there were occasional birdcalls and cries from monkeys, but otherwise a profound stillness settled over them. And it was oddly monotonous: although he saw every shade of green in the foliage and the clinging creeper vines, there were few flowers or blooms. Even the occasional orchids seemed pale and muted.

He had expected rotting decay at every turn, but that was not true either. The ground underfoot was often firm, and the air had a neutral smell. But it was incredibly hot, and it seemed as though everything was wet—the leaves, the ground, the trunks of the trees, the oppressively still air itself, trapped under the overhanging trees.

Elliot would have agreed with Stanley's description from a century before: "Overhead the wide-spreading branches absolutely shut out the daylight. . . . We marched in a feeble twilight. . . . The dew dropped and pattered on us incessantly. . . . Our clothes were heavily saturated with it. . . . Perspiration exuded from every pore, for the atmosphere was stifling. . . . What a forbidding aspect had the Dark Unknown which confronted us!"

Because Elliot had looked forward to his first experience of the equatorial African rain forest, he was surprised at how quickly he felt oppressed—and how soon he entertained thoughts of leaving again. Yet the tropical rain forests had spawned most new life forms, including man. The jungle was not one uniform environment but many different microenvironments, arranged vertically like a layer cake. Each microenvironment supported a bewildering profusion of plant and animal life, but there were typically few members of each species. The tropical jungle supported four times as many species of animal life as a comparable temperate forest. As he walked through the forest, Elliot found himself thinking of it as an enormous hot, dark womb, a place where new species were nourished in unchanging conditions until they were ready to migrate out to the harsher and more variable temperate zones. That was the way it had been for millions of years.

Amy's behavior immediately changed as she entered the vast humid darkness of her original home. In retrospect, Elliot believed he could have predicted her reaction, had he thought it through clearly.

Amy no longer kept up with the group.

She insisted on foraging along the trail, pausing to sit and chew tender shoots and grasses. She could not be budged or hurried, and ignored Elliot's requests that she stay with them. She ate lazily, a pleasant, rather vacant expression on her face. In shafts of sunlight, she would lie on her back, and belch, and sigh contentedly.

"What the hell is this all about?" Ross asked, annoyed. They were not making good time.

"She's become a gorilla again," Elliot said. "Gorillas are vegetarians, and they spend nearly all day eating; they're large animals, and they need a lot of food." Amy had immediately reverted to these traits.

"Well, can't you make her keep up with us?"

"I'm trying. She won't pay attention to me." And he knew why—Amy was finally back in a world where Peter Elliot was irrelevant, where she herself could find food and security and shelter, and everything else that she wanted.

"School's out," Munro said, summarizing the situation. But he had a solution. "Leave her," he said crisply, and he led the party onward. He took Elliot firmly by the elbow. "Don't look back," he said. "Just walk on. Ignore her."

They continued for several minutes in silence.

Elliot said, "She may not follow us."

"Come, come, Professor," Munro said. "I thought you knew about gorillas."

"I do," Elliot said.

"Then you know there are none in this part of the rain forest."

Elliot nodded; he had seen no nests or spoor. "But she has everything she needs here."

"Not everything," Munro said. "Not without other gorillas around."

Like all higher primates, gorillas were social animals. They lived in a group, and they were not comfortable—or safe— in isolation. In fact, most primatologists assumed that there was a need for social contact as strongly perceived as hunger, thirst, or fatigue.

"We're her troop," Munro said. "She won't let us get far."

Several minutes later, Amy came crashing through the underbrush fifty yards ahead. She watched the group, and glared at Peter.

"Now come here, Amy," Munro said, "and I'll tickle you." Amy bounded up and lay on her back in front of him. Munro tickled her.

"You see, Professor? Nothing to it."

Amy never strayed far from the group again.

If Elliot had an uncomfortable sense of the rain forest as the natural domain of his own animal, Karen Ross viewed it in terms of earth resources—in which it was poor. She was not fooled by the luxuriant, oversized vegetation, which she knew represented an extraordinarily efficient ecosystem built in virtually barren soil.*

---

* The rain forest ecosystem is an energy utilization complex far more efficient than any energy conversion system developed by man. See C. F. Higgins et al., *Energy Resources and Ecosystem Utilization* (Englewood Cliffs, N.J.: Prentice Hall, 1977), pp. 232–255.

The developing nations of the world did not understand this fact; once cleared, the jungle soil yielded disappointing crops. Yet the rain forests were being cleared at the incredible rate of fifty acres a minute, day and night. The rain forests of the world had circled the equator in a green belt for at least sixty million years—but man would have cleared them within twenty years.

This widespread destruction had caused some alarm Ross did not share. She doubted that the world climate would change or the atmospheric oxygen be reduced. Ross was not an alarmist, and not impressed by the calculations of those who were. The only reason she felt uneasy was that the forest was so little understood. A clearing rate of fifty acres a minute meant that plant and animal species were becoming extinct at the incredible rate of *one species per hour*. Life forms that had evolved for millions of years were being wiped out every few minutes, and no one could predict the consequences of this stupendous rate of destruction. The extinction of species was proceeding much faster than anybody recognized, and the publicized lists of "endangered" species told only a fraction of the story; the disaster extended all the way down the animal phyla to insects, worms, and mosses.

The reality was that entire ecosystems were being destroyed by man without a care or a backward glance. And these ecosystems were for the most part mysterious, poorly understood. Karen Ross felt herself plunged into a world entirely different from the exploitable world of mineral resources; this was an environment in which plant life reigned supreme. It was no wonder, she thought, that the Egyptians called this the Land of Trees. The rain forest provided a hothouse environment for plant life, an environment in which gigantic plants were much superior to—and much favored over—mammals, including the insignificant human mammals who were now picking their way through its perpetual darkness.

. . .

The Kikuyu porters had an immediate reaction to the forest: they began to laugh and joke and make as much noise as possible. Ross said to Kahega, "They certainly are jolly."

"Oh, no," Kahega said. "They are warning."

"Warning?"

Kahega explained that the men made noise to warn off the buffalo and leopards. And the *tembo*, he added, pointing to the trail.

"Is this a *tembo* trail?" she asked.

Kahega nodded.

"The *tembo* live nearby?"

Kahega laughed. "I hope no," Kahega said. "*Tembo*. Elephant."

"So this is a game trail. Will we see elephants?"

"Maybe yes, maybe no," Kahega said. "I hope no. They are very big, elephants."

There was no arguing with his logic. Ross said, "They tell me these are your brothers," nodding down the line of porters.

"Yes, they are my brothers."

"Ah."

"But you mean that my brothers, we have the same mother?"

"Yes, you have the same mother."

"No," Kahega said.

Ross was confused. "You are not real brothers?"

"Yes, we are real brothers. But we do not have the same mother."

"Then why are you brothers?"

"Because we live in the same village."

"With your father and mother?"

Kahega looked shocked. "*No*," he said emphatically. "Not the same village."

"A different village, then?"

"Yes, of course—we are Kikuyu."

Ross was perplexed. Kahega laughed.

Kahega offered to carry the electronic equipment that Ross had slung over her shoulder, but she declined. Ross was obliged to try and link up with Houston at intervals throughout the day, and at noon she found a clear window, probably because the consortium jamming operator took a break for lunch. She managed to link through and register another Field Time-Position.

The console read: FILD TME-POSITN CHEK - 10:03 H

They had lost nearly an hour since the previous check the night before. "We've got to go faster," she told Munro.

"Perhaps you'd prefer to jog," Munro said. "Very good exercise." And then, because he decided he was being too hard on her, he added, "A lot can happen between here and Virunga."

They heard the distant growl of thunder and minutes later were drenched in a torrential rain, the drops so dense and heavy that they actually hurt. The rain fell solidly for the next hour, then stopped as abruptly as it had begun. They were all soaked and miserable, and when Munro called a halt for food, Ross did not protest.

Amy promptly went off into the forest to forage; the porters cooked curried meat gravy on rice; Munro, Ross, and Elliot burned leeches off their legs with cigarettes. The leeches were swollen with blood. "I didn't even notice them," Ross said.

"Rain makes 'em worse," Munro said. Then he looked up sharply, glancing at the jungle.

"Something wrong?"

"No, nothing," Munro said, and he went into an explanation of why leeches had to be burned off; if they were pulled off, a part of the head remained lodged in the flesh and caused an infection.

Kahega brought them food, and Munro said in a low voice, "Are the men all right?"

"Yes," Kahega said. "The men are all right. They will not be afraid."

"Afraid of what?" Elliot said.

"Keep eating. Just be natural," Munro said.

Elliot looked nervously around the little clearing.

"Eat!" Munro whispered. "Don't insult them. You're not supposed to know they're here."

The group ate in silence for several minutes. And then the nearby brush rustled and a pygmy stepped out.

2. The Dancers of God

He was a light-skinned man about four and a half feet tall, barrel-chested, wearing only a loincloth, with a bow and arrow over his shoulder. He looked around the expedition, apparently trying to determine who was the leader.

Munro stood, and said something quickly in a language that was not Swahili. The pygmy replied. Munro gave him one of the cigarettes they had been using to burn off the leeches. The pygmy did not want it lit; instead he dropped it into a small leather pouch attached to his quiver. A brief conversation followed. The pygmy pointed off into the jungle several times.

"He says a white man is dead in their village," Munro said. He picked up his pack, which contained the first-aid kit. "I'll have to hurry."

Ross said, "We can't afford the time."

Munro frowned at her.

"Well, the man's dead anyway."

"He's not *completely* dead," Munro said. "He's not dead-for-ever."

The pygmy nodded vigorously. Munro explained that pygmies graded illness in several stages. First a person was hot, then he was with fever, then ill, then dead, then completely dead—and finally dead-for-ever.

From the bush, three more pygmies appeared. Munro nodded. "Knew he wasn't alone," he said. "These chaps never are alone. Hate to travel alone. The others were watching us; if we'd made a wrong move, we'd get an arrow for our trouble. See those brown tips? Poison."

Yet the pygmies appeared relaxed now—at least until Amy came crashing back through the underbrush. Then there were shouts and swiftly drawn bows; Amy was terrified and ran to Peter, jumping up on him and clutching his chest—and making him thoroughly muddy.

The pygmies engaged in a lively discussion among themselves, trying to decide what Amy's arrival meant. Several questions were asked of Munro. Finally, Elliot set Amy back down on the ground and said to Munro, "What did you tell them?"

"They wanted to know if the gorilla was yours, and I said yes. They wanted to know if the gorilla was female, and I said yes. They wanted to know if you had relations with the gorilla; I said no. They said that was good, that you should not become too attached to the gorilla, because that would cause you pain."

"Why pain?"

"They said when the gorilla grows up, she will either run away into the forest and break your heart or kill you."

Ross still opposed making a detour to the pygmy village, which was several miles away on the banks of the Liko River.

"We're behind on our timeline," she said, "and slipping further behind every minute."

For the first and last time during the expedition, Munro lost his temper. "Listen, Doctor," he said, "this isn't downtown Houston, this is the middle of the goddamn Congo and it's no place to be injured. We have medicines. That man may need it. You don't leave him behind. You just don't."

"If we go to that village," Ross said, "we blow the rest of the day. It puts us nine or ten hours further back. Right now we can still make it. With another delay, we won't have a chance."

One of the pygmies began talking quickly to Munro. He nodded, glancing several times at Ross. Then he turned to the others.

"He says that the sick white man has some writing on his shirt pocket. He's going to draw the writing for us."

Ross glanced at her watch and sighed.

The pygmy picked up a stick and drew large characters in the muddy earth at their feet. He drew carefully, frowning in concentration as he reproduced the alien symbols: E R T S.

"Oh, God," Ross said softly.

The pygmies did not walk through the forest: they ran at a brisk trot, slipping through the forest vines and branches, dodging rain puddles and gnarled tree roots with deceptive ease. Occasionally they glanced over their shoulders and giggled at the difficulties of the three white people who followed.

For Elliot, it was a difficult pace—a succession of roots to stumble over, tree limbs to strike his head on, thorny vines to tear at his flesh. He was gasping for breath, trying to keep up with the little men who padded effortlessly ahead of him. Ross was doing no better than he, and even Munro, although surprisingly agile, showed signs of fatigue.

Finally they came to a small stream and a sunlit clearing.

The pygmies paused on the rocks, squatting and turning their faces up to the sun. The white people collapsed, panting and gasping. The pygmies seemed to find this hilarious, their laughter good-natured.

The pygmies were the earliest human inhabitants of the Congo rain forest. Their small size, distinctive manner, and deft agility had made them famous centuries before. More than four thousand years ago, an Egyptian commander named Herkouf entered the great forest west of the Mountains of the Moon; there he found a race of tiny men who sang and danced to their god. Herkouf's amazing report had the ring of fact, and Herodotus and later Aristotle insisted that these stories of the tiny men were true, and not fabulous. The Dancers of God inevitably acquired mythical trappings as the centuries passed.

As late as the seventeenth century, Europeans remained unsure whether tiny men with tails who had the power to fly through the trees, make themselves invisible, and kill elephants actually existed. That skeletons of chimpanzees were sometimes mistaken for pygmy skeletons added to the confusion. Colin Turnbull notes that many elements of the fable are actually true: the pounded-bark loincloths hang down and look like tails; the pygmies can blend into the forest and become virtually invisible; and they have always hunted and killed elephants.

The pygmies were laughing now as they got to their feet and padded off again. Sighing, the white people struggled up and lumbered after them. They ran for another half hour, never pausing or hesitating, and then Elliot smelled smoke and they came into a clearing beside a stream where the village was located.

He saw ten low rounded huts no more than four feet high, arranged in a semicircle. The villagers were all outside in the afternoon light, the women cleaning mushrooms and berries picked during the day, or cooking grubs and turtles on crackling fires; children tottered around, bothering the men who sat before their houses and smoked tobacco while the women worked.

At Munro's signal, they waited at the edge of the camp until they were noticed, and then they were led in. Their arrival provoked great interest; the children giggled and pointed; the men wanted tobacco from Munro and Elliot; the women touched Ross's blonde hair, and argued about it. A little girl crawled between Ross's legs, peering up her trousers. Munro explained that the women were uncertain whether Ross painted her hair, and the girl had taken it upon herself to settle the question of artifice.

"Tell them it's natural," Ross said, blushing.

Munro spoke briefly to the women. "I told them it was the color of your father's hair," he told Ross. "But I'm not sure they believe it." He gave Elliot cigarettes to pass out, one to each man; they were received with broad smiles and odd girlish giggles.

Preliminaries concluded, they were taken to a newly constructed house at the far end of the village where the dead white man was said to be. They found a filthy, bearded man of thirty, sitting cross-legged in the small doorway, staring outward. After a moment Elliot realized the man was catatonic —he was not moving at all.

"Oh, my God," Ross said. "It's Bob Driscoll."

"You know him?" Munro said.

"He was a geologist on the first Congo expedition." She leaned close to him, waved her hand in front of his face. "Bobby, it's me, Karen. Bobby, what happened to you?"

Driscoll did not respond, did not even blink. He continued to stare forward.

One of the pygmies offered an explanation to Munro. "He came into their camp four days ago," Munro said. "He was wild and they had to restrain him. They thought he had blackwater fever, so they made a house for him and gave him some medicines, and he was not wild any more. Now he lets them feed him, but he never speaks. They think perhaps he was captured by General Muguru's men and tortured, or else he is *agudu*—a mute."

Ross moved back in horror.

"I don't see what we can do for him," Munro said. "Not in his condition. Physically he's okay, but . . ." He shook his head.

"I'll give Houston the location," Ross said, "and they'll send help from Kinshasa."

During all this, Driscoll never moved. Elliot leaned forward to look at his eyes, and as he approached, Driscoll wrinkled his nose. His body tensed. He broke into a high-pitched wail—"Ah-ah-ah-ah"—like a man about to scream.

Appalled, Elliot backed off, and Driscoll relaxed, falling silent again. "What the hell was that all about?"

One of the pygmies whispered to Munro. "He says," Munro said, "that you smell like gorilla."

3. Ragora

Two hours later, they were reunited with Kahega and the others, led by a pygmy guide across the rain forest south of Gabutu. They were all sullen, uncommunicative—and suffering from dysentery.

The pygmies had insisted they stay for an early dinner, and Munro felt they had no choice but to accept. The meal was mostly a slender wild potato called *kitsombe*, which looked like a shriveled asparagus; forest onions, called *otsa*; and *modoke*, wild manioc leaves, along with several kinds of mushrooms. There were also small quantities of sour, tough turtle meat and occasional grasshoppers, caterpillars, worms, frogs, and snails.

This diet actually contained twice as much protein by weight as beefsteak, but it did not sit well on unaccustomed stomachs. Nor was the news around the campfire likely to improve their spirits.

According to the pygmies, General Muguru's men had established a supply camp up at the Makran escarpment, which was where Munro was headed. It seemed wise to avoid the troops. Munro explained there was no Swahili word for chivalry or sportsmanship, and the same was true of the Congolese variant, Lingala. "In this part of the world, it's kill or be killed. We'd best stay away."

Their only alternate route took them west, to the Ragora River. Munro frowned at his map, and Ross frowned at her computer console.

"What's wrong with the Ragora River?" Elliot asked.

"Maybe nothing," Munro said. "Depends on how hard it's rained lately."

Ross glanced at her watch. "We're now twelve hours behind," she said. "The only thing we can do is continue straight through the night on the river."

"I'd do that anyway," Munro said.

Ross had never heard of an expedition guide leading a party through a wilderness area at night. "You would? Why?"

"Because," Munro said, "the obstacles on the lower river will be much easier at night."

"What obstacles?"

"We'll discuss them when we come to them," Munro said.

A mile before they reached the Ragora, they heard the distant roar of powerful water. Amy was immediately anxious, signing *What water?* again and again. Elliot tried to reassure her, but he was not inclined to do much; Amy was going to have to put up with the river, despite her fears.

But when they got to the Ragora they found that the

sound came from tumbling cataracts somewhere u
directly before them, the river was fifty feet wide anc
muddy brown.

"Doesn't look too bad," Elliot said.

"No," Munro said, "it doesn't."

But Munro understood about the Congo. The fourth
largest river in the world (after the Nile, the Amazon, and the
Yangtze) was unique in many ways. It twisted like a giant
snake across the face of Africa, twice crossing the equator—
the first time going north, toward Kisangani, and later going
south, at Mbandaka. This fact was so remarkable that even a
hundred years ago geographers did not believe it was true. Because the Congo flowed both north and south of the equator,
there was always a rainy season somewhere along its path; the
river was not subject to the seasonal fluctuations that characterized rivers such as the Nile. The Congo poured a steady
1,500,000 cubic feet of water every second into the Atlantic
Ocean, a flow greater than any river except the Amazon.

But this tortuous course also made the Congo the least
navigable of the great rivers. Serious disruptions began with
the rapids of Stanley Pool, three hundred miles from the
Atlantic. Two thousand miles inland, at Kisangani, where the
river was still a mile wide, the Wagenia Cataract blocked all
navigation. And as one moved farther upriver along the fan of
tributaries, the impediments became even more pronounced,
for above Kisangani the tributaries were descending rapidly
into the low jungle from their sources—the highland savannahs to the south, and the 16,000-foot snow-capped Ruwen-
zori Mountains to the east.

The tributaries cut a series of gorges, the most striking of
which was the Portes d'Enfer—the Gates of Hell—at Kon-
golo. Here the placid Lualaba River funneled through a gorge
half a mile deep and a hundred yards wide.

The Ragora was a minor tributary of the Lualaba, which
it joined near Kisangani. The tribes along the river referred to

it as *baratawani*, "the deceitful road," for the Ragora was notoriously changeable. Its principal feature was the Ragora Gorge, a limestone cut two hundred feet deep and in places only ten feet wide. Depending on recent rainfall, the Ragora Gorge was either a pleasant scenic spectacle or a boiling white-water nightmare.

At Abutu, they were still fifteen miles upriver from the gorge, and conditions on the river told them nothing about conditions within the gorge. Munro knew all that, but he did not feel it necessary to explain it to Elliot, particularly since at the moment Elliot was fully occupied with Amy.

Amy had watched with growing uneasiness as Kahega's men inflated the two Zodiac rafts. She tugged Elliot's sleeve and demanded to know *What balloons?*

"They're boats, Amy," he said, although he sensed she had already figured that out, and was being euphemistic. "Boat" was a word she had learned with difficulty; since she disliked water, she had no interest in anything intended to ride upon it.

Why boat? she asked.

"We ride boat now," Elliot said.

Indeed, Kahega's men were pushing the boats to the edge of the water, and loading the equipment on, lashing it to the rubber stanchions at the gunwales.

Who ride? she asked.

"We all ride," Elliot said.

Amy watched a moment longer. Unfortunately, everyone was nervous, Munro barking orders, the men working hastily. As she had often shown, Amy was sensitive to the moods of those around her. Elliot always remembered how she had in-sisted that something was wrong with Sarah Johnson for days before Sarah finally told the Project Amy staff that she had split up with her husband. Now Elliot was certain that Amy sensed their apprehension. *Cross water in boat?* she asked.

"No, Amy," he said. "Not cross. Ride boat."

No, Amy signed, stiffening her back, tightening her shoulders.

"Amy," he said, "we can't leave you here."

She had a solution for that. *Other people go. Peter stay Amy.*

"I'm sorry, Amy," he said. "I have to go. You have to go."

No, she signed. *Amy no go.*

"Yes, Amy." He went to his pack and got his syringe and a bottle of Thoralen.

With her body stiff and angry, she tapped the underside of her chin with a clenched fist.

"Watch your language, Amy," he warned her.

Ross came over with orange life vests for him and Amy. "Something wrong?"

"She's swearing," Elliot said. "Better leave us alone." Ross took one look at Amy's tense, rigid body, and left hurriedly.

Amy signed Peter's name, then tapped the underside of her chin again. This was the Ameslan sign politely translated in scholarly reports as "dirty," although it was most often employed by apes when they needed to go to the potty. Primate investigators were under no illusions about what the animals really meant. Amy was saying, *Peter shitty.*

Nearly all language-skilled primates swore, and they employed a variety of words for swearing. Sometimes the pejorative seemed to be chosen at random, "nut" or "bird" or "wash." But at least eight primates in different laboratories had independently settled on the clenched-fist sign to signify extreme displeasure. The only reason this remarkable coincidence hadn't been written up was that no investigator was willing to try and explain it. It seemed to prove that apes, like people, found bodily excretions suitable terms to express denigration and anger.

Peter shitty, she signed again.

"Amy . . ." He doubled the Thoralen dose he was drawing into the syringe.

Peter shitty boat shitty people shitty.

"Amy, cut it out." He stiffened his own body and hunched over, imitating a gorilla's angry posture; that often made her back off, but this time it had no effect.

Peter no like Amy. Now she was sulking, turned away from him, signing to nobody.

"Don't be ridiculous," Elliot said, approaching her with the syringe held ready. "Peter like Amy."

She backed away and would not let him come close to her. In the end he was forced to load the CO_2 gun and shoot a dart into her chest. He had only done this three or four times in all their years together. She plucked out the dart with a sad expression. *Peter no like Amy.*

"Sorry," Peter Elliot said, and ran forward to catch her as her eyes rolled back and she collapsed into his arms.

Amy lay on her back in the second boat at Elliot's feet, breathing shallowly. Ahead, Elliot saw Munro standing in the first boat, leading the way as the Zodiacs slid silently downstream.

Munro had divided the expedition into two rafts of six each; Munro went in the first, and Elliot, Ross, and Amy went in the second, under Kahega's command. As Munro put it, the second boat would "learn from our misfortunes."

But for the first two hours on the Rangora, there were no misfortunes. It was an extraordinarily peaceful experience to sit in the front of the boat and watch the jungle on both sides of the river glide past them in timeless, hypnotic silence. It was idyllic, and very hot; Ross began to trail her hand over the side in the muddy water, until Kahega put a stop to it.

"Where there is water, there is always *mamba*," he said.

Kahega pointed to the muddy banks, where crocodiles basked in the sunshine, indifferent to their approach. Occasionally one of the huge reptiles yawned, lifting jagged jaws into the air, but for the most part they seemed sluggish, hardly noticing the boats.

Elliot was secretly disappointed. He had grown up on the jungle movies where the crocodiles slithered menacingly into the water at the first approach of boats. "Aren't they going to bother us?" he asked.

"Too hot," Kahega said. "*Mamba* sleepy except at cool times, eat morning and night, not now. In daytime, Kikuyu say *mamba* have joined army, one-two-three-four." And he laughed.

It took some explaining before it was clear that Kahega's tribesmen had noticed that during the day the crocodiles did pushups, periodically lifting their heavy bodies off the ground on their stubby legs in a movement that reminded Kahega of army calisthenics.

"What is Munro so worried about?" Elliot asked. "The crocodiles?"

"No," Kahega said.

"The Ragora Gorge?"

"No," Kahega said.

"Then what?"

"*After* the gorge," Kahega said.

Now the Ragora twisted, and they came around a bend, and they heard the growing roar of the water. Elliot felt the boat gathering speed, the water rippling along the rubber gunwales. Kahega shouted, "Hold fast, Doctors!"

And they were into the gorge.

Afterward, Elliot had only fragmented, kaleidoscopic impressions: the churning muddy water that boiled white in the sun-

light; the erratic wrenching of his own boat, and the way
Munro's boat up ahead seemed to reel and upend, yet miracu-
lously remain upright.

They were moving so fast it was hard to focus on the
passing blur of craggy red canyon walls, bare rock except for
sparse green clinging scrub; the hot humid air and the shock-
ingly cold muddy water that smashed over them, drenching
them time and again; the pure white surge of water boiling
around the black protruding rocks, like the bald heads of
drowned men.

Everything was happening too fast.

Ahead, Munro's boat was often lost from sight for minutes
at a time, concealed by giant standing waves of leaping, roaring muddy water. The roar echoed off the rock walls, re-
verberating, becoming a constant feature of their world; in the
depths of the gorge, where the afternoon sun did not reach the
narrow strip of dark water, the boats moved through a rushing, churning inferno, careening off rocky walls, spinning end
around end, while the boatmen shouted and cursed and
fended off the rock walls with paddles.

Amy lay on her back, lashed to the side of the boat, and
Elliot was in constant fear that she would drown from the
muddy waves that crashed over the gunwales. Not that Ross
was doing much better; she kept repeating "Oh my God oh
my God oh my God" over and over, in a low monotone, as
the water smashed down on them in successive waves, soaking
them to the skin.

Other indignities were forced upon them by nature. Even
in the boiling, pounding heart of the gorge, black clouds of
mosquitoes hung in the air, stinging them again and again.
Somehow it did not seem possible that there could be mosquitoes in the midst of the roaring chaos of the Ragora Gorge,
but they were there. The boats moved with gut-wrenching
fury through the standing waves, and in the growing darkness

the passengers baled out the boats and slapped at the mosquitoes with equal intensity.

And then suddenly the river broadened, the muddy water slowed, and the walls of the canyon moved apart. The river became peaceful again. Elliot slumped back in the boat, exhausted, feeling the fading sun on his face and the water moving beneath the inflated rubber of the boat.

"We made it," he said.

"So far," Kahega said. "But we Kikuyu say no one escapes from life alive. No relaxing now, Doctors!"

"Somehow," Ross said wearily, "I believe him."

They drifted gently downstream for another hour, and the rock walls receded farther away on each side, until finally they were in flat African rain forest once more. It was as if the Ragora Gorge had never existed; the river was wide and sluggish gold in the descending sun.

Elliot stripped off his soaking shirt and changed it for a pullover, for the evening air was chilly. Amy snored at his feet, covered with a towel so she would not get too cold. Ross checked her transmitting equipment, making sure it was all right. When she was finished, the sun had set and it was rapidly growing dark. Kahega broke out a shotgun and inserted yellow stubby shells.

"What's that for?" Elliot said.

"*Kiboko*," Kahega said. "I do not know the word in English." He shouted, "*Mzee! Nini maana kiboko?*"

In the lead boat, Munro glanced back. "Hippopotamus," he said.

"Hippo," Kahega said.

"Are they dangerous?" Elliot asked.

"At night, we hope no," Kahega said. "But me, I think yes."

. . .

The twentieth century had been a period of intensive wild-life study, which overturned many long-standing conceptions about animals. It was now recognized that the gentle, soft-eyed deer actually lived in a ruthless, nasty society, while the supposedly vicious wolf was devoted to family and offspring in exemplary fashion. And the African lion—the proud king of beasts—was relegated to the status of slinking scavenger, while the loathed hyena assumed new dignity. (For decades, observers had come upon a dawn kill to find lions feeding on the carcass, while the scavenging hyenas circled at the periphery, awaiting their chance. Only after scientists began night tracking the animals did a new interpretation emerge: hyenas actually made the kill, only to be driven off by opportunistic and lazy lions; hence the traditional dawn scene. This coincided with the discovery that lions were in many ways erratic and mean, while the hyenas had a finely developed social structure—yet another instance of long-standing human prejudice toward the natural world of animals.)

But the hippopotamus remained a poorly understood animal. Herodotus's "river horse" was the largest African mammal after the elephant, but its habit of lying in the water with just eyes and nostrils protruding made it difficult to study. Hippos were organized around a male. A mature male had a harem of several females and their offspring, a group of eight to fourteen animals altogether.

Despite their obese, rather humorous appearance, hippos were capable of unusual violence. The bull hippopotamus was a formidable creature, fourteen feet long and weighing nearly ten thousand pounds. Charging, he moved with extraordinary speed for such a large animal, and his four stubby, blunted tusks were actually razor sharp on the sides. A hippo attacked by slashing, moving his cavernous mouth from side to side, rather than biting. And, unlike most animals, a fight between bulls often resulted in the death of one animal from deep slashing wounds. There was nothing symbolic about a hippopotamus fight.

The animal was dangerous to man, as well. In river areas where herds were found, half of native deaths were attributed to hippos; elephants and predatory cats accounted for the remainder. The hippopotamus was vegetarian, and at night the animals came onto the land, where they ate enormous quantities of grass to sustain their great bulk. A hippo separated from the water was especially dangerous; anyone finding himself between a landed hippo and the river he was rushing to return to did not generally survive the experience.

But the hippo was essential to Africa's river ecology. His fecal matter, produced in prodigious quantities, fertilized the river grasses, which in turn allowed river fish and other creatures to live. Without the hippopotamus African rivers would be sterile, and where they had been driven away, the rivers died.

This much was known, and one thing more. The hippopotamus was fiercely territorial. Without exception, the male defended his river against any intruder. And as had been recorded on many occasions, intruders included other hippos, crocodiles, and passing boats. And the people in them.

DAY 7: MUKENKO

June 19, 1979

1. Kiboko

Munro's intention in continuing through the night was two-fold. First, he hoped to make up precious time, for all the computer projections assumed that they would stop each night. But it took no effort to ride the river in the moonlight; most of the party could sleep, and they would advance themselves another fifty or sixty miles by dawn.

But more important, he hoped to avoid the Ragora hippos, which could easily destroy their flimsy rubber boats. During the day, the hippos were found in pools beside the river-banks, and the bulls would certainly attack any passing boat. At night, when the animals went ashore to forage, the expedition could slip down the river and avoid a confrontation entirely.

It was a clever plan, but it ran into trouble for an unexpected reason—their progress on the Ragora was too rapid. It was only nine o'clock at night when they reached the first hippo areas, too early for the animals to be eating. The hippos would attack the boats—but they would attack in the dark.

The river twisted and turned in a series of curves. At each curve there was a still pool, which Kahega pointed out as the kind of quiet water that hippos liked to inhabit. And he

pointed to the grass on the banks, cut short as if the banks had
been mown.

"Soon now," Kahega said.

They heard a low grunting *"Haw-huh-huh-huh."* It
sounded like an old man trying to clear his throat of phlegm.
Munro tensed in the lead boat. They drifted around another
curve, carried smoothly in the flow of current. The two boats
were now about ten yards apart. Munro held his loaded shotgun ready.

The sound came again, this time in a chorus: *"Haw-huh-
huh-huh."*

Kahega plunged his paddle into the water. It struck bottom quickly. He pulled it out; only three feet of it was wet.
"Not deep," he said, shaking his head.

"Is that bad?" Ross said.

"Yes, I think it is bad."

They came around the next bend, and Elliot saw a half-
dozen partially submerged black rocks near the shore, gleaming in the moonlight. Then one of the "rocks" crashed upward
and he saw an enormous creature lift entirely out of the shallow water so that he could see the four stubby legs, and the
hippo churned forward toward Munro's boat.

Munro fired a low magnesium flare as the animal charged;
in the harsh white light Elliot saw a gigantic mouth, four huge
glistening blunted teeth, the head lifted upward as the animal
roared. And then the hippo was engulfed in a cloud of pale
yellow gas. The gas drifted back, and stung their eyes.

"He's using tear gas," Ross said.

Munro's boat had already moved on. With a roar of pain
the male hippo had plunged down into the water and disappeared from sight. In the second boat, they blinked back tears
and watched for him as they approached the pool. Overhead,
the magnesium flare sizzled and descended, lengthening sharp
shadows, glaring off the water.

"Perhaps he's given up," Elliot said. They could not see the hippo anywhere. They drifted in silence.

And suddenly the front of the boat bucked up, and the hippo roared and Ross screamed. Kahega toppled backward, discharging his gun into the air. The boat slapped down with a wrenching crash and a spray of water over the sides, and Elliot scrambled to his feet to check Amy and found himself staring into a huge pink cavernous mouth and hot breath. The mouth came down with a lateral slash on the side of the rubber boat, and the air began to hiss and sizzle in the water.

The mouth opened again, and the hippo grunted, but then Kahega had got to his feet and fired a stinging cloud of gas. The hippo backed off and splashed down, rocking the boat and propelling them onward, down the river. The whole right side of the boat was collapsing swiftly as the air leaked out of the huge cuts in the rubber. Elliot tried to pull them shut with his hands; the hissing continued unabated. They would sink within a minute.

Behind them, the bull hippo charged, racing down the shallow river like a powerboat, churning water in a wake from both sides of his body, bellowing in anger.

"Hold on, hold on!" Kahega shouted, and fired again. The hippo disappeared behind a cloud of gas, and the boat drifted around another curve. When the gas cleared the animal was gone. The magnesium flare sputtered into the water and they were plunged into darkness again. Elliot grabbed Amy as the boat sank, and they found themselves standing knee-deep in the muddy water.

They managed to beach the Zodiac on the dark riverbank. In the lead boat, Munro paddled over, surveyed the damage, and announced that they would inflate another boat and go on. He called for a rest, and they all lay in the moonlight on the river's edge swatting mosquitoes away.

. . .

Their reverie was interrupted by the screaming whine of ground-to-air rockets, blossoming explosions in the sky over-head. With each explosion, the riverbank glowed bright red, casting long shadows, then fading black once more.

"Muguru's men firing from the ground," Munro said, reaching for his field glasses.

"What're they shooting at?" Elliot said, staring up into the sky.

"Beats me," Munro said.

Amy touched Munro's arm, and signed, *Bird come.* But they heard no sound of an aircraft, only the bursting of rock-ets in the sky.

Munro said, "You think she hears something?"

"Her hearing is very acute."

And then they heard the drone of a distant aircraft, ap-proaching from the south. As it came into view, they saw it twist, maneuvering among the brilliant yellow-red explosions that burst in the moonlight and glinted off the metal body of the aircraft.

"Those poor bastards are trying to make time," Munro said, scanning the plane through field glasses. "That's a C-130 transport with Japanese markings on the tail. Supply plane for the consortium base camp—if it makes it through."

As they watched, the transport twisted left and right, run-ning a zigzag course through the bursting fireballs of explod-ing missiles.

"Breaking a snake's back," Munro said. "The crew must be terrified; they didn't buy into this."

Elliot felt a sudden sympathy for the crew; he imagined them staring out the windows as the fireballs exploded with brilliant light, illuminating the interior of the plane. Were they chattering in Japanese? Wishing they had never come?

A moment later, the aircraft droned onward to the north, out of sight, a final missile with a red-hot tail chasing after it, but it was gone over the jungle trees, and he listened to the distant explosion of the missile.

"Probably got through," Munro said, standing. "We'd better move on." And he shouted in Swahili for Kahega to put the men on the river once more.

2. Mukenko

Elliot shivered, zipped his parka tighter, and waited for the hailstorm to stop. They were huddled beneath a stand of evergreen trees above 8,000 feet on the alpine slopes of Mount Mukenko. It was ten o'clock in the morning, and the air temperature was 38 degrees. Five hours before, they had left the river behind and begun their pre-dawn climb in 100-degree steaming jungle.

Alongside him, Amy watched the golfball-sized white pellets bounce on the grass and slap the branches of the tree over their heads. She had never seen hail before.

She signed, *What name?*

"Hail," he told her.

Peter make stop.

"I wish I could, Amy."

She watched the hail for a moment, then signed, *Amy want go home.*

She had begun talking about going home the night before. Although the Thoralen had worn off, she remained depressed and withdrawn. Elliot had offered her some food to cheer her up. She signed that she wanted milk. When he told her they had none (which she knew perfectly well), she signed that she wanted a banana. Kahega had produced a bunch of small, slightly sour jungle bananas. Amy had eaten them without objection on previous days, but she now threw them into the water contemptuously, signing she wanted "real bananas."

When Elliot told her that they had no real bananas, she signed, *Amy want go home.*

"We can't go home now, Amy."

Amy good gorilla Peter take Amy home.

She had only known him as the person in charge, the final arbiter of her daily life in the experimental setting of Project Amy. He could think of no way to make clear to her that he was no longer in charge, and that he was not punishing her by keeping her here.

In fact, they were all discouraged. Each of the expedition members had looked forward to escaping the oppressive heat of the rain forest, but now that they were climbing Mukenko, their enthusiasm had quickly faded. "Christ," Ross said. "From hippos to hail."

As if on cue, the hail stopped. "All right," Munro said, "let's get moving."

Mukenko had never been climbed until 1933. In 1908, a German party under von Ranke ran into storms and had to descend; a Belgian team in 1913 reached 10,000 feet but could not find a route to the summit; and another German team was forced to quit in 1919 when two team members fell and died, above 12,000 feet. Nevertheless Mukenko was classified as a fairly easy (non-technical) climb by most mountaineers, who generally devoted a day to the ascent; after 1943, a new route up the southeast was found which was frustratingly slow but not dangerous, and it was this route that most climbers followed.

Above 9,000 feet, the pine forest disappeared and they crossed weak grassy fields cloaked in chilly mist; the air was thinner, and they called frequently for a rest. Munro had no patience with the complaints of his charges. "What did you expect?" he demanded. "It's a mountain. Mountains are high."

He was especially merciless with Ross, who seemed the most easily fatigued. "What about your timetable?" he would ask her. "We're not even to the difficult part. It's not even interesting until eleven thousand feet. You quit now and we'll never make it to the summit before nightfall, and that means we lose a full day."

"I don't care," Ross said finally, dropping to the ground, gasping for breath.

"Just like a woman," Munro said scornfully, and smiled when Ross glared at him. Munro humiliated them, chided them, encouraged them—and somehow kept them moving.

Above 10,000 feet, the grass disappeared and there was only mossy ground cover; they came upon the solitary peculiar fat-leafed lobelia trees, emerging suddenly from the cold gray mist. There was no real cover between 10,000 feet and the summit, which was why Munro pushed them; he did not want to get caught in a storm on the barren upper slopes.

The sun broke out at 11,000 feet, and they stopped to position the second of the directional lasers for the ERTS laser-fix system. Ross had already set the first laser several miles to the south that morning, and it had taken thirty minutes.

The second laser was more critical, since it had to be matched to the first. Despite the electronic jamming, the transmitting equipment had to be connected with Houston, in order that the little laser—it was the size of a pencil eraser, mounted on a tiny steel tripod—could be accurately aimed. The two lasers on the volcano were positioned so that their beams crossed many miles away, above the jungle. And if Ross's calculations were correct, that intersection point was directly over the city of Zinj.

Elliot wondered if they were inadvertently assisting the consortium, but Ross said no. "Only at night," she said, "when they aren't moving. During the day, they won't be able to lock on our beacons—that's the beauty of the system."

Soon they smelled sulfurous volcanic fumes drifting down from the summit, now 1,500 feet above them. Up here there was no vegetation at all, only bare hard rock and scattered patches of snow tinged yellow from the sulfur. The sky was clear dark blue, and they had spectacular views of the south Virunga range—the great cone of Nyiragongo, rising steeply from the deep green of the Congo forests, and, beyond that, Mukenko, shrouded in fog.

The last thousand feet were the most difficult, particularly for Amy, who had to pick her way barefoot among the sharp lava rocks. Above 12,000 feet, the ground was loose volcanic scree. They reached the summit at five in the afternoon, and gazed over the eight-mile-wide lava lake and smoking crater of the volcano. Elliot was disappointed in the landscape of black rock and gray steam clouds. "Wait until night," Munro said.

That night the lava glowed in a network of hot red through the broken dark crust; hissing red steam slowly lost its color as it rose into the sky. On the crater rim, their little tents reflected the red glow of the lava. To the west scattered clouds were silver in the moonlight, and beneath them the Congo jungle stretched away for miles. They could see the straight green laser beams, intersecting over the black forest. With any luck they would reach that intersection tomorrow.

Ross connected her transmitting equipment to make the nightly report to Houston. After the regular six-minute delay, the signal linked directly through to Houston, without interstitial encoding or other evasive techniques.

"Hell," Munro said.

"But what does it mean?" Elliot asked.

"It means," Munro said gloomily, "the consortium has stopped jamming us."

"Isn't that good?"

"No," Ross said. "It's bad. They must already be on the site, and they've found the diamonds." She shook her head, and adjusted the video screen:

HUSTN CONFRMS CONSRTUM ONSITE ZINJ PROBABILTY 1.000. TAK NO FURTHR RSKS. SITUTN HOPELSS.

"I can't believe it," Ross said. "It's all over."
Elliot sighed. "My feet hurt," he said.
"I'm tired," Munro said.
"The hell with it," Ross said.
Utterly exhausted, they all went to bed.

DAY 8: KANYAMAGUFA

June 20, 1979

1. Descent

Everyone slept late on the morning of June 20. They had a leisurely breakfast, taking the time to cook a hot meal. They relaxed in the sun, and played with Amy, who was delighted by this unexpected attention. It was past ten o'clock before they started down Mukenko to the jungle.

Because the western slopes of Mukenko are sheer and impassable, they descended inside the smoking volcanic crater to a depth of half a mile. Munro led the way, carrying a porter's load on his head; Asari, the strongest porter, had to carry Amy, because the rocks were much too hot for her bare feet.

Amy was terrified, and regarded the human persons trekking single-file down the steep inner cone to be mad. Elliot was not sure she was wrong: the heat was intense; as they approached the lava lake, the acrid fumes made eyes water and nostrils burn; they heard the lava pop and crackle beneath the heavy black crust.

Then they reached the formation called Naragema—the Devil's Eye. It was a natural arch 150 feet high, and so smooth it appeared polished on the inside. Through this arch a fresh breeze blew, and they saw the green jungle below. They paused to rest in the arch, and Ross examined the smooth inner surface. It was part of a lava tube formed in some earlier eruption; the main body of the tube had been blown away, leaving just the slender arch.

"They call it the Devil's Eye," Munro said, "because from below, during an eruption, it glows like a red eye."

From the Devil's Eye they descended rapidly through an alpine zone, and from there across the unworldly jagged terrain of a recent lava flow. Here they encountered black craters of scorched earth, some as deep as five or six feet. Munro's first thought was that the Zaire army had used this field for mortar practice. But on closer examination, they saw a scorched pattern etched into the rock, extending like tentacles outward from the craters. Munro had never seen anything like it; Ross immediately set up her antenna, hooked in the computer, and got in touch with Houston. She seemed very excited.

The party rested while she reviewed the data on the little screen. Munro said, "What are you asking them?"

"The date of the last Mukenko eruption, and the local weather. It was in March— Do you know somebody named Seamans?"

"Yes," Elliot said. "Tom Seamans is the computer programmer for Project Amy. Why?"

"There's a message for you," she said, pointing to the screen.

Elliot came around to look: SEMNS MESG FOR ELYT STNDBY.

"What's the message?" Elliot asked.

"Push the transmit button," she said.

He pushed the button and the message flashed:REVUWD ORGNL TAPE HUSTN NU M.

"I don't understand," Elliot said. Ross explained that the "M" meant that there was more message, and he had to press the transmit button again. He pushed the button several times before he got the message, which in its entirety read:

REVUWD ORGNL TAPE HUSTN NU FINDNG RE AURL SIGNL INFO-COMPUTR ANLYSS COMPLTE THNK ITS LNGWGE.

Elliot found he could read the compressed shortline language by speaking it aloud: "Reviewed original tape Houston, new finding regarding aural signal information, computer analysis complete think it's language." He frowned. "Language?"

Ross said, "Didn't you ask him to review Houston's original tape material from the Congo?"

"Yes, but that was for visual identification of the animal on the screen. I never said anything to him about aural information." Elliot shook his head. "I wish I could talk to him."

"You can," Ross said. "If you don't mind waking him up." She pushed the interlock button, and fifteen minutes later Elliot typed, Hello Tom How Are You? The screen printed HLO TOM HOWRU.

"We don't usually waste satellite time with that kind of thing," Ross said.

The screen printed SLEPY WHRERU.

He typed, Virunga. VIRNGA.

"Travis is going to scream when he sees this transcript," Ross said. "Do you realize what the transmission costs are?" But Ross needn't have worried; the conversation soon became technical:

RECVD MESG AURL INFO PLS XPLN.

AXIDENTL DISKVRY VRY XCITNG-DISCRIMNT FUNXN COMPTR ANLSS 99 CONFDNCE LIMTS TAPD AURL INFO {BRETHNG SOUNS} DEMNSTRTS CHRCTRISTX SPECH.

SPSFY CHRCTRISTX.

REPETNG ELMNTS-ARBTRARY PATRN-STRXRAL RLATNSHPS-PROBLY THRFOR SPOKN LNGWGE.

KN U TRNSLTE?

NOT SOFR.

WHT RESN?

COMPUTR HAS INSFSNT INFO IN AURL MESG-WNT MOR DATA-STL WORKNG-MAYB MOR TOMORO-FINGRS X.

RLY THNK GORILA LNGWGE?

YES IF GORILA.

"I'll be damned," Elliot said. He ended the satellite transmission, but the final message from Seamans remained on the
screen, glowing bright green:

YES IF GORILA.

2. The Hairy Men

Within two hours of receiving this unexpected news, the expedition had its first contact with gorillas.

They were by now back in the darkness of the equatorial
rain forest. They proceeded directly toward the site, following
the overhead laser beams. They could not see these beams directly, but Ross had brought a wired optical track guide, a
cadmium photocell filtered to record the specific laser wave-
length emission. Periodically during the day, she inflated a
small helium balloon, attached the track guide with a wire,
and released it. Lifted by the helium, the guide rose into the
sky above the trees. There it rotated, sighted one of the laser
lines, and transmitted coordinates down the wire to the computer. They followed the track of diminishing laser intensity
from a single beam, and waited for the "blip reading," the
doubled intensity value that would signal the intersection of
two beams above them.

This was a slow job and their patience was wearing thin
when, toward midday, they came upon the characteristic three-
lobed feces of gorilla, and they saw several nests made of
eucalyptus leaves on the ground and in the trees.

Fifteen minutes later, the air was shattered by a deafening
roar. "Gorilla," Munro announced. "That was a male telling
somebody off."

Amy signed, *Gorilla say go away.*

"We have to continue, Amy," he said.

Gorilla no want human people come.

"Human people won't harm gorillas," Elliot assured her. But Amy just looked blank at this, and shook her head, as if Elliot had missed the point.

Days later he realized that he had indeed missed the point. Amy was not telling him that the gorillas were afraid of being harmed by people. She was saying that the gorillas were afraid that the people would be harmed, by gorillas.

They had progressed halfway across a small jungle clearing when the large silverback male reared above the foliage and bellowed at them.

Elliot was leading the group, because Munro had gone back to help one of the porters with his pack. He saw six animals at the edge of the clearing, dark black shapes against the green, watching the human intruders. Several of the females cocked their heads and compressed their lips in a kind of disapproval. The dominant male roared again.

He was a large male with silver hair down his back. His massive head stood more than six feet above the ground, and his barrel chest indicated that he weighed more than four hundred pounds. Seeing him, Elliot understood why the first explorers to the Congo had believed gorillas to be "hairy men," for this magnificent creature looked like a gigantic man, both in size and shape.

At Elliot's back Ross whispered, "What do we do?"

"Stay behind me," Elliot said, "and don't move."

The silverback male dropped to all fours briefly, and began a soft *ho-ho-ho* sound, which grew more intense as he leapt to his feet again, grabbing handfuls of grass as he did so. He threw the grass in the air, and then beat his chest with flat palms, making a hollow thumping sound.

"Oh, no," Ross said.

The chest-beating lasted five seconds, and then the male dropped to all fours again. He ran sideways across the grass, slapping the foliage and making as much noise as possible, to frighten the intruders off. Finally he began the *ho-ho-ho* sound once more.

The male stared at Elliot, expecting that this display would send him running. When it did not, the male leapt to his feet, pounded his chest, and roared with even greater fury.

And then he charged.

With a howling scream he came crashing forward at frightening speed, directly toward Elliot. Elliot heard Ross gasp behind him. He wanted to turn and run, his every bodily instinct screamed that he should run, but he forced himself to stand absolutely still—and to look down at the ground.

Staring at his feet while he listened to the gorilla crashing through the tall grass toward him, he had the sudden sensation that all his abstract book knowledge was wrong, that everything that scientists around the world thought about gorillas was wrong. He had a mental image of the huge head and the deep chest and the long arms swinging wide as the powerful animal rushed toward an easy kill, a stationary target foolish enough to believe all the academic misinformation sanctified by print. . . .

There was silence.

The gorilla (who must have been quite close) made a snorting noise, and Elliot could see his heavy shadow on the grass near his feet. But he did not look up until the shadow moved away.

When Elliot raised his head, he saw the male gorilla retreating backward, toward the far edge of the clearing. There the male turned, and scratched his head in a puzzled way, as if wondering why his terrifying display had not driven off the intruders. He slapped the ground a final time, and then he and the rest of the troop melted away into the tall grass. It was silent in the clearing until Ross collapsed into Elliot's arms.

"Well," Munro said as he came up, "it seems you know a thing or two about gorillas after all." Munro patted Ross's arm. "It's all right. They don't do anything unless you run away. Then they bite you on the ass. That's the native mark for cowardice in these regions—because it means you ran away."

Ross was sobbing quietly, and Elliot discovered that his own knees were shaky; he went to sit down. It had all happened so fast that it was a few moments before he realized that these gorillas had behaved in exactly the textbook manner, which included not making any verbalizations even remotely like speech.

3. The Consortium

An hour later they found the wreckage of the C-130 transport. The largest airplane in the world appeared in correct scale as it lay half buried in the jungle, the gigantic nose crushed against equally gigantic trees, the enormous tail section twisted toward the ground, the massive wings buckled casting shadows on the jungle floor.

Through the shattered cockpit windshield, they saw the body of the pilot, covered with black flies. The flies buzzed and thumped against the glass as they peered in. Moving aft, they tried to look into the fuselage windows, but even on crumpled landing gear the body of the plane stood too high above the jungle floor.

Kahega managed to climb an overturned tree, and from there moved onto one wing and looked into the interior. "No people," he said.

"Supplies?"

"Yes, many supplies. Boxes and containers."

Munro left the others, walking beneath the crushed tail section to examine the far side of the plane. The port wing, concealed from their view, was blackened and shattered, the engines gone. That explained why the plane had crashed—the last FZA missile had found its target, blowing away most of the port wing. Yet the wreck remained oddly mysterious to Munro; something about its appearance was wrong. He looked along the length of the fuselage, from the crushed nose, down the line of windows, past the stump of wing, past the rear exit doors. . . .

"I'll be damned," Munro said softly.

He hurried back to the others, who were sitting on one of the tires, in the shadow of the starboard wing. The tire was so enormous that Ross could sit on it and swing her feet in the air without touching the ground.

"Well," Ross said, with barely concealed satisfaction. "They didn't get their damn supplies."

"No," Munro said. "And we saw this plane the night before last, which means it's been down at least thirty-six hours."

Munro waited for Ross to figure it out.

"Thirty-six hours?"

"That's right. Thirty-six hours."

"And they never came back to get their supplies. . . ."

"They didn't even *try* to get them," Munro said. "Look at the main cargo doors, fore and aft—no one has tried to open them. I wonder why they never came back?"

In a section of dense jungle, the ground underfoot crunched and crackled. Pushing aside the palm fronds, they saw a carpeting of shattered white bones.

"*Kanyamagufa,*" Munro said. The place of bones. He glanced quickly at the porters to see what their reaction was, but they showed only puzzlement, no fear. They were East African Kikuyu and they had none of the superstitions of the tribes that bordered the rain forest.

Amy lifted her feet from the sharp bleached fragments. She signed, *Ground hurt.*

Elliot signed, What place this?

We come bad place.

What bad place?

Amy had no reply.

"These are bones!" Ross said, staring down at the ground.

"That's right," Munro said quickly, "but they're not human bones. Are they, Elliot?"

Elliot was also looking at the ground. He saw bleached skeletal remains from several species, although he could not immediately identify any of them.

"Elliot? Not human?"

"They don't look human," Elliot agreed, staring at the ground. The first thing he noticed was that the majority of the bones came from distinctly small animals—birds, monkeys, and tiny forest rodents. Other small pieces were actually fragments from larger animals, but how large was hard to say. Perhaps large monkeys—but there weren't any large monkeys in the rain forest.

Chimpanzees? There were no chimps in this part of the Congo. Perhaps they might be gorillas: he saw one fragment from a cranium with heavy supraorbital ridging; he picked it up and turned it over in his hands.

It was a fragment of gorilla skull, no question. He felt the thickness of bone over the frontal sinuses, and he saw the beginning of the characteristic sagittal crest.

"Elliot?" Munro said, his voice tense, insistent. "Non-human?"

"Definitely non-human," Elliot said, staring. *What could shatter a gorilla skull?* It must have happened after death, he decided. A gorilla had died and after many years the bleached skeleton had been crushed in some fashion. Certainly it could not have happened during life.

"Not human," Munro said, looking at the ground. "Hell of a lot of bones, but nothing human." As he walked past Elliot, he gave him a look. *Keep your mouth shut.* "Kahega

and his men know that you are expert in these matters,"
Munro said, looking at him steadily.

What had Munro seen? Certainly he had been around
enough death to know a human skeleton when he saw one.
Elliot's glance fell on a curved bone. It looked a bit like a tur-
key wishbone, only much larger and broader, and white with
age. He picked it up. It was a fragment of the zygomatic arch
from a human skull. A cheekbone, from beneath the eye.

He turned the fragment in his hands. He looked back at
the jungle floor, and the creepers that spread reaching tentacles
over the white carpet of bones. He saw many very fragile
bones, some so thin they were translucent—bones that he assumed had come from small animals.

Now he was not sure.

A question from graduate school returned to him. What
seven bones compose the orbit of the human eye? Elliot tried
to remember. The zygoma, the nasal, the inferior orbital, the
sphenoid—that was four—the ethmoid, five—something must
come from beneath, from the mouth—the palatine, six—
one more to go—he couldn't think of the last bone. Zygoma,
nasal, inferior orbital, sphenoid, ethmoid, palatine . . . delicate bones, translucent bones, small bones.

Human bones.

"At least these aren't human bones," Ross said.

"No," Elliot agreed. He glanced at Amy.

Amy signed, *People die here.*

"What did she say?"

"She said people don't benefit from the air here."

"Let's push on," Munro said.

Munro led him a little distance ahead of the others. "Well
done," he said. "Have to be careful about the Kikuyu. Don't
want to panic them. What'd your monkey say?"

"She said people died there."

"That's more than the others know," Munro said, nodding grimly. "Although they suspect."

Behind them, the party walked single-file, nobody talking.

"What the hell happened back there?" Elliot said.

"Lot of bones," Munro said. "Leopard, colobus, forest rat, maybe a bush baby, human . . ."

"And gorilla," Elliot said.

"Yes," Munro said. "I saw that, too. Gorilla." He shook his head. "What can kill a gorilla, Professor?"

Elliot had no answer.

The consortium camp lay in ruins, the tents shredded and shattered, the dead bodies covered with dense black clouds of flies. In the humid air, the stench was overpowering, the buzzing of the flies an angry monotonous sound. Everybody except Munro hung back at the edge of the camp.

"No choice," he said. "We've got to know what happened to these—" He went inside the camp itself, stepping over the flattened fence.

As Munro moved inside, the perimeter defenses were set off, emitting a screaming high-frequency signal. Outside the fence, the others cupped their hands over their ears and Amy snorted her displeasure.

Bad noise.

Munro glanced back at them. "Doesn't bother me," he said. "That's what you get for staying outside." Munro went to one dead body, turning it over with his foot. Then he bent down, swatting away the cloud of buzzing flies, and carefully examined the head.

Ross glanced over at Elliot. He seemed to be in shock, the typical scientist, immobilized by disaster. At his side, Amy covered her ears and winced. But Ross was not immobilized; she took a deep breath and crossed the perimeter. "I have to know what defenses they installed."

"Fine," Elliot said. He felt detached, light-headed, as if he might faint; the sight and the smells made him dizzy. He saw Ross pick her way across the compound, then lift up a black box with an odd baffled cone. She traced a wire back toward the center of the camp. Soon afterward the high-frequency signal ceased; she had turned it off at the source.

Amy signed, *Better now.*

With one hand, Ross rummaged through the electronics equipment in the center of the units in the camp, while with the other she held her nose against the stench.

Kahega said, "I'll see if they have guns, Doctor," and he, too, moved into the camp. Hesitantly, the other porters followed him.

Alone, Elliot remained with Amy. She impassively surveyed the destruction, although she reached up and took his hand. He signed, Amy what happen this place?

Amy signed, *Things come.*

What things?

Bad things.

What things?

Bad things come things come bad.

What things?

Bad things.

Obviously he would get nowhere with this line of questioning. He told her to remain outside the camp, and went in himself, moving among the bodies and the buzzing flies.

Ross said, "Anybody find the leader?"

Across the camp, Munro said, "Menard."

"Out of Kinshasa?"

Munro nodded. "Yeah."

"Who's Menard?" Elliot asked.

"He's got a good reputation, knows the Congo." Ross picked her way through the debris. "But he wasn't good enough." A moment later she paused.

Elliot went over to her. She stared at a body lying face down on the ground.

"Don't turn it over," she said. "It's Richter."

Elliot did not understand how she could be sure. The body was covered with black flies. He bent over.

"Don't touch him!"

"Okay," Elliot said.

"Kahega," Munro shouted, raising a green plastic twenty-liter can. The can sloshed with liquid in his hand. "Let's get this done."

Kahega and his men moved swiftly, splashing kerosene over the tents and dead bodies. Elliot smelled the sharp odor.

Ross, crouched under a torn nylon supply tent, shouted, "Give me a minute!"

"Take all the time you want," Munro said. He turned to Elliot, who was watching Amy outside the camp.

Amy was signing to herself: *People bad. No believe people bad things come.*

"She seems very calm about it," Munro said.

"Not really," Elliot said. "I think she knows what took place here."

"I hope she'll tell us," Munro said. "Because all these men died in the same way. Their skulls were crushed."

The flames from the consortium camp licked upward into the air, and the black smoke billowed as the expedition moved onward through the jungle. Ross was silent, lost in thought. Elliot said, "What did you find?"

"Nothing good," she said. "They had a perfectly adequate peripheral system, quite similar to our ADP—animal defense perimeter. Those cones I found are audio-sensing units, and when they pick up a signal, they emit an ultra-high-frequency signal that is very painful to auditory systems. Doesn't work for reptiles, but it's damn effective on mammalian systems. Send a wolf or a leopard running for the hills."

"But it didn't work here," Elliot said.

"No," Ross said. "And it didn't bother Amy very much."

Elliot said, "What does it do to human auditory systems?"

"You felt it. It's annoying, but that's all." She glanced at Elliot. "But there aren't any human beings in this part of the Congo. Except us."

Munro asked, "Can we make a better perimeter defense?"

"Damn right we can," Ross said. "I'll give you the next generation perimeter—it'll stop anything except elephants and rhinos." But she didn't sound convinced.

Late in the afternoon, they came upon the remains of the first ERTS Congo camp. They nearly missed it, for during the intervening eight days the jungle vines and creepers had already begun to grow back over it, obliterating all traces. There was not much left—a few shreds of orange nylon, a dented aluminum cooking pan, the crushed tripod, and the broken video camera, its green circuit boards scattered across the ground. They found no bodies, and since the light was fading they pressed on.

Amy was distinctly agitated. She signed, *No go.*

Peter Elliot paid no attention.

Bad place old place no go.

"We go, Amy," he said.

Fifteen minutes later they came to a break in the over-hanging trees. Looking up, they saw the dark cone of Mu-kenko rising above the forest, and the faint crossed green beams of the lasers glinting in the humid air. And directly beneath the beams were the moss-covered stone blocks, half concealed in jungle foliage, of the Lost City of Zinj.

Elliot turned to look at Amy.

Amy was gone.

4. WEIRD

He could not believe it.

At first he thought she was just punishing him, running off to make him sorry for shooting the dart at her on the river. He explained to Munro and Ross that she was capable of such things, and they spent the next half hour wandering through the jungle, calling her name. But there was no response, just the eternal silence of the rain forest. The half hour became an hour, then almost two hours.

Elliot was panic-stricken.

When she still did not emerge from the foliage, another possibility had to be considered. "Maybe she ran off with the last group of gorillas," Munro said.

"Impossible," Elliot said.

"She's seven, she's near maturity." Munro shrugged. "She *is* a gorilla."

"Impossible," Elliot insisted.

But he knew what Munro was saying. Inevitably, people who raised apes found at a certain point they could no longer keep them. With maturity the animals became too large, too powerful, too much their own species to be controllable. It was no longer possible to put them in diapers and pretend they were cute humanlike creatures. Their genes coded inevitable differences that ultimately became impossible to overlook.

"Gorilla troops aren't closed," Munro reminded him. "They accept strangers, particularly female strangers."

"She wouldn't do that," Elliot insisted. "She couldn't."

Amy had been raised from infancy among human beings. She was much more familiar with the Westernized world of freeways and drive-ins than she was with the jungle. If Elliot drove his car past her favorite drive-in, she was quick to tap his shoulder and point out his error. What did she know of the jungle? It was as alien to her as it was to Elliot himself. And not only that—

"We'd better make camp," Ross said, glancing at her watch. "She'll come back—if she wants to. After all," she said, "we didn't leave her. She left us."

They had brought a bottle of Dom Pérignon champagne but nobody was in a mood to celebrate. Elliot was remorseful over the loss of Amy; the others were horrified by what they had seen of the earlier camp; with night rapidly falling, there was much to do to set up the ERTS system known as WEIRD (wilderness environment intruder response defenses).

The exotic WEIRD technology recognized the fact that perimeter defenses were traditional throughout the history of Congo exploration. More than a century before, Stanley observed that "no camp is to be considered complete until it is fenced around by bush or trees." In the years since there was little reason to alter the essential nature of that instruction. But defensive technology had changed, and the WEIRD system incorporated all the latest innovations.

Kahega and his men inflated the silvered Mylar tents, arranging them close together. Ross directed the placement of the tubular infrared night lights on telescoping tripods. These were positioned shining outward around the camp.

Next the perimeter fence was installed. This was a lightweight metalloid mesh, more like cloth than wire. Attached to stakes, it completely enclosed the campsite, and when hooked to the transformer carried 10,000 volts of electrical current. To reduce drain on the fuel cells, the current was pulsed at four cycles a second, creating a throbbing, intermittent hum.

Dinner on the night of June 21 was rice with rehydrated Creole shrimp sauce. The shrimps did not rehydrate well, remaining little cardboard-tasting chunks in the mix, but no-

body complained about this failure of twentieth-century technology as they glanced around them at the deepening jungle
darkness.

Munro positioned the sentries. They would stand four-
hour watches; Munro announced that he, Kahega, and Elliot
would take the first watch.

With night goggles in place, the sentries looked like mysterious grasshoppers peering out at the jungle. The night goggles
intensified ambient light and overlaid this on the pre-existing
imagery, rimming it in ghostly green. Elliot found the goggles
heavy, and the electronic view through them difficult to adjust
to. He pulled them off after several minutes, and was astonished to see that the jungle was inky black around him. He put
them back on hastily.

The night passed quietly, without incident.

DAY 9: ZINJ

June 21, 1979

1. Tiger Tail

Their entrance into the Lost City of Zinj on the morning of June 21 was accomplished with none of the mystery and romance of nineteenth-century accounts of similar journeys. These twentieth-century explorers sweated and grunted under a burdensome load of technical equipment—optical range finders, data-lock compasses, RF directionals with attached transmitters, and microwave transponders—all deemed essential to the modern high-speed evaluation of a ruined archaeological site.

They were only interested in diamonds. Schliemann had been only interested in gold when he excavated Troy, and he had devoted three years to it. Ross expected to find her diamonds in three days.

According to the ERTS computer simulation the best way to do this was to draw up a ground plan of the city. With a plan in hand, it would be relatively simple to deduce mine locations from the arrangement of urban structures.

They expected a usable plan of the city within six hours. Using RF transponders, they had only to stand in each of the four corners of a building, pressing the radio beeper at each corner. Back in camp, two widely spaced receivers recorded their signals so that their computer could plot them in two dimensions. But the ruins were extensive, covering more than

three square kilometers. A radio survey would separate them
widely in dense foliage—and, considering what had happened
to the previous expedition, this seemed unwise.

Their alternative was what ERTS called the non-
systematic survey, or "the tiger-tail approach." (It was a joke
at ERTS that one way to find a tiger was to keep walking until
you stepped on its tail.) They moved through the ruined
buildings, avoiding slithering snakes and giant spiders that
scurried into dark recesses. The spiders were the size of a
man's hand, and to Ross's astonishment made a loud clicking
noise.

They noticed that the stonework was of excellent quality,
although the limestone in many places was pitted and crumbling. And everywhere they saw the half-moon curve of doors
and windows, which seemed to be a cultural design motif.

But aside from that curved shape, they found almost nothing distinctive about the rooms they passed through. In general, the rooms were rectangular and roughly the same size;
the walls were bare, lacking decoration. After so many intervening centuries they found no artifacts at all—although Elliot
finally came upon a pair of disc-shaped stone paddles, which
they presumed had been used to grind spices or grain.

The bland, characterless quality of the city grew more
disturbing as they continued; it was also inconvenient, since
they had no way to refer to one place or another; they began
assigning arbitrary names to different buildings. When Karen
Ross found a series of cubby holes carved into the wall of one
room, she announced that this must be a post office, and from
then on it was referred to as "the post office."

They came upon a row of small rooms with postholes for
wooden bars. Munro thought these were cells of a jail, but the
cells were extremely small. Ross said that perhaps the people
were small, or perhaps the cells were intentionally small for
punishment. Elliot thought perhaps they were cages for a zoo.
But in that case, why were all the cages of the same size? And

Munro pointed out there was no provision for viewing the animals; he repeated his conviction that it was a jail, and the rooms became known as "the jail."

Near to the jail they found an open court they called "the gymnasium." It was apparently an athletic field or training ground. There were four tall stone stakes with a crumbling stone ring at the top; evidently these had been used for some kind of game like tetherball. In a corner of the court stood a horizontal overhead bar, like a jungle gym, no more than five feet off the ground. The low bar led Elliot to conclude that this was a playground for children. Ross repeated her belief that the people were small. Munro wondered if the gymnasium was a training area for soldiers.

As they continued their search, they were all aware that their reactions simply mirrored their preoccupations. The city was so neutral, so uninformative, that it became a kind of Rorschach for them. What they needed was objective information about the people who had built the city, and their life.

It was there all along, although they were slow to realize it. In many rooms, one wall or another was overgrown with black-green mold. Munro noticed that this mold did not grow in relation to light from a window, or air currents, or any other factor they could identify. In some rooms, the mold grew thickly halfway down a wall, only to stop in a sharp horizontal line, as if cut by a knife.

"Damn strange," Munro said, peering at the mold, rubbing his finger against it. His finger came away with traces of blue paint.

That was how they discovered the elaborate bas-reliefs, once painted, that appeared throughout the city. However, the overgrowth of mold on the irregular carved surface and the pitting of the limestone made any interpretation of the images impossible.

At lunch, Munro mentioned that it was too bad they hadn't brought along a group of art historians to recover the bas-relief images. "With all their lights and machines, they could see what's there in no time," he said.

It gave Ross an idea.

The most recent examination techniques for artwork, as devised by Degusto and others, employed infrared light and image intensification, and the Congo expedition had the necessary equipment to contrive such a method on the spot. At least it was worth a try. After lunch they returned to the ruins, lugging in the video camera, one of the infrared night lights, and the tiny computer display screen.

After an hour of fiddling they had worked out a system. By shining infrared light on the walls and recording the image with the video camera—and then feeding that image via satellite through the digitizing computer programs in Houston, and returning it back to their portable display unit—they were able to reconstitute the pictures on the walls.

Seeing the bas-reliefs in this way reminded Peter Elliot of the night goggles. If you looked directly at the walls, you saw nothing but dark moss and lichen and pitted stone. But if you looked at the little computer screen, you saw the original painted scenes, vibrant and lifelike. It was, he remembered, "very peculiar. There we were in the middle of the jungle, but we could only examine our environment indirectly, with the machines. We used goggles to see at night, and video to see during the day. We were using machines to see what we could not see otherwise, and we were totally dependent on them."

He also found it odd that the information recorded by the video camera had to travel more than twenty thousand miles before returning to the display screen, only a few feet away. It was, he said later, the "world's longest spinal cord," and it produced an odd effect. Even at the speed of light, the transmission required a tenth of a second, and since there was a short processing time in the Houston computer, the images did not appear on the screen instantaneously, but arrived about half a second late. The delay was just barely noticeable. The scenes they saw provided them with their first insight into the city and its inhabitants.

The people of Zinj were relatively tall blacks, with round heads and muscular bodies; in appearance they resembled the Bantu-speaking people who had first entered the Congo from the highland savannahs to the north, two thousand years ago. They were depicted here as lively and energetic: despite the climate, they favored elaborately decorated, colorful long robes; their attitudes and gestures were expansive; in all ways they contrasted sharply with the bland and crumbling structures, now all that remained of their civilization.

The first decoded frescoes showed marketplace scenes: sellers squatted on the ground beside beautiful woven baskets containing round objects, while buyers stood and bargained with them. At first they thought the round objects were fruit, but Ross decided they were stones.

"Those are uncut diamonds in a surrounding matrix," she said, staring at the screen. "They're selling diamonds."

The frescoes led them to consider what had happened to the inhabitants of the city of Zinj, for the city was clearly abandoned, not destroyed—there was no sign of war or invaders, no evidence of any cataclysm or natural disaster.

Ross, voicing her deepest fears, suspected the diamond mines had given out, turning this city into a ghost town like so many other mining settlements in history. Elliot thought that a plague or disease had overcome the inhabitants. Munro said he thought the gorillas were responsible.

"Don't laugh," he said. "This is a volcanic area. Eruptions, earthquakes, drought, fires on the savannah—the animals go berserk, and don't behave in the ordinary way at all."

"Nature on the rampage?" Elliot asked, shaking his head. "There are volcanic eruptions here every few years, and we know this city existed for centuries. It can't be that."

"Maybe there was a palace revolution, a coup."

"What would that matter to gorillas?" Elliot laughed.

"It happens," Munro said. "In Africa, the animals always get strange when there's a war on, you know." He then told them stories of baboons attacking farmhouses in South Africa and buses in Ethiopia.

Elliot was unimpressed. These ideas of nature mirroring the affairs of man were very old—at least as old as Aesop, and about as scientific. "The natural world is indifferent to man," he said.

"Oh, no question," Munro said, "but there isn't much natural world left."

Elliot was reluctant to agree with Munro, but in fact a well-known academic thesis argued just that. In 1955, the French anthropologist Maurice Cavalle published a controversial paper entitled "The Death of Nature." In it he said:

> One million years ago the earth was characterized by a pervasive wildness which we may call "nature." In the midst of this wild nature stood small enclaves of human habitation. Whether caves with artificial fire to keep men warm, or later cities with dwellings and artificial fields of cultivation, these enclaves were distinctly unnatural. In the succeeding millennia, the area of untouched nature surrounding artificial human enclaves progressively declined, although for centuries the trend remained invisible.
>
> Even 300 years ago in France or England, the great cities of man were isolated by hectares of wilderness in which untamed beasts roamed, as they had for thou-

sands of years before. And yet the expansion of man continued inexorably.

One hundred years ago, in the last days of the great European explorers, nature had so radically diminished that it was a novelty: it is for this reason that African explorations captured the imagination of nineteenth-century man. To enter a truly natural world was exotic, beyond the experience of most mankind, who lived from birth to death in entirely man-made circumstances.

In the twentieth century the balance has shifted so far that for all practical purposes one may say that nature has disappeared. Wild plants are preserved in hothouses, wild animals in zoos and game parks: artificial settings created by man as a souvenir of the once-prevalent natural world. But an animal in a zoo or a game park does not live its natural life, any more than a man in a city lives a natural life.

Today we are surrounded by man and his creations. Man is inescapable, everywhere on the globe, and nature is a fantasy, a dream of the past, long gone.

Ross called Elliot away from his dinner. "It's for you," she said, pointing to the computer next to the antenna. "That friend of yours again."

Munro grinned. "Even in the jungle, the phone never stops ringing."

Elliot went over to look at the screen: COMPUTR LNGWAGE ANALYSS NG REQUIR MOR INPUT KN PROVIDE?

WHT INPUT? Elliot typed back.

MOR AURL INPUT-TRNSMIT RECORDNGS.

Elliot typed back, Yes If Occurs. YES IF OCRS.

RCORD FREQNCY 22-50,000 CYCLS-CRITICL

Elliot typed back, Understood. UNDRSTOD.

There was a pause, then the screen printed: HOWS AMY?
Elliot hesitated. FINE.

STAF SNDS LOV came the reply, and the transmission was momentarily interrupted.

HOLD TRSNMSN.

There was a long pause.

INCREDIBL NWZ , Seamans printed. HAV FOUND MRS SWENSN.

2. Swensn NWZ

For a moment Elliot did not recognize the name. Swensn? Who was Swensn? A transmission error? And then he realized: *Mrs. Swenson!* Amy's discoverer, the woman who had brought her from Africa and had donated her to the Minneapolis zoo. The woman who had been in Borneo all these weeks. IF WE HAD ONLY KNON AMY MOTHR NOT KILD BY NATIVS.

Elliot waited impatiently for the next message from Seamans.

Elliot stared at the message. He had always been told that Amy's mother had been killed by natives in a village called Bagimindi. The mother had been killed for food, and Amy was orphaned. . . .

WHT MEANS?

MOTHR ALREDY DED NOT EATN.

The natives hadn't killed Amy's mother? She was already dead?

XPLN.

SWENSN HAS PICTR CAN TRANSMT?

Hastily, Elliot typed, his fingers fumbling at the keyboard.

TRANSMT.

There was a pause that seemed interminable, and then the video screen received the transmission, scanning it from top to bottom. Long before the picture filled the screen, Elliot realized what it showed.

A crude snapshot of a gorilla corpse with a crushed skull. The animal lay on its back in a packed-earth clearing, presumably in a native village.

In that moment Elliot felt as if the puzzle that preoccupied him, that had caused so much anguish for so many months, was explained. If only they had been able to reach her before. . . .

The glowing electronic image faded to black.

Elliot was confronted by a rush of sudden questions. Crushed skulls occurred in the remote—and supposedly uninhabited—region of the Congo, *kanyamagufa*, the place of bones. But Bagimindi was a trading village on the Lubula River, more than a hundred miles away. How had Amy and her dead mother reached Bagimindi?

Ross said, "Got a problem?"

"I don't understand the sequence. I need to ask—"

"Before you do," she said, "review the transmission. It's all in memory." She pressed a button marked REPEAT.

The earlier transmitted conversation was repeated on the screen. As Elliot watched Seaman's answers, one line struck him: MOTHR ALREDY DED NOT EATN.

Why wasn't the mother eaten? Gorilla meat was an acceptable—indeed a prized—food in this part of the Congo basin. He typed in a question:

WHY MOTHR NOT EATN.

MOTHR / INFNT FWND BY NATIV ARMY PATRL DOWN FRM SUDAN CARRIED CRPSE / INFNT 5 DAYS TO BAGMINDI VILLAG FOR SALE TOURISTS. SWENSN THERE.

Five days! Quickly, Elliot typed the important question:
WHER FWND?

The answer came back: UNKNWN AREA CONGO.

SPECFY.

NO DETALS. A short pause, then: THERS MOR PICTRS.

SND, he typed back.

The screen went blank, and then filled once more, from top to bottom. Now he saw a closer view of the female gorilla's crushed skull. And alongside the huge skull, a small black creature lying on the ground, hands and feet clenched, mouth open in a frozen scream.

Amy.

Ross repeated the transmission several times, finishing on the image of Amy as an infant—small, black, screaming.

"No wonder she's been having nightmares," Ross said. "She probably saw her mother killed."

Elliot said, "Well, at least we can be sure it wasn't gorillas. They don't kill each other."

"Right now," Ross said, "we can't be sure of anything at all."

The night of June 21 was so quiet that by ten o'clock they switched off the infrared night lights to save power. Almost at once they became aware of movement in the foliage outside the compound. Munro and Kahega swung their guns around. The rustling increased, and they heard an odd sighing sound, a sort of wheeze.

Elliot heard it too, and felt a chill: it was the same wheezing that had been recorded on the tapes from the first Congo expedition. He turned on the tape recorder, and swung the microphone around. They were all tense, alert, waiting.

But for the next hour nothing further happened. The foliage moved all around them, but they saw nothing. Then shortly before midnight the electrified perimeter fence erupted in sparks. Munro swung his gun around and fired; Ross hit the switch for the night lights and the camp was bathed in deep red.

"Did you see it?" Munro said. "Did you see what it was?" They shook their heads. Nobody had seen anything. Elliot checked his tapes; he had only the harsh rattle of gunfire, and the sound of sparks. No breathing.

The rest of the night passed uneventfully.

DAY 10: ZINJ
June 22, 1979

1. Return

The morning of June 22 was foggy and gray. Peter Elliot awoke at 6 a.m. to find the camp already up and active. Munro was stalking around the perimeter of the camp, his clothing soaked to the chest by the wet foliage. He greeted Elliot with a look of triumph, and pointed to the ground.

There, on the ground, were fresh footprints. They were deep and short, rather triangular-shaped, and there was a wide space between the big toe and the other four toes—as wide as the space between a human thumb and fingers.

"Definitely not human," Elliot said, bending to look closely.

Munro said nothing.

"Some kind of primate."

Munro said nothing.

"It can't be a gorilla," Elliot finished, straightening. His video communication from the night before had hardened his belief that gorillas were not involved. Gorillas did not kill other gorillas as Amy's mother had been killed. "It can't be a gorilla," he repeated.

"It's a gorilla, all right," Munro said. "Have a look at this." He pointed to another area of the soft earth. There were four indentations in a row. "Those are the knuckles, when they walk on their hands."

"But gorillas," Elliot said, "are shy animals that sleep at night and avoid contact with men."

"Tell the one that made this print."

"It's small for a gorilla," Elliot said. He examined the fence nearby, where the electrical short had occurred the night before. Bits of gray fur clung to the fence. "And gorillas don't have gray fur."

"Males do," Munro said. "Silverbacks."

"Yes, but the silverback coloring is whiter than this. This fur is distinctly gray." He hesitated. "Maybe it's a *kakundakari*."

Munro looked disgusted.

The *kakundakari* was a disputed primate in the Congo. Like the yeti of the Himalayas and bigfoot of North America, he had been sighted but never captured. There were endless native stories of a six-foot-tall hairy ape that walked on his hind legs and otherwise behaved in a manlike fashion.

Many respected scientists believed the *kakundakari* existed; perhaps they remembered the authorities who had once denied the existence of the gorilla.

In 1774, Lord Monboddo wrote of the gorilla that "this wonderful and frightful production of nature walks upright like man; is from 7 to 9 feet high . . . and amazingly strong; covered with longish hair, jet black over the body, but longer on the head; the face more like the human than the Chimpenza, but the complexion black; and has no tail."

Forty years later, Bowditch described an African ape "generally five feet high, and four across the shoulders; its paw was said to be even more disproportionate than its breadth, and one blow of it to be fatal." But it was not until 1847 that Thomas Savage, an African missionary, and Jeffries Wyman, a Boston anatomist, published a paper describing "a second species in Africa . . . not recognized by naturalists," which they proposed to call *Troglodytes gorilla*. Their announcement caused enormous excitement in the scientific world, and a rush in London, Paris, and Boston to procure skeletons; by 1855, there was no longer any doubt—a second, very large ape existed in Africa.

Even in the twentieth century, new animal species were discovered in the rain forest: the blue pig in 1944, and the red-breasted grouse in 1961. It was perfectly possible that a rare, reclusive primate might exist in the jungle depths. But there was still no hard evidence for the *kakundakari*.

"This print is from a gorilla," Munro insisted. "Or rather a group of gorillas. They're all around the perimeter fence. They've been scouting our camp."

"Scouting our camp," Elliot repeated, shaking his head.

"That's right," Munro said. "Just look at the bloody prints."

Elliot felt his patience growing short. He said something about white-hunter campfire tales, to which Munro said something unflattering about people who knew everything from books.

At that point, the colobus monkeys in the trees overhead began to shriek and shake the branches.

They found Malawi's body just outside the compound. The porter had been going to the stream to get water when he had been killed; the collapsible buckets lay on the ground nearby. The bones of his skull had been crushed; the purple, swelling face was distorted, the mouth open.

The group was repelled by the manner of death; Ross turned away, nauseated; the porters huddled with Kahega, who tried to reassure them; Munro bent to examine the injury. "You notice these flattened areas of compression, as if the head was squeezed between something. . . ."

Munro then called for the stone paddles that Elliot had

found in the city the day before. He glanced back at Kahega.

Kahega stood at his most erect and said, "We go home now, boss."

"That's not possible," Munro said.

"We go home. We must go home, one of our brothers is dead, we must make ceremony for his wife and his children, boss."

"Kahega . . ."

"Boss, we must go now."

"Kahega, we will talk." Munro straightened, put his arm over Kahega and led him some distance away, across the clearing. They talked in low voices for several minutes.

"It's awful," Ross said. She seemed genuinely affected with human feeling and instinctively Elliot turned to comfort her, but she continued, "The whole expedition is falling apart. It's awful. We have to hold it together somehow, or we'll *never* find the diamonds."

"Is that all you care about?"

"Well, they *do* have insurance. . . ."

"For Christ's sake," Elliot said.

"You're just upset because you've lost your damned monkey," Ross said. "Now get hold of yourself. They're watching us."

The Kikuyu were indeed watching Ross and Elliot, trying to sense the drift of sentiment. But they all knew that the real negotiations were between Munro and Kahega, standing off to one side. Several minutes later Kahega returned, wiping his eyes. He spoke quickly to his remaining brothers, and they nodded. He turned back to Munro.

"We stay, boss."

"Good," Munro said, immediately resuming his former imperious tone. "Bring the paddles."

When they were brought, Munro placed the paddles to either side of Malawi's head. They fitted the semicircular indentations on the head perfectly.

Munro then said something quickly to Kahega in Swahili, and Kahega said something to his brothers, and they nodded. Only then did Munro take the next horrible step. He raised his arms wide, and then swung the paddles back hard against the already crushed skull. The dull sound was sickening; droplets of blood spattered over his shirt, but he did not further damage the skull.

"A man hasn't the strength to do this," Munro said flatly. He looked up at Peter Elliot. "Care to try?"

Elliot shook his head.

Munro stood. "Judging by the way he fell, Malawi was standing when it happened." Munro faced Elliot, looking him in the eye. "Large animal, the size of a man. Large, strong animal. A gorilla."

Elliot had no reply.

There is no doubt that Peter Elliot felt a personal threat in these developments, although not a threat to his safety. "I simply couldn't accept it," he said later. "I knew my field, and I simply couldn't accept the idea of some unknown, radically violent behavior displayed by gorillas in the wild. And in any case, it didn't make sense. Gorillas making stone paddles that they used to crush human skulls? It was impossible."

After examining the body, Elliot went to the stream to wash the blood from his hands. Once alone, away from the others, he found himself staring into the clear running water and considering the possibility that he might be wrong. Certainly primate researchers had a long history of misjudging their subjects.

Elliot himself had helped eradicate one of the most famous misconceptions—the brutish stupidity of the gorilla. In their first description, Savage and Wyman had written, "This animal exhibits a degree of intelligence inferior to that of the Chimpanzee; this might be expected from its wider departure from the organization of the human subject." Later observers saw the gorilla as "savage, morose, and brutal." But now there was abundant evidence from field and laboratory studies that the gorilla was in many ways brighter than the chimpanzee.

Then, too, there were the famous stories of chimpanzees kidnapping and eating human infants. For decades, primate researchers had dismissed such native tales as "wild and superstitious fantasy." But there was no longer any doubt that chimpanzees occasionally kidnapped—and ate—human infants; when Jane Goodall studied Gombe chimpanzees, she locked away her own infant to prevent his being taken and killed by the chimps.

Chimpanzees hunted a variety of animals, according to a complicated ritual. And field studies by Dian Fossey suggested that gorillas also hunted from time to time, killing small game and monkeys, whenever—

He heard a rustling in the bushes across the stream, and an enormous silverback male gorilla reared up in chest-high foliage. Peter was startled, although as soon as he got over his fright he realized that he was safe. Gorillas never crossed open water, even a small stream. Or was that a misconception, too?

The male stared at him across the water. There seemed to be no threat in his gaze, just a kind of watchful curiosity. Elliot smelled the musty odor of the gorilla, and he heard the breath hiss through his flattened nostrils. He was wondering what he should do when suddenly the gorilla crashed noisily away through the underbrush, and was gone.

This encounter perplexed him, and he stood, wiping the sweat from his face. Then he realized that there was still movement in the foliage across the stream. After a moment, another gorilla rose up, this one smaller: a female, he thought, though he couldn't be sure. The new gorilla gazed at him as implacably as the first. Then the hand moved.

Peter come give tickle.

"Amy!" he shouted, and a moment later he had splashed

across the stream, and she had leapt into his arms, hugging
him and delivering sloppy wet kisses and grunting happily.

Amy's unexpected return to camp nearly got her shot by the
jumpy Kikuyu porters. Only by blocking her body with his
own did Elliot prevent gunfire. Twenty minutes later, however,
everyone had adjusted to her presence—and Amy promptly
began making demands.

She was unhappy to learn that they had not acquired milk
or cookies in her absence, but when Munro produced the
bottle of warm Dom Pérignon, she agreed to accept champagne instead.

They all sat around her, drinking champagne from tin
cups. Elliot was glad for the mitigating presence of the others,
for now that Amy was sitting there, safely restored to him,
calmly sipping her champagne and signing *Tickle drink Amy
like*, he found himself overcome with anger toward her.

Munro grinned at Elliot as he gave him his champagne.
"Calmly, Professor, calmly. She's just a child."

"The hell she is," Elliot said. He conducted the subsequent
conversation entirely in sign language, not speaking.

Amy, he signed. Why Amy leave?

She buried her nose in her cup, signing *tickle drink good
drink*.

Amy, he signed. Amy tell Peter why leave.

Peter not like Amy.

Peter like Amy.

*Peter hurt Amy Peter fly ouch pin Amy no like Peter no
like Amy Amy sad sad.*

In a detached corner of his mind, he thought he would
have to remember that "ouch pin" had now been extended to
the Thoralen dart. Her generalization pleased him, but he
signed sternly, Peter like Amy. Amy know Peter like Amy.
Amy tell Peter why—

*Peter no tickle Amy Peter not nice Amy Peter not nice
human person Peter like woman no like Amy Peter not like
Amy Amy sad Amy sad.*

This increasingly rapid signing was itself an indication that
she was upset. Where Amy go?

Amy go gorillas good gorillas. Amy like.

Curiosity overcame his anger. Had she joined a troop of
wild gorillas for several days? If so, it was an event of major
importance, a crucial moment in modern primate history—a
language-skilled primate had joined a wild troop and had come
back again. He wanted to know more.

Gorillas nice to Amy?

With a smug look: *Yes.*

Amy tell Peter.

She stared off into the distance, not answering.

To catch her attention Elliot snapped his fingers. She
turned to him slowly, her expression bored.

Amy tell Peter, Amy stay gorillas?

Yes.

In her indifference was the clear recognition that Elliot
was desperate to learn what she knew. Amy was always very
astute at recognizing when she had the upper hand—and she
had it now.

Amy tell Peter, he signed as calmly as he could.

Good gorillas like Amy Amy good gorilla.

That told him nothing at all. She was composing phrases
by rote: another way of ignoring him.

Amy.

She glanced at him.

Amy tell Peter. Amy come see gorillas?

Yes.

Gorillas do what?

Gorillas sniff Amy.

All gorillas?

Big gorillas white back gorillas sniff Amy baby sniff Amy all gorillas sniff gorillas like Amy.

So silverback males had sniffed her, then infants, then all the members of the troop. That much was clear—remarkably clear, he thought, making a mental note of her extended syntax. Afterward had she been accepted in the troop? He signed, What happen Amy then?

Gorillas give food.

What food?

No name Amy food give food.

Apparently they had shown her food. Or had they actually fed her? Such a thing had never been reported in the wild, but then no one had ever witnessed the introduction of a new animal into a troop. She was a female, and nearly of reproductive age. . . .

What gorillas give food?

All give food Amy take food Amy like.

Apparently it was not males, or not males exclusively. But what had caused her acceptance? Granted that gorilla troops were not as closed to outsiders as monkey troops—what actually had happened?

Amy stay with gorillas?

Gorillas like Amy.

Yes. What Amy do?

Amy sleep Amy eat Amy live gorillas gorillas good gorillas Amy like.

So she had joined in the life of the troop, living the daily existence. Had she been totally accepted?

Amy like gorillas?

Gorillas dumb.

Why dumb?

Gorillas no talk.

No talk sign talk?

Gorillas no talk.

Evidently she had experienced frustration with the gorillas because they did not know her sign language. (Language-using primates were commonly frustrated and annoyed when thrown among animals who did not understand the signs.)

Gorillas nice to Amy?

Gorillas like Amy Amy like gorillas like Amy like gorillas.

Why Amy come back?

Want milk cookies.

"Amy," he said, "you know we don't have any damn milk or cookies." His sudden verbalization startled the others. They looked questioningly at Amy.

For a long time she did not answer. *Amy like Peter. Amy sad want Peter.*

He felt like crying.

Peter good human person.

Blinking his eyes he signed, Peter tickle Amy. She jumped into his arms.

Later, he questioned her in more detail. But it was a painstakingly slow process, chiefly because of Amy's difficulty in handling concepts of time.

Amy distinguished past, present, and future—she remembered previous events, and anticipated future promises—but the Project Amy staff had never succeeded in teaching her exact differentiations. She did not, for example, distinguish yesterday from the day before. Whether this reflected a failing in teaching methods or an innate feature of Amy's conceptual world was an open question. (There was evidence for a conceptual difference. Amy was particularly perplexed by spatial metaphors for time, such as "that's behind us" or "that's coming up." Her trainers conceived of the past as behind them and the future ahead. But Amy's behavior seemed to indicate that she conceived of the past as in front of her—because she could see it—and the future behind her—because it was still invisible. Whenever she was impatient for the promised arrival of a friend, she repeatedly looked over her shoulder, even if she was facing the door.)

In any case, the time problem was a difficulty in talking to her now, and Elliot phrased his questions carefully. He asked, "Amy, what happened at night? With the gorillas?"

She gave him the look she always gave him when she thought a question was obvious. *Amy sleep night.*

"And the other gorillas?"

Gorillas sleep night.

"All the gorillas?"

She disdained to answer.

"Amy," he said, "gorillas come to our camp at night."

Come this place?

"Yes, this place. Gorillas come at night."

She thought that over. *No.*

Munro said, "What did she say?"

Elliot said, "She said 'No.' Yes, Amy, they come."

She was silent a moment, and then she signed, *Things come.*

Munro again asked what she had said.

"She said, 'Things come.' " Elliot translated the rest of her responses for them.

Ross asked, "What things, Amy?"

Bad things.

Munro said, "Were they gorillas, Amy?"

Not gorillas. Bad things. Many bad things come forest come. Breath talk. Come night come.

Munro said, "Where are they now, Amy?"

Amy looked around at the jungle. *Here. This bad old place things come.*

Ross said, "What things, Amy? Are they animals?"

Elliot told them that Amy could not abstract the category "animals." "She thinks people are animals," he explained. "Are the bad things people, Amy? Are they human persons?"

No.

Munro said, "Monkeys?"

No. Bad things, not sleep night.

Munro said, "Is she reliable?"

What means?

"Yes," Elliot said. "Perfectly."

"She knows what gorillas are?"

Amy good gorilla, she signed.

"Yes, you are," Elliot said. "She's saying she's a good gorilla."

Munro frowned. "So she knows what gorillas are, but she says these things are not gorillas?"

"That's what she says."

2. Missing Elements

Elliot got Ross to set up the video camera at the outskirts of the city, facing the campsite. With the videotape running he led Amy to the edge of the camp to look at the ruined buildings. Elliot wanted to confront Amy with the lost city, the reality behind her dreams—and he wanted a record of her responses to that moment. What happened was totally unexpected.

Amy had no reaction at all.

Her face remained impassive, her body relaxed. She did not sign. If anything she gave the impression of boredom, of suffering through another of Elliot's enthusiasms that she did not share. Elliot watched her carefully. She wasn't displacing; she wasn't repressing; she wasn't doing anything. She stared at the city with equanimity.

"Amy know this place?"

Yes.

"Amy tell Peter what place."

Bad place old place.
"Sleep pictures?"
This bad place.
"Why is it bad, Amy?"
Bad place old place.
"Yes but why, Amy?"
Amy fear.
She showed no somatic indication of fear. Squatting on the ground alongside him she gazed forward, perfectly calm.
"Why Amy fear?"
Amy want eat.
"Why Amy fear?"
She would not answer, in the way that she did not deign to answer him whenever she was completely bored; he could not provoke her to discuss her dreams further. She was as closed on the subject as she had been in San Francisco. When he asked her to accompany them into the ruins, she calmly refused to do so. On the other hand, she did not seem distressed that Elliot was going into the city, and she cheerfully waved goodbye before going to demand more food from Kahega.

Only after the expedition was concluded and Elliot had returned to Berkeley did he find the explanation to this perplexing event—in Freud's *Interpretation of Dreams*, first published in 1887.

> It may happen on rare occasions that a patient may be confronted by the reality behind his dreams. Whether a physical edifice, a person, or a situation that has the tenor of deep familiarity, the subjective response of the dreamer is uniformly the same. The emotive content held in the dream—whether frightening, pleasurable, or mysterious—is drained away upon sight of the reality. . . . We may be certain that the apparent boredom of the subject does not prove the dream-content is false.

Boredom may be most strongly felt when the dream-content is *real*. The subject recognizes on some deep level his inability to alter the conditions that he feels, and so finds himself overcome by fatigue, boredom, and indifference, to conceal from him *his fundamental helplessness in the face of a genuine problem which must be rectified.*

Months later, Elliot would conclude that Amy's bland reaction only indicated the depth of her feeling, and that Freud's analysis was correct; it protected her from a situation that had to be changed, but that Amy felt powerless to alter, especially considering whatever infantile memories remained from the traumatic death of her mother.

Yet at the time, Elliot felt disappointment with Amy's neutrality. Of all the possible reactions he had imagined when he first set out for the Congo, boredom was the least expected, and he utterly failed to grasp its significance—that the city of Zinj was so fraught with danger that Amy felt obliged in her own mind to push it aside, and to ignore it.

Elliot, Munro, and Ross spent a hot, difficult morning hacking their way through the dense bamboo and the clinging, tearing vines of secondary jungle growth to reach new buildings in the heart of the city. By midday, their efforts were rewarded as they entered structures unlike any they had seen before. These buildings were impressively engineered, enclosing vast cavernous spaces descending three and four stories beneath the ground.

Ross was delighted by the underground constructions, for it proved to her that the Zinj people had evolved the technology to dig into the earth, as was necessary for diamond mines.

Munro expressed a similar view: "These people," he said, "could do anything with earthworks."

Despite their enthusiasm, they found nothing of interest in the depths of the city. They ascended to higher levels later in the day, coming upon a building so filled with reliefs that they termed it "the gallery." With the video camera hooked to the satellite linkup, they examined the pictures in the gallery.

These showed aspects of ordinary city life. There were domestic scenes of women cooking around fires, children playing a ball game with sticks, scribes squatting on the ground as they kept records on clay tablets. A whole wall of hunting scenes, the men in brief loincloths, armed with spears. And finally scenes of mining, men carrying baskets of stones from tunnels in the earth.

In this rich panorama, they noticed certain missing elements. The people of Zinj had dogs, used for hunting, and a variety of civet cat, kept as household pets—yet it had apparently never occurred to them to use animals as beasts of burden. All manual labor was done by human slaves. And they apparently never discovered the wheel for there were no carts or rolling vehicles. Everything was carried by hand in baskets.

Munro looked at the pictures for a long time and finally said "Something else is missing."

They were looking at a scene from the diamond mines, the dark pits in the ground from which men emerged carrying baskets heaped with gems.

"Of course!" Munro said, snapping his fingers. "No police!"

Elliot suppressed a smile: he considered it only too predictable that a character like Munro would wonder about police in this long-dead society.

But Munro insisted his observation was significant. "Look here," he said. "This city existed because of its diamond mines. It had no other reason for being, out here in the jungle. Zinj was a mining civilization—its wealth, its trade, its daily life, everything depended upon mining. It was a classic one-crop economy—and yet they didn't guard it, didn't regulate it, didn't control it?"

Elliot said, "There are other things we haven't seen—pictures of people eating, for example. Perhaps it was taboo to show the guards."

"Perhaps," Munro said, unconvinced. "But in every other mining complex in the world guards are ostentatiously prominent, as proof of control. Go to the South African diamond mines or the Bolivian emerald mines and the first thing you are made aware of is the security. But here," he said, pointing to the reliefs, "*there are no guards.*"

Karen Ross suggested that perhaps they didn't need guards, perhaps the Zinjian society was orderly and peaceful. "After all, it was a long time ago," she said.

"Human nature doesn't change," Munro insisted.

When they left the gallery, they came to an open courtyard, overgrown with tangled vines. The courtyard had a formal quality, heightened by the pillars of a temple-like building to one side. Their attention was immediately drawn to the courtyard floor. Strewn across the ground were dozens of stone paddles, of the kind Elliot had previously found.

"I'll be damned," Elliot said. They picked their way through this field of paddles, and entered the building they came to call "the temple."

It consisted of a single large square room. The ceiling had been broken in several places, and hazy shafts of sunlight filtered down. Directly ahead, they saw an enormous mound of vines perhaps ten feet high, a pyramid of vegetation. Then they recognized that it was a statue.

Elliot climbed up on the statue and began stripping away the clinging foliage. It was hard work; the creepers had dug tenaciously into the stone. He glanced back at Munro. "Better?"

"Come and look," Munro said, with an odd expression on his face.

Elliot climbed down, stepped back to look. Although the statue was pitted and discolored, he could clearly see an enormous standing gorilla, the face fierce, the arms stretched wide. In each hand, the gorilla held stone paddles like cymbals, ready to swing them together.

"My God," Peter Elliot said.

"Gorilla," Munro said with satisfaction.

Ross said, "It's all clear now. These people worshiped gorillas. It was their religion."

"But why would Amy say they weren't gorillas?"

"Ask her," Munro said, glancing at his watch. "I have to get us ready for tonight."

3. Attack

They dug a moat outside the perimeter fence with collapsible metalloid shovels. The work continued long after sundown; they were obliged to turn on the red night lights while they filled the moat with water diverted from the nearby stream. Ross considered the moat a trivial obstacle—it was only a few inches deep and a foot wide. A man could step easily across it. In reply, Munro stood outside the moat and said, "Amy, come here, I'll tickle you."

With a delighted grunt, Amy came bounding toward him, but stopped abruptly on the other side of the water. "Come on, I'll tickle you," Munro said again, holding out his arms. "Come on, girl."

Still she would not cross. She signed irritably; Munro

stepped over and lifted her across. "Gorillas hate water," he told Ross. "I've seen them refuse to cross a stream smaller than this." Amy was reaching up and scratching under his arms, then pointing to herself. The meaning was perfectly clear. "Women," Munro sighed, and bent over and tickled her vigorously. Amy rolled on the ground, grunting and snuffling and smiling broadly. When he stopped, she lay expectantly on the ground, waiting for more.

"That's all," Munro said.

She signed to him.

"Sorry, I don't understand. No," he laughed, "signing slower doesn't help." And then he understood what she wanted, and he carried her back across the moat again, into the camp. She kissed him wetly on the cheek.

"Better watch your monkey," Munro said to Elliot as he sat down to dinner. He continued in this light bantering fashion, aware of the need to loosen everybody up; they were all nervous, crouching around the fire. But when the dinner was finished, and Kahega was off setting out the ammunition and checking the guns, Munro took Elliot aside and said, "Chain her in your tent. If we start shooting tonight, I'd hate to have her running around in the dark. Some of the lads may not be too particular about telling one gorilla from another. Explain to her that it may get very noisy from the guns but she should not be frightened."

"Is it going to get very noisy?" Elliot said.

"I imagine," Munro said.

He took Amy into his tent and put on the sturdy chain leash she often wore in California. He tied one end to his cot, but it was a symbolic gesture; Amy could move it easily if she chose to. He made her promise to stay in the tent.

She promised. He stepped to the tent entrance, and she signed, *Amy like Peter.*

"Peter like Amy," he said, smiling. "Everything's going to be fine."

. . .

He emerged into another world.

The red night lights had been doused, but in the flickering glow of the campfire he saw the goggle-eyed sentries in position around the compound. With the low throbbing pulse of the electrified fence, this sight created an unearthly atmosphere. Peter Elliot suddenly sensed the precariousness of their position—a handful of frightened people deep in the Congo rain forest, more than two hundred miles from the nearest human habitation.

Waiting.

He tripped over a black cable on the ground. Then he saw a network of cables, snaking over the compound, running to the guns of each sentry. He noticed then that the guns had an unfamiliar shape—they were somehow too slender, too insubstantial—and that the black cables ran from the guns to squat, snub-nosed mechanisms mounted on short tripods at intervals around the camp.

He saw Ross near the fire, setting up the tape recorder. "What the hell is all this?" he whispered, pointing to the cables.

"That's a LATRAP. For laser-tracking projectile," she whispered. "The LATRAP system consists of multiple LGSDs attached to sequential RFSDs."

She told him that the sentries held guns which were actually laser-guided sight devices, linked to rapid-firing sensor devices on tripods. "They lock onto the target," she said, "and do the actual shooting once the target is identified. It's a jungle warfare system. The RFSDs have marlan-baffle silencers so the enemy won't know where the firing is coming from. Just make sure you don't step in front of one, because they automatically lock onto body heat."

Ross gave him the tape recorder, and went off to check the fuel cells powering the perimeter fence. Elliot glanced at the sentries in the outer darkness; Munro waved cheerfully to him. Elliot realized that the sentries with their grasshopper goggles and their acronymic weapons could see him far better that he could see them. They looked like beings from another universe, dropped into the timeless jungle.

Waiting.

The hours passed. The jungle perimeter was silent except for the murmur of water in the moat. Occasionally the porters called to one another softly, making some joke in Swahili; but they never smoked because of the heat-sensing machinery. Eleven o'clock passed, and then midnight, and then one o'clock.

He heard Amy snoring in his tent, her noisy rasping audible above the throb of the electrified fence. He glanced over at Ross sleeping on the ground, her finger on the switch for the night lights. He looked at his watch and yawned; nothing was going to happen tonight; Munro was wrong.

Then he heard the breathing sound.

The sentries heard it too, swinging their guns in the darkness. Elliot pointed the recorder microphone toward the sound but it was hard to determine its exact location. The wheezing sighs seemed to come from all parts of the jungle at once, drifting with the night fog, soft and pervasive.

He watched the needles wiggle on the recording gauges. And then the needles bounced into the red, as Elliot heard a dull thud, and the gurgle of water. Everyone heard it; the sentries clicked off their safeties.

Elliot crept with his tape recorder toward the perimeter fence and looked out at the moat. Foliage moved beyond the fence. The sighing grew louder. He heard the gurgle of water and saw a dead tree trunk lying across the moat.

That was what the slapping sound had been: a bridge being placed across the moat. In that instant Elliot realized they had vastly underestimated whatever they were up against. He signaled Munro to come and look, but Munro was waving

him away from the fence and pointing emphatically to the
squat tripod on the ground near his feet. Before Elliot could
move, the colobus monkeys began to shriek in the trees overhead—and the first of the gorillas silently charged.

He had a glimpse of an enormous animal, distinctly gray
in color, racing up to him as he ducked down; a moment later,
the gorilla hit the electrified fence with a shower of spitting
sparks and the odor of burning flesh.

It was the start of an eerie, silent battle.

Emerald laser beams flashed through the air; the tripod-
mounted machine guns made a soft *thew-thew-thew* as the
bullets spit outward, the aiming mechanisms whining as the
barrels spun and fired, spun and fired again. Every tenth
bullet was a white phosphorous tracer; the air was crisscrossed
green and white over Elliot's head.

The gorillas attacked from all directions; six of them simultaneously hit the fence and were repelled in a crackling
burst of sparks. Still more charged, throwing themselves on
the flimsy perimeter mesh, yet the sizzle of sparks and the
shriek of the colobus monkeys was the loudest sound they
heard. And then he saw gorillas in the trees overhanging the
campsite. Munro and Kahega began firing upward, silent laser
beams streaking into the foliage. He heard the sighing sound
again. Elliot turned and saw more gorillas tearing at the
fence, which had gone dead—there were no more sparks.

And he realized that this swift, sophisticated equipment
was not holding the gorillas back—they needed the noise.
Munro had the same thought, because he shouted in Swahili
for the men to hold their fire, and called to Elliot, "Pull the
silencers! The silencers!"

Elliot grabbed the black barrel on the first tripod mechanism and plucked it away, swearing—it was very hot. Immediately as he stepped away from the tripod, a stuttering sound
filled the air, and two gorillas fell heavily from the trees, one
still alive. The gorilla charged him as he pulled away the si-

lencer from the second tripod. The stubby barrel swung around and blasted the gorilla at very close range; warm liquid spattered Elliot's face. He pulled the silencer from the third tripod and threw himself to the ground.

Deafening machine-gun fire and clouds of acrid cordite had an immediate effect on the gorillas; they backed off in disorder. There was a period of silence, although the sentries fired laser shots that sent the tripod machines scanning rapidly across the jungle landscape, whirring back and forth, searching for a target.

Then the machines stopped hunting, and paused. The jungle around them was still.

The gorillas were gone.

DAY 11: ZINJ
June 23, 1979

1. Gorilla Elliotensis

The gorilla corpses lay stretched on the ground, the bodies already stiffening in the morning warmth. Elliot spent two hours examining the animals, both adult males in the prime of life.

The most striking feature was the uniform gray color. The two known races of gorilla, the mountain gorilla in Virunga, and the lowland gorilla near the coast, both had black hair. Infants were often brown with a white tuft of hair at the rump, but their hair darkened within the first five years. By the age of twelve, adult males had developed the silver patch along their back and rump, the sign of sexual maturity.

With age, gorillas turned gray—as did people—in much the same way. Male gorillas first developed a spot of gray above each ear, and as the years passed more body hair turned gray. Old animals in their late twenties and thirties sometimes turned entirely gray except for their arms, which remained black.

But from their teeth Elliot estimated that these males were no more than ten years old. All their pigmentation seemed lighter, eye and skin color as well as hair. Gorilla skin was black, and eyes were dark brown. But here the pigmentation was distinctly gray, and the eyes were light yellow brown.

As much as anything it was the eyes that set him thinking.

Next Elliot measured the bodies. The crown-heel length

was 139.2 and 141.7 centimeters. Male mountain gorillas had been recorded from 147 to 205 centimeters, with an average height of 175 centimeters—five feet eight inches. But these animals stood about four feet six inches tall. They were distinctly small for gorillas. He weighed them: 255 pounds and 347 pounds. Most mountain gorillas weighed between 280 and 450 pounds.

Elliot recorded thirty additional skeletal measurements for later analysis by the computer back in San Francisco. Because now he was convinced that he was onto something. With a knife, he dissected the head of the first animal, cutting away the gray skin to reveal the underlying muscle and bone. His interest was the sagittal crest, the bony ridge running along the center of the skull from the forehead to the back of the neck. The sagittal crest was a distinctive feature of gorilla skull architecture not found in other apes or man; it was what gave gorillas a pointy-headed look.

Elliot determined that the sagittal crest was poorly developed in these males. In general, the cranial musculature resembled a chimpanzee's far more than a gorilla's. Elliot made additional measurements of the molar cusps, the jaw, the simian shelf, and the brain case.

By midday, his conclusion was clear: this was at least a new race of gorilla, equal to the mountain and lowland gorilla —and it was possibly a new species of animal entirely.

"Something happens to the man who discovers a new species of animal," wrote Lady Elizabeth Forstmann in 1879. "At once he forgets his family and friends, and all those who were near and dear to him; he forgets colleagues who supported his professional efforts; most cruelly he forgets parents and children; in short, he abandons all who knew him prior to his insensate lust for fame at the hands of the demon called Science."

Lady Forstmann understood, for her husband had just left her after discovering the Norwegian blue-crested grouse in 1878. "In vain," she observed, "does one ask what it matters that another bird or animal is added to the rich panoply of God's creations, which already number—by Linnaean reckoning—in the millions. There is no response to such a question, for the discoverer has joined the ranks of the immortals, at least as he imagines it, and he lies beyond the power of mere people to dissuade him from his course."

Certainly Peter Elliot would have denied that his own behavior resembled that of the dissolute Scottish nobleman.* Nevertheless he found he was bored by the prospect of further exploration of Zinj; he had no interest in diamonds, or Amy's dreams; he wished only to return home with a skeleton of the new ape, which would astonish colleagues around the world. He suddenly remembered he did not own a tuxedo, and he found himself preoccupied with matters of nomenclature; he imagined in future three species of African apes:

> *Pan troglodytes*, the chimpanzee.
> *Gorilla gorilla*, the gorilla.
> *Gorilla elliotensis*, a new species of gray gorilla.

Even if the species category and name were ultimately rejected, he would have accomplished far more than most scientists studying primates could ever hope to achieve.

Elliot was dazzled by his own prospects.

In retrospect, no one was thinking clearly that morning. When Elliot said he wanted to transmit the recorded breathing sounds to Houston, Ross replied it was a trivial detail that could wait. Elliot did not press her; they both later regretted their decision.

---

* Sir Antony Forstmann died of gambling debts and syphilis in 1880.

And when they heard booming explosions like distant artillery fire that morning, they paid no attention. Ross assumed it was General Muguru's men fighting the Kigani. Munro told her that the fighting was at least fifty miles away, too far for the sound to carry, but offered no alternative explanation for the noise.

And because Ross skipped the morning transmission to Houston, she was not informed of new geological changes that might have given new significance to the explosive detonations.

They were seduced by the technology employed the night before, secure in their sense of indomitable power. Only Munro remained immune. He had checked their ammunition supplies with discouraging results. "That laser system is splendid but it uses up bullets like there's no tomorrow," Munro said. "Last night consumed half of our total ammunition."

"What can we do?" Elliot asked.

"I was hoping you'd have an answer for that," Munro said. "You examined the bodies."

Elliot stated his belief that they were confronted with a new species of primate. He summarized the anatomical findings, which supported his beliefs.

"That's all well and good," Munro said. "But I'm interested in how they act, not how they look. You said it yourself —gorillas are usually diurnal animals, and these are nocturnal. Gorillas are usually shy and avoid men, while these are aggressive and attack men fearlessly. Why?"

Elliot had to admit that he didn't know.

"Considering our ammunition supplies, I think we'd better find out," Munro said.

2. The Temple

The logical place to begin was the temple, with its enormous, menacing gorilla statue. They returned that afternoon, and found behind the statue a succession of small cubicle-like rooms. Ross thought that priests who worshiped the cult of the gorilla lived here.

She had an elaborate explanation: "The gorillas in the surrounding jungle terrorized the people of Zinj, who offered sacrifices to appease the gorillas. The priests were a separate class, secluded from society. Look here, at the entrance to the line of cubicles, there is this little room. A guard stayed here to keep people away from the priests. It was a whole system of belief."

Elliot was not convinced, and neither was Munro. "Even religion is practical," Munro said. "It's supposed to benefit you."

"People worship what they fear," Ross said, "hoping to control it."

"But how could they control the gorillas?" Munro asked. "What could they do?"

When the answer finally came it was startling, for they had it all backward.

They moved past the cubicles to a series of long corridors, decorated with bas-reliefs. Using their infrared computer system, they were able to see the reliefs, which were scenes arranged in a careful order like a picture textbook.

The first scene showed a series of caged gorillas. A black man stood near the cages holding a stick in his hand.

The second picture showed an African standing with two gorillas, holding ropes around their necks.

A third showed an African instructing the gorillas in a

courtyard. The gorillas were tethered to vertical poles, each with a ring at the top.

The final picture showed the gorillas attacking a line of straw dummies, which hung from an overhead stone support. They now knew the meaning of what they had found in the courtyard of the gymnasium, and the jail.

"My God," Elliot said. "They *trained* them."

Munro nodded. "Trained them as guards to watch over the mines. An animal élite, ruthless and incorruptible. Not a bad idea when you think about it."

Ross looked at the building around her again, realizing it wasn't a temple but a school. An objection occurred to her: these pictures were hundreds of years old, the trainers long gone. Yet the gorillas were still here. "Who teaches them now?"

"They do," Elliot said. "They teach each other."

"Is that possible?"

"Perfectly possible. Conspecific teaching occurs among primates."

This had been a longstanding question among researchers. But Washoe, the first primate in history to learn sign language, taught ASL to her offspring. Language-skilled primates freely taught other animals in captivity; for that matter, they would teach people, signing slowly and repeatedly until the stupid uneducated human person got the point.

So it was possible for a primate tradition of language and behavior to be carried on for generations. "You mean," Ross said, "that the people in this city have been gone for centuries, but the gorillas they trained are still here?"

"That's the way it looks," Elliot said.

"And they use stone tools?" she asked. "Stone paddles?"

"Yes," Elliot said. The idea of tool use was not as far-fetched as it first seemed. Chimpanzees were capable of elaborate tool use, of which the most striking example was "termite fishing." Chimps would make a twig, carefully bending it to their specifications, and then spend hours over a termite mound, fishing with the stick to catch succulent grubs.

Human observers labeled this activity "primitive tool use" until they tried it themselves. It turned out that making a satisfactory twig and catching termites was not primitive at all; at least it proved to be beyond the ability of people who tried to duplicate it. Human fishermen quit, with a new respect for the chimpanzees, and a new observation—they now noticed that younger chimps spent days watching their elders make sticks and twirl them in the mound. Young chimps literally *learned* how to do it, and the learning process extended over a period of years.

This began to look suspiciously like culture; the apprenticeship of young Ben Franklin, printer, was not so different from the apprenticeship of young Chimpanzee, termite fisher. Both learned their skills over a period of years by observing their elders; both made mistakes on the way to ultimate success.

Yet manufactured stone tools implied a quantum jump beyond twigs and termites. The privileged position of stone tools as the special province of mankind might have remained sacrosanct were it not for a single iconoclastic researcher. In 1971, the British scientist R. V. S. Wright decided to teach an ape to make stone tools. His pupil was a five-year-old orangutan named Abang in the Bristol zoo. Wright presented Abang with a box containing food, bound with a rope; he showed Abang how to cut the rope with a flint chip to get the food. Abang got the point in an hour.

Wright then showed Abang how to make a stone chip by striking a pebble against a flint core. This was a more difficult lesson; over a period of weeks, Abang required a total of three hours to learn to grasp the flint core between his toes, strike a sharp chip, cut the rope, and get the food.

The point of the experiment was not that apes used stone tools, but that the ability to make stone tools was literally within their grasp. Wright's experiment was one more reason to think that human beings were not as unique as they had previously imagined themselves to be.

"But why would Amy say they weren't gorillas?"

"Because they're not," Elliot said. "These animals don't look like gorillas and they don't act like gorillas. They are physically and behaviorally different." He went on to voice his suspicion that not only had these animals been trained, they had been *bred*—perhaps interbred with chimpanzees or, more strangely still, with men.

They thought he was joking. But the facts were disturbing. In 1960, the first blood protein studies quantified the kinship between man and ape. Biochemically man's nearest relative was the chimpanzee, much closer than the gorilla. In 1964, chimpanzee kidneys were successfully transplanted into men; blood transfusions were also possible.

But the degree of similarity was not fully known until 1975, when biochemists compared the DNA of chimps and men. It was discovered that chimps differed from men by only 1 percent of their DNA strands. And almost no one wanted to acknowledge one consequence: with modern DNA hybridization techniques and embryonic implantation, ape-ape crosses were certain, and man-ape crosses were possible.

Of course, the fourteenth-century inhabitants of Zinj had no way to mate DNA strands. But Elliot pointed out that they had consistently underestimated the skills of the Zinj people, who at the very least had managed, five hundred years ago, to carry out sophisticated animal-training procedures only duplicated by Western scientists within the last ten years.

And as Elliot saw it, the animals the Zinjians had trained presented an awesome problem.

"We have to face the realities," he said. "When Amy was given a human IQ test, she scored ninety-two. For all practical purposes, Amy is as smart as a human being, and in many ways she is smarter—more perceptive and sensitive. She can manipulate us at least as skillfully as we can manipulate her.

"These gray gorillas possess that same intelligence, yet they have been single-mindedly bred to be the primate equivalent of Doberman pinschers—guard animals, attack animals, trained for cunning and viciousness. But they are much brighter and more resourceful than dogs. And they will continue their attacks until they succeed in killing us all, as they have killed everyone who has come here before."

3.
Looking Through the Bars

In 1975, the mathematician S. L. Berensky reviewed the literature on primate language and reached a startling conclusion. "There is no doubt," he announced, "that primates are far superior in intelligence to man."

In Berensky's mind, "The salient question—which every human visitor to the zoo intuitively asks—is, who is behind the bars? Who is caged, and who is free? . . . On both sides of the bars primates can be observed making faces at each other. It is too facile to say that man is superior because he has made the zoo. We impose our special horror of barred captivity—a form of punishment among our species—and assume that other primates feel as we do."

Berensky likened primates to foreign ambassadors. "Apes have for centuries managed to get along with human beings, as ambassadors from their species. In recent years, they have even learned to communicate with human beings using sign language. But it is a one-sided diplomatic exchange; no human being has attempted to live in ape society, to master their language and customs, to eat their food, to live as they do. The apes have learned to talk to us, but we have never learned to talk to them. Who, then, should be judged the greater intellect?"

Berensky added a prediction. "The time will come," he said, "when circumstances may force some human beings to communicate with a primate society on its own terms. Only then human beings will become aware of their complacent egotism with regard to other animals."

The ERTS expedition, isolated deep in the Congo rain forest, now faced just such a problem. Confronted by a new species of gorilla-like animal, they somehow had to deal with it on its own terms.

During the evening, Elliot transmitted the taped breath sounds to Houston, and from there they were relayed to San Francisco. The transcript which followed the transmission was brief:

Seamans wrote: RECVD TRNSMISN. SHLD HELP.

IMPORTNT–NEED TRNSLATION SOON, Elliot typed back. WHN HAVE?

COMPUTR ANALYSS DIFICLT–PROBLMS XCEED MGNITUDE CSL / JSL TRNSLATN.

"What does that mean?" Ross said.

"He's saying that the translation problems exceed the problem of translating Chinese or Japanese sign language."

She hadn't known there was a Chinese or Japanese sign language, but Elliot explained that there were sign languages for all major languages, and each followed its own rules. For instance, BSL, British sign language, was totally different from ASL, American sign language, even though spoken and written English language was virtually identical in the two countries.

Different sign languages had different grammar and syntax, and even obeyed different sign traditions. Chinese sign language used the middle finger pointing outward for several signs, such as TWO WEEKS FROM NOW and BROTHER, although this configuration was insulting and unacceptable in American sign language.

"But this is a spoken language," Ross said.

"Yes," Elliot said, "but it's a complicated problem. We aren't likely to get it translated soon."

By nightfall, they had two additional pieces of information. Ross ran a computer simulation through Houston which came back with a probability course of three days and a standard deviation of two days to find the diamond mines. That meant they should be prepared for five more days at the site. Food was not a problem, but ammunition was: Munro proposed to use tear gas.

They expected the gray gorillas to try a different approach, and they did, attacking immediately after dark. The battle on the night of June 23 was punctuated by the coughing explosions of canisters and the sizzling hiss of the gas. The strategy was effective; the gorillas were driven away, and did not return again that night.

Munro was pleased. He announced that they had enough tear gas to hold off the gorillas for a week, perhaps more. For the moment, their problems appeared to be solved.

DAY 12: ZINJ
June 24, 1979

1. The Offensive

Shortly after dawn, they discovered the bodies of Mulewe and Akari near their tent. Apparently the attack the night before had been a diversion, allowing one gorilla to enter the compound, kill the porters, and slip out again. Even more disturbing, they could find no clue to how the gorilla had got through the electrified fence and back out again.

A careful search revealed a section of fence torn near the bottom. A long stick lay on the ground nearby. The gorillas had used the stick to lift the bottom of the fence, enabling one to crawl through. And before leaving, the gorillas had carefully restored the fence to its original condition.

The intelligence implied by such behavior was hard to accept. "Time and again," Elliot said later, "we came up against our prejudices about animals. We kept expecting the gorillas to behave in stupid, stereotyped ways but they never did. We never treated them as flexible and responsive adversaries, though they had already reduced our numbers by one fourth."

Munro had difficulty accepting the calculated hostility of the gorillas. His experience had taught him that animals in nature were indifferent to man. Finally he concluded that "these animals had been trained by men, and I had to think

of them as men. The question became what would I do if they
were men?"

For Munro the answer was clear: take the offensive.

Amy agreed to lead them into the jungle where she said the
gorillas lived. By ten o'clock that morning, they were moving
up the hillsides north of the city armed with machine guns. It
was not long before they found gorilla spoor—quantities of
dung, and nests on the ground and in the trees. Munro was
disturbed by what he saw; some trees held twenty or thirty
nests, suggesting a large population of animals.

Ten minutes later, they came upon a group of ten gray
gorillas feeding on succulent vines: four males and three females, a juvenile, and two scampering infants. The adults were
lazy, basking in the sun, eating in desultory fashion. Several
other animals slept on their backs, snoring loudly. They all
seemed remarkably unguarded.

Munro gave a hand signal; the safeties clicked off the
guns. He prepared to fire into the group when Amy tugged at
his trouser leg. He looked off and "had the shock of my bloody
life. Up the slope was another group, perhaps ten or twelve
animals—and then I saw another group—and another—and
another still. There must have been three hundred or more.
The hillside was *crawling* with gray gorillas."

The largest gorilla group ever sighted in the wild had been
thirty-one individuals, in Kabara in 1971, and even that sighting was disputed. Most researchers thought it was actually two
groups seen briefly together, since the usual group size was
ten to fifteen individuals. Elliot found three hundred animals
"an awesome sight." But he was even more impressed by the
behavior of the animals. As they browsed and fed in the sun-

light, they behaved very much like ordinary gorillas in the wild, but there were important differences.

"From the first sighting, I never had any doubt that they had language. Their wheezing vocalizations were striking and clearly constituted a form of language. In addition they used sign language, although nothing like what we knew. Their hand gestures were delivered with outstretched arms in a graceful way, rather like Thai dancers. These hand movements seemed to complement or add to the sighing vocalizations. Obviously the gorillas had been taught, or had elaborated on their own, a language system far more sophisticated than the pure sign language of laboratory apes in the twentieth century."

Some abstract corner of Elliot's mind considered this discovery tremendously exciting, while at the same time he shared the fear of the others around him. Crouched behind the dense foliage they held their breath and watched the gorillas feed on the opposite hillside. Although the gorillas seemed peaceful, the humans watching them felt a tension approaching panic at being so close to such great numbers of them. Finally, at Munro's signal, they slipped back down the trail, and returned to the camp.

The porters were digging graves for Akari and Mulewe in camp. It was a grim reminder of their jeopardy as they discussed their alternatives. Munro said to Elliot, "They don't seem to be aggressive during the day."

"No," Elliot said. "Their behavior looks quite typical—if anything, it's more sluggish than that of ordinary gorillas in daytime. Probably most of the males are sleeping during the day."

"How many animals on the hillside are males?" Munro asked. They had already concluded that only male animals participated in the attacks; Munro was asking for odds.

Elliot said, "Most studies have found that adult males

constitute fifteen percent of gorilla groupings. And most studies show that isolated observations underestimate troop size by twenty-five percent. There are more animals than you see at any given moment."

The arithmetic was disheartening. They had counted three hundred gorillas on the hillside, which meant there were probably four hundred, of which 15 percent were males. That meant that there were sixty attacking animals—and only nine in their defending group.

"Hard," Munro said, shaking his head.

Amy had one solution. She signed, *Go now.*

Ross asked what she said and Elliot told her, "She wants to leave. I think she's right."

"Don't be ridiculous," Ross said. "We haven't found the diamonds. We can't leave now."

Go now, Amy signed again.

They looked at Munro. Somehow the group had decided that Munro would make the decision of what to do next. "I want the diamonds as much as anyone," he said. "But they won't be much use to us if we're dead. We have no choice. We must leave if we can."

Ross swore, in florid Texan style.

Elliot said to Munro, "What do you mean, if we can?"

"I mean," Munro said, "that they may not let us leave."

2. Departure

Following Munro's instructions, they carried only minimal supplies of food and ammunition. They left everything else— the tents, the perimeter defenses, the communications equipment, everything, in the sunlit clearing at midday.

Munro glanced back over his shoulder and hoped he was doing the right thing. In the 1960s, the Congo mercenaries had had an ironic rule: "Don't leave home." It had multiple meanings, including the obvious one that none of them should ever have come to the Congo in the first place. It also meant that once established in a fortified camp or colonial town you were unwise to step out into the surrounding jungle, whatever the provocation. Several of Munro's friends had bought it in the jungle because they had foolishly left home. The news would come to them: "Digger bought it last week outside Stanleyville." "Outside? Why'd he leave home?"

Munro was leading the expedition outside now, and home was the little silver camp with its perimeter defense behind them. Back in that camp, they were sitting ducks for the attacking gorillas. The mercenaries had had something to say about that, too: "Better a sitting duck than a dead duck."

As they marched through the rain forest, Munro was painfully aware of the single-file column strung out behind him, the least defensible formation. He watched the jungle foliage move in as their path narrowed. He did not remember this track being so narrow when they had come to the city. Now they were hemmed in by close ferns and spreading palms. The gorillas might be only a few feet away, concealed in the dense foliage, and they wouldn't know it until it was too late.

They walked on.

Munro thought if they could reach the eastern slopes of Mukenko, they would be all right. The gray gorillas were localized near the city, and would not follow them far. One or two hours walking, and they would be beyond danger.

He checked his watch: they had been gone ten minutes.

And then he heard the sighing sound. It seemed to come from all directions. He saw the foliage moving before him, shifting as if blown by a wind. Only there was no wind. He heard the sighing grow louder.

The column halted at the edge of a ravine, which followed a streambed past sloping jungle walls on both sides. It was the perfect spot for an ambush. Along the line he heard the safeties click on the machine guns. Kahega came up. "Captain, what do we do?"

Munro watched the foliage move, and heard the sighing. He could only guess at the numbers concealed in the bush. Twenty? Thirty? Too many, in any case.

Kahega pointed up the hillside to a track that ran above the ravine. "Go up there?"

For a long time, Munro did not answer. Finally, he said, "No, not up there."

"Then where, Captain?"

"Back," Munro said. "We go back."

When they turned away from the ravine, the sighing faded and the foliage ceased its movement. When he looked back over his shoulder for a last glimpse, the ravine appeared an ordinary passage in the jungle, without threat of any kind. But Munro knew the truth. They could not leave.

3. Return

Elliot's idea came in a flash of insight. "In the middle of the camp," he later related, "I was looking at Amy signing to Kahega. Amy was asking him for a drink, but Kahega didn't know Ameslan, and he kept shrugging helplessly. It occurred to me that the linguistic skill of the gray gorillas was both their great advantage and their Achilles' heel."

Elliot proposed to capture a single gray gorilla, learn its language, and use that language to establish communication with the other animals. Under normal circumstances it would take several months to learn a new ape language, but Elliot thought he could do it in a matter of hours.

Seamans was already at work on the gray-gorilla verbalizations; all he needed was further input. But Elliot had decided that the gray gorillas employed a combination of spoken sounds and sign language. And the sign language would be easy to work out.

Back at Berkeley, Seamans had developed a computer program called APE, for animal pattern explanation. APE was capable of observing Amy and assigning meanings to her signs. Since the APE program utilized declassified army software subroutines for code-breaking, it was capable of identifying new signs, and translating these as well. Although APE was intended to work with Amy in ASL, there was no reason why it would not work with an entirely new language.

If they could forge satellite links from the Congo to Houston to Berkeley, they could feed video data from a captive animal directly into the APE program. And APE promised a speed of translation far beyond the capacity of any human observer. (The army software was designed to break enemy codes in minutes.)

Elliot and Ross were convinced it would work; Munro was not. He made some disparaging comments about interrogating prisoners of war. "What do you intend to do," he said, "torture the animal?"

"We will employ situational stress," Elliot said, "to elicit language usage." He was laying out test materials on the ground: a banana, a bowl of water, a piece of candy, a stick, a succulent vine, stone paddles. "We'll scare the hell out of her if we have to."

"Her?"

"Of course," Elliot said, loading the Thoralen dart gun. "Her."

4. Capture

He wanted a female without an infant. An infant would create difficulties.

Pushing through waist-high undergrowth, he found himself on the edge of a sharp ridge and saw nine animals grouped below him: two males, five females, and two juveniles. They were foraging through the jungle twenty feet below. He watched the group long enough to be sure that all the females used language, and that there were no infants concealed in the foliage. Then he waited for his chance.

The gorillas fed casually among the ferns, plucking up tender shoots, which they chewed lazily. After several minutes, one female moved up from the group to forage nearer the top of the ridge where he was crouching. She was separated from the rest of the group by more than ten yards.

Elliot raised the dart pistol in both hands and squinted down the sight at the female. She was perfectly positioned. He watched, squeezed the trigger slowly—and lost his footing on the ridge. He fell crashing down the slope, right into the midst of the gorillas.

Elliot lay unconscious on his back, twenty feet below, but his chest was moving, and his arm twitched; Munro felt certain that he was all right. Munro was only concerned about the gorillas.

The gray gorillas had seen Elliot fall and now moved toward the body. Eight or nine animals clustered around him, staring impassively, signing.

Munro slipped the safety off his gun.

Elliot groaned, touched his head, and opened his eyes. Munro saw Elliot stiffen as he saw the gorillas, but he did not move. Three mature males crouched very close to him, and he understood the precariousness of his situation. Elliot lay motionless on the ground for nearly a minute. The gorillas whispered and signed, but they did not come any closer.

Finally Elliot sat up on one elbow, which caused a burst of signing but no direct threatening behavior.

On the hillside above, Amy tugged at Munro's sleeve, signing emphatically. Munro shook his head: he did not understand; he raised his machine gun again, and Amy bit his kneecap. The pain was excruciating. It was all Munro could do to keep from screaming.

Elliot, lying on the ground below, tried to control his breathing. The gorillas were very close—close enough for him to touch them, close enough to smell the sweet, musty odor of their bodies. They were agitated; the males had started grunting, a rhythmic *ho-ho-ho.*

He decided he had better get to his feet, slowly and methodically. He thought that if he could put some distance between himself and the animals, their sense of threat would be reduced. But as soon as he began to move the grunting grew louder, and one of the males began a sideways crablike movement, slapping the ground with his flat palms.

Immediately Elliot lay back down. The gorillas relaxed, and he decided he had done the correct thing. The animals were confused by this human being crashing down in their midst; they apparently did not expect contact with men in foraging areas.

He decided to wait them out, if necessary remaining on his back for several hours until they lost interest and moved off. He breathed slowly, regularly, aware that he was sweating. Probably he smelled of fear—but like men, gorillas had a poorly developed sense of smell. They did not react to the odor of fear. He waited. The gorillas were sighing and signing swiftly, trying to decide what to do. Then one male abruptly resumed his crabwise movements, slapping the ground and staring at Elliot. Elliot did not move. In his mind, he reviewed the stages of attack behavior: grunting, sideways movement, slapping, tearing up grass, beating chest—

Charging.

The male gorilla began tearing up grass. Elliot felt his heart pounding. The gorilla was a huge animal, easily three hundred pounds. He reared up on his hind legs and beat his chest with flat palms, making a hollow sound. Elliot wondered what Munro was doing above. And then he heard a crash, and he looked up to see Amy tumbling down the hillside, breaking her fall by grabbing at branches and ferns. She landed at Elliot's feet.

The gorillas could not have been more surprised. The large male ceased beating his chest, dropped down from his upright posture, and glowered at Amy.

Amy grunted.

The large male moved menacingly toward Peter, but he never took his eyes off Amy. Amy watched him without response. It was a clear test of dominance. The male moved closer and closer, without hesitation—

Amy bellowed, a deafening sound; Elliot jumped in surprise. He had only heard her do it once or twice before in moments of extreme rage. It was unusual for females to roar, and the other gorillas were alarmed. Amy's forearms stiffened, her back went rigid, her face became tense. She stared aggressively at the male and roared again.

The male paused, tilted his head to one side. He seemed to be thinking it over. Finally he backed off, rejoining the semicircle of gray apes around Elliot's head.

Amy deliberately rested her hand on Elliot's leg, establishing possession. A juvenile male, four or five years old, impulsively scurried forward, baring his teeth. Amy slapped him across the face, and the juvenile whined and scrambled back to the safety of his group.

Amy glowered at the other gorillas. And then she began signing. *Go away leave Amy go away.*

The gorillas did not respond.

Peter good human person. But she seemed to be aware that the gorillas did not understand, for she then did something remarkable: she sighed, making the same wheezing sound that the gorillas made.

The gorillas were startled, and stared at one another.

But if Amy was speaking their language, it was without effect: they remained where they were. And the more she sighed, the more their reaction diminished, until finally they stared blandly at her.

She was not getting through to them.

Amy now came alongside Peter's head and began to groom him, plucking at his beard and scalp. The gray gorillas signed rapidly. Then the male began his rhythmic *ho-ho-ho* once more. When she saw this Amy turned to Peter and signed, *Amy hug Peter*. He was surprised: Amy never volunteered to hug Peter. Ordinarily she only wanted Peter to hug and tickle Amy.

Elliot sat up and she immediately pulled him to her chest, pressing his face into her hair. At once the male gorilla ceased grunting. The gray gorillas began to backpedal, as if they had committed some error. In that moment, Elliot understood: *she was treating him like her infant.*

This was classic primate behavior in aggressive situations. Primates carried strong inhibitions against harming infants, and this inhibition was invoked by adult animals in many contexts. Male baboons often ended their fight when one male grabbed an infant and clutched it to his chest; the sight of the small animal inhibited further attack. Chimpanzees showed more subtle variations of the same thing. If juvenile chimp play turned too brutal, a male would grab one juvenile and clutch it maternally, even though in this case both parent and child were symbolic. Yet the posture was sufficient to evoke the inhibition against further violence. In this case Amy was not only halting the male's attack but protecting Elliot as well, by treating him as an infant—if the gorillas would accept a bearded six-foot-tall infant.

They did.

They disappeared back into the foliage. Amy released Elliot

from her fierce grip. She looked at him and signed, *Dumb things.*

"Thank you, Amy," he said and kissed her.

Peter tickle Amy Amy good gorilla.

"You bet," he said, and he tickled her for the next several minutes, while she rolled on the ground, grunting happily.

It was two o'clock in the afternoon when they returned to camp. Ross said, "Did you get a gorilla?"

"No," Elliot said.

"Well, it doesn't matter," Ross said, "because I can't raise Houston."

Elliot was stunned: "More electronic jamming?"

"Worse than that," Ross said. She had spent an hour trying to establish a satellite link with Houston, and had failed. Each time the link was broken within seconds. Finally, after confirming that there was no fault with her equipment, she had checked the date. "It's June 24," she said. "And we had communications trouble with the last Congo expedition on May 28. That's twenty-seven days ago."

When Elliot still didn't get it, Munro said, "She's telling you it's solar."

"That's right," Ross said. "This is an ionospheric disturbance of solar origin." Most disruptions of the earth's ionosphere—the thin layer of ionized molecules 50–250 miles up—were caused by phenomena such as sunspots on the surface of the sun. Since the sun rotated every twenty-seven days, these disturbances often recurred a month later.

"Okay," Elliot said, "it's solar. How long will it last?"

Ross shook her head. "Ordinarily, I would say a few hours, a day at most. But this seems to be a severe disturbance and it's come up very suddenly. Five hours ago we had perfect communications—and now we have none at all. Something unusual is going on. It could last a week."

"No communications for a week? No computer tie-ins, no nothing?"

"That's right," Ross said evenly. "From this moment on, we are entirely cut off from the outside world."

5. Isolation

The largest solar flare of 1979 was recorded on June 24, by the Kitt Peak Observatory near Tucson, Arizona, and duly passed on to the Space Environment Services Center in Boulder, Colorado. At first the SESC did not believe the incoming data: even by the gigantic standards of solar astronomy, this flare, designated 78/06/414aa, was a monster.

The cause of solar flares in unknown, but they are generally associated with sunspots. In this case the flare appeared as an extremely bright spot ten thousand miles in diameter, affecting not only alpha hydrogen and ionized calcium spectral lines but also the white light spectrum from the sun. Such a "continuous spectrum" flare was extremely rare.

Nor could the SESC believe the computed consequences. Solar flares release an enormous amount of energy; even a modest flare can double the amount of ultraviolet radiation emitted by the entire solar surface. But flare 78/06/414aa was almost *tripling* ultraviolet emissions. Within 8.3 minutes of its first appearance along the rotating rim—the time it takes light to reach the earth from the sun—this surge of ultraviolet radiation began to disrupt the ionosphere of the earth.

The consequence of the flare was that radio communications on a planet ninety-three million miles away were seriously disrupted. This was especially true for radio transmissions which utilized low signal strengths. Commercial radio stations generating kilowatts of power were hardly inconvenienced, but the Congo Field Survey, transmitting signals on the order of twenty thousand watts, was unable to establish satellite links. And since the solar flare also ejected X-rays and atomic particles which would not reach the earth for a full day, the radio disruption would last at least one day, and perhaps longer. At ERTS in Houston, technicians reported to Travis that the SESC predicted a time course of ionic disruption of four to eight days.

"You mean we're going to be out of contact with them for four to eight days?" Travis said.

"That's how it looks. Ross'll probably figure it out," the technician said, "when she can't re-establish today."

"They need that computer hookup," Travis said. The ERTS staff had run five computer simulations and the outcome was always the same—short of airlifting in a small army, Ross's expedition was in serious trouble. Survival projections were running "point two four four and change" —only one chance in four that the Congo expedition would get out alive, assuming the help of the computer link which was now broken.

Travis wondered if Ross and the others realized how grave their situation was. "Any new Band Five on Mukenko?" Travis asked.

Band 5 on Landsat satellites recorded infrared data. On its last pass over the Congo, Landsat had acquired significant new information on Mukenko. The volcano had become much hotter in the nine days since the previous Landsat pass; the temperature increase was on the order of 8 degrees.

"Nothing new," the technician said. "And the computers don't project an eruption. Four degrees of orbital change are within sensor error on that system, and the additional four degrees have no predictive value."

"Well, that's something," Travis said. "But what are they going to do about the apes now that they're cut off from the computer?"

. . .

That was the question the Congo Field Survey had been asking themselves for the better part of an hour. With communications disrupted the only computers available were the computers in their own heads. And those computers were not powerful enough. Elliot found it strange to think that his own brain was inadequate. "We had all become accustomed to the availability of computing power," he said later. "In any decent laboratory you can get all the memory and all the computation speed you could want, day or night. We were so used to it we had come to take it for granted."

Of course they could have eventually worked out the ape language, but they were up against a time factor: they didn't have months to puzzle it out; they had hours. Cut off from the APE program their situation was ominous. Munro said that they could not survive another night of frontal attack, and they had every reason to expect an attack that night.

Amy's rescue of Elliot suggested their plan. Amy had shown some ability to communicate with the gorillas; perhaps she could translate for them as well. "It's worth a try," Elliot insisted.

Unfortunately, Amy herself denied that this was possible. In response to the question "Amy talk thing talk?" she signed, *No talk.*

"Not at all?" Elliot said, remembering the way she had sighed. "Peter see Amy talk thing talk."

No talk. Make noise.

He concluded from this that she was able to mimic the gorilla verbalizations but had no knowledge of their meaning. It was now past two; they had only four or five hours until nightfall.

Munro said, "Give it up. She obviously can't help us."

Munro preferred to break camp and fight their way out in day-light. He was convinced that they could not survive another night among the gorillas.

But something nagged at Elliot's mind.

After years of working with Amy, he knew she had the maddening literal-mindedness of a child. With Amy, especially when she was feeling uncooperative, it was necessary to be exact to elicit the appropriate response. Now he looked at Amy and said, "Amy talk thing talk?"

No talk.

"Amy understand thing talk?"

Amy did not answer. She was chewing on vines, preoc-cupied.

"Amy, listen to Peter."

She stared at him.

"Amy understand thing talk?"

Amy understand thing talk, she signed back. She did it so matter-of-factly that at first he wondered if she realized what he was asking her.

"Amy watch thing talk, Amy understand talk?"

Amy understand.

"Amy sure?"

Amy sure.

"I'll be goddamned," Elliot said.

Munro was shaking his head. "We've only got a few hours of daylight left," he said. "And even if you do learn their lan-guage, how are you going to talk to them?"

6. Amy Talk Thing Talk

At 3 p.m., Elliot and Amy were completely concealed in the foliage along the hillside. The only sign of their presence was the slender cone of the microphone that protruded through the foliage. The microphone was connected to the videotape recorder at Elliot's feet, which he used to record the sounds of the gorillas on the hills beyond.

The only difficulty was trying to determine which gorilla the directional microphone had focused on—and which gorilla Amy had focused on, and whether they were the same gorilla. He could never be quite sure that Amy was translating the verbal utterances of the same animal that he was recording. There were eight gorillas in the nearest group and Amy kept getting distracted. One female had a six-month-old infant, and at one point, when the baby was bitten by a bee, Amy signed, *Baby mad.* But Elliot was recording a male.

Amy, he signed. Pay attention.

Amy pay attention. Amy good gorilla.

Yes, he signed. Amy good gorilla. Amy pay attention man thing.

Amy not like.

He swore silently, and erased half an hour of translations from Amy. She had obviously been paying attention to the wrong gorilla. When he started the tape again, he decided that this time he would record whatever Amy was watching. He signed, What thing Amy watch?

Amy watch baby.

That wouldn't work, because the baby didn't speak. He signed, Amy watch woman thing.

Amy like watch baby.

This dependency on Amy was like a bad dream. He was in the hands of an animal whose thinking and behavior he barely understood; he was cut off from the wider society of human beings and human machinery, thus increasing his dependency on the animal; and yet he had to trust her.

After another hour, with the sunlight fading, he took Amy back down the hillside to the camp.

. . .

Munro had planned as best he could.

First he dug a series of holes like elephant traps outside the camp; they were deep pits lined with sharp stakes, covered with leaves and branches.

He widened the moat in several places, and cleared away dead trees and underbrush that might be used as bridges.

He cut down the low tree branches overhanging the camp, so that if gorillas went into the trees, they would be kept at least thirty feet above the ground—too high to jump down.

He gave three of the remaining porters, Muzezi, Amburi, and Harawi, shotguns along with a supply of tear-gas canisters.

With Ross, he boosted power on the perimeter fence to almost 200 amps. This was the maximum the thin mesh could handle without melting; they had been obliged to reduce the pulses from four to two per second. But the additional current changed the fence from a deterrent to a lethal barrier. The first animals to hit that fence would be immediately killed, although the likelihood of shorts and a dead fence was considerably increased.

At sunset, Munro made his most difficult decision. He loaded the stubby tripod-mounted RFSDs with half their remaining ammunition. When that was gone, the machines would simply stop firing. From that point on, Munro was counting on Elliot and Amy and their translation.

And Elliot did not look very happy when he came back down the hill.

7. Final Defense

"How long until you're ready?" Munro asked him.

"Couple of hours, maybe more." Elliot asked Ross to help him, and Amy went to get food from Kahega. She seemed

very proud of herself, and behaved like an important person in
the group.

Ross said, "Did it work?"

"We'll know in a minute," Elliot said. His first plan was
to run the only kind of internal check on Amy that he could,
by verifying repetitions of sounds. If she had consistently translated sounds in the same way, they would have a reason for
confidence.

But it was painstaking work. They had only the half-inch
VTR and the small pocket tape recorder; there were no con-
necting cables. They called for silence from the others in the
camp and proceeded to run the checks, taping, retaping, listening to the whispering sounds.

At once they found that their ears simply weren't capable
of discriminating the sounds—everything sounded the same.
Then Ross had an idea.

"These sounds taped," she said, "as electrical signals."

"Yes . . ."

"Well, the linkup transmitter has a 256K memory."

"But we can't link up to the Houston computer."

"I don't mean that," Ross said. She explained that the
satellite linkup was made by having the 256K computer onsite match an internally generated signal—like a video test
pattern—to a transmitted signal from Houston. That was how
they locked on. The machine was built that way, but they
could use the matching program for other purposes.

"You mean we can use it to compare these sounds?" Elliot
said.

They could, but it was incredibly slow. They had to transfer the taped sounds to the computer memory, and rerecord
it in the VTR, on another portion of the tape bandwidth.
Then they had to input that signal into the computer memory,
and run a second comparison tape on the VTR. Elliot found
that he was standing by, watching Ross shuffle tape cartridges

and mini floppy discs. Every half hour, Munro would wander over to ask how it was coming; Ross became increasingly snappish and irritable. "We're going as fast as we can," she said.

It was now eight o'clock.

But the first results were encouraging: Amy was indeed consistent in her translations. By nine o'clock they had quantified matching on almost a dozen words:

FOOD	.9213	.112
EAT	.8844	.334
WATER	.9978	.004
DRINK.	.7743	.334
{AFFIRMATION} YES	.6654	.441
{NEGATION} NO	.8883	.220
COME	.5459	.440
GO	.5378	.404
SOUND COMPLEX: ? AWAY	.5444	.343
SOUND COMPLEX: ? HERE	.6344	.344
SOUND COMPLEX: ? ANGER		
? BAD	.4232	.477

Ross stepped away from the computer. "All yours," she said to Elliot.

Munro paced across the compound. This was the worst time. Everyone waiting, on edge, nerves shot. He would have joked with Kahega and the other porters, but Ross and Elliot needed silence for their work. He glanced at Kahega.

Kahega pointed to the sky and rubbed his fingers together. Munro nodded.

He had felt it too, the heavy dampness in the air, the almost palpable feeling of electrical charge. Rain was coming. That was all they needed, he thought. During the afternoon, there had been more booming and distant explosions, which he had thought were far-off lightning storms. But the sound was not right; these were sharp, single reports, more like a sonic boom than anything else. Munro had heard them before, and he had an idea about what they meant.

He glanced up at the dark cone of Mukenko, and the faint glow of the Devil's Eye. He looked at the crossed green laser beams overhead. And he noticed one of the beams was moving where it struck foliage in the trees above.

At first he thought it was an illusion, that the leaf was moving and not the beam. But after a moment he was sure: the beam itself was quivering, shifting up and down in the night air.

Munro knew this was an ominous development, but it would have to wait until later; at the moment, there were more pressing concerns. He looked across the compound at Elliot and Ross bent over their equipment, talking quietly and in general behaving as if they had all the time in the world.

Elliot actually was going as fast as he could. He had eleven reliable vocabulary words recorded on tape. His problem now was to compose an unequivocal message. This was not as easy as it first appeared.

For one thing, the gorilla language was not a pure verbal language. The gorillas used sign and sound combinations to convey information. This raised a classic problem in language structure—how was the information actually conveyed? (L. S. Verinski once said that if alien visitors watched Italians speaking they would conclude that Italian was basically a gestural sign language, with sounds added for emphasis only.) Elliot needed a simple message that did not depend on accompanying hand signs.

But he had no idea of gorilla syntax, which could critically alter meaning in most circumstances—the difference between "me beat" and "beat me." And even a short message could be ambiguous in another language. In English, "Look out!" generally meant the opposite of its literal meaning.

Faced with these uncertainties, Elliot considered broadcasting a single word. But none of the words on his list was suitable. His second choice was to broadcast several short messages, in case one was inadvertently ambiguous. He eventually decided on three messages: GO AWAY, NO COME, and BAD HERE; two of these combinations had the virtue of being essentially independent of word order.

By nine o'clock, they had already isolated the specific sound components. But they still had a complicated task ahead. What Elliot needed was a loop, repeating the sounds over and over. The closest they would come was the VCR, which rewound automatically to play its message again. He could hold the six sounds in the 256K memory and play them out, but the timing was critical. For the next hour, they frantically punched buttons, trying to bring the word combinations close enough together to sound—to their ears—correct.

By then it was after ten.

Munro came over with his laser gun. "You think all this will work?"

Elliot shook his head. "There's no way to know." A dozen objections had come to mind. They had recorded a female voice, but would the gorillas respond to a female? Would they accept voice sounds without accompanying hand signals? Would the message be clear? Would the spacing of the sounds be acceptable? Would the gorillas pay attention at all?

There was no way to know. They would simply have to try.

Equally uncertain was the problem of broadcasting. Ross had made a speaker, removing the tiny speaker from the pocket tape recorder and gluing it to an umbrella on a collapsible tripod. This makeshift speaker produced surprisingly loud volume, but reproduction was muffled and unconvincing.

Shortly afterward, they heard the first sighing sounds.

. . .

Munro swung the laser gun through the darkness, the red activation light glowing on the electronic pod at the end of the barrel. Through his night goggles he surveyed the foliage. Once again, the sighing came from all directions; and although he heard the jungle foliage shifting, he saw no movement close to the camp. The monkeys overhead were silent. There was only the soft, ominous sighing. Listening now, Munro was convinced that the sounds represented a language of some form, and—

A single gorilla appeared and Kahega fired, his laser beam streaking arrow-straight through the night. The RFSD chattered and the foliage snapped with bullets. The gorilla ducked silently back into a stand of dense ferns.

Munro and the others quickly took positions along the perimeter, crouching tensely, the infrared night lights casting their shadows on the mesh fence and the jungle beyond.

The sighing continued for several minutes longer, and then slowly faded away, until all was silent again.

"What was that about?" Ross said.

Munro frowned. "They're waiting."

"For what?"

Munro shook his head. He circled the compound, looking at the other guards, trying to work it out. Many times he had anticipated the behavior of animals—a wounded leopard in the bush, a cornered buffalo—but this was different. He was forced to admit he didn't know what to expect. Had the single gorilla been a scout to look at their defenses? Or had an attack actually begun, only for some reason to be halted? Was it a maneuver designed to fray nerves? Munro had watched parties of hunting chimpanzees make brief threatening forays toward baboons, to raise the anxiety level of the entire troop before the actual assault, isolating some young animal for killing.

Then he heard the rumble of thunder. Kahega pointed to the sky, shaking his head. That was their answer.

"Damn," Munro said.

At 10:30 a torrential tropical rain poured down on them. Their fragile speaker was immediately soaked and drooping. The rain shorted the electrical cables and the perimeter fence went dead. The night lights flickered, and two bulbs exploded. The ground turned to mud; visibility was reduced to five yards. And worst of all, the rain splattering the foliage was so noisy they had to shout to each other. The tapes were unfinished; the loudspeaker probably would not work, and certainly would not carry over the rain. The rain would interfere with the lasers and prevent the dispersal of tear gas. Faces in camp were grim.

Five minutes later, the gorillas attacked.

The rain masked their approach; they seemed to burst out of nowhere, striking the fence from three directions simultaneously. From that first moment, Elliot realized the attack would be unlike the others. The gorillas had learned from the earlier assaults, and now were intent on finishing the job.

Primate attack animals, trained for cunning and viciousness: even though that was Elliot's own assessment, he was astonished to see the proof in front of him. The gorillas charged in waves, like disciplined shock troops. Yet he found it more horrifying than an attack by human troops. To them we are just animals, he thought. An alien species, for which they have no feeling. We are just pests to be eliminated.

These gorillas did not care why human beings were there, or what reasons had brought them to the Congo. They were not killing for food, or defense, or protection of their young. They were killing because they were trained to kill.

The attack proceeded with stunning swiftness. Within seconds, the gorillas had breached the perimeter and trampled the mesh fence into the mud. Unchecked, they rushed into the compound, grunting and roaring. The driving rain matted their hair, giving them a sleek, menacing appearance in the red night lights. Elliot saw ten or fifteen animals inside the compound, trampling the tents and attacking the people. Azizi was killed immediately, his skull crushed between paddles.

Munro, Kahega, and Ross all fired laser bursts, but in the confusion and poor visibility their effectiveness was limited. The laser beams fragmented in the slashing rain; the tracer bullets hissed and sputtered. One of the RFSDs went haywire, the barrel swinging in wide arcs, bullets spitting out in all directions, while everyone dived into the mud. Several gorillas were killed by the RFSD bursts, clutching their chests in a bizarre mimicry of human death.

Elliot turned back to the recording equipment and Amy flung herself on him, panicked, grunting in fear. He pushed her away and switched on the tape replay.

By now the gorillas had overwhelmed everyone in the camp. Munro lay on his back, a gorilla on top of him. Ross was nowhere to be seen. Kahega had a gorilla clinging to his chest as he rolled in the mud. Elliot was hardly aware of the hideous scratching sounds now emanating from the loudspeaker, and the gorillas themselves paid no attention.

Another porter, Muzezi, screamed as he stepped in front of a firing RFSD; his frame shook with the impact of the bullets and he fell backward to the ground, his body smoking from the tracers. At least a dozen gorillas were dead or lying wounded in the mud, groaning. The haywire RFSD had run out of ammunition; the barrel swung back and forth, the empty chamber clicking. A gorilla kicked it over, and it lay writhing on its side in the mud like a living thing as the barrel continued to swing.

Elliot saw one gorilla crouched over, methodically tearing a tent apart, shredding the silver Mylar into strips. Across

the camp, another arrival banged aluminum cook pans together, as if they were metal paddles. More gorillas poured
into the compound, ignoring the rasping broadcast sounds.
He saw a gorilla pass beneath the loudspeaker, very close, and
pay no attention at all. Elliot had the sickening realization
that their plan had failed.

They were finished; it was only a matter of time.

A gorilla charged him, bellowing in rage, swinging stone
paddles wide. Terrified, Amy threw her hands over Elliot's
eyes. "Amy!" he shouted, pulling her fingers away, expecting
to feel at any moment the impact of the paddles and the instant of blinding pain.

He saw the gorilla bearing down on him. He tensed his
body. Six feet away, the charging gorilla stopped so abruptly
that he literally skidded in the mud and fell backward. He sat
there surprised, cocking his head, listening.

Then Elliot realized that the rain had nearly stopped, that
there was now only a light drizzle sifting down over the campsite. Looking across the compound, Elliot saw another gorilla
stop to listen—then another—and another—and another.
The compound took on the quality of a frozen tableau, as the
gorillas stood silent in the mist.

They were listening to the broadcast sounds.

He held his breath, not daring to hope. The gorillas
seemed uncertain, confused by the sounds they heard. Yet
Elliot sensed that at any moment they could arrive at some
group decision and resume their attack with the same intensity
as before.

That did not happen. The gorillas stepped away from the
people, listening. Munro scrambled to his feet, raising his gun
from the mud. But he did not shoot; the gorilla standing over
him seemed to be in a trance, to have forgotten all about the
attack.

In the gentle rain, with the flickering night lights, the gorillas moved away, one by one. They seemed perplexed, off balance. The rasping continued over the loudspeaker.

The gorillas left, moving back across the trampled perimeter fence, disappearing once more into the jungle. And then the expedition members were alone, staring at each other, shivering in the misty rain. The gorillas were gone.

Twenty minutes later, as they were trying to rebuild their shattered campsite, the rain poured down again with unabated fury.

DAY 13: MUKENKO

June 25, 1979

1. Diamonds

In the morning a fine layer of black ash covered the campsite, and in the distance Mukenko was belching great quantities of black smoke. Amy tugged at Elliot's sleeve.

Leave now, she signed insistently.

"No, Amy," he said.

Nobody in the expedition was in a mood to leave, including Elliot. Upon arising, he found himself thinking of additional data he needed before leaving Zinj. Elliot was no longer satisfied with a skeleton of one of these creatures; like men, their uniqueness went beyond the details of physical structure to their behavior. Elliot wanted videotapes of the gray apes, and more recordings of verbalizations. And Ross was more determined than ever to find the diamonds, with Munro no less interested.

Leave now.

"Why leave now?" he asked her.

Earth bad. Leave now.

Elliot had no experience with volcanic activity, but what he saw did not impress him. Mukenko was more active than it had been in previous days, but the volcano had ejected smoke and gas since their first arrival in Virunga.

He asked Munro, "Is there any danger?"

Munro shrugged. "Kahega thinks so, but he probably just wants an excuse to go home."

Amy came running over to Munro raising her arms, slapping them down on the earth in front of him. Munro recognized this as her desire to play; he laughed and began to tickle Amy. She signed to him.

"What's she saying?" Munro asked. "What are you saying, you little devil?"

Amy grunted with pleasure, and continued to sign.

"She says leave now," Elliot translated.

Munro stopped tickling her. "Does she?" he asked sharply. "What *exactly* does she say?"

Elliot was surprised at Munro's seriousness—although Amy accepted his interest in her communication as perfectly proper. She signed again, more slowly, for Munro's benefit, her eyes on his face.

"She says the earth is bad."

"Hmm," Munro said. "Interesting." He glanced at Amy and then at his watch.

Amy signed, *Nosehair man listen Amy go home now.*

"She says you listen to her and go home now," Elliot said.

Munro shrugged. "Tell her I understand."

Elliot translated. Amy looked unhappy, and did not sign again.

"Where is Ross?" Munro asked.

"Here," Ross said.

"Let's get moving," Munro said, and they headed for the lost city. Now they had another surprise—Amy signed she was coming with them, and she hurried to catch up with them.

This was their final day in the city, and all the participants in the Congo expedition described a similar reaction: the city, which had been so mysterious before, was somehow stripped of its mystery. On this morning, they saw the city for what it was: a cluster of crumbling old buildings in a hot stinking uncomfortable jungle.

They all found it tedious, except for Munro. Munro was worried.

Elliot was bored, talking about verbalizations and why he wanted tape recordings, and whether it was possible to preserve a brain from one of the apes to take back with them. It seemed there was some academic debate about where language came from; people used to think language was a development of animal cries, but now they knew that animal barks and cries were controlled by the limbic system of the brain, and that real language came from some other part of the brain called Broca's area. . . . Munro couldn't pay attention. He kept listening to the distant rumbling of Mukenko.

Munro had firsthand experience with volcanoes; he had been in the Congo in 1968, when Mbuti, another of the Virunga volcanoes, erupted. When he had heard the sharp explosions the day before, he had recognized them as brontides, the unexplained accompaniments of coming earthquakes. Munro had assumed that Mukenko would soon erupt, and when he had seen the flickering laser beam the night before, he had known there was new rumbling activity on the upper slopes of the volcano.

Munro knew that volcanoes were unpredictable—as witnessed by the fact that this ruined city at the base of an active volcano had been untouched after more than five hundred years. There were recent lava fields on the mountain slopes above, and others a few miles to the south, but the city itself was spared. This in itself was not so remarkable—the configuration of Mukenko was such that most eruptions occurred on the gentle south slopes. But it did not mean that they were now in any less danger. The unpredictability of volcanic eruptions meant that they could become life-threatening in a matter of minutes. The danger was not from lava, which rarely flowed faster than a man could walk; it would take hours for lava to flow down from Mukenko's summit. The real danger from volcanic eruptions was ash and gas.

Just as most people killed by fires actually died from smoke inhalation, most deaths from volcanoes were caused by asphyxiation from dust and carbon monoxide. Volcanic gases were heavier than air; the Lost City of Zinj, located in a valley, could be filled in minutes with a heavy, poisonous atmosphere, should Mukenko discharge a large quantity of gas.

The question was how rapidly Mukenko was building toward a major eruptive phase. That was why Munro was so interested in Amy's reactions: it was well known that primates could anticipate geological events such as earthquakes and eruptions. Munro was surprised that Elliot, babbling away about freezing gorilla brains, didn't know about that. And he was even more surprised that Ross, with her extensive geological knowledge, did not regard the morning ashfall as the start of a major volcanic eruption.

Ross knew a major eruption was building. That morning, she had routinely tried to establish contact with Houston; to her surprise, the transmission keys immediately locked through. After the scrambler notations registered, she began typing in field updates, but the screen went blank, and flashed:

HUSTN STATN OVRIDE CLR BANX.

This was an emergency signal; she had never seen it before on a field expedition. She cleared the memory banks and pushed the transmit button. There was a burst transmission delay, then the screen printed:

COMPUTR DESIGNATN MAJR ERUPTN SIGNATR MUKENKO ADVIS LEAV SITE NOW EXPEDN JEPRDY DANGR REPET ALL LEAV SITE NOW.

Ross glanced across the campsite. Kahega was making breakfast; Amy squatted by the fire, eating a roasted banana (she had got Kahega to make special treats for her); Munro and Elliot were having coffee. Except for the black ashfall, it was a perfectly normal morning at the camp. She looked back at the screen.

MAJR ERUPTN SIGNATR MUKENKO ADVIS LEAV SITE NOW.

Ross glanced up at the smoking cone of Mukenko. The hell with it, she thought. She wanted the diamonds, and she had gone too far to quit now.

The screen blinked: PLS SIGNL REPLY.

Ross turned the transmitter off.

As the morning progressed they felt several sharp jolting earth tremors, which released clouds of dust from the crumbling buildings. The rumblings of Mukenko became more frequent. Ross paid no attention. "It just means this is elephant country," she said. That was an old geological adage: "If you're looking for elephants, go to elephant country." Elephant country meant a likely spot to find whatever minerals you were looking for. "And if you want diamonds," Ross said, shrugging, "you go to volcanoes."

The association of diamonds with volcanoes had been recognized for more than a century, but it was still poorly understood. Most theories postulated that diamonds, crystals of pure carbon, were formed in the intense heat and pressure of the upper mantle one thousand miles beneath the earth's surface. The diamonds remained inaccessible at this depth except in volcanic areas where rivers of molten magma carried them to the surface.

But this did not mean that you went to erupting volcanoes to catch diamonds being spewed out. Most diamond mines were at the site of extinct volcanoes, in fossilized cones called kimberlite pipes, named for the geological formations in Kimberley, South Africa. Virunga, near the geologically unstable Rift Valley, showed evidence of continuous volcanic activity for more than fifty million years. They were now looking for the same fossil volcanoes which the earlier inhabitants of Zinj had found.

Shortly before noon they found them, halfway up the hills east of the city—a series of excavated tunnels running into the mountain slopes of Mukenko.

Elliot felt disappointed. "I don't know what I was expecting," he said later, "but it was just a brown-colored tunnel in the earth, with occasional bits of dull brown rock sticking out. I couldn't understand why Ross got so excited." Those bits of dull brown rock were diamonds; when cleaned, they had the transparency of dirty glass.

"They thought I was crazy," Ross said, "because I began jumping up and down. But they didn't know what they were looking at."

In an ordinary kimberlite pipe, diamonds were distributed sparsely in the rock matrix. The average mine recovered only thirty-two karats—a fifth of an ounce—for every hundred tons of rock removed. When you looked down a diamond mineshaft, you saw no diamonds at all. But the Zinj mines were lumpy with protruding stones. Using his machete, Munro dug out six hundred karats. And Ross saw six or seven stones protruding from the wall, each as large as the one Munro had removed. "Just looking," she said later, "I could see easily four or five thousand karats. With no further digging, no separation, nothing. Just sitting there. It was a richer mine than the Premier in South Africa. It was *unbelievable*."

Elliot asked the question that had already formed in Ross's

own mind. "If this mine is so damn rich," he said, "why was it abandoned?"

"The gorillas got out of control," Munro said. "They staged a coup." He was laughing, plucking diamonds out of the rock.

Ross had considered that, as she had considered Elliot's earlier suggestion that the city had been wiped out by disease. She thought a less exotic explanation was likely. "I think," she said, "that as far as they were concerned, the diamond mines had dried up." Because as gemstones, these crystals were very poor indeed—blue, streaked with impurities.

The people of Zinj could not have imagined that five hundred years in the future these same worthless stones would be more scarce and desirable than any other mineral resources on the planet.

"What makes these blue diamonds so valuable?"

"They are going to change the world," Ross said, in a soft voice. "They are going to end the nuclear age."

2.
War at the Speed of Light

In January, 1979, testifying before the Senate Armed Services Subcommittee, General Franklin F. Martin of the Pentagon Advanced Research Project Agency said, "In 1939, at the start of World War II, the most important country in the world to the American military effort was the Belgian Congo." Martin explained that as a kind of "accident of geography" the Congo, now Zaire, has for forty years remained vital to American interests—and will assume even more importance in the future. (Martin said bluntly that "this country will go to war over Zaire before we go to war over any Arab oil state.")

During World War II, in three highly secret shipments,

the Congo supplied the United States with uranium used to build the atomic bombs exploded over Japan. By 1960 the U.S. no longer needed uranium, but copper and cobalt were strategically important. In the 1970s the emphasis shifted to Zaire's reserves of tantalum, wolframite, germanium—substances vital to semiconducting electronics. And in the 1980s, "so-called Type IIb blue diamonds will constitute the most important military resource in the world"—and the presumption was that Zaire had such diamonds. In General Martin's view, blue diamonds were essential because "we are entering a time when the brute destructive power of a weapon will be less important than its speed and intelligence."

For thirty years, military thinkers had been awed by intercontinental ballistic missiles. But Martin said that "ICBMs are crude weapons. They do not begin to approach the theoretical limits imposed by physical laws. According to Einsteinian physics, nothing can happen faster than the speed of light, 186,000 miles a second. We are now developing high-energy pulsed lasers and particle beam weapons systems which operate *at the speed of light*. In the face of such weapons, ballistic missiles travelling a mere 17,000 miles an hour are slow-moving dinosaurs from a previous era, as inappropriate as cavalry in World War I, and as easily eliminated."

Speed-of-light weapons were best suited to space, and would first appear in satellites. Martin noted that the Russians had made a "kill" of the American spy satellite VV/02 as early as 1973; in 1975, Hughes Aircraft developed a rapid aiming and firing system which locked onto multiple targets, firing eight high-energy pulses in less than one second. By 1978, the Hughes team had reduced response time to fifty nanoseconds—fifty billionths of a second—and increased beam accuracy to five hundred missile knockdowns in less than one minute. Such developments presaged the end of the ICBM as a weapon.

"Without the gigantic missiles, miniature, high-speed computers will be vastly more important in future conflicts than nuclear bombs, and their speed of computation will be the single most important factor determining the outcome of World War III. Computer speed now stands at the center of the armament race, as megaton power once held the center twenty years ago.

"We will shift from electronic circuit computers to light circuit computers simply because of speed—the Fabry-Perot Interferometer, the optical equivalent of a transistor, can respond in 1 picosecond (10^{-12} seconds), at least 1,000 times faster than the fastest Josephson junctions." The new generation of optical computers, Martin said, would be dependent on the availability of Type IIb boron-coated diamonds.

Elliot recognized at once the most serious consequence of the speed-of-light weapons—they were much too fast for human comprehension. Men were accustomed to mechanized warfare, but a future war would be a war of machines in a startlingly new sense: machines would actually govern the moment-to-moment course of a conflict which lasted only minutes from start to finish.

In 1956, in the waning years of the strategic bomber, military thinkers imagined an all-out nuclear exchange lasting 12 hours. By 1963, ICBMs had shrunk the time course to 3 hours. By 1974, military theorists were predicting a war that lasted just 30 minutes, yet this "half-hour war" was vastly more complex than any earlier war in human history.

In the 1950s, if the Americans and the Russians launched all their bombers and rockets at the same moment, there would still be no more than 10,000 weapons in the air, attacking and counterattacking. Total weapons interaction events would peak at 15,000 in the second hour. This represented the impressive figure of 4 weapons interactions every second around the world.

But given diversified tactical warfare, the number of weapons and "systems elements" increased astronomically. Modern estimates imagined 400 million computers in the field, with total weapons interactions at more than 15 billion in the first half hour of war. This meant there would be 8 million weapons interactions every second, in a bewildering ultra-fast conflict of aircraft, missiles, tanks, and ground troops.

Such a war was only manageable by machines; human response times were simply too slow. World War III would not be a push-button war because as General Martin said, "It takes too long for a man to push the button—at least 1.8 seconds, which is an eternity in modern warfare."

This fact created what Martin called the "rock problem." Human responses were geologically slow, compared to a high-speed computer. "A modern computer performs 2,000 calculations in the time it takes a man to blink. Therefore, from the point of view of computers fighting the next war, human beings will be essentially fixed and unchanging elements, like rocks. Human wars have never lasted long enough to take into account the rate of geological change. In the future, computer wars will not last long enough to take into account the rate of human change."

Since human beings responded too slowly, it was necessary for them to relinquish decision-making control of the war to the faster intelligence of computers. "In the coming war, we must abandon any hope of regulating the course of the conflict. If we decide to 'run' the war at human speed, we will almost surely lose. Our only hope is to put our trust in machines. This makes human judgment, human values, human thinking utterly superfluous. World War III will be war by proxy: a pure war of machines, over which we dare exert no influence for fear of so slowing the decision-making mechanism as to cause our defeat." And the final, crucial transition—the transition from computers working at nanoseconds to computers working at picoseconds—was dependent on Type IIb diamonds.

Elliot was appalled by this prospect of turning control over to the creations of men.

Ross shrugged. "It's inevitable," she said. "In Olduvai Gorge in Tanzania, there are traces of a house two million years old. The hominid creature wasn't satisfied with caves and other natural shelters; he created his own accommodations. Men have always altered the natural world to suit their purposes."

"But you can't give up control," Elliot said.

"We've been doing it for centuries," Ross said. "What's a domesticated animal—or a pocket calculator—except an attempt to give up control? We don't want to plow fields or do square roots so we turn the job over to some other intelligence, which we've trained or bred or created."

"But you can't let your creations take over."

"We've been doing it for centuries," Ross repeated. "Look: even if we refused to develop faster computers, the Russians would. They'd be in Zaire right now looking for diamonds, if the Chinese weren't keeping them out. You can't stop technological advances. As soon as we know something is possible, we have to carry it out."

"No," Elliot said. "We can make our own decisions. I won't be a part of this."

"Then leave," she said. "The Congo's no place for academics, anyway."

She began unpacking her rucksack, taking out a series of white ceramic cones, and a number of small boxes with antennae. She attached a box to each ceramic cone, then entered the first tunnel, placing the cones flat against the walls, moving deeper into darkness.

Peter not happy Peter.

"No," Elliot said.

Why not happy?

"It's hard to explain, Amy," he said.

Peter tell Amy good gorilla.

"I know, Amy."

Karen Ross emerged from one tunnel, and disappeared into the second. Elliot saw the glow of her flashlight as she placed the cones, and then she was hidden from view.

Munro came out into the sunlight, his pockets bulging with diamonds. "Where's Ross?"

"In the tunnels."

"Doing what?"

"Some kind of explosive test, looks like." Elliot gestured to three remaining ceramic cones on the ground near her pack.

Munro picked up one cone, and turned it over. "Do you know what these are?" he asked.

Elliot shook his head.

"They're RCs," Munro said, "and she's out of her mind to place them here. She could blow the whole place apart."

Resonant conventionals, or RCs, were timed explosives, a potent marriage of microelectronics and explosive technology. "We used RCs two years ago on bridges in Angola," Munro explained. "Properly sequenced, six ounces of explosive can bring down fifty tons of braced structural steel. You need one of those sensors"—he gestured to a control box lying near her pack—"which monitors shock waves from the early charges, and detonates the later charges in the timed sequence to set up resonating waves which literally shake the structure to pieces. Very impressive to see it happen." Munro glanced up at Mukenko, smoking above them.

At that moment, Ross emerged from the tunnel, all smiles. "We'll soon have our answers," she said.

"Answers?"

"About the extent of the kimberlite deposits. I've set twelve seismic charges, which is enough to give us definitive readings."

"You've set twelve *resonant* charges," Munro said.

"Well, they're all I brought. We've got to make do."

"They'll do," Munro said. "Perhaps too well. That volcano"—he pointed upwards—"is in an eruptive phase."

"I've placed a total of eight hundred grams of explosive," Ross said. "That's less than a pound and a half. It can't make the slightest difference."

"Let's not find out."

Elliot listened to their argument with mixed feelings. On the face of it, Munro's objections seemed absurd—a few trivial explosive charges, however timed, could not possibly trigger a volcanic eruption. It was ridiculous; Elliot wondered why Munro was so adamant about the dangers. It was almost as if Munro knew something that Elliot and Ross did not—and could not even imagine.

3.
DOD/ARPD/VULCAN 7021

In 1978, Munro had led a Zambia expedition which included Robert Perry, a young geologist from the University of Hawaii. Perry had worked on PROJECT VULCAN, the most advanced program financed under the Department of Defense Advanced Research Project Division.

VULCAN was so controversial that during the 1975 House Armed Services Subcommittee hearings, project DOD/ARPD/VULCAN 7021 was carefully buried among "miscellaneous long-term fundings of national security significance." But the following year, Congressman David Inaga (D., Hawaii) challenged DOD/ARPD/VULCAN, demanding to know "its exact military purpose, and why it should be funded entirely within the state of Hawaii."

Pentagon spokesmen explained blandly that VULCAN was a "tsunami warning system" of value to the residents of the Hawaiian islands, as well as to military installations there. Pentagon experts reminded Inaga that in 1948 a tsunami had swept across the Pacific Ocean, first devastating Kauai, but moving so swiftly along the Hawaiian island chain that when it struck Oahu and Pearl Harbor twenty minutes later, no effective warning had been given.

"That tsunami was triggered by an underwater volcanic avalanche off the coast of Japan," they said. "But Hawaii has its own active volcanoes, and now Honolulu is a city of half a million, and naval presence valued at more than thirty-five billion dollars, the ability to predict tsunami activity secondary to eruptions by Hawaiian volcanoes assumes major long-term significance."

In truth, PROJECT VULCAN was not long-term at all; it was intended to be carried out at the next eruption of Mauna Loa, the largest active volcano in the world, located on the big island of Hawaii. The designated purpose of VULCAN was to control volcanic eruptions as they progressed; Mauna Loa was chosen because its eruptions were relatively mild and gentle.

Although it rose to an altitude of only 13,500 feet, Mauna Loa was the largest mountain in the world. Measured from its origin at the depths of the ocean floor, Mauna Loa had more than twice the cubic volume of Mount Everest; it was a unique and extraordinary geological formation. And Mauna Loa had long since become the most carefully studied volcano in history, having a permanent scientific observation station on its crater since 1928. It was also the most interfered-with volcano in history, since the lava that flowed down its slopes at three-year intervals had been diverted by everything from aerial bombers to local crews with shovels and sandbags.

VULCAN intended to alter the course of a Mauna Loa eruption by "venting" the giant volcano, releasing the enormous
quantities of molten magma by a series of timed, non-nuclear
explosions detonated along fault lines in the shield. In October,
1978, VULCAN was carried out in secret, using navy helicopter
teams experienced in detonating high-explosive resonant conic
charges. The VULCAN project lasted two days; on the third day,
the civilian Mauna Loa Volcanic Laboratory publicly announced that "the October eruption of Mauna Loa has been
milder than anticipated, and no further eruptive episodes are
expected."

PROJECT VULCAN was secret but Munro had heard all about it
one drunken night around the campfire near Bangazi. And he
remembered it now as Ross was planning a resonant explosive
sequence in the region of a volcano in its eruptive phase. The
basic tenet of VULCAN was that enormous, pent-up geological
forces—whether the forces of an earthquake, or a volcano, or
a Pacific typhoon—could be devastatingly unleashed by a relatively small energy trigger.

Ross prepared to fire her conical explosives.

"I think," Munro said, "that you should try again to contact Houston."

"That's not possible," Ross said, supremely confident. "I'm
required to decide on my own—and I've decided to assess the
extent of diamond deposits in the hillsides now."

As the argument continued, Amy moved away. She picked
up the detonating device lying alongside Ross's pack. It was a
tiny handheld device with six glowing LEDs, more than
enough to fascinate Amy. She raised her fingers to push the
buttons.

Karen Ross looked over. "Oh God."

Munro turned. "Amy," he said softly. "Amy, no. No.
Amy no good."

Amy good gorilla Amy good.

Amy held the detonating device in her hand. She was captivated by the winking LEDs. She glanced over at the humans.

"No, Amy," Munro said. He turned to Elliot. "Can't you stop her?"

"Oh, what the hell," Ross said. "Go ahead, Amy."

A series of rumbling explosions blasted gleaming diamond dust from the mine shafts, and then there was silence. "Well," Ross said finally, "I hope you're satisfied. It's perfectly clear that such a minimal explosive charge could not affect the volcano. In the future you can leave the scientific aspects to me, and—"

And then Mukenko rumbled, and the earth shook so hard that they were all knocked to the ground.

4. ERTS Houston

At 1 a.m. Houston time, R. B. Travis frowned at the computer monitor in his office. He had just received the latest photosphere imagery from Kitt Peak Observatory, via GSFC telemetry. GSFC had kept him waiting all day for the data, which was only one of several reasons why Travis was in a bad humor.

The photospheric imagery was negative—the sphere of the sun appeared black on the screen, with a glowing white chain of sunspots. There were at least fifteen major sunspots across the sphere, one of which originated the massive solar flare that was making his life hell.

For two days now, Travis had been sleeping at ERTS. The entire operation had gone to hell. ERTS had a team in northern Pakistan, not far from the troubled Afghan border; another in central Malaysia, in an area of Communist insurrection; and the Congo team, which was facing rebelling natives and some unknown group of gorilla-like creatures.

Communications with all teams around the world had been cut off by the solar flare for more than twenty-four hours. Travis had been running computer simulations on all of them with six-hour updates. The results did not please him. The Pakistan team was probably all right, but would run six days over schedule and cost them an additional two hundred thousand dollars; the Malaysia team was in serious jeopardy; and the Congo team was classified CANNY—ERTS computer slang for "can not estimate." Travis had had two CANNY teams in the past—in the Amazon in 1976, and in Sri Lanka in 1978 —and he had lost people from both groups.

Things were going badly. Yet this latest GSFC was much better than the previous report. They had—it seemed—managed a brief transmission contact with the Congo several hours earlier, although there was no verification response from Ross. He wondered whether the team had received the warning or not. He stared at the black sphere with frustration.

Richards, one of the main data programmers, stuck his head in the door. "I have something relevant to the CFS."

"Fire away," Travis said. Any news relevant to the Congo Field Survey was of interest.

"The South African seismological station at the University of Jo'burg reports tremors initiating at twelve oh four p.m. local time. Estimated epicenter coordinates are consistent with Mount Mukenko in the Virunga chain. The tremors are multiple, running Richter five to eight."

"Any confirmation?" Travis asked.

"Nairobi is the nearest station, and they're computing a Richter six to nine, or a Morelli Nine, with heavy downfall of ejecta from the cone. They are also predicting that the LAC, the local atmospheric conditions, are conducive to severe electrical discharges."

Travis glanced at his watch. "Twelve oh four local time is nearly an hour ago," he said. "Why wasn't I informed?"

Richards said, "It didn't come in from the African stations until now. I guess they figure it's no big deal, another volcano."

Travis sighed. That was the trouble—volcanic activity was now recognized as a common phenomenon on the earth's surface. Since 1965, the first year that global records were kept, there had been twenty-two major eruptions each year, roughly one eruption every two weeks. Outlying stations were in no hurry to report such "ordinary" occurrences—to delay was proof of fashionable boredom.

"But they have problems," Richards said. "With the satellites disrupted by the sunspots, everybody has to transmit surface cable. And I guess as far as they're concerned, the northeast Congo is uninhabited."

Travis said, "How bad is a Morelli Nine?"

Richards paused. "It's pretty bad, Mr. Travis."

5.
"Everything Was Moving"

In the Congo, earth movement was Richter scale 8, a Morelli scale IX. At this severity, the earth shakes so badly a man has difficulty standing. There are lateral shifts in the earth and rifts open up; trees and even steel-frame buildings topple.

For Elliot, Ross, and Munro, the five minutes following the onset of the eruption were a bizarre nightmare. Elliot recalled that *"everything* was moving. We were all literally knocked off our feet; we had to crawl on our hands and knees, like babies. Even after we got away from mine-shaft tunnels, the city swayed like a wobbling toy. It was quite a while —maybe half a minute—before the buildings began to collapse. Then everything came down at once: walls caving in, ceilings collapsing, big blocks of stone crashing down into the jungle. The trees were swaying too, and pretty soon they began falling over."

The noise of this collapse was incredible, and added to that was the sound from Mukenko. The volcano wasn't rumbling any more; they heard staccato explosions of lava blasting from the cone. These explosions produced shock waves; even when the earth was solid under their feet, they were knocked over without warning by blasts of hot air. "It was," Elliot recalled, "just like being in the middle of a war."

Amy was panic-stricken. Grunting in terror, she leapt into Elliot's arms—and promptly urinated on his clothes—as they began to run back toward the camp.

A sharp tremor brought Ross to the ground. She picked herself up, and stumbled onward, acutely aware of the humidity and the dense ash and dust ejected by the volcano. Within minutes, the sky above them was dark as night, and the first flashes of lightning cracked through the boiling clouds. It had rained the night before; the jungle surrounding them was wet, the air supersaturated with moisture. In short, they had all the requisites for a lightning storm. Ross felt herself torn between the perverse desire to watch this unique theoretical phenomenon and the desire to run for her life.

In a searing burst of blue-white light, the lightning storm struck. Bolts of electricity crackled all around them like rain; Ross later estimated there were two hundred bolts within the first minute—nearly three every second. The familiar shattering crack of lightning was not punctuation but a continuous sound, a roar like a waterfall. The booming thunder caused sharp ear pains, and the accompanying shock waves literally knocked them backward.

Everything happened so fast that they had little chance to absorb sensations. Their ordinary expectations were turned upside down. One of the porters, Amburi, had come back toward the city to find them. They saw him standing in a clearing, waving them ahead when a lightning bolt crashed *up* through a nearby tree into the sky. Ross had known that the lightning flash came after the invisible downward flow of electrons and actually ran upward from the ground to the clouds above. But to see it! The explosive flash lifted Amburi off his feet and tossed him through the air toward them; he scrambled to his feet, shouting hysterically in Swahili.

All around them trees were cracking, splitting and hissing clouds of moisture as the lightning bolts shot upward through them. Ross later said, "The lightning was everywhere, the blinding flashes were continuous, with this terrible sizzling sound. That man [Amburi] was screaming and the next instant the lightning grounded through him. I was close enough to touch him but there was very little heat, just white light. He went rigid and there was this terrible smell as his whole body burst into flame, and he fell to the ground. Munro rolled on him to put out the fire but he was dead, and we ran on. There was no time to react; we kept falling down from the [earthquake] tremors. Soon we were all half-blinded from the lightning. I remember hearing somebody screaming but I didn't know who it was. I was sure we would all die."

Near camp, a gigantic tree crashed down before them, presenting an obstacle as broad and high as a three-story building. As they clambered through it, lightning sizzled through the damp branches, stripping off bark, glowing and scorching. Amy howled when a white bolt streaked across her hand as she gripped a wet branch. Immediately she dived to the ground, burying her head in the low foliage, refusing to move. Elliot had to drag her the remaining distance to the camp.

Munro was the first to reach camp. He found Kahega trying to pack the tents for their departure, but it was impossible with the tremors and the lightning crashing down through the dark ashen sky. One Mylar tent burst into flames. They smelled the harsh burning plastic. The dish antenna, resting on the ground, was struck and split apart, sending metal fragments flying.

"Leave!" Munro shouted. "Leave!"

"*Ndio mzee!*" Kahega shouted, grabbing his pack hastily. He glanced back toward the others, and in that moment Elliot stumbled out of the black gloom with Amy clinging to his chest. He had injured his ankle and was limping slightly. Amy quickly dropped to the ground.

"Leave!" Munro shouted.

As Elliot moved on, Ross emerged from the darkness of the ashen atmosphere, coughing, bent double. The left side of her body was scorched and blackened, and the skin of her left hand was burned. She had been struck by lightning, although she had no later memory of it. She pointed to her nose and throat, coughing. "Burns . . . hurts . . ."

"It's the gas," Munro shouted. He put his arm around her and half-lifted her from her feet, carrying her away. "We have to get uphill!"

An hour later, on higher ground, they had a final view of the city engulfed with smoke and ash. Farther up on the slopes of the volcano, they saw a line of trees burst into flames as an unseen dark wave of lava came sliding down the mountainside. They heard agonized bellows of pain from the gray gorillas on the hillside as hot lava rained down on them. As they watched, the foliage collapsed closer and closer to the city, until finally the city itself crumbled under a darkly descending cloud, and disappeared.

The Lost City of Zinj was buried forever.

Only then did Ross realize that her diamonds were buried forever as well.

6. Nightmare

They had no food, no water, and very little ammunition. They dragged themselves through the jungle, clothes burned and torn, faces haggard, exhausted. They did not speak to one another, but silently pressed on. Elliot said later they were "living through a nightmare."

The world through which they passed was grim and colorless. Sparkling white waterfalls and streams now ran black with soot, splashing into scummy pools of gray foam. The sky was dark gray, with occasional red flashes from the volcano. The very air became filmy gray; they coughed and stumbled through a world of black soot and ash.

They were all covered with ash—their packs gritty on their backs, their faces grimy when they wiped them, their hair many shades darker. Their noses and eyes burned. There was nothing to do about it; they could only keep going.

As Ross trudged through the dark air, she was aware of an ironic ending to her personal quest. Ross had long since acquired the expertise to tap into any ERTS databank she wanted, including the one that held her own evaluation. She knew her assigned qualities by heart:

YOUTHFUL-ARROGANT (probably) / TENUOUS HUMAN RAPPORT (she particularly resented that one) / DOMINEERING (maybe) / INTELLECTUALLY ARROGANT (only natural) / INSENSITIVE (whatever that meant) / DRIVEN TO SUCCEED AT ANY COST (was that so bad?)

And she knew her late-stage conclusions. All that flopover matrix garbage about parental figures and so on. And the last line of her report: SUBJECT MUST BE MONITORED IN LATE STAGE GOAL ORIENTED PROCEDURES.

But none of that was relevant. She had gone after the diamonds only to be beaten by the worst volcanic eruption in Africa in a decade. Who could blame her for what had happened? It wasn't her fault. She would prove that on her next expedition. . . .

Munro felt the frustration of a gambler who has placed every bet correctly but still loses. He had been correct to avoid the Euro-Japanese consortium; he had been correct to go with ERTS; and yet he was coming out empty-handed. Well, he reminded himself, feeling the diamonds in his pockets, not *quite* empty handed. . . .

Elliot was returning without photographs, videotapes, sound recordings, or the skeleton of a gray gorilla. Even his measurements had been lost. Without such proofs, he dared not claim a new species—in fact, he would be unwise even to discuss the possibility. A great opportunity had slipped away from him, and now, walking through the dark landscape, he had only a sense of the natural world gone mad: birds fell screeching from the sky, flopping at their feet, asphyxiated by the gases in the air above; bats skittered through the midday air; distant animals shrieked and howled. A leopard, fur burning on its hindquarters, ran past them at noon. Somewhere in the distance, elephants trumpeted with alarm.

They were trudging lost souls in a grim sooty world that seemed like a description of hell; perpetual fire and darkness, where tormented souls screamed in agony. And behind them Mukenko spat cinders and glowing rain. At one point, they were engulfed in a shower of red-hot embers that sizzled as they struck the damp canopy overhead, then turned the wet ground underfoot smoky, burning holes in their clothing, scorching their skin, setting hair smoldering as they danced in pain and finally sought shelter beneath tall trees, huddled together, awaiting the end of the fiery rain from the skies.

Munro planned from the first moments of the eruption to head directly for the wrecked C-130 transport, which would afford them shelter and supplies. He estimated they would reach the aircraft in two hours. In fact, six hours passed before the gigantic ash-covered hulk of the plane emerged from the murky afternoon darkness.

One reason it had taken them so long to move away from Mukenko was that they were obliged to avoid General Muguru and his troops. Whenever they came across jeep tracks, Munro led them farther west, into the depths of the jungle. "He's not a fellow you want to meet," Munro said. "And neither are his boys. And they'd think nothing of cutting your liver out and eating it raw."

Dark ash on wings and fuselage made the giant transport look as if it had crashed in black snow. Off one bent wing, a kind of waterfall of ash hissed over the metal down to the ground. Far in the distance, they heard the soft beating of Kigani drums, and thumping mortar from Muguru's troops. Otherwise it was ominously quiet.

Munro waited in the forest beyond the wreckage, watching the airplane. Ross took the opportunity to try to transmit on the computer, continuously brushing ash from the video screen, but she could not reach Houston.

Finally Munro signaled, and they all began to move forward. Amy, panicked, tugged at Munro's sleeve. *No go*, she signed. *People there.*

Munro frowned at her, glanced at Elliot. Elliot pointed to the airplane. Moments later, there was a crash, and two white-painted Kigani warriors emerged from the aircraft, onto the high wing. They were carrying cases of whiskey and arguing about how to get them down to the jungle floor below. After a moment, five more Kigani appeared beneath the wing, and the cases were passed to them. The two men above jumped down, and the group moved off.

Munro looked at Amy and smiled.

Amy good gorilla, she signed.

They waited another twenty minutes, and when no further Kigani appeared, Munro led the group to the airplane. They were just outside the cargo doors when a rain of white arrows began to whistle down on them.

"Inside!" Munro shouted, and hurried them all up the crumpled landing gear, onto the upper wing surface, and from there into the airplane. He slammed the emergency door; arrows clattered on the outer metal surface.

Inside the transport it was dark; the floor tilted at a crazy angle. Boxes of equipment had slid across the aisles, toppled over, and smashed. Broken glassware crunched underfoot. Elliot carried Amy to a seat, and then noticed that the Kigani had defecated on the seats.

Outside, they heard drums, and the steady rain of arrows on the metal and windows. Looking out through the dark ash, they glimpsed dozens of white-painted men, running through the trees, slipping under the wing.

"What are we going to do?" Ross asked.

"Shoot them," Munro said briskly, breaking open their supplies, removing machine-gun clips. "We aren't short of ammunition."

"But there must be a hundred men out there."

"Yes, but only one man is important. Kill the Kigani with red streaks painted beneath his eyes. That'll end the attack right away."

"Why?" Elliot asked.

"Because he's the *Angawa* sorcerer," Munro said, moving forward to the cockpit. "Kill him and we're off the hook."

Poison-tipped arrows clattered on the plastic windows and rang against the metal; the Kigani also threw feces, which thudded dully against the fuselage. The drums beat constantly.

Amy was terrified, and buckled herself into a seat, signing, *Amy leave now bird fly.*

Elliot found two Kigani concealed in the rear passenger compartment. To his own amazement he killed both without hesitation, firing the machine gun which bucked in his hands, blasting the Kigani back into the passenger seats, shattering windows, crumpling their bodies.

"Very good, Doctor." Kahega grinned, although by then Elliot was shaking uncontrollably. He slumped into a seat next to Amy.

People attack bird bird fly now bird fly Amy want go.

"Soon, Amy," he said, hoping it would prove true.

By now, the Kigani had abandoned their frontal assault; they were attacking from the rear, where there were no windows. Everyone could hear the sound of bare feet moving over the tail section and up onto the fuselage above their heads. Two warriors managed to climb through the open aft cargo door. Munro, who was in the cockpit, shouted, "If they get you, they eat you!"

Ross fired at the rear door, and blood spattered on her clothes as the intruding Kigani were knocked out backward.

Amy no like, she signed. *Amy want go home.* She clutched her seat belt.

"There's the son of a bitch," Munro shouted, and fired his machine gun. A young man of about twenty, his eyes smeared with red, fell onto his back, shuddering with machine-gun fire. "Got him," Munro said. "Got the *Angawa.*" He sat back and allowed the warriors to remove the body.

It was then the Kigani attack ended, the warriors retreating into the silent bush. Munro bent over the slumped body of the pilot and stared out at the jungle.

"What happens now?" Elliot asked. "Have we won?"

Munro shook his head. "They'll wait for nightfall. Then they'll come back to kill us all."

Elliot said, "What will we do then?"

Munro had been thinking about that. He saw no possibility of their leaving the aircraft for a least twenty-four hours. They needed to defend themselves at night and they needed a wider clearing around the plane during the day. The obvious solution was to burn the waist-high bush in the immediate vicinity of the plane—if they could do that without exploding the residual fuel in the airplane tanks.

"Look for flamethrowers," he told Kahega, "or gas canisters." And he began to check for documents that would tell him tank locations on the C-130.

Ross approached him. "We're in trouble, aren't we."

"Yes," Munro said. He didn't mention the volcano.

"I suppose I made a mistake."

"Well, you can atone," Munro said, "by thinking of some way out."

"I'll see what I can do," she said seriously, and went aft.

Fifteen minutes later, she screamed.

Munro spun back into the passenger compartment, his machine gun raised to fire. But he saw that Ross had collapsed into a seat, laughing hysterically. The others stared at her, not sure what to do. He grabbed her shoulders and shook her: "Get a grip on yourself," he said, but she just went on laughing.

Kahega stood next to a gas cylinder marked PROPANE. "She see this, and she ask how many more, I tell her six more, she begins to laugh."

Munro frowned. The cylinder was large, 20 cubic feet. "Kahega, what'd they carry that propane for?"

Kahega shrugged. "Too big for cooking. They need only five, ten cubic feet for cooking."

Munro said, "And there are six more like this?"

"Yes, boss. Six."

"That's a hell of a lot of gas," Munro said, and then he

realized that Ross with her instinct for planning would have grasped at once the significance of all that propane, and Munro also knew what it meant, and he broke into a grin.

Annoyed, Elliot said, "Will someone please tell us what this means?"

"It means," Munro said through his laughter, "it means things are looking up."

Buoyed by 50,000 pounds of heated air from the propane gas ring, the gleaming plastic sphere of the consortium balloon lifted off from the jungle floor, and climbed swiftly into the darkening night air.

The Kigani came running from the forest, the warriors brandishing spears and arrows. Pale white arrows sliced up in the fading light, but they fell short, arcing back down to the ground again. The balloon rose steadily into the sky.

At an altitude of 2,000 feet, the sphere caught an easterly wind which carried it away from the dark expanse of the Congo forest, over the smoking red volcanic heart of Mount Mukenko, and across the sharp depression of the Rift Valley, vertical walls shimmering in the moonlight.

From there, the balloon slid across the Zaire border, moving southeast toward Kenya—and civilization.

Epilogue:
The Place of Fire

On September 18, 1979, the Landsat 3 satellite, at a nominal altitude of 918 kilometers, recorded a 185-kilometer-wide scan on Band 6 (.7–.8 millimicrons in the infrared spectrum) over central Africa. Penetrating cloud cover over the rain forest, the acquired image clearly showed the eruption of Mount Mukenko still continuing after three months. A computer projection of ejecta estimated 6–8 cubic kilometers of debris dispersed into the atmosphere, and another 2–3 cubic kilometers of lava released down the western flanks of the mountain. The natives called it *Kanyalifeka*, "the place of fire."

On October 1, 1979, R. B. Travis formally canceled the Blue Contract, reporting that no natural source of Type IIb diamonds could be anticipated in the foreseeable future. The Japanese electronics firm of Hakamichi revived interest in the Nagaura artificial boron-doping process. American firms had also begun work on doping; it was expected that the process would be perfected by 1984.

On October 23, Karen Ross resigned from ERTS to work for the U.S. Geological Survey EDC in Sioux Falls, South Dakota, where no military work was conducted, and no field-work was possible. She has since married John Bellingham, a scientist at EDC.

Peter Elliot took an indefinite leave of absence from the Berkeley Department of Zoology on October 30. A press release cited "Amy's increasing maturity and size . . . making further laboratory research difficult . . ." Project Amy was formally disbanded, although most of the staff accompanied Elliot and Amy to the Institut d'Etudes Ethnologiques at Bukama, Zaire. Here Amy's interaction with wild gorillas continues to be studied in the field. In November, 1979, she was thought to be pregnant; by then she was spending most of her time with a local gorilla troop, so it was difficult to be sure. She disappeared in May 1980.*

The institute conducted a census of mountain gorillas from March to August 1980. The estimate was five thousand animals in all, approximately half the estimate of George Schaller, field biologist, twenty years before. These data confirm that the mountain gorilla is disappearing rapidly. Zoo reproduction rates have increased, and gorillas are unlikely to become technically extinct, but their habitats are shrinking under the press of mankind, and researchers suspect that the gorilla will vanish as a wild, free-roaming animal in the next few years.

Kahega returned to Nairobi in 1979, working in a Chinese restaurant which went bankrupt in 1980. He then joined the National Geographic Society expedition to Botswana to study hippos.

Aki Ubara, the eldest son of the porter Marawani and a radio astronomer at Cambridge, England, won the Herskovitz Prize in 1980 for research on X-ray emissions from the galactic source M322.

* In May, 1980, Amy disappeared for four months, but in September she returned with a male infant clinging to her chest. Elliot signed to her, and had the unexpected satisfaction of seeing the infant sign back to him *Amy like Peter like Peter*. The signing was crisp and correct and has been recorded on videotape. Amy would not approach closely with her infant; when the infant moved toward Elliot, Amy grabbed him to her chest, disappearing into the bush. She was later sighted among a troop of twelve gorillas on the slopes of Mt. Kyambara in northeastern Zaire.

At a handsome profit, Charles Munro sold 31 karats of blue Type IIb diamonds on the Amsterdam *bourse* in late 1979; the diamonds were purchased by Intel, Inc., an American micronics company. Subsequently he was stabbed by a Russian agent in Antwerp in January, 1980; the agent's body was later recovered in Brussels. Munro was arrested by an armed border patrol in Zambia in March, 1980, but charges were dropped. He was reported in Somalia in May, but there is no confirmation. He still resides in Tangier.

A Landsat 3 image acquired on January 8, 1980, showed that the eruption of Mount Mukenko had ceased. The faint signature of crossed laser beams, recorded on some earlier satellite passes, was no longer visible. The projected intersection point now marked a field of black quatermain lava with an average depth of eight hundred meters—nearly half a mile—over the Lost City of Zinj.

References

BALANDIER, GEORGES. *Daily Life in the Kingdom of the Kongo from the Sixteenth to the Eighteenth Century.* New York: Pantheon, 1968.

BANCHOFF, THOMAS F., and STRAUSS, CHARLES M. "Real-Time Computer Graphics Analysis of Figures in Four-Space." In *Hypergraphics*, edited by David W. Brisson, pp. 159–169. AAAS Selected Symposium 24. Boulder, Colo.: Westview Press, 1978.

BLEIBTREU, JOHN N. *The Parable of the Beast.* New York: Macmillan, 1967.

BROWN, HARRISON; BONNER, JAMES; and WEIR, JOHN. *The Next Hundred Years.* New York: Viking Press, 1963.

BURCHETT, WILFRED, and ROEBUCK, DEREK. *The Whores of War.* Harmondsworth, England: Penguin, 1977.

CAPLAN, ARTHUR L. "Ethics, Evolution and the Milk of Human Kindness." In *The Sociobiology Debate*, edited by Arthur L. Caplan, pp. 304–314. New York: Harper & Row, 1978.

CHURCHMAN, C. WEST. *The Systems Approach and Its Enemies.* New York: Basic Books, 1979.

CLARK, W. E. *The Antecedents of Man.* Edinburgh: University of Edinburgh Press, 1962.

COX, KEITH G. "Kimberlite Pipes." *Scientific American* 238, no. 4 (1978): 120–134.

DEACON, RICHARD. *The Chinese Secret Service.* New York: Taplinger, 1974.

DERJAGUIN, B. V., and FEDOSEEV, D. B. "The Synthesis of Diamonds at Low Pressure." *Scientific American* 233, no. 5 (1975): 102–110.

DESMOND, ADRIAN J. *The Ape's Reflexion.* New York: Dial, 1979.

DOUGLAS-HAMILTON, IAIN and ORIA. *Among the Elephants.* New York: Viking, 1975.

EVANS-PRITCHARD, E. E. "The Morphology and Function of Magic: A Comparative Study of Trobriand and Zande Ritual and Spells." In *Magic, Witchcraft and Curing,* edited by John Middleton, pp. 1–22. Garden City, N.Y.: Natural History Press, 1967.

————. *Witchcraft, Oracles and Magic Among the Azande.* Oxford: Clarendon Press, 1937.

FORBATH, PETER. *The River Congo.* New York: Harper & Row, 1977.

FOUTS, ROGER S. "Sign Language in Chimpanzees: Implications of the Visual Mode and the Comparative Approach." In *Sign Language and Language Acquisition in Man and Ape: New Dimensions in Comparative Pedolinguistics,* edited by Fred C. C. Peng, pp. 121–137. AAAS Selected Symposium 16. Boulder, Colo.: Westview Press, 1978.

FRANCIS, PETER. *Volcanoes.* Harmondsworth, England: Penguin, 1976.

GOLD, THOMAS, and SOTER, STEVEN. "Brontides: Natural Explosive Noises." *Science* 204, no. 4391 (1979): 371–375.

GOULD, R. G., and LUM, L. F., eds. *Communications Satellite Systems: An Overview of the Technology.* New York: Institute of Electrical and Electronics Engineers Press, 1976.

GRIBBIN, JOHN. "What Future for Futures?" *New Scientist* 84, no. 1187, pp. 21–23.

HALLET, JEAN-PIERRE. *Congo Kitabu.* New York: Random House, 1964.

HARRIS, MARVIN. *Cannibals and Kings: The Origins of Cultures.* New York: Random House, 1977.

HAWTHORNE, J. B. "Model of a Kimberlite Pipe." *Physics and Chemistry of the Earth* 9 (1975): 1–15.

HOARE, COLONEL MIKE. *Congo Mercenary.* London: Hale, 1967.

HOFF, CHRISTINA. "Immoral and Moral Uses of Animals." *New England Journal of Medicine* 302, no. 2, pp. 115–118.

HOGG, GARRY. *Cannibalism and Human Sacrifice.* New York: Citadel Press, 1966.

JENSEN, HOMER; GRAHAM, L. C.; PORCELLO, L. J.; and LEITH, E. N. "Side-Looking Airborne Radar." *Scientific American* 237, no. 4 (1977): 84–96.

JONES, ROGER. *The Rescue of Emin Pasha.* New York: St. Martin's Press, 1972.

KAHN, HERMAN; BROWN, WILLIAM; and MARTEL, LEON. *The Next Two Hundred Years.* New York: Morrow, 1976.

LILLESAND, THOMAS M., and KIEFER, RALPH W. *Remote Sensing and Image Interpretation.* New York: Wiley, 1979.

LINDEN, EUGENE. *Apes, Men and Language.* New York: E. P. Dutton, 1975.

MARTIN, JAMES. *Telecommunications and the Computer.* Englewood Cliffs, N.J.: Prentice-Hall, 1969.

MARWICK, M. G. "The Sociology of Sorcery in a Central African Tribe." In *Magic, Witchcraft and Curing,* edited by John Middleton. Garden City, N.Y.: Natural History Press, 1967.

MIDGLEY, MARY. *Beast and Man: The Roots of Human Nature.* Ithaca, N.Y.: Cornell University Press, 1978.

MOORE, C. B., ed. *Chemical and Biochemical Applications of Lasers.* Vol. 3. New York: Academic Press, 1977.

MOOREHEAD, ALAN. *The White Nile.* New York: Harper & Brothers, 1960.

MOSS, CYNTHIA. *Portraits in the Wild: Animal Behavior in East Africa.* London: Hamilton, 1976.

NOYCE, ROBERT N. "Microelectronics." *Scientific American* 237, no. 3 (1977): 62–70.

NUGENT, JOHN PEER. *Call Africa 999.* New York: Coward-McCann, 1965.

ORLOV, YU L. *The Mineralogy of the Diamond.* New York: Wiley, 1977.

PATTERSON, FRANCINE. "Conversations with a Gorilla." *National Geographic* 154, no. 4 (1978): 438–467.

———. "Linguistic Capabilities of a Lowland Gorilla." In *Sign Language and Language Acquisition in Man and Ape: New Dimensions in Comparative Pedolinguistics,* edited by Fred C. C. Peng, pp. 161–202. AAAS Selected Symposium 16. Boulder, Colo.: Westview Press, 1978.

PETERS, WILLIAM C. *Exploration and Mining Geology.* New York: Wiley, 1978.

PREMACK, ANN JAMES and DAVID. "Teaching Language to an Ape." *Scientific American* 227, no. 4 (1972): 92–100.

PREMACK, DAVID. "Language in a Chimpanzee?" *Science* 172, no. 3985 (1971): 808–822.

RICHARDS, PAUL W. "The Tropical Rain Forest." *Scientific American* 229, no. 6 (1973): 58–69.

ROTH, H. M., and others. *Zaire: A Country Study.* Area Handbook Series. Washington, D.C.: U.S. Government Printing Office, 1977.

RUMBAUGH, DUANE M., ed. *Language Learning by a Chimpanzee: The Lana Project.* New York: Academic Press, 1977.

SABINS, FLOYD F. *Remote Sensing Principles and Interpretation.* San Francisco: W. H. Freeman, 1978.

SANDVED, KJELL B., and EMSLEY, MICHAEL. *Rain Forests and Cloud Forests.* New York: Abrams, 1979.

SAPOLSKY, HARVEY M. *The Polaris System Development.* Cambridge, Mass.: Harvard, 1972.

SCHALLER, GEORGE B. *The Mountain Gorilla, Ecology and Behavior.* Chicago: University of Chicago Press, 1963.

————. *The Year of the Gorilla.* Chicago: University of Chicago Press, 1964.

SPUHLER, J. N. "Somatic Paths to Culture." In *The Evolution of Man's Capacity for Culture*, edited by J. N. Spuhler, pp. 1–13. Detroit: Wayne State University Press, 1959.

STANLEY, HENRY M. *In Darkest Africa*, 2 vols. New York: 1890.

TERRACE, H. S. *Nim.* New York: Alfred A. Knopf, 1979.

————. "How Nim Chimpsky Changed My Mind." *Psychology Today*, November, 1979, pp. 65–76.

TURNBULL, COLIN M. *The Forest People.* London: Jonathan Cape, 1961.

————. *Man in Africa.* Garden City, N.Y.: Doubleday, 1976.

————. *The Mountain People.* London: Jonathan Cape, 1973.

VAUGHAN, JAMES H. "Environment, Population, and Traditional Society." In *Africa*, edited by Phyllis M. Martin and Patrick O'Meara, pp. 9–23. Bloomington: Indiana University Press, 1977.

WILSON, EDWARD O. *On Human Nature.* Cambridge, Mass: Harvard, 1978.

YERKES, ROBERT M. and ADA W. *The Great Apes: A Study of Anthropoid Life.* New Haven: Yale University Press, 1929.

ZUCKERMAN, ED. "You Talkin' to Me?" *Rolling Stone*, June 16, 1977, pp. 45–48.

A NOTE ON THE TYPE

The text of this book was set in Electra, a type face designed by
William Addison Dwiggins for the Mergenthaler Linotype Company and first made available in 1935. Electra cannot be classified
as either "modern" or "old-style." It is not based on any historical
model, and hence does not echo any particular period or style of
type design. It avoids the extreme contrast between thick and thin
elements that marks most modern faces, and is without eccen-
tricities that catch the eye and interfere with reading. In general,
Electra is a simple, readable typeface that attempts to give a feeling
of fluidity, power, and speed.
    W. A. Dwiggins (1880–1956) began an association with the
Mergenthaler Linotype Company in 1929 and over the next
twenty-seven years designed a number of book types, including
the Metro, Electra, Caledonia, Eldorado, and Falcon.

Composed by Maryland Linotype Composition Company, Inc.,
Baltimore, Maryland. Printed and bound by The Haddon Crafts-
men, Scranton, Pennsylvania. Typography and binding design by
Virginia Tan.